IT'S ONLY LOVE

Also from Linda Cashdan

Special Interests

IT'S ONLY LOVE
LINDA CASHDAN

ST. MARTIN'S PRESS
NEW YORK

Design by Tanya M. Pérez

Library of Congress Cataloging-in-Publication Data

Cashdan, Linda.
    It's only love / Linda Cashdan.
      p. cm.
    ISBN 0-312-07811-0
    I. Title.
    PS3553.A7938I85   1992
    813'.54—dc20   92-2678
                                                            CIP

First Edition: July 1992

10 9 8 7 6 5 4 3 2 1

To my husband, David . . .
living proof of the lasting power of teenage summer romances

Special thanks to my "literary midwife," Molly McKitterick, with whom I have shared criticism, support, and, happily, the birth of several books now—both hers and mine . . . to my exuberant, ever-helpful agent, Elaine Markson . . . and to my St. Martin's editor, Maureen Baron, who has nurtured, guided, and cut with brilliant precision.

I also want to thank Washington attorney James (Jim) Wilson Greene for being just what I needed—a close friend who was also a toxic tort litigator . . . and Louise Krumm, Beverly Nadel, and Marcia Sprinkle, my best friends and intrepid readers and rereaders . . . and Eve Cashdan, my ever-bolstering, unfatigable mother-in-law.

1

"She's your cousin," Marci Courbienne's mother insisted over the telephone one week after Salvatore Durone's funeral. "If she needs help, then, Baby, you gotta help."

Francine Durone was Marci's "cousin" because their mothers had been born two houses from each other, because their fathers had played on the same high-school football team and set up a contracting business together and failed in the contracting business together and died within two years of each other. Such was the stuff of "cousinhood" in Fallsville, Massachusetts.

And "Baby" would help. No matter that "Baby" was now thirty-eight years old, the mother of two, and a partner in a law firm. She was also a woman who supported her widowed mother and was helping her older sister financially. Still, in Fallsville, you were for life what you were at birth, and the last born, the runt of the litter, would always be "Baby."

Marci knew she had to do it. It was part of the escape fee. She'd done it a million times before—helped out other "cousins." The problem was, this time she had no idea what "it" was.

Marci glanced at the digital clock on her dashboard as she pulled her car out of the office parking lot, estimating: twenty minutes to get to Francine's, twenty minutes back. How *many* minutes listening and consoling in the middle? It all added up to a helluva lot of nonbillable time.

She smiled ruefully at the idea that she was one of a kind—an attorney who made house calls.

It was, she had to admit, a sensational day for a drive. The sun was bright, the skies clear blue, and the trees proudly displayed autumnal hues of red, orange, and gold. The sight conjured up childhood memories. Adults watched the seasons change. Children participated. She thought back to those leaf-raking Saturdays—four piles, one per child, and intense competition over whose pile was highest.

They were permitted to play in their piles for a while, tumbling down into the soft, crinkling leaves (*"Mine*'s better! Oooh, my pile's so *deep!"*), but the "falling" only lasted for a limited interval—until Papa gave them the signal: "Time for burning!"

Then they raked the leaves back up and watched from a safe distance as Papa lit matches, creating four fires that crackled and sent red sparks up to clash with the setting sun.

Rosy cheeks. Icy noses. Cold fingers, but sweaty bodies underneath their clothes from all the raking. Apples. Pumpkins. Autumn. And, a prize for their hard work: marshmallows, toasted on sticks in the living-room fireplace, as Mama cooked dinner in the kitchen.

Marci Courbienne inhaled deeply, and then laughed a little at the scent her memory had conjured: garlic. Not toasted marshmallows, but garlic—always garlic, pouring out of her mother's kitchen. Garlic, the incense of home, the aroma of family happiness.

Not family tranquility. Never tranquility. Always turmoil, sibling discord.

"Mama, he took my—"

"Mama, make her give it back!"

"Mama, she won't let me—"

Family dinners with four children fighting for center stage, never permitting one another to finish a sentence, complaining, whining, shouting, and sniping, uniting only to worry together about that chronic family problem: no money.

How ridiculously wonderful it all seemed now. Had there ever been a moment, a single moment, when she had realized what she had, the incredible emotional wealth that existed in that humble, chaotic household?

She swallowed hard. Maybe one—just before the wonderful world of childhood had come crashing down around her. At least there had been one moment. . . .

Her hands squeezed the steering wheel. Another full circle. She had been going around in circles ever since Salvatore Durone's funeral, first remembering that part of her suppressed past, then realizing, painfully, why it had been suppressed.

ENTERING FALLSVILLE.

As she pulled off the highway at the familiar little sign and proceeded on automatically, past the church, left over the hill, right to the creek, then right again, she wondered if she could ever give another person, a stranger, specific directions to the Durone house.

The yellow school bus ahead of her stopped and turned on its flashing lights, forbidding her to pass.

A sure sign of change.

When she was a child, they had all gone to neighborhood schools. But Fallsville's population decline and the population explosion in neighboring communities had caused the closing of the local elementary and high school and the busing of Fallsville's young to the same big all-county schools Marci's children attended.

She waited patiently behind the school bus, scrutinizing the children getting off to see how many she could pick out by name. About fifteen kids got off. She spotted a tall, thin boy with straggly, greasy black hair that was almost shoulder length. Wearing tight jeans, a black jacket with metal adornments, and a silver earring in his left earlobe, he was standing alone. Unlike the others, he carried no books. Well, what do you know, another "cousin."

When the school bus moved on, Marci pulled up her car next to the boy and tooted her horn. He squinted, and then, recognizing her, nodded uncomfortably. She rolled down the window. "I'm going to your house, Frankie. Hop in and I'll give you a ride."

He looked around, searching for an escape, but then shrugged self-consciously and climbed in. She remembered that Frankie was just a year younger than her son, Tommy, who was getting tired of the little-boy appelation, and realized she probably shouldn't have called him "Frankie."

3

"That must be a pretty long bus ride to take two times a day, Frank," she said as they pulled off.

He shrugged. "Twenty-five minutes."

"How do you like Oakland High?"

"It's great," he snorted. "Just great."

The hostile tone unnerved her because she felt as if the ghost of Salvatore Durone were riding next to her in the car. Frank Durone certainly looked just like his father—the same harsh facial configuration, the chin curving up, the long thin nose curving down. The two features, aimed at each other that way, created a permanent sneer.

Not his fault, Marci reminded herself. The child was just the biological recipient, after all. She tried to ignore the fact that his demeanor appeared to be like Sal's too—tough, kind of raw.

"Do you see Tommy much? At school?"

"Yup." Frank snarled slightly. "Can't miss him."

The tone pricked her maternal sensitivity. "How's that?"

"Tom Courbienne, football star? Mr. Prep? Mr. Stuck-up?"

Her fingers tightened on the steering wheel.

"The view's kinda one way." Frank laughed gruffly and turned back to her, his eyes flashing. "He don't see me much."

She stared at the road ahead, uncomfortable in the heat of the anger she sensed filtering over from the passenger's seat. "How are things at home?" she asked softly after a while.

"Better."

"Better?"

Frank shrugged. "Dead's better than dying." He leaned toward her, and she reproached herself for finding the gesture menacing. "Know what I mean?"

Marci pulled up the dirt slope into the Durones' yard, grateful there was no time to pursue that one.

The house, a large, modern pre-fab, had been Francine and Sal Durone's honeymoon dream home, its shipped parts received with great excitement when Sal had returned from Vietnam imbued with anticipation of a "new beginning."

The new beginning had never come off, and it showed. The paint on the house was peeling, the shutters falling off. The yard was littered with discards—a broken washing machine under a blanket of dead leaves in one corner, a rusted metal porch swing in

4

another. Old tires and metal car parts lay strewn under the big elm tree next to Sal's pickup truck. *Better Homes and Gardens*, Fallsville style.

Marci's eyes wandered over to another car, parked close to the house.

"Grandma Durone," Frank grunted by way of explanation. "She came for the dying, and she seems to be stickin' around for the dead part too." He got out of the car.

Just what she needed. A house call that included Old Lady Durone.

Francine opened the door as Marci walked up the front steps. She was wearing a flowered house dress with a sweater draped over her shoulders. The dress was too big and gave her thin frame an extra air of fragility. She smiled at Marci, but then frowned quizzically when she spotted Frank behind her.

"She gave me a ride from the bus stop," Frank said, answering his mother's look.

"What about your sisters?" Francine asked.

"Don't ask me, ask her," Frank said, nodding toward Marci. "She didn't invite them." He sauntered through the living room to the kitchen.

Marci stopped dead in the doorway, feeling like an idiot. "My God, they were on the same bus! I didn't think of that . . . I just saw Frank and stopped!"

"It's okay," Francine said, ushering her in. "*They* at least have *friends* to walk home with!" she shouted in a shrill voice over her shoulder in Frank's direction.

"He's just impossible," Francine whimpered as she helped Marci off with her coat. "I don't know what I'm going to do with him. He don't listen. He don't obey." Francine dropped Marci's coat over a chair next to the front door and began wringing her hands. "Oh, Marci, I just . . . I don't know."

Marci experienced a strong sense of déjà vu as she put a comforting arm around Francine. Would there ever come a time in life when Francine Durone knew what to do? "He'll be okay," she consoled out of reflex. "This is just a difficult time for everyone."

Francine dug her fingernails into Marci's suit jacket, pulling her closer.

"Sal's mother," she whispered frantically, "she's living here!"

"For how long?"

"I don't know!" Francine shut her eyes as her body trembled slightly. "I don't know!"

Marci started to read Francine her rights—it was *her* house and she was entitled to kick the old bag out anytime she wanted—but then swallowed the sentence. Action was not Francine's strong suit.

The living room was dimly lit and stuffy, the furniture's dark, shabby upholstery intensifying the drabness. As Marci's eyes adjusted to the lack of light, the room's Buddha-like centerpiece came into focus: large, overstuffed Old Lady Durone in a large, overstuffed chair. Draped in black, her thick lips rigid, her eyes grim, Mrs. Durone sat purposefully, registering silent, nonspecific disapproval.

There it was, Marci realized giddily, the genetic origin of the sneering Durone facial configuration. The woman's nose and chin were thicker than both Sal's and Frank's, but they were curved toward each other in the same nasty way.

Time to behave like the good little girl her mother had sent on this mission. Marci walked over to the Buddha. "I'm so sorry . . ." she mumbled, reaching out instinctively toward the woman.

Mrs. Durone nodded curtly and kept her hands folded tightly across her chest. Her eyes crept slowly from Marci's spiked heels up her legs to her skirt and suit jacket, but looked away when they got to Marci's face.

Nice to see you again, too, Marci thought

Marci sat down on the sofa and turned to Francine, suddenly even more anxious to get the meeting over with as quickly as possible. "What's the problem?"

Francine floated down next to her and began fidgeting with her fingers. "You gotta help me, Marci . . ." she whimpered.

It was the usual lead-in sentence to an interview with Francine Durone. Marci nodded, waiting for the follow-up. But Francine began interacting fervently with the pile of Kleenex in her lap, dabbing her eyes with one, and then blowing her nose with another.

The unbillable-time clock ticked away in Marci's head, causing her mind to accelerate impatiently. The circumstances precluded wife-beating, Francine's chronic problem. Money. That had to be it. "I assume you're entitled to survivor's benefits from the company?"

Marci asked. Sal Durone's last job had been as a truck driver with Sherrington, a new firm with a regional reputation as a beneficent employer.

"Well, yes . . ." Francine looked down at her lap.

"Not enough to live on!" interjected Mrs. Durone.

"Well, yes, that's right . . . not enough . . . but that's not what I need your help on." Francine's eyes returned to Marci's. The corners of her mouth turned down, but her chin went up defiantly. *"Someone killed Sal!"*

"Killed? Now, Francine—"

"He was on the track! He was tracing whoever it was down when he died. 'They'll pay!' He told me, 'Don't worry, you'll have plenty of money to live on. They're gonna pay for what they did to me!' "

Dumfounded, Marci leaned forward. "Who?"

Francine collapsed against the back of the chair and pressed a new Kleenex to her eyes. "I don't know!" she screamed. "He never told me! He *died* without telling me!" She succumbed to sobs.

Waiting for the histrionics to subside, Marci coolly tabulated the facts: Salvatore Durone had died of cancer, of that she was certain because the information had come from her mother, certified, over the years, as a thoroughly reliable source. So what are we talking about here? A cancer-producing pill someone had slipped into one of Sal's beers? Extremely doubtful such a high-tech murder weapon even existed, less likely still that it would be wasted on a man who could have been knocked off without suspicion during one of the barroom brawls he was famous for provoking.

If she were to get any real work done this afternoon, she had to prick this melodramatic balloon, thoroughly and quickly. "Facts, Francine," she ordered, "Give me facts. Number one, Sal died of cancer—right?"

"Yes and no," Francine whimpered.

"The doctor!" Mrs. Durone instructed from her perch. "Tell her about the doctor."

Francine nodded and tried to pull herself together. "It was a funny kind of cancer. 'Unnatural causes,' the doctor said."

"Meaning what?"

"I don't know!" Francine wailed. "He told Sal—not me! Sal said the doctor gave him information to help him figure out who it was

7

that killed him. That's all he did, after he found out about the cancer . . . all the time, he was running around tracking down the killers."

"How?" Marci asked, bewildered.

"Always making phone calls."

"Phone calls?" Marci leaned forward alertly. "Long-distance phone calls?"

"Um, maybe." Francine wadded up a Kleenex nervously. "Once I think I heard him ask what the area code for Washington, D.C., was—"

Marci frowned. "He was calling Washington? Why would he—"

"*Do I know?*" Francine threw up her hands.

"If he made long-distance phone calls, there would be a record," Marci pointed out, "on the telephone bill. Think, Francine." The order only created a new stream of tears. "Well, then, did you hear him say anything on the phone?"

"I don't remember," Francine moaned. "Besides, most of the checking he did outside the house. 'Won't be home until late tonight,' he'd tell me. 'Got some checking to do!' You know how Sal was," she sighed, "stubborn. Always the mystery man, involved in all these little projects, doing everything on his own!"

A mystery man? The Sal Durone Marci had known was a teenage hoodlum whose only "project" had been terrorizing the inhabitants of Fallsville. Granted, those memories were a good two decades old.

She realized she had no recent knowledge about "how Sal was," not firsthand. She only knew what she'd heard over the years from her mother, and from Francine's visits to her office.

"But he knew he was dying, Francine," Marci protested. "Everybody knew! He must have known he might not live long enough to find out. He must have told someone!"

"The doctor lied!" Francine screeched. "A year to a year and a half was what he told him! Sal died in less than four months! It came very quick, the end. A cold that turned into pneumonia."

Marci opened her purse and pulled out a pen and pad. "What's the doctor's name?"

"Goldstein . . . Goldberg . . . Goldsomething." Francine waved the specifics away with a Kleenex. "You know, Jewish. A big specialist."

"Specialist!" Mrs. Durone hissed from her throne. "Lotta good he did, the specialist!"

Marci looked at Francine irritably. "His name and office number, Francine. I need his name and office number."

"Okay, okay," Francine sighed, "I'll get it for you."

"Len," Mrs. Durone grunted. "Tell her about Len!"

"Oh, yeah!" Francine's countenance brightened. "Lennie might know something!"

Marci looked up with interest. "Who's Lennie?"

"You know, Lennie Lucinski?"

Marci shook her head.

"*Of course* you remember! Sal's best friend, Lennie!"

"No. But what does he have to do with this?"

"Whoever did it to Sal did it to Lennie too. He's got the same form of cancer. Sal mighta told him about tracing the murderers. Sal told Lennie everything."

"And this Lennie, he's still alive?" Marci asked hopefully.

"Barely." Francine pulled out another Kleenex and pressed it to her lips. "He's in Orange County Hospital."

Marci handed Francine the pad and pen. "Write down his name for me." Just what she needed: a nonpaying assignment to track down a murderer who inflicted cancer on his victims, with the only assistance coming from the deceased man's scatterbrained wife, a specialist doctor with a nonspecific name, and a second, probably already-comatose victim.

Her eyes wandered around the dark, dismal room. "How are you fixed financially?" she asked, attempting to reenter reality.

Francine cowered in her widow's role. "He had a small pension . . . not enough, but something." She sighed. "Frankie'll be working soon, so I guess that'll help."

Marci's eyes lit up. A silver lining! A show of familial responsibility from the gangster son she had just chauffeured. "Frank's going to start an after-school job?"

"No. Better. He's gonna quit school when he turns sixteen, so he'll be able to—"

"*Quit school!*" Marci sat up abruptly. "No, Francine. You don't want him to quit school."

"He don't study!" Mrs. Durone thundered from her throne. "He don't study, he quits!"

9

Ignoring the witch, Marci zeroed in on Francine with a look that commanded attention. "If he quits school, then there's no hope," she announced tersely. "No hope for the future—his or yours. He's got to get an education."

Francine wrung her hands.

"Francine, you are the parent. He is the child," Marci said sternly. "It is *your* responsibility to see to it that he continues with school. You've got to stop crying and acting helpless and assume control of the family. It is—"

"Show her whatcha found," Mrs. Durone broke in.

Francine reached into a pocket and handed Marci a folded piece of paper.

Marci unfolded it and blinked as she scanned the familiar program: *1969 to 1989: The Collier Chamber of Commerce salutes B. J. Courbienne.* She looked up and found Francine and Old Lady Durone staring at her smugly. "So?"

"You tell us!" Mrs. Durone said.

Marci shrugged. "Where did you find this?"

"In Sal's jacket pocket."

Marci frowned. "Sal went to the celebration for B.J.?"

Francine stood up and began strutting around the room, victim turned cross-examiner. "Sallie *never* went over to that side of the county. 'Newcomers,' that's what he always called the people there."

"*Your* people," Mrs. Durone accused. "Where you live."

"So, he didn't go?"

"I don't know." Francine sighed. "Did he? B.J.'s *your* father-in-law. You were there."

"And so were *hundreds* of other people," Marci laughed. "It was a celebration of the twentieth anniversary of B.J.'s shopping mall! I was up on the podium, with the rest of the family. I have no idea—"

"Seemed funny is all." Francine played with her fingernails. "Him having the program like that."

Marci's head hurt. "I don't see what this has to do with Sal's death, Francine."

Francine shrugged. "Thought maybe it would help." She smiled hopefully. "You find Sal's murderers and we'll have enough money. Frankie won't have to quit school."

10

This was the moment to inform both women she was a lawyer, not a private detective. But she knew they would not understand, and, more to the point, neither would her mother. Marci slumped down in her chair. "That's a fantasy, Francine. I really don't see how—"

"You'll see." Mrs. Durone squinted her eyes into tiny slits. "A educated girl like you, you'll figure it out!"

Marci stared at the woman coldly. She could figure it out already. Old Lady Durone should be sent to live in her own home. Francine should get off her ass and look for a job. Someone should speak to Frank's teachers to find out why he was not studying. Oh, she could figure it all out.

She stood up. "Come on, Francine." Marci sighed. "Let's find the doctor's name and go look at those telephone bills."

2

A gust of wind rustled the window panes of the apartment on New York City's Central Park West. The thin, muscular blond man lying nude on the bed opened his eyes in response to the noise, but then shut them to the glare of daylight. He winced and scratched the light stubble on his square jaw. "You are Rod Bingham", he reminded himself, "Rodney Everett Bingham, to be precise, and you're in bed."

He stretched and then shivered slightly. "And you are bare-assed," he told himself. "You need a blanket." His eyes still closed, he reached to the left until his hand came in contact with a quilt. He sensed something solid under it. Frowning, he turned his head in the direction of the mass. His eyes opened slowly as he tried to focus on the object before him.

Well, well. Rodney Everett Bingham opened his eyes and found himself face to face with a woman's buttock.

A lousy opening line if ever there was one. "Cheek to cheek." That's it.

Applauding his own pun, he studied the pink roundness and healthy skin tone of the flesh before him and continued the silent narrative: *Summoning his expertise, Bingham judged this to be a vintage twenty-eight-year-old buttock: carefully worked over on jogging paths and health clubs, but too young to be the beneficiary of a tuck or liposuction.*

Rod heard the doorbell buzz, but he ignored it, just as he had the previous buzzes. He stared at the sheets and blankets covering the rest of the body in the bed beside him and tried to remember the name that went with the anatomically perfect rear end. Linda? Lucy? No, but he was close. Something with an "L." It would come to him when he needed to know it. Names always did.

The doorbell buzzed and buzzed, angry, frantic, determined buzzes. Rod frowned. A persistent son-of-a-bitch, this buzzer.

He sat up very slowly, taking care to lift his enormously heavy head into an upright position as gingerly as possible. Placing his feet firmly on the floor next to the bed, he waited for the whirling sensation behind his eyes to go away.

No time. The doorbell noise was taking on a life of its own. Resigning himself to dizziness, he stood up, grabbed the gray velour bathrobe draped over the chair next to the bed, and cast one more glance back at the bundle beside him.

"Farewell, sweet ass."

The huge cathedral bedroom windows ushered in aggressive rays of sunshine, assaulting his vision. He closed his eyes and stepped uneasily across the thick oriental rug, guiding himself by the touch of familiar objects—the side bureau, then the cluttered dresser top, then a lampshade, then the wall, then the thick, carved molding of the doorway—to the central hall.

He grimaced as his toes smashed against a small hard object in his pathway. Angrily, he picked up the culprit, a VCR remote control.

The doorbell buzzed again.

"I'm coming!" Operating in slow motion, he took the empty liquor bottles off the top of the bar, shoved them on a shelf below, slammed the cabinet door shut, and winced at the reflection he encountered in the mirror behind the bar.

His face looked a little gray, but he told himself his skin was just picking up the hue of the bathrobe. The bloodshot whites surrounding his deep green eyes were more difficult to dismiss.

"I *said* I'm coming!" He smoothed a few stubbornly errant strands of blond hair back in place and checked the mirror: final inspection. The hair was okay, but over his left shoulder in the reflection he spied two half-filled highball glasses, one embedded

13

with thick purple lipstick. He turned around, picked them up off the table, and searched the room for an appropriate disposal.

He walked over to a little alcove and placed the glasses carefully on the blue felt blotter of the opened eighteenth-century cubbyhole desk, along with the black cummerbund and white dress shirt that were draped over the side. Then he pulled the antique desktop up, covering it all.

Pleased with the masterfully executed cleanup process, he strode jauntily to the front door and opened it. There he encountered a short, dark-haired man of about fifty pacing back and forth in the hallway. The man glowered at him.

Bingham's eyes lit up. "Since when does my hotshot agent make house calls?"

Stanley Kurtz barreled past Bingham into the apartment's foyer. "When he gets tired of sitting alone for an hour at a table for two at Mortimers!" Kurtz yelled angrily. *"That's* when your agent makes house calls!" Kurtz pulled off his gray cashmere muffler and began peeling his leather gloves from his hands in a gesture that came close to being threatening.

Rod put his hand to his mouth. "Shit, it must be Tuesday."

"Shit, it must be Tuesday!" Kurtz gritted his teeth as his voice mimicked Bingham's.

"Gee, Stan, I'm sorry. Really, I don't know what could have—"

"You don't *know?*" Kurtz screamed. His eyes made a panoramic scan of the room, taking in the evidence Bingham had missed in his hasty cleanup: the pair of pantyhose dangling from the corner of an ornately framed oil painting, the BVDs on the green velvet cushion of the armchair, the needlepoint pillows scattered all over the floor. "It's easy to forget it's Tuesday when every night is Saturday night, for Christ's sake!"

Rod laughed good-naturedly and flopped down on a nearby loveseat. "Hey, Stan . . ." The voice was soft, affectionate. "I'm sorry. Really I am."

"Do you know how many times I rang your doorbell?" Kurtz accused. "What the hell were you? Unconscious?"

"I was . . . just involved, that's all."

"Involved in what? Were you writing?"

Rod looked into the face of a man who was willing to be convinced, dying, actually, to be convinced. For a moment he toyed

14

with the idea of lying, but he couldn't. Honesty had long been a hallmark of his relationship with Stanley Kurtz. It set the relationship off from just about every other one Rod had going. He shrugged and pulled his bathrobe around him tighter.

Kurtz took off his coat and threw it over a chair. "I swear to God, if you hadn't answered this time, I was going to go down and get the doorman to let me in."

"You suspected foul play?" Bingham's eyes sparkled. " 'Pulitzer-Prize–Winning Author's Bludgeoned Body Discovered by Well-Known Agent!' "

"*Former* author, present hack-off."

"Hey, hold on, Stan. You know this is a first for me—forgetting a lunch date."

"This wasn't just a lunch date! This was an appointment to discuss a manuscript you've been working on for months!" Kurtz shot him a look. "Supposedly."

"Now, wait a minute—"

"Go!" Kurtz ordered. "Put on some clothes and we'll discuss it."

Obediently, Rod went into the bathroom. He came out a few minutes later, scrubbed but still barefoot, wearing a navy blue sweatsuit.

Stan Kurtz was sitting on a bar stool at the kitchen counter, a thick manila envelope before him, a freshly brewed pot of coffee on his right. "I see Stephanie won custody of the fancy cappuccino machine," he grumbled.

Rod shrugged as he picked up the percolator and poured himself a cup. "I figured it was only right. *She* was the one who knew how to use it." He sat down on a stool across the counter from Kurtz.

"Using that criteria, I'm surprised you got anything but the king-size bed."

Rod winced. "Sardonic humor first thing in the morning?"

Kurtz held out his watch. "It's two-thirty P.M." He put on his glasses, pulled an enormous stack of paper out of the manila envelope, and placed it between them on the counter.

Bingham stared uncomfortably at the manuscript for a moment and then walked over and opened a drawer behind Kurtz.

"Even when I smoked, I didn't smoke first thing in the morning," Kurtz growled without turning around.

"First thing in the morning? Why, it's two-thirty P.M.!" Rod pulled a pack of Dunhill cigarettes out of the drawer, lit one, and then choked on it as his eyes traveled through the kitchen doorway to the woman waving to him cheerfully from the living room. She was wearing a low-cut, clingy black dress and spike heels. Tangled brown curls spilled irregularly around her face, framing the dark lines of run mascara embedded beneath her eyes.

Stanley Kurtz sat up stiffly on the stool and inhaled.

"Uh, Lorraine," Rod said. (Sure enough, the name had come to him.) "This is Stan Kurtz. Stan, meet Lorraine."

Rod watched as Stan's head moved slowly up and down, his small brown eyes glaring out over the sagging bags.

"Well, I'll be going!" Lorraine trilled, and she fled toward the front door.

"Thanks," Rod called after her. "Uh, thanks for coming!"

They heard the door slam.

Rod grabbed the cigarettes and an ashtray and resumed his seat opposite Stanley Kurtz at the counter.

Invisible strings in Kurtz's face tugged his loose jowls into an expression of total disgust.

"She means nothing to me."

"I believe you," Kurtz growled. "A hundred percent. That makes her one of a long line of people and things that mean nothing to you. One former wife, one former live-in, plus countless other young female bodies, a cappuccino maker, a wrecked BMW, let's count up all the things that mean nothing to Rodney Bingham! And what's left on the other side? Huh? Invitations to the right beach parties in East Hampton? Balling and boozing with the jet set?"

"Stan? What is this? All of a sudden, after ten years of friendship—"

"Us? Friends? The Jewish junk dealer's son and Mister Patrician? Mister Card-Carrying Member of every restricted social club that exists, he's suddenly my big buddy?"

Bingham gaped at him in disbelief.

"It's time to face facts, Roddy. What we've had for ten years is a business relationship. You got an aggressive agent who could get you top dollar on your work, and I got a talent—a talent that

16

happens, quite frankly, to be housed inside a client I've never been able to understand, a man who steps nimbly over every human being who has ever entered his real life, but can treat the people he writes about with an empathy and perception that borders on genius."

Bingham grinned. "What did you do, write this all down on a napkin at Mortimers?"

"An emotionless snob with a passionate pen! Well, the pen's run dry, my boy, the pen's run dry! The young reporter who broke his ass to uncover the details behind the well-hidden fifteen-year-old murder of a black civil-rights activist in Mississippi and layed out those facts brilliantly and painstakingly in an award-winning book . . . the thirty-four-year-old who delved into the passions and anguish of working-class families in middle America and created a poignant novel in the process . . . the thirty-six-year-old who spent a year and a half uncovering a corporate scandal no one even knew existed, and then exposed it in a bestseller . . . this author of talent has finally permitted *who he is* to permeate his creation. And who is he? A forty-year-old jerk-off, part health fadist, part socialite, both parts replete with affectation and devoid of meaning!"

"Jesus, Stan . . ."

"Jogging and cigarettes, bean sprouts and Scotch. Even your affectations are in conflict! You've got a much labored-over perfect exterior that belies what *have* to be disintegrating insides and, worst of all, a disintegrating talent! *This*"—Kurtz snarled contemptuously, pounding the manuscript—"badly written, clichéd hyperbole, that's all it is!" He shrugged. "Debauchery in the jet set? Drugs, booze, extravagance? It's all been done before, *and done better.*"

Bingham watched his cigarette burning in the ashtray for a while and then looked up testily. "I wager it'll sell."

Kurtz stared at the ceiling. "It'll sell."

"So, then!"

Stan held up a finger. "It'll sell on the basis of your past. It'll sell, but it will be pointed to in the future—mark my words—as your first inferior work, the beginning of your downfall."

Rod yawned. "So you want me to rewrite a little, change some of the clichéd hyperbole?"

"You don't want to hear what *I* want." Kurtz played with the pen on the counter before him, and Rod did not want to hear. "I

17

think you're cracking up, Rod. This . . . this dichotomy I've been talking about between Mister Teflon in real life and Mister Passion in prose, it's always bothered me because it never fit. I've always felt the written Bingham had to be the *real* Bingham, the other some kind of cover-up. A person just can't write like that, empathize like that, and—"

"Be a total shit in person?"

Kurtz's eyes zeroed in on him. "Have no soul."

Bingham looked away.

"This manuscript . . ." Kurtz shook his head and shoved the stack of papers down the counter. "This tells me you're going in the wrong direction. You're letting the lesser half take over from the better half." A stone-faced Stanley Kurtz sat very still, his breath coming in labored wheezes as his thick fingers strummed the counter. After a minute or so, he looked up. "Take some time off, Rod. Get out of New York City. Get away from everything that's messing up your judgment, away from the balling and the boozing, which, you admit, is not giving you any great pleasure. Go some place where you'll be able to spend all your energy searching things through."

Bingham shifted uncomfortably on his stool. "You want me to try living the life of a monk? That's your panacea for minor burnout?"

"I think getting yourself off booze and cigarettes would be an accomplishment in itself. I don't know whether anything will help, to tell the truth." Kurtz looked at him point-blank. "I dare you to go off by yourself and either find something that matters to you or figure out why nothing does. I dare you. Hell, if you want, you can use my condo in Florida. We won't be going down there until January. Just go off someplace and think. Be alone. Suffer, maybe, a little. Whatever it takes. Write." Kurtz shrugged. "Try drawing again."

"Drawing?" Rod winced. "I'm a writer!"

"Yeah? Well, you've got an apartment full of watercolors that attest to the fact you're also a damn good artist!"

"I used to like to paint," Rod scoffed. "That hardly qualifies me as an artist."

"All I'm saying is you were a man of many talents, but they were all motivated by a rich quantity of inner passion. You've lost it . . . but maybe it's only temporary." He leaned across the counter. "What do you say?"

Bingham took a long drag on his cigarette and exhaled. "Out of the question."

3

When she walked in the front door of her split-level home, Marci Courbienne heard loud male voices coming from the kitchen. "Hello!"

"Eh, Mom . . . Jack's here!"

"I know, I saw the car. I'll be right in." She hung her coat in the closet, cast a disparaging eye at the jacket and books strewn over the sofa in the living room, and headed for the kitchen, smoothing the bottom of her blouse into her skirt as she walked.

Tommy was bent over the kitchen table scribbling notes on a yellow pad, as Jack Whelan, a gray-haired man of about fifty, dictated. Whelan was wearing a suit and tie, but his shirt collar was opened, his tie pulled down.

"Jack," Marci said softly, "you didn't have to—"

"Well, when I returned your call, they said you were out." Jack Whelan winked and held up a beer can. "I figured I could find out what you wanted and get a free drink if I just came here and waited until you got home from work."

"Oh, it wasn't that important!" She smiled at him. "I just wanted to let you know a team from Boston will arrive at the plant next Tuesday."

Tommy's head shot up from the legal pad. "A team's coming here from Boston?"

"Not the kind of team you're thinking about," Marci laughed. "This is a team of job-evaluation experts!"

"Huh?"

"Just some legal business your mother's handling for my labor union," Whelan explained. "A comparable-worth lawsuit."

"A what?"

"Comparable worth." Whelan went on, "We're trying to get more pay for the women we represent at an electrical plant in Briarcliff."

"Just the women?" Tom frowned suspiciously. "How about the men?"

"It's the *women* who are being discriminated against," Marci snapped. "They're performing jobs every bit as difficult as the men, but they are being paid less, solely because they happen to be women!"

Tom grinned at Jack Whelan. "Guess I stepped on her feminist toes a little, huh?"

"*When* are you going to start putting your stuff away?" Marci demanded. "The living room looks as though—"

"Hey! I remembered to put the casserole in the oven!" Tom shouted. "C'mon, Mom, you wouldn't want me to be a hundred percent perfect."

"The hell I wouldn't, I—"

"And Jack and I have just figured out a great idea for the speech contest."

"Speech contest?" Marci frowned as she opened the refrigerator and took out a soda. "I thought you decided not to enter."

"Yeah, well, that's the problem. Everyone decided not to enter, so the dorks went ahead and made it mandatory." He stood up and picked up the pen and pad on the kitchen table. "That leaves Number One Man here with no choice." He turned toward her in an exaggerated swagger. "I gotta win."

Marci raised an eyebrow and nodded toward Jack Whelan. "With help."

"No sweat," Tom laughed. "I plan to mention Jack in my acceptance speech." He slapped Whelan "five" and headed out of the kitchen. "It'll just take me a couple of minutes to clean it up. Wait'll you hear it!"

Marci opened the soda can and plopped down in a kitchen chair. "What am I gonna do with him?"

"You already did it."

"What do you mean?"

"You've told him all his life he was terrific." Whelan's eyes twinkled. "You can't blame him for believing it." He leaned across the table. "Know what?" he whispered. "He is."

"A cocky son of a bitch!"

"Right on both counts." Whelan grinned mischievously, and then patted her hand. "But a good kid."

Marci sat up abruptly, looking around. "Where's Lindsay?"

"Babysitting." He took a sip of beer and looked at his watch. "She just called a few minutes ago. Said she'll be home by seven."

Marci relaxed in her chair. "Well, you certainly seem to have everything under control." She looked across the table at him, finding comfort as she always did in the warm, familiar face etched with smile lines. "Will you stay for dinner?"

"Depends." His gray eyes studied her.

"On what?"

"Is that really the only reason you called me? To discuss progress on the lawsuit?"

"Yes. Why else?" She looked at him quizzically and then, suddenly understanding, she became uncomfortable. "Oh, Jack . . ." Her fingers were fiddling with her suit jacket, her eyes darting around the walls and ceiling. "I thought that other matter was settled."

"It'll never be settled. Not that way. Not for me." His eyes were targeted on hers, mining them for guilt.

Once she realized that, she stared him down, meeting his Irish melancholia with stubborn show of Italian defiance. "That group of lawyers I told you about who specialize in comparable-worth issues? They're the ones who gave me the name of these Boston job-evaluation experts. I thought that would be good news—good *professional* news for both of us."

"It is! It is!" Whelan shifted around uncomfortably in his chair. "I was just hoping . . ."

"No." Marci held up her hand. "None of that tonight. We've talked it over a thousand times, and I happen to have one colossal headache this evening." She closed her eyes and took a deep breath. "It's been a hell of an afternoon."

"Where were you? I called a couple of times. Your secretary just said 'out.' "

She took a long swig of soda. "I blew about two hours on a nonpaying client, and then blew another thirty minutes trying unsuccessfully to communicate with a hairless, fleshless, unconscious cancer patient on the terminal ward at Orange County Hospital."

"What in the blazes for?"

Marci looked up at Jack Whelan somberly and then cast furtive glances around the kitchen to make sure they were not being overheard. "Promise not to tell?" she whispered. "The information I am about to impart will go no further?"

"No further." He leaned forward expectantly.

"A forty-five-year-old truck driver named Salvatore Durone was killed—administered a cancer-causing pill—by the C.I.A., and the only person who can finger the specific C.I.A. agent that did it is three-quarters dead himself from an equally deadly dose, unable to talk, being kept alive by life-support systems at Orange County Hospital." She flopped back in her chair and pressed her hand over her mouth to keep a straight face.

"Marci?" Whelan's frown melted into a look of suspicious amusement. He raised an eyebrow. "Just what sort of proof do you have?"

Marci choked on her soda and broke out giggling. "Well, the evidence *is* a tad flimsy! Durone died last week of cancer. In diagnosing his cancer, the doctor told him it was unnatural."

"Isn't *all* cancer unnatural?"

"The doctor offered to help Durone track down the killer—the person who had unnaturally afflicted him. Whatever information the deceased man uncovered before he became deceased, however, he took with him to his grave. And the same thing appears to be on the verge of happening to his friend, Lennie Lucinski, who, it seems, was another victim of this very nonspecific murder weapon. Lucinski is the almost-cadaver I visited this afternoon at the hospital."

"And the C.I.A. involvement?"

"A bit of original sleuthing." Marci grinned broadly. "My own deduction."

"Deduced from what?"

"Salvatore Durone's widow—who not only knows nothing but can't even find her old phone bills—thinks she once heard Durone ask the operator for the area code for Washington, D.C."

Jack Whelan chuckled. "That's it?"

"Well," Marci laughed, "can you think of any *other* reason Salvatore Durone might have asked for the area code for Washington, D.C.?"

"No. Sounds right to me."

Marci grew serious, closed her eyes, and shook her head slowly. "I've been asked by my cousin, Durone's widow, to track down the murderer and make him pay—in cash—for what he did to Sal."

Whelan smiled affectionately and reached over and patted Marci's hand. "Well," he said softly. "It makes perfect sense."

Her eyes opened abruptly. "*What* makes perfect sense?"

"The fact that you have a colossal headache!"

Marci laughed, but then, gradually, her face sobered again. She stared into space.

"Marci . . . what is it now?"

"I was just thinking. I mean, the whole thing is a joke, easily dismissable, really, as a fantasy created by a lazy widow and her greedy mother-in-law in some irrational hope of getting life-long support. Insane . . . completely off the wall." She turned her gaze to Whelan. "Except for one thing."

"What's that?"

"I asked Francine—Durone's widow—for the phone bill. When she went to get it from the dumpy old desk where Sal kept all the bills and, supposedly, all his personal business records, the drawer was empty! Cleaned out! Not a thing in it!"

"Well, maybe she was wrong. Maybe he didn't keep the bills there."

"No. She was visibly shocked! Said she had just looked inside the drawer yesterday and it was full of stuff! And when I got back to my office and called the doctor whose name she had given me—the one who diagnosed Salvatore Durone? They told me he'd left the country yesterday! Left for a half-year sabbatical in Scandinavia!"

Whelan frowned. "All of which means what?"

"Damned if I know. It's just weird. The circumstances. You have to admit, it's peculiar."

Whelan shook his head. "Well, what do you know about the dead man?"

"Salvatore Durone was an off-again, on-again alcoholic, for starters." She handed Jack Whelan another beer and shrugged. "He beat his wife."

He opened the can. "Well, now, isn't that nice?"

Marci sat very still for a while and then looked up at Whelan. "You want to know something awful?" she whispered across the table. "Sometimes I feel like beating his wife, too!"

"Marci!"

"No, really. She . . . she almost provokes it, the way she flutters about helplessly, whining, whimpering, manipulating people through her own inability to cope. I spend five, ten minutes with her and suddenly I understand completely how a frustrated, angry, down-on-his-luck big hulk of a loser who had only muscles going for him would be unable to resist bashing her one."

Jack chuckled. "It's really a shame you can't represent the dead man on a battering charge!"

"Her oldest child—a boy around Tom's age—is having trouble in school. The kid's a physical replica of his old man, and, believe me, he's heading in exactly the same direction." Her eyes flashed fury. "Does she worry about him? Does she do anything to help? *No!* She decides he should quit school so he can bring home some money!"

Marci stood up and began pacing around the kitchen, her high heels clicking on the floor tiles, her petite body pulsating. "Her *son,* for God's sake!" She whirled around to face Jack. The suddenness of the gesture caused a lock of her short dark brown hair to tumble down over her right eye. "And the boy is bright. He's flunking school, but his aptitude scores are unusually high. Just . . ." Her eyes seemed to drift off. "Just like his father."

"How long did you know his father?"

"All my life."

Whelan grunted. "Ah, another dreg from the old neighborhood, eh?"

"That doesn't make me very unusual," she said pointedly.

25

"You're always telling me about dregs you bump into from *your* old neighborhood."

"The difference is my old Boston neighborhood isn't even there anymore. So my dregs have at least gone out into the world, on to new lives." He laughed a little. "You have to admit you have the only old neighborhood that still exists—intact—with all the dregs frozen in time."

She did not seem to hear him. "I knew him all my life, but not at all. Know what I mean? One time, I remember, Sal Durone accused me—behind my back—of having the biggest mouth in Fallsville, Massachusetts."

"No!" Jack Whelan feigned shock. "You? A big mouth? Never!" He grinned at her. "I, for one, think of you as a person with a very little, delicate mouth . . . a hell of a lot of *words* spilling out of it all the time, but a very little mouth."

Marci kept pacing. "He was always there—one of the guys— but he was always in the background, an anecdote. 'Sallie Durone and the boys got into trouble last night at Delgado's . . .' that kind of thing. He was about seven years older than I, and we had nothing in common. I knew *about* him all my life but mostly secondhand, from other people."

"What did they say?"

"I can only remember bits and pieces. He had several different incarnations, a weird life, going from rotten to 'finally figured out what to do with his life,' back to rotten. He was always kind of larger-than-life. But it's all hazy." She flopped back into the chair and opened the soda can. "Would you believe, I've spent the last couple of hours obsessed with trying to remember the bits and pieces of the life of Salvatore Durone?"

"Why ever?"

"Because all of a sudden, coming back in the car this afternoon, I *understood* why he wanted to splatter his wife's head all over the walls and ceilings! Because you have to feel sorry for a man who started out life with a terrible handicap like Old Lady Durone for a mother. Because . . . well, it was his desk, maybe. The house is a shambles—a testimonial to Francine's abysmal homemaking capabilities—but the one little shabby room in the house that belonged to Salvatore Durone was completely different. Neat. Organized. Sentimental. There were pictures of his kids in varying

26

stages of growth all over the place. Tacked on the walls were school papers—spelling tests and such, with high marks or gold stars they had gotten. And then . . . then that totally empty drawer." She shook her head slowly and sighed. "Oh, I don't know. Perhaps it's just because I didn't realize until this afternoon that Salvatore Durone might have had other dimensions. He was always there, in my life, but never there." She looked up at Whelan sheepishly. "Crazy, huh?"

"Oh, yeah. No doubt about it." He grinned at her affectionately. "Crazy, but vintage Marci Courbienne." He studied her for a while, thinking. Then he gave her a suspicious look. "How do you know about his son's high I.Q. scores?"

She looked away. "Common knowledge."

"No go." He leaned across the table. "If he were *your* son and he had a fancy I.Q., the whole world would know. But this lady you described, she's not the type to even know herself."

Marci shrugged uncomfortably. "Well, I guess I left out one other stop I made this afternoon," she mumbled. "I went to the high school and talked to the guidance counselor." She turned on him. "Jack, the boy is a time bomb about to go off! *Someone* had to—"

"Marci, Marci. There you go again, trying to save the world."

"This boy is about to go from little hope to out and out hopeless, just because his mother's too lazy to get a job! Once he quits school—"

"Hey, Mom, I've got to run over and drop something off at Jim Burrough's house." It was Tommy's voice coming from the hallway. "I'll be right back."

"How's my speech?" Jack Whelan called out.

"Oh, man, it's perfect!" Tom leaned through the kitchen doorway giving Whelan the thumbs-up sign. "Achieving greatness comes from meeting the little challenges as much as the big ones." Tom turned to his mother. "See, the dweeby topic is 'Challenge and Achievement.' Jack and I figured everyone's gonna write about finding a cure for cancer, winning the Olympics, that kind of thing. *Mine*"—he put his hand over his heart and stared up at the ceiling— "mine deals with the small, day-to-day challenges, the kind you don't get big recognition for, and are often things you would rather not do, but that can have a major impact on another human being."

Standing there, his white teeth glistening, his face earnest, his dark blond hair falling softly above large, sincere brown eyes, he

27

looked like a model for the perfect all-American high school student.

"Like what?" Marci asked.

"Huh?"

"Name me one 'small, day-to-day challenge!' "

He thought for a moment. "Say you're real good at football," Tom began seriously, "and there's this kid who's dying to learn how to play. Now, it's a pain in the neck to take the time to teach the kid, right? And you probably feel like a twerp doing it in front of all the other guys on the team, but by just taking a little time, making a small sacrifice, you could make a big difference in that kid's life."

Jack applauded.

Tommy hopped about the kitchen, pretending to spike the ball and shuffle the way he always did in the end zone after scoring a touchdown.

Marci took a long swig of soda. "Tom, do you see much of Frank Durone at school?"

Jack Whelan studied her for a moment and then put his hand over his eyes.

"Not if I can help it," Tom snickered. "The guy's real creepy, know what I mean? Creepy in a nasty way. Everyone thinks so." He looked from his mother to Whelan. "What does Frank Durone have to do with my speech?"

"A lamb to the slaughter," Whelan moaned.

Marci's dark brown eyes sparkled warmly. "We'll talk about it later, honey, over dinner . . . after you do your errand."

"You staying for dinner, Jack?"

"Naw," Jack Whelan drawled, shaking his head as he gave Marci a significant look. "I helped with the speech. You're on your own now, Tommy."

4

Ten days.

No boozing, no balling, no cigarettes.

Had it only been ten days?

Tanned and bare-chested in a pair of blue swim trunks, Rodney Bingham leaned against the railing of the sixth-floor balcony, his back to the Atlantic Ocean, eyeing the huge white stucco buildings on either side of Stanley Kurtz's Miami Beach condominium. One structure was slightly Spanish in design, the other squarely American. The "skyline" looked like a herd of concrete elephants, creeping ominously forward, competing with one another for position on the dwindling beach.

He turned around on the balcony and faced the ocean. Ten days, each one lengthened interminably by abstinence. Whereas in the very recent past, huge hunks of time had been blotted out by his excesses, he now faced daylight in unmitigating sobriety, acutely aware of every passing minute . . . counting, in fact, many of those passing minutes.

And what had it yielded, this taste of stoicism? This life-change prescribed by Doctor Kurtz?

He bent his head down and feasted his eyes on the only tangible result: his taut bronze abdomen. He had been running regularly. Actually, he noted wryly, even that was becoming a bit of a problem. The more he cleansed his system through healthy living and exercise, the more his jogging speed picked up. He could now run his four miles in less time than he had when he'd first arrived in condo land. That meant he now had an additional three minutes of "extra" time to fill each day.

His eyes roamed down six floors to the beach below, scanning the morning beach walkers, looking for his man, "the dreamer."

Sure enough. There he was again today, standing at water's edge in the same beige sweatsuit that always looked brand-new, the shiny bald spot on the top of his head reflecting the gleaming sun above. Every day "the dreamer" put in a good hour or so in ankle-high surf, all by himself, staring out at the placid turquoise waters beyond the breaking waves, patiently waiting, Rod imagined, for the boat that would come to rescue him.

Kurtz had been right on one front: Once his head cleared, the old reportorial senses had clicked in. Rod Bingham had effectively reentered the category of "acute observer." However, the geographical choice for reentry was unfortunate: He had returned to life in a place, it seemed, where everyone else had come to await death, amid balmy temperatures and infuriatingly clear blue skies.

He was a stand-out in this land of eternal sun, a forty-year-old fair-haired Christian surrounded by a virtual army of Jewish geriatrics, burned out by excessive exposure to the almighty sun. Why bother living the good clean life if longevity meant nothing but a few extra years preparing for purgatory by frying the flesh?

Or fighting. Rod Bingham, astute observer, had deduced in only ten days' time that Florida's senior citizens broke down easily into two broad categories: comatose and bellicose. Those who didn't look as though they should be put on leashes seemed to be in a perpetually snarling state. Elderly couples—the golden anniversary set—came off as appropriate candidates for "Can this marriage be saved?" columns, as they bickered and whined and practically came to blows in the aisles of local supermarkets.

"Look, Emma, they got a special on tuna. Two cans for ninety-two cents!"

"You didn't eat it when I made it last week, Harry."

"At two for ninety-two cents, I'll be hungrier."

"Yeah? I can see it now, rotting in the frig—"

"I'll eat it, Emma. *Goddamn it, I'll eat it!*"

Bingham picked up the sketchpad and brush, sat down in the chair facing the beach, and studied the assortment of watercolors on the table next to him. It was time to try again. Time for Stanley Kurtz's very own Leonardo Da Vinci to pursue one of his many underutilized talents. The ocean. How about the ocean as today's subject matter? Nature's still life . . . rendered by a human still life.

Ten days of introspection had done little more than confirm to him that Kurtz's accusations were on the mark. The more he scrutinized his present life, the more certain he became that there was no one in it he really cared about.

Oh, there was a fondness for friends, for his relatives, certainly. Take his niece, Lola, for example. Hadn't he spent an entire afternoon at the family beach house playing Uncle Roddy with her last summer, enjoying her antics? Making up stories and becoming immersed in the way a five-year-old's mind worked?

He studied the sketchpad and wrinkled his nose. The blue-green was off. He searched the table for a better shade.

The truth was, of course, that he had not seen niece Lola since early July, had not even thought of her since then.

He looked at the sketchpad and nodded approval. A better shade of blue-green.

And wasn't it just possible, since we were being totally honest here—that was, after all, the mission Kurtz had sent him on: total honesty—that he had enjoyed being Uncle Roddy so much because he found it preferable that day to the other roles available at the family reunion, like brother Rod, or son Rodney.

Another dead end in the search for emotion. And he'd been grasping for straws to begin with. No passion, Stan, still no passion. Monkhood was tedious, but not excruciating. He was bored, but not in the least bit hungry for something else.

He moved the brush across the page in short light strokes.

Face facts. He had spent ten days now, in solitary confinement, searching for something that mattered, and all he'd done was confirm the accusations of all the people with whom he'd had long-term relationships, including Stanley Kurtz, namely: *"You don't give a damn about anything!"*

Former wife Susanna had blamed his smoking dope, and former apartment mate Stephanie had fingered alcohol. Two more accusations thoroughly supported by deep thinking à la Miami. But he was not a booze head or a druggie. The years with Susanna and Stephanie had accounted for a total of only seven of his twenty years of adulthood.

And what had he done during the sober moments?

Written, that's what! Writing had always been his real drug of preference. Writing had taken him to the only people who really mattered. Had he cared about any human being in his personal life as much as he'd cared about Jeremiah Pruitt's aged black grandfather?

No. Definitely not.

And wasn't it just possible *that's* what made him a good writer? Reserving all his passion for his subjects rather than getting bogged down in personal involvements? (Eh, Susanna? Eh, Stephanie? Eh, Kurtz?) After all, it takes a hell of a lot of emotional energy to zero in on a human being—way in—and then be able to pick up the details, the minutia that matter but are invisible to the average observer, and describe what you see, feel, smell, sense, and translate it all into words that make that human being fascinate other people the way he fascinated you.

Jeremiah Pruitt's grandfather was real, but Cicero, Illinois, steelworker Franklin Dober had been fiction—a made-up man, a Rod Bingham creation. True, Stephanie and Susanna had merely figured as pass-throughs in his life, but Franklin Dober? Franklin Dober had fascinated him, excited him, driven him to emotional ranges of anger and sorrow he'd never known possible.

Shit. What was he doing? Painting the ocean and rehashing his glorious résumé?

He had grown up with enough of everything—not too little or too much, those passion-whetters. There had always been plenty of money, just enough to suppress the urge to "make it big," but not enough to make great wealth a necessity. And there were trust funds that assured no one had to worry.

He smiled as he swirled his paintbrush in water and picked up a new color.

Being born financially comfortable had obviously made him passion-handicapped. Take Kurtz. What pushed old Stanley forward to make a million, if not the vivid recollections of an impoverished childhood? What made him worry and seethe and writhe in his love and hatred? Paranoid perceptions of an anti-Semitic world and an early-in-life indoctrination in Jewish emotionalism that had been perpetuated into middle age by his hyperactive wife and his two volatile offspring.

Bad news, Stanley. It's WASP material you're dealing with here. The passion has been sanded down through countless generations, replaced by "good taste," a.k.a. "no feelings."

He smiled a little, idly stroking the brush along the sketchpad.

Passion, Stan, that's for the Jews, the Italians, the Greeks, the Armenians, all you people of the swarthy-skinned set, you . . . you dreadful *ethnics*, you!

Uh-uh-uh. Bingham held up an index finger. There you go again, Kurtz. I can hear you, all the way from New York City, screaming accusations of "Patrician prejudice!"

Well, you're wrong. By definition, "prejudice" is an unfavorable opinion formed without sufficient investigation. *My* unfavorable opinions, on the other hand, are steeped in experience. Ahh, yes, I have sampled ethnic passion, Stan—gagged on it, in fact. And the aftertaste was enough to make me seek lifelong refuge up here on the patrician plateau! You could say history has built up in me an aversion to all things *ethnic!*

The merriment vanished from his eyes. "Eye-talian," he whispered disparagingly. "The menaces in *my* life were Italian."

He threw the paintbrush onto the table next to him.

Around and around in mounting mental hyperbole, that's where he was heading on this, his eleventh day of captivity. And why, why in God's name had he come up with something so distant, so buried, so thoroughly meaningless to his present-day life?

He yawned. Perhaps it wasn't so meaningless. Give it a chance, just in case. Give *ethnic* passion the "mental picture test."

Obediently, he sat back in the chair, folded his arms across his chest, and stared out at the oceanic expanse in the distance, daring an image to unfold before him. Any image. Gradually, the lethargic gaze in his green eyes became more alert, focusing, almost . . . almost seeing something. It was very far away—a face—getting clearer, acquiring features.

He squinted, to see it better. Yes. Yes, it was coming into focus: the bushy eyebrows, the sneering lips, the glimmer in the deep brown eyes. He couldn't believe it. Clear and unmistakable, even after all these years. It hung there, taunting him, daring him, it seemed, to render it on paper.

The doorbell rang, and he snapped back.

Who could it be? he wondered as he made his way off the balcony. One of the many new friends he had made in his tenure in Miami?

He opened the door and found himself staring at what could only be called a "sweet young thing." She was about nineteen, with soft, sun-streaked auburn hair, a tanned, lean frame topped off with the roundest, firmest breasts he had seen in his ten days in Miami. They were displayed bralessly in a breathtakingly skimpy white sundress.

"I heard—like, uh—they said downstairs at the desk you were looking for a cleaning woman?"

"Do you clean?" He asked, emphasizing each word and complimenting himself on pulling it off with a straight face.

"Yeah. I . . . I work Mondays for the Gellmans?" Her eyes opened to enormous proportions. "Mr. Gellman's the really nice man in the wheelchair in number seven-thirty? And Wednesdays I do the Silvermans? They're just down the hall."

"Won't you come in?"

She walked all the way into the living room. "Oh, you've got a real nice place here," she said, turning around. "It's just like the Gellmans', only, you know, different furniture."

"How much do you charge?"

"Fifty dollars a day. That's the going rate, and I'm real thorough." Her eye caught sight of his word processor over in the corner. "Oh, wow! You've got a computer!"

"A word processor. I'm a writer." He said it with a certain degree of pomp that he attributed to overcompensation. He had not touched the thing since he'd set it down on the desk upon his arrival.

She beamed. "I'm a model! I just, you know, clean to support myself in my spare time."

He toyed with the idea of telling her he was in the midst of writing a commercial that called for a leggy brunette with good tits. "What day do you have free?"

"I have Fridays free. I could start next week, or—" She giggled. "I could start today, right now."

It must be Friday, he told himself. "Today's fine."

34

"Do you have any specific preferences?"

Her lips were so moist. "No," he said, looking away from them quickly. "Just a thorough cleaning, that's all." He gave her a tour of the two-bedroom apartment, completed the prework interview, and then headed back to the balcony.

"I know what you're thinking, Stan," he chortled as he slid the glass balcony door shut behind him. "But just have faith, Kurtz. Have faith."

He picked up the sketchpad and looked at the watercolor on it. It was a factual reproduction of the scene before him—a foaming but nonetheless listless-looking blue-green ocean. He studied it for a while and then broke out laughing.

"Mark down a big zero in the passion department next to 'ocean view,' Stan!"

But then, remembering the vision he'd seen before the doorbell had rung, he looked out, over the balcony, into the distance, and stared for a while searching for the face.

Yes. He found it. It was still there, begging, once again, to be rendered.

The vacuum cleaner roared in the hallway, and, on the other side of the closed door, in the Kurtzs' second bedroom, Rodney Bingham pictured the agile female body tilting gently forward as the young woman pushed the suction nozzle back and forth, back and forth across the thick wall-to-wall carpeting.

Brandy Devine. He bet he was the only man in the world with a cleaning woman named Brandy Devine. He chomped on his chewing gum. His eyes wandered down to the failed attempts at sketching crumpled up into balls on the floor next to his stool, and then he looked at the blank piece of paper on the tablet resting on the table before him.

He picked up the pencil. "You almost had it last time," he told himself. "This time you'll get it right." He bent over the paper and started in, his eyes squinting, his brow furrowed, his hand moving briskly around the paper, leaving short, light pencil marks in its wake. "If this one doesn't work out, there's always Brandy Devine as a consolation prize."

After a while, his body relaxed, as did his facial muscles. His green eyes opened wider, hypnotized by the strokes and what was coming from the strokes. The chewing gum crackled as his jaw moved up and down, faster and faster.

He leaned so far forward he was half-sitting, half-standing, and his hand took on a life of its own, moving around the paper quickly, almost frantically. It was all so clear in his head, and this time the translation was working. This time it was coming out on paper. Gradually the lines were forming eyes—eyes that were both hostile and playful, brown eyes, dark eyes—a nose, a jaw.

Not the right jaw. He grabbed the eraser and then began again. Better, narrower, much better. His hand began drawing to the rhythm of his gum chewing. He sketched the lips—thick, and drawn into a barely discernible snarl—and when he looked at them, he knew they were right, because he could hear in his head the words coming through them: "Whadya, crazy?"

He smiled in remembrance.

It was a magic wand, this pencil he held in his hand, scrambling up and around the paper with unerring precision, filling in the details here, smoothing out the angles there, bringing back the past in breathtaking detail. His hand couldn't stop scampering around, following the pencil's will. He felt his heart pound as his eyes watched in awe.

A few minutes later he stopped abruptly, put the tablet down, and walked away from the table. His T-shirt was damp with sweat, his body shaky, as though he'd just run four miles. He walked around the room, examining the floral print on the curtains, the matching print on the lampshade, looking everywhere but back at the sketch on the table, afraid to look, afraid of being disappointed.

There was a knock on the door. "Uh, Mr. Bingham?"

He opened the door. "Yes, Brandy?" He looked at her without seeing her.

"Do you want me to clean in here?" She walked into the room and looked around. "Oh, who did these pictures?" she asked, moving over to one of the beds.

"I did."

She picked up the ocean view. "Isn't that pretty," she said politely. "Looks just like the view, you know, uh, from your balcony." She picked up another one. "And this is . . . this is the sunset."

She reminded him of a mother trying to decipher the clumsy crayoned lines on colored construction paper her child had brought

36

home from kindergarten. Then he heard her say, "Wow!" He looked up.

She was standing very still by the table, holding the pencil sketch. "Did you do this too?"

"Yes." He stood without moving, right where he was, still afraid to look at it.

"Jeez, it's awful good."

"Why—" His voice squeaked. He swallowed. "Why do you think it's good?"

"I pick it up and I'm thinking *'Hold on!'* In just, like, a lot of pencil marks going in funny directions, you got a real person's face here! It's like he has a personality and all."

He turned and faced her. "What is he like?"

"Wise guy." She smiled coquettishly at the drawing. "Big shot. Guy in his twenties. Macho-macho, know what I mean?" She giggled. "Boy, I sure wouldn't trust *him.*"

That gave him the strength. He walked slowly over to the table and examined the drawing in her hands. He took a deep breath, pulling all the air in the room in to fortify his rumpled body, and then he exhaled it slowly in a relieved grunt.

Victory, at last. It worked. God damn, this one really worked. It was just like the image in his head. No, not an image, a real person, one he could see so clearly.

Passion returneth, Stanley Kurtz. *Passion returneth.*

"Who is he?" she asked.

He stared at the drawing for a long time, curious, wondering, suddenly wanting to ask it all kinds of questions, silently welcoming something—something lost—back into his life.

"Who?" she prodded.

"Huh?" He looked up and blinked, startled to find Brandy Devine standing before him. "Oh, he's . . . um . . . he's a central character in the book I'm going to write."

"Really? Wow, that's great. Like, does, does this, uh, character have a name?"

Rodney Bingham nodded, his eyes never leaving the drawing. "Salvatore Durone," he told her. "His name is Salvatore Durone."

5

1968 The Brooklyn Dodgers won their first World Series in 1955, when they defeated the New York Yankees in the seventh game. I was only six years old, but I was there—in a box along the first base line with my family.

I remember my starched shirt collar rubbed uncomfortably against my neck, and my sister got ketchup on my pants and told everyone I'd done it. I remember the baseball diamond grass looked like bright green velvet, and everything smelled like hot dogs. I remember my mother kept telling me not to press my nose against the metal railing because I'd get germs. Mostly I remember feeling the way I always felt on family outings—left out of the lineup.

I was the youngest of four children, preceded in this world by two strapping brothers and a sister who looked like Alice-in-Wonderland.

There appeared to be two distinct sets of genes in operation: My older brothers were carbon copies of my tall, dark, robust father. My older sister was a replica of my dainty, fair, small-boned mother. The fact that I looked like the women in the family was unfortunate because I was a boy.

I had other unfortunate characteristics. I was sickly, small, and solitary in a family of hearty extroverts. I liked to draw and read, and hated to run, kick, and catch. "Puny" was the adjective the male members of the household used to describe me. I did not need a dictionary definition to sense it was not uttered in admiration.

The momentous import of the seventh game of the 1955 World Series was lost on a six-year-old who did not understand baseball. I knew we had come to watch the Yankees win, partly because we always wanted the Yankees to win, but also because losing to the Brooklyn Dodgers would be worse than losing to anyone else. It had something to do with their being the first team to let "knee-grows" play. That's what I heard my father tell my brothers.

But that was only part of the reason. It was also because they were "burns" and "losers" and "low-class creeps." All of this I overheard. As usual, no one was talking to me.

"Where's Brooklyn?" I asked, turning around, trying to gain entry to the all-male club.

"No place," my brother Todd sneered. Everyone got a big laugh out of that one. I shriveled a little.

"Who's winning?" I tried again.

"Haven't you been watching?" my father stormed.

Shattered, I turned back to the field.

"Who's number fifteen again?" Todd asked my father. "You know, their left fielder?"

"Over there!" I shouted victoriously, pointing to a man with a "15" on his shirt.

"I know *where* he is, silly. I was asking what his *name* was."

"Sandy Amoros," my father said, ignoring my brilliance. "He's a Cuban knee-grow, can't even speak English."

They chuckled, man to man.

"Little runt, look at him."

"Puny, isn't he?"

"Yup."

Puny. As my eyes watched number 15 trot out onto the field, a terrible realization came to me: I was a Dodger in a family of Yankees, a puny knee-grow loser who came from noplace.

Batters started swinging, and balls were flying, and Yankees were running to bases, and my brothers and my father were saying strange things like "Bases loaded!" and "Bye-bye Podres!" and "We're gonna pull this game out of the fire!"

39

But my eyes were glued to number 15, out there in the field. I felt just the way number 15 looked—little and lonely. Then I heard the crack of the bat, and my father yelling "That's it!" and my whole family screaming as they jumped up and down around me.

But I was watching number 15. He ran like crazy—ran and ran and ran all the way over to the corner of the field farthest away from us, right by the white line, and he stretched his small body as if it were a rubber band and reached out his glove . . .

And the ball fell right into it! *Smack.*

There was a giant *woooosh* as the whole crowd took in a breath, and then—real fast—number 15 fired the ball back to number 1, and number 1 threw it to number 14, and the umpire screamed, "Ow-wooooot!"

My mother whimpered and my brothers groaned and my father kept shouting "No!" But a whole lot of other people sitting near us were jumping up and down and clapping and yelling: "He caught it!" "Can you believe that?" "And he made it a double play!"

And out on the field, number 15 was being pounded and patted by all the other numbers, like he was a hero.

"Thegoddamncatch." That's what they called it over and over again in the car going home from the game. That was about the only thing anybody said in the car. No one was talking much. Everyone was pretty miserable.

Except me. I stared out the car window, watching the city lights go by, replaying little number 15 all alone out there, catching the ball, and digesting an important message: It didn't just happen in story books like *The Little Engine That Could* and *Tiny Jim and the Giant.* It could happen in *real life* too. Puny knee-grow losers from noplace—like me—could triumph.

That day marked the beginning of a preoccupation that lasted thirteen years. Realizing it could happen, I began devoting large amounts of time and energy secretly searching for real-life examples.

I found them all over—on television ("The Green family is alive tonight, thanks to quick thinking on the part of the Green's five-year-old son, Jimmy . . ."), and even in the course of family dinners ("Stan Christopher, that jerk I fired? They say he started his own company and is making a pile of money!").

By the time I was ten, I had found biblical justification (David and Goliath), and my preoccupation had turned into an obsession. It had also become essential therapy at home, where, no matter how hard I tried, I always ended up feeling like a Dodger in a family of Yankees.

I poured over the feature pages of newspapers and magazines searching for stories. The *New York Post*, disdained by my father as "that pinko paper," offered endless examples of the downtrodden overcoming adversity. I began sneaking the *Post* into my bedroom, much the way I had watched my older brothers sneak *Playboy* into theirs.

By the time I was sent to the family prep school, the obsession had become more specific: I was looking for stories about people who overcame oppression through brainpower and diplomacy. The obsession had also become even more crucial to my survival, as it was a sports-dominated school populated by sneering, nasty, aggressive jocks who seemed to derive great pleasure out of torturing me.

I spent the four most miserable years of my life there, as I cowered in my room, ferreting out news accounts of uprisings against tyranny in little countries around the world.

I was the first male in three generations of my family who did not attend the Naval Academy at Annapolis. Indeed, when I entered Harvard College in the fall of 1967, I suspected I had the dubious distinction of being the only one in the freshman class whose family considered him a failure for going to Harvard.

No matter. At Harvard I found the cocoon I had been seeking all my life, a place where jocks hung out with jocks, intellectuals hung out with intellectuals, and both groups were too absorbed in themselves to notice my by then well-developed failings.

My freshman year not only afforded me the comfort of being permitted to exist in relative obscurity. It yielded the best David and Goliath story of my life. In the fall of 1967, a new reformist leader, Alexander Dubcek, managed to rally support in Czechoslovakia against the Czech Communist Party's First Secretary, Antonin Novotny.

By January of 1968, Dubcek had succeeded in replacing Novotny, promising the Czechoslovaks "Socialism with a human face." In February, March, and April, he proved himself true to that

41

promise, introducing liberal reforms, loosening censorship, and courageously rehabilitating the Czech victims of the Stalin era.

It says something about my fragile, introverted, Walter Mitty nature that I chose to dream about a distant revolution when I could have participated in a real one. My Harvard classmates were actively protesting the war in Vietnam and fighting for students' rights. They were rushing off to New Hampshire to campaign for Eugene McCarthy in the Presidential primary, tasting new sexual freedoms, and passing around joints. Hair kept getting longer, draft cards were burned, and debates on equality went on into the early-morning hours in smoke-filled rooms.

However, by that time I had learned that public contact yielded private pain. Thus, as demonstrations erupted daily outside my dorm window, I spent my freshman year closeted in my room, clandestinely devouring each and every newspaper report I could get my hands on about Czechoslovakia. I cheered from the sidelines as Alexander Dubcek, my personal hero, courageously and with disciplined persistence managed to temper Marxist doctrine with democracy.

Gradually, my inner world began to blend in harmoniously with the outer world. Even the greening of the grass and the sprouting of flowers on the Harvard campus seemed to me, one more manifestation of "Prague Spring"—the dramatic rebirth in the arts and politics taking place in a country half a world away.

Somehow, Dubcek's success in Czechoslovakia, combined with my lack of personal failure at Harvard, created an internal euphoria I had never known before. For the first time in my life, in "Prague Spring"—the spring of 1968—I was comfortable, relaxed, at peace with the world.

Unfortunately, I made the mistake of letting the happiness show on a weekend visit to my family.

While the old values were being ridiculed on campus, they were being maintained with a vengeance at home. I arrived in New York City with a grown-out version of the haircut I had gotten at Christmas. The wavy wisps of blond curling around my ears and jaw, coupled with my unprecedented contentment, were enough to convince my father that Harvard was just reinforcing my weaknesses, and the still-elusive goal of "putting hair on my chest" would only be accomplished if he took action.

Action came in the form of a summer job. A friend of one of my uncles owned a plant about an hour's drive from Boston that was going to be closed down in September and transported to the South, where labor costs were cheaper. The Massachusetts natives, it seemed, were a volatile lot—high-tempered Italians and Greeks, the second generation in a downtrodden area to experience a rash of plant closings. When the textile factory up the road had closed two years earlier, there had been a series of arsons just before the last day. My uncle's friend felt it might be useful to have a contact in the plant to let management know about any attempts at sabotage as September approached.

In return for offering me up as a spy, my father got assurances that I would work my tail off on the loading platform and either sink or learn to swim amid a gang of seasoned toughies.

Delighted at having discovered a means of compensating for Harvard's lack of a proper introduction to life—in other words, the "hazing" period or "hell week" offered by many of the nation's enlightened universities—my father told me in the form of an order from high command exactly how I would be spending my summer vacation.

And thus, in May of 1968, praying Alexander Dubcek would help me get through what I saw as three difficult months ahead, I found myself packing my "Prague Spring" clippings into a suitcase and heading in my yellow VW bug up to a tiny town north of Boston with instructions to "make a man" out of myself.

Rodney Bingham stared at the computer screen for a while and then took his hands off the keyboard. He got up and walked slowly around Stanley Kurtz's living room, idly picking up ashtrays, fiddling with them and then putting them down, turning on lamps.

He stopped at the big sliding doors leading to the balcony and stood for a while staring out at the darkening beach below. Then he walked back to his word processor and sat down.

"The only thing more preposterous than the idea," he wrote, "was that it worked."

6

"Oh, you're here!" Francine Durone gasped as Marci opened the front door. "It being Saturday night and all, I was afraid you wouldn't be home!"

"The kids are out. I was taking advantage of the quiet to get some work done." Marci stepped aside in the doorway. "Come on in."

"No. Can't stay." Francine seemed more disturbed than usual. "I borrowed Sal's mother's car. Gotta get it back. I just . . ." She thrust a thick manila envelope at Marci. "Just wanted you to see this."

Marci's face it up. "The bills! You found the old telephone bills!"

"No." Francine shook her head resolutely. "Marci, I have combed that house from top to bottom. I swear, they're gone. Someone *stole* them! That's the only possible—"

"Then," Marci asked, looking down in confusion at the manila envelope in her hands, "what's this?"

"Don't know." Francine's upper lip curled slightly. "Apparently, uh, Sal Durone had a private side."

"What?"

"I sold Sal's pickup truck today. The man who bought it found that envelope stuck away in the glove compartment. It's bank statements."

"Bank statements?" Marci frowned.

"From a private account!" Francine whined. "An account he opened a few days *after we got married*. His mother says he received some money for his Vietnam duty right around then. *She* knew, but not *me!* I, his wife, never knew such an account existed!" She pointed her finger accusingly at Marci. "Fifteen hundred dollars he had in there, gathering interest over the years. Money I coulda used to get a dishwasher or a decent television——"

"Is it still intact?" Marci asked hopefully. "Is there still money in the account?"

"Not much." Francine nibbled on her lower lip. "He took out a whole bunch this year." She turned around and began walking down Marci's front steps.

"For what?" Marci called after her. "What did he use it for?"

"Some floosie probably!" Francine screamed over her shoulder. "Do I know? Did he tell *me?*" She scampered down the front walk. "For months this year he was coming home late every Wednesday night. *That* I know!" She climbed into the car and slammed the door.

Marci watched as the car sped off. What can of worms had she opened? Had she become Francine Durone's personal accountant? Called in to clean up, to service all the Durone family's loose ends?

She slammed her front door. One night, one Saturday evening free to catch up on her legal work, was that too much to ask?

No, it was not. She hurled the envelope on the coffee table in the living room and began climbing the stairs. Back to the study. Back to the planned agenda. But she stopped halfway up the stairs. Salvatore Durone, keeper of mysterious bank accounts? It didn't figure. But using the glove compartment to store secret information, *that* figured. The only consistency in Durone's life had been his trucks. Always, from the time he got his driving license, Durone had driven pickup trucks. It was his trademark—tires squealing, followed by someone muttering, "Here comes Sallie."

She turned around and went back to the living room. Chastizing herself, she plopped down on the sofa and emptied the envelope out onto the coffee table.

There were three stacks of papers, each stack stapled together. She picked up the top pile. The first bank statement was dated

January 23, 1972, and indicated the account had been opened with a deposit of $1,500. She flipped through sixteen different year-end statements, 1973 through 1989, each one a documentation of interest accrued on the original lump sum. No withdrawals.

It was the orderliness that floored her, the meticulousness of the bookkeeping. It fit in with the man whose workroom she had visited in the Durone house, but it most certainly did not fit the wild, rough, reckless man she had known as Salvatore Durone all these years. Or *thought* she had known.

The next stack of papers were monthly statements for 1989. On February 3, 1989, Durone had withdrawn a hundred dollars. On February 10, 1989, he had withdrawn seventy-five. On February 17, a hundred. On February 24, seventy-five.

Marci scanned the next three monthly statements: March, April, May. The February pattern was duplicated in each one: alternating weekly withdrawals. A hundred dollars one week, seventy-five the next. She checked the dates on a calendar. All the withdrawals were made on Wednesdays, the nights when, according to Francine, Durone always stayed out late.

She reexamined the first statement. Francine was right. He had set the account up just after they got married, obviously intending it to be his private financial reserve. But why, all of a sudden, after seventeen years of nonwithdrawals, had he begun taking money out of the account? She went on to the pack of more recent monthly statements: June, July, August, September. No withdrawals.

The doorbell rang. She cringed. Please, she begged the ceiling, no more Francine Durone tonight! She breathed a sigh of relief when she saw Jack's face smiling self-consciously through the windowpane in the front door.

"Busy?" The word turned into vapor in the cold night air.

She opened the door. "Nope. Come on in."

"You're sure I'm not keeping you from working?" Jack Whelan's square frame held its ground on the front stoop. "I saw there was a light on in your study."

"I'm finished. Still reeling from an earlier interruption, in fact." She shivered. "Come *in*, for God's sake, before I freeze to death!"

Jack Whelan crossed the threshold and took off his coat, revealing a dark green sportshirt and clashing green pants. Marci smiled indulgently.

46

He noticed the look. "They don't go together, huh?"

"It's not your fault." Marci giggled as she hung up his coat. "I've decided you just have a closet in which nothing goes together." Her nose picked up Old Spice aftershave cologne mixed with a dab of bourbon.

"Where're the kids?"

"Lindsay's at a slumber party and Tommy's out on a date."

"What are you doing? Your bills?" He pointed to the clutter of bank statements on the living-room coffee table.

"No," she laughed, "just keeping tabs on my murder victim's sex life!" She explained Francine's visit and Sal's previously unknown bank account.

Whelan began perusing the statements. "Where did he come up with the original deposit?"

"Vietnam veteran's benefits."

Whelan frowned. "And the withdrawals stopped this June?"

"Yup. That's the month Durone found out he had cancer." Marci shrugged. "Maybe he decided it was time for the fun to end." She tossed her hands up into the air. "It's bad enough that I seem to have turned into Francine Durone's private accountant. I don't want—"

"Well, it's your own fault for asking for the phone bill!" He pointed an accusing finger at her. "You should have told this Durone lady what you would have told any client who entered your office with an off-the-wall murder theory—that there was *nothing* you could do. Period. End of interview. *Fini!*"

She forced an ingratiating smile. "Jack," she purred lightly, "would you like a drink?"

"Why, that would be most delightful, my dear," he responded, mimicking her tone.

When Marci returned to the living room with a glass of bourbon and a glass of wine, Jack was staring at a picture. He quickly put it back in place on the fireplace mantel. "So!" he said jocularly. "How did that tutoring project of yours work out?"

She handed him the bourbon, kicked off her shoes, and curled up coyly on the sofa. "Tutoring project?"

"Don't malarcky me, Courbienne." He leaned back and put his elbow on the mantel. "When I left here the other night, your son

47

was well on his way to tutoring the Durone kid. He just didn't know it yet."

She ran her finger around the top of the wineglass. "First session is next Tuesday."

"Just like that? No fight? No protest?"

"There were a few problems to work out, but they're settled. The high-school guidance counselor officially asked Tom to do it, and then announced it as her decision to Frank Durone."

"Saving face on both sides."

Marci beamed. "And giving Tom a unique opportunity to live out the stellar words you wrote in his 'challenge and achievement' speech!"

She giggled, but Jack just grunted and sipped his drink. He seemed unusually restless, distracted. "You have the look of a man with an agenda, Jack."

"I've been thinking . . ." He took the picture off the mantel again and waved it in her direction. "This is the whole problem."

Marci looked up at him mischievously. "By 'this' are you referring to the silver frame that has been in my mother-in-law's family for generations, or the picture of my husband?"

"Deceased husband!" he stormed, slamming the frame back on the mantel. "Good heavens, girl, the man's been dead for twelve years now."

Dinner in the oven, the kitchen table set for two. Lindsay sound asleep. Tommy calling down from upstairs for one more good-night kiss. And then the vision—just the sight of those two policemen through the window of the front door, seeing them there . . . knowing— Had it really been twelve years? It came back to her as though it had happened yesterday.

"It's time to face, it, Marci, face it and go on!"

"Go *on?*" Her eyes flashed. "I began going on the minute Tom died, Jack! On to one more year of law school, and then the bar exam, and then balancing—"

"I mean *personally* go on."

She shook her head and closed her eyes. Oh, the unwavering audacity of the male ego. "Meaning, marry you."

"It's not just me. It's—"

"Really?" She leaned back on the sofa. "You're here pleading for an end to Marci Courbienne's widowhood on behalf of *all* the

48

single men in Orange County who have asked for her hand in marriage?"

"Was I the first who asked?"

Knowing full well it was intended as a rhetorical question, she contemplated it seriously. "You were—let me see now—the fourth." She looked up at Whelan brightly. "You are, however, the only man who *stopped* sleeping with me when I said 'no.' "

He looked away.

"Jack," she said softly, "you are my best friend and I love you very, very much."

"But not enough to marry me." He turned back to the mantel. "The problem is him! You were married to a saint, a long, lean, handsome, loving young god who died in a freak car accident at the age of twenty-seven, and whose memory you've preserved intact for twelve years now."

She clamped her mouth shut. Better that than the truth.

"Don't you see, Marci, I can't compete with that. No one can."

"I don't see why we can't just maintain the same relationship we've always had."

"When I'm obviously not good enough to—"

"You're good enough!" She shifted uncomfortably on the sofa. "You're *too* good, if anything."

"But not rich enough. Is that it?"

She blinked. "What?"

"I know the score. I know I'm no flashy entrepreneur like him!" He pointed at the mantel.

"My God, Tom was *hardly* a flashy—"

"I admit it! I'm just a salaried labor union official. I don't have his drive to make a million." Whelan spit the words out contemptuously. "I'm not fancy stock either."

Marci threw her head back in laughter. "Fancy stock? Gee, Tom would be a bit surprised to hear himself described that way!"

"Thomas H. Courbienne? Only child of B. J. Courbienne, Collier's esteemed—"

"Now you're getting ridiculous. If you only *knew* how off-base you are."

"You know what I mean! He was all American! He had the type of credentials that appeal to little Italian girls hoping to better themselves!"

49

Marci's visage hardened. "That's your game plan for winning my hand in marriage, Jack? Walking in here and suggesting that I choose my husbands on the grounds of financial promise and social elevation?"

"No," Whelan groaned, putting his hand over his eyes. "It came out wrong. All wrong. I'm sorry." He looked up at her, his eyes pleading. "Marci, we have good times together. We understand each other. We—"

"—are good friends," Marci interrupted. "Close friends. The best of friends."

"And that's all it can ever be?"

"Why can't that be enough?"

He drowned his drink and stood up.

She looked up at him, wide-eyed and hurt. "That's it, Jack? You come, make your accusations and your pronouncement, and then exit? All or nothing?"

"That's it," he said hoarsely, heading out to the hall.

When Jack Whelan walked back into the living room, he was wearing his coat. He paused and fingered the papers on the coffee table. "I, uh, didn't realize until you said so tonight that Durone was a Vietnam veteran."

Marci shook her head to adjust to the abrupt change of topic. "How's that for a sudden shift in gears?"

"Well." He stepped awkwardly from foot to foot. "I was just thinking, that might explain his asking for the area code for Washington, D.C. Might have been calling some veterans organization for information."

Marci squinted up at him, totally perplexed.

"I bet *Vietnam's* where he picked up his fancy form of cancer."

Her face froze. Oh, no. Not Vietnam. She drew the line at Vietnam. She wrapped her fingers tightly around the base of the wineglass.

Her reaction confused him. "It's just that a whole lot of people from around here have been afflicted in funny ways. You might not know, but this Agent Orange they used—"

"I know." She inhaled abruptly. "Don't talk to me about the Vietnam War. Please."

"What do you know?"

She stared into space. "I know that Jimmy Fresco—the boy

who sent me a most elaborate Valentine in the third grade—Jimmy Fresco's daughter was born with her heart in the wrong place, outside where it was supposed to be." She said the words slowly, in a monotone. "I know Bruno Burgesi's son was born with a contorted lung that snuffed out his life in two days." She looked up angrily at Whelan. "And Bruno and Jimmy, those were the *survivors*. Two of the few who came back.

"I grew up in one of those rare communities in this patriotic country of ours," she said, "a place where all the young men searching for a better life rushed off to serve in Vietnam, while all those rich, educated boys in other places were either evading or protesting the draft. And the boys from Fallsville were either killed or scarred for life or sent home to make babies who did not survive. I simply can't sit here and listen to—"

"Marci." His voice was gentle. "All I'm saying is—"

"Salvatore Durone was just about the only winner. Sal came home a hero without scars, at least ostensibly without scars, to a town that has *never* recovered from the Vietnam War." Her voice was choked. "If he had latent scars, I don't want to know about them."

"Admit, at least, that you're being a little melodramatic here! I mean, everybody's got neighborhood tragedies. You're acting like it's *personal* or something."

She stared straight ahead.

"Marci?"

She did not move. "I had two brothers who were killed in Vietnam."

"What?" His face became pale. "Three years I've known you, and you never once told me that?"

So many things she'd never told Jack Whelan. So many things she'd tried to forget herself.

"Didn't even know you *had* brothers," he accused. "You and your sister, that's all I ever heard about!

"So? Sue me for withholding information."

"I'm so sorry, Marci." He sat down beside her on the sofa in silence. She knew he wanted to put his arms around her, and at the moment, she felt a desperate need to feel his arms wrapped around her. But she also knew there would be a quid for the show of affection, and that transformed her angst into anger.

He gazed at the hands lying limply in his lap. "I'm just an old-fashioned Irishman," he whispered, reading her thoughts. "I did one thing in my whole life no other Whelan had ever done. I got a divorce. That was my great gesture to the modern world, and it tore me apart, even though I knew I'd go out of my mind if I didn't."

He shook his head slowly. "What you want me to do, it's just something I can't do. I can't feel the way I do about you and your children and keep being an outsider, Marci. I want to be a part of you—make you all a part of me. I want to . . . no, I'm not gonna say take care of you, because I know you'll run me out of town if I do. You're very good at taking care of things yourself. I guess I want the chance to help you, to make you all happy, because being with you makes me so very happy. If I can't become a part of you, then I just can't have it any other way." He looked at her. "Can you understand that?"

She avoided his eyes. "I understand how you feel. It is you who are refusing to understand me."

"Well, you don't leave me any choice!" He kept looking at her, and she kept looking away. "Outspoken Marci Courbienne, the woman who puts into words things most people don't even have the guts to think to themselves. Marci Courbienne refuses to tell me honestly and out loud why she will not marry me!"

He waited for several minutes for her eyes to meet his. When they did not, he stood up and stalked out of the living room.

She heard the front door slam, and then the car motor turn on. It was only when the sound of the car's engine faded away into the night that she got up off the sofa.

She walked resolutely over to the cabinet in the corner of the living room. She opened the door and without looking, reached in to pull out a framed picture of a smiling, dashing, young dark-haired man in a military uniform. She looked at it, just for a moment, but that was enough. Tears began streaming down her face.

Time to stop trying to bury the past, she instructed herself. Time for the kids to get a daily look at their uncle, time for Tommy to see the man his mother patterned him after. She put the picture on the oval side table, next to photos of the children when they were small, their grandparents.

Then she walked around in circles on the oriental rug in the middle of the living room trying to figure out how old her brother

Vince would be right now if he had survived Vietnam, wondering why the fact was so important to her, knowing rationally that it was easy to figure out. It was just that her mind was all confused with so many different emotions.

Forty-one. That was it. A ridiculous thought: Vince at forty-one. Vince would always be twenty, "at his peak," one of the many men who'd left her life at their peak.

She moved over to the fireplace mantel, picked up the picture Jack Whelan had waved in front of her, and gazed down at the sincere young man of twenty-seven with the soft dark blond hair and the face that was a replica of her son's, except the eyes. They lacked the devilish sparkle her son had in his. A saint. Jack was right. Tom was a saint. What Jack Whelan didn't realize was that he was every bit as much a saint as Thomas Courbienne, and a woman could only stand to be married to a saint once in a lifetime.

She looked into the sweet innocent young eyes that were willing to do anything to make her happy, but unable to understand what it took to make her happy, and when she could stand their stare no more, she shut hers. She knew only too well the unbearable guilt that came from being married to a man who loved you more than you loved him.

That was what she had been unwilling to tell Jack Whelan.

7

The balcony doors were open, and the Florida sunshine was pouring into the living room along with gusts of warm air. Rodney Bingham took a few gulps of orange juice, put the glass back down next to him on the desk, and returned to the word processor.

1968 The information my father gave me was minimal. "The town is Fallsville. Mrs. Stompous on Winslow Street rents rooms. The factory's name is Kelso. You're to report to work on Monday morning at eight o'clock."

The charred carcasses of two empty factory buildings heralded the beginning of Fallsville's Main Street. They were followed by a string of sleepy storefronts with CLOSED SUNDAY signs in their windows. A big parking lot set the Kelso plant off at the other end of the two-block spread.

Main Street was surrounded by clusters of run-down houses splattered across the town's hills and valleys. The terrain was woodsy, but much of the "foliage" seemed to be man-made. Discarded objects—a doorless car here, a wheelless truck there, a baby carriage, a stack of tires—vied with trees and bushes for room on the landscape.

Mrs. Stompous, a squat woman with a dour visage and thin

gray hair fastened into little bobby-pinned curls all over her head, led me to a small structure in her backyard. It housed a single, unheated room with a lumpy bed, a dresser, and a light bulb with a metal chain that dangled down, forming a little silvery pile in the middle of the bed. The room had a tiny bathroom with an old, yellowish tub that stood on feet.

The expression on Mrs. Stompous's face dared me to express my real feelings.

I signed on for the summer.

With even less enthusiasm, I signed the register in Kelso's main office at 8 A.M. the next day. The shift chief gave me the run-down: Kelso's day shift was made up of three sections. I would be put in the section with the "young guys." Each section was subdivided into three groups: cleaners, processors, and loaders. There were two cleaners in each section, two loaders, and all the rest were processors, who worked the assembly line. Since cleaning chores only happened at the beginning and end of each shift, the cleaners doubled as supervisors. I would work as a loader.

Then he led me to my section's locker room.

Sensitive about my small size, I usually measured myself against new peers by height and weight, but something else hit me about the locker-room group: ears. I saw a whole room full of ears. The trend toward long hair had, apparently, not made it to Fallsville. Nor had body shirts and bell-bottom pants. These guys were changing out of shirts that had the collars pulled up in the back and the sleeves rolled up above the elbows, sort of like the 1950s street gangs I had seen in movies.

The banter froze to silence when we walked in, and I felt all eyes in the room directed at the hair running down the sides of my face.

"Where's Sallie?" the shift chief asked, frowning as he scanned the room.

"Finishin' up the cleanin'."

"Well, this here's the college boy I been tellin' you about," the supervisor said.

I looked at the faces and begged silently for the chance to rewrite my introduction.

"Rodney Bingham's his name." He gave it six syllables. "So? Just 'cause Sallie ain't here's no reason for bad manners!"

Sallie, I decided, had to be a kind of house mother.

"Introduce yourselves to the new man!"

Obediently, going around the room, each guy stepped forward and uttered a name. Only one name. Each appellation was rendered matter-of-factly, which was very strange, given the utterances.

"Fatso," declared an expressionless six-footer. "Pimp." "Con man." "Nasty." "Turd."

I was Snow White meeting the dwarfs, only the dwarfs were twice my size and hostile. Some of the names fit and some didn't. One of Cripple's legs was shorter than the other, and Tooth was missing his top front teeth. Lucky, on the other hand, seemed an unfortunate kind of guy—short and very fat with a face full of pimples and a ripe odor.

Big and greasy from his short black hair and shiny face down to his soiled undershirt, Slime definitely fit his name. Hard-on, on the other hand, had no readily discernible lump at his crotch. The fact that the supervisor pointed out to me, parenthetically, that Hard-on had a high-school diploma, made me guess he was the only one in the group who did.

Suddenly the locker-room door burst open, and a long, lean guy with the biggest set of upper arm muscles I'd ever seen sauntered in.

"Sallie!" The men gravitated toward him, whispering and laughing, their backs to me, beckoning over their shadows, and Sallie stood very still, nodding at the information he was receiving, never taking his eyes off me. His hair, closely cropped on the sides, erupted into a well-greased pompadour on the top of his head. He had a thin, long nose that snarled at his mouth and an aura of raw masculinity. Very raw.

So much for my house-mother theory.

I knew instinctively as I gazed across the room that this was the bully. This was to be my summer nemesis.

"This here's your supervisor, Salvatore Durone, Roduhney," the day chief explained. "Sallie," he said, patting Durone on the shoulder as he turned to leave, "you know what to do."

The door slammed behind him, and the only sound in the room was Salvatore Durone's footsteps as he made his way toward me.

He reached into his shirt pocket, pulled out a pack of cigarettes, and lit one.

"Roduhney," he said, staring down his crooked nose at me, a cigarette dangling from his lips. "We got a problem. Lotta dese guys, see, 'ey're dumb. 'Ey can't say big words like 'Roduhney.' "

Cackles from the other end of the room.

He exhaled a cloud of smoke in my face. "We gotta give you a simple name."

"How 'bout Goldilocks?" shrieked Lucky.

"Naaaah," Durone drawled, tugging on a lock of my hair. "Ee'll probably cut this faggot stuff off real quick." He grinned, unshielding a mouthful of pointy teeth just about an inch above my nose. "We need a name 'at'll stick."

The gang offered unfriendly epithets.

"College boy, huh?" Sallie snorted, standing so close I felt the heat of his breath.

The whistle blew for the shift to start and the guys scrambled for their work clothes.

"Smarts," Durone announced as I put on my shirt. "We'll call him Smarts." The snickers on the other side of the room told me it was the ultimate insult.

Durone grabbed me by the collar of the workshirt I was buttoning up. "You get out they-ah on that loading dock and you work your butt off, Smarts!"

Nothing motivates like terror. I not only worked my butt off that first day, I got my hair shorn right after work. By some coincidence the local barber's specialty was the razored look popular at the factory.

Work hard and hide. That, I decided in my room after my first day at Kelso, would be my strategy. I would become an exemplary employee on the loading dock and as invisible as possible everywhere else. The last part was the most difficult. The locker room felt a lot like a locked ward, a meeting place for high-strung zombies itching for a fight.

"Wassamattah? You don't like my shirt?"

"Dint say nothin' 'bout you-ah shirt!"

"You was looking at it ahful funny."

"I c'n lookit what I wanna lookit!"

"Not if I'm in it you can't!"

This was brittle kindling that did not need a match to ignite it. I spent a lot of time, my first days at Kelso, staring at my fingers as they buttoned and unbuttoned my workshirts, trying to ignore both the hostilities and the strange idiosyncrasies of my coworkers.

Slime, for example, entertained himself as he changed clothes with a monologue on the television show he'd watched the night before. Or there was Lucky, who loved to sing, but only one song. "You gotta talk to the animals," he'd chant as he untied his shoelaces, "walk with the animals."

And then, of course, there was the landmine in the corner, our commanding officer, who only had eyes for me. The locker room could be in a state of total chaos, with four arguments going on simultaneously, and a furtive glance at Durone would find him staring at me, his upper lip curling slightly, a growling dog about to bite.

Nonetheless, my strategy worked. After two weeks working on the loading dock beside the taciturn Hard-on, I was performing flawlessly and the guys had practically forgotten I existed.

Unfortunately, Salvatore Durone had not forgotten. "Ey, Smarts!" he yelled from across the room at closing time one night. "Think it's time you joined us at Mongon's for some fun."

All talk stopped. I felt a sea of hostile eyes focused on me, daring me to say "no."

"Sure," I squeaked.

I'd heard a lot about this place called Mongon's. "Meetcha at Mongon's!" "We was at Mongon's, see, and—" "Me and Turd seen him last week at Mongon's."

I had heard enough to know it was a place to avoid. I was barely holding my own with the animals when they were sober. I had no intention of offering myself up as a target when they'd had a few beers at the local bar. But now I had no choice. I followed haltingly as Durone led the pack out of the factory, down the street, and around the corner. I was a little surprised when they sauntered into a drugstore.

"This is Mongon's?" I wondered out loud.

"Yah," Fatso grunted. "Doc Mongon—the pharmacist? He'sa owner."

On the other side of the swinging doors was an old-fashioned soda counter with about twenty rotating stools. I saw a bunch of girls sitting together at one end of the counter.

Or rather I saw one girl. The rest was backdrop. The centerpiece was a well-tanned brunette with long, silky straight hair that hung down to waist level. She was wearing a sleeveless aqua-and-white checkered dress with a thick white zipper that ran from the hem up to the collar, but had only made it halfway up the bust.

The dress stopped midthigh, where the aqua shade of the checkers was carried on by a matching pair of aqua fishnet stockings that caressed the curves of the thigh and calf all the way down to white flats.

"Ooooooo, Looooo," the boys began to bellow at the shapely brunette, "Bella Louella!"

The object of the roars placed a handful of long, painted fingernails to her brow and winced, but only slightly. This was a girl accustomed to flamboyant attention and she was enjoying it.

"Eh," Sallie ordered, "at's enough."

Slowly, Bella Louella raised her lowered eyelids, causing her long, thick eyelashes to flutter a little, and my stomach along with them. Her moist bubble gum–pink lips smiled around a set of perfect teeth as she patted the stool next to her. Durone sat down on it, thereby snuffling out my internal sparks.

The animals began pounding their fists on the counter in unison.

"I do not respond to subhuman behavior!" The words came out in a high-decibel screech. It took me a second to locate their source: a small, heavily made-up girl with long black hair, standing behind the counter, her hands on her hips. She was tiny—not much more than five feet tall—wearing snug white hip-huggers, a yellow headband that matched her yellow blouse, and an expression on her face that said she could take on any man in the room.

"Eh, how 'bout a little action!" Pimp shouted.

"Pimp wants action? Sell will give him action!" The girl grabbed the whipped cream spritzer and aimed it at Pimp. "Where yah want it, Pimp?" she snarled. "Across that ugly face of yours?"

"Aw, c'mon, Sell!"

"Ey, Sell," Durone called out from his stool. "We brought you a present tonight." He beckoned to me. "A college boy to talk to!"

"Yeah?" She put the spritzer down and turned to me. Her eyes roamed expressionlessly up and down my body as I cringed in the unexpected spotlight. "Gee, thanks, Sallie."

"Sell here's the genius of Fallsville," Sallie hollered over to me. "She has trouble findin' people ta understand her in the summer when there ain't no teachers 'round!"

The boys cracked up on cue. Thankful for the distraction, I walked over to a stool at the opposite end of the counter from Durone and plopped down.

"So, Sell," Durone baited, "talk to him!"

"Yeah, Sell," the guys joined in. "G'wan! Talk to him fancy!"

The girl walked over to where I was sitting, gazed down at me through mascara-clogged eyelashes, and said: "Antisestablishmentarianism."

"Pneumonoultramicroscopicsiliconvolcanoconiosis," I replied.

"Aaaaaaaah" went the thigh-slapping male chorus at the other end of the counter.

"Told yah you two would hit it off!" howled Sallie.

Sell leaned her elbow on the counter and stared Durone down. "What can I get you, Sallie?" It was said in the manner of a saloon keeper.

"The usual, all 'round."

Sell went to work with impressive energy and alacrity, grabbing glasses, working first one machine, then another, swirling and mixing and pouring. "Seven large root beer floats!" she announced as she set a tray of drinks down on the counter.

I bit my lip. Root beer floats? The drugstore as the gangsters' watering hole?

Then Sell headed in my direction, and nothing seemed the least bit amusing. "Okay, college boy, what can I get you?"

"The same." I tried to say it like the Marlboro Man, but it came out in a Virginia Slims voice.

Sell went to work again at her machinery.

"What's new, Sell?" Pimp called out.

"Maryanne and Billie're gonna have a baby," she announced over her shoulder.

"That's not new!"

"Nah, you told us that last week!"

"I told you she was going to have a baby. What's new is they're doing it together. Got married yesterday."

60

"No kidding."

"Never thought Billie'd be so dumb!"

"What else, Sell?"

I felt her eyes linger on me, and then dart back to the guys. It happened so quickly, the look, I wondered if I'd imagined it.

"Kelso is selling the plant manager's residence," she announced.

"Yeah?"

"Then where's the manager gonna live?"

"Beats me," she sighed, taking out a glass. "Maybe there's not going to be a manager."

"Whatcha talkin' about?" Deke shouted. "How can you have a plant without a manager?"

"Good question, Deke." She took her eyes off the machine for a split second and gave me another look. That one definitely was aimed at me. "How can you have a plant without a manager?"

"Never know what old Kelso's gonna do."

The guys were off in small talk, totally missing the point. The crazy little girl was telling them the plant was closing. Or rather, she was telling me, using those side looks and words she knew they wouldn't get, to let me know that she knew that I knew. What else did she know? Did she know it was my uncle's friend who was closing down the plant, thereby removing my coworkers' steady incomes? That I had been hired as a spy?

"I just heard they're expecting trouble at Kelso," she announced over her shoulder. "They're afraid you guys might burn the place down or something."

"Why would we do that?"

"Don't know." Her back was to the group. "Maybe because you got upset about something Kelso management told you."

"Like what?"

"Sell, you're not makin' sense!"

"Talks in puzzles alla time!"

"I hear they're bringing spies in from the outside," she said, carrying my glass over to the counter. "Management spies they're hiring as plant workers to alert them if you guys decide to start something."

My heart was pounding so hard I was sure the pulsations were

61

visible through my T-shirt. Who was this miniature witch, and what was she trying to do?

"Well, if there's spies, they gotta be invisible," laughed Pimp.

"Yeah," Con Man chimed in. "We ain't seen no spies at the plant!"

"You guys wouldn't know a spy if you were working next to him." She slapped the root beer float down in front of me. "Would they?" she whispered.

I gulped and shrugged.

The guys were really talking now, about spies and Crazy Sell and how you could never tell what she was talking about. But Sell lingered at my end of the counter. My hands were ice, my armpits rapidly filling with sweat. Talk to her, I ordered myself. Small talk, idiot, distract her with small talk!

I played with the straw for a while, flicking it around in the glass, sipping through it, then flicking it around some more, all the time trying to figure out what to say. "You, uh, you work here?" I asked finally.

She sneered. "You have blond hair?" she asked scathingly.

I felt my face flash heat. "It was a dumb question."

"Surely *Smarts* can come up with a better ice breaker than that!" She wiped the counter with a sponge.

"How, uh, how did you know about my nickname being Smarts?"

"I'm clairvoyant."

She scared me, this mean little witch-bitch with the crystal ball. I cast a nervous eye down at the other end of the counter. "What else do you know about me?"

She bent over close to me. "Your name is Rodney Bingham," she said. "You're entering your sophomore year at Harvard. You're from New York City. You drive a yellow VW bug. You wear brand-new BVDs, write letters to your sister, and you're rich."

Now I really could not breathe. Out. I had to get out. And fast. "How much do I owe you for the float?"

"But you haven't finished—"

"How much?"

She stared at the sponge. "Sixty-two cents with tax."

I reached into my pocket and, with trembling hands, I put

exactly sixty-two cents down on the counter. Telling myself that rich people were notorious nontippers, I walked out.

"She's got the goods on you!" Slime yelled out when I walked into the locker room the next day. I jumped and rushed over to my locker, my nightmares confirmed. That urchin, Sell, had told them everything.

"She's got the goods on you!" Slime screeched again as I cowered next to my locker. "She's got the—"

"What the fuck you talkin' 'bout?" Durone roared.

"That's just what the little blond girl said on 'Laugh-In' last night," Slime chortled. "You know, that part at the end when they all pop outta their windows?"

Durone made a face and went back to dressing.

"She's my favorite." Slime smiled at no one in particular. "The way she's always poppin' outta that window with that fuzzy yella hair a hers and that li'l giggle. She's got the goods on you!" he chirped in falsetto, slapping his thigh. "She's got the goods on you!"

8

The candles' flames were burning their way down uncluttered white stalks. She remembered how she had loved to finger the hot wax as it spilled down the sides of candles. She marveled at this modern invention, dripless candles, and assured herself the visual splendor of the torches gleaming before her more than compensated for lost tactile pleasures. Then she admitted she had imbibed far too much wine.

"Marci, darling . . ." Priscilla Courbienne's taut lips curved upward slightly as she scrutinized her daughter-in-law. "I like you in that color." The words floated across the dining-room table, a puff of warm air from a usually icy source.

"Dark red," Priscilla continued, inclining her head as though evaluating a museum canvas. "It gives you a regal look."

Marci moved her shoulders back and lifted her chin, attempting to verify the compliment. "Why, thank you, Priscilla."

"Aw, c'mon now, Pris, it's not the *color!*" B. J. Courbienne bellowed, shifting his potbelly around uncomfortably in the delicate antique chair and pointing an accusing finger at the tabletop display. "Long-stemmed glassware, sterling silverware, Limoges china, and candles! Who in hell *wouldn't* look regal in this setting?"

"You." Priscilla cast a cold eye on B.J.'s massive elbows resting on the place setting in front of him.

"Will he never learn?" B.J. crooned in falsetto, spreading his stubby fingers delicately across his eyes the way his wife always did in moments of despair. "Would I have married the man if I'd known he'd make it all the way to the age of seventy without developing any real *class?"*

"Don't push it," Priscilla warned drily.

Marci and B.J. laughed loudly, Priscilla politely.

"Never will forget," B.J. drawled slowly, leaning back in his chair and signaling the onset of a vintage B.J. anecdote, "never will forget that cold, miserable afternoon in January, Nineteen forty-seven . . ."

Marci assumed her listening pose. B.J. anecdotes were usually reruns, greatly enhanced in each telling by the man's gift for spontaneous embellishment. They were handy time-fillers, and Marci guessed this one was designed to serve that purpose. All three adults were pretending not to notice the two empty chairs at the table, fully aware that what was going on behind the closed kitchen door was supposed to come as a surprise.

"I was just a lonesome farm boy who'd run away from home to find a job," B.J. was saying, "and I'd found one too—as a ditch digger."

Ah, yes. It was the ditch-digger-meets-school-teacher story. The gist was that poor, dumb, pudgy Canadian farm boy, B.J., had fallen head over heels for the amply educated, long-legged Priscilla Hampshire Hardon. Through charm, pluck, and artful diplomacy (tinged with a tad of misrepresentation), B.J. had managed to win his beloved's hand in marriage.

"She was a haughty one, I'll tell you that. The Hardon family was patrician stock all the way."

Marci smiled, silently substituting "patrician poverty" for "patrician stock." It made more sense that, having fallen on hard times, the distinguished Hardon family of Boston had been willing to hand over its somewhat spinsterly (Priscilla had been, Marci figured, close to thirty) daughter to a charismatic fast talker with big plans, an Elmer Gantry extolling the glory of capitalism rather than God.

"Just over the horizon!" B.J. orated, raising his hands up majestically. " 'I am certain,' I told her crusty old man, 'that fortune is waiting for me just over the horizon!' "

"Little did he know you just were just dreaming of the pot of gold at the end of the rainbow," Priscilla quipped.

"*You* knew!" B.J. laughed. "And you came anyway!"

Marci could imagine her mother-in-law running off with an enterprising capitalist, but with a dreamer looking for a pot of gold? Hard to believe.

She watched the two of them bickering—Priscilla with her well-placed monosyllables, and B.J. with blustering diatribes and demonstrative gestures. Four decades after that cold January afternoon, B.J. was still an inch shorter than his statuesque wife but many, many inches wider. His thick black hair was now almost entirely white, and just as unruly as Marci guessed it had been back then. He was still an irrepressible loose cannon, and Priscilla was still trying to control him.

In the end, it had been Priscilla who had managed to locate the pot of gold. B.J. had the flamboyance and charm, but Priscilla had the drive. And she had fortunately passed it on in the gene pool, along with her long, lean frame, fair coloring, and pale blue eyes, to her son, Thomas Courbienne.

Indeed, it had taken the two of them—Priscilla and Tom, mother and son—to harness B.J.'s energy and channel it for profit. The pudgy farmer who had left Canada in search of fortune in the 1940s had not realized his dream until the 1970s, and then only because his son, Tom, had reached adulthood and was able to bring his mother's disciplined push to his father's workplace.

The kitchen door opened and a hand came out and flicked off the light switch on the wall.

"Oh, my," Priscilla exclaimed, staring up at the darkened overhead chandelier, "looks like there's some kind of electrical failure."

"Seems to happen every year," B.J. quipped, winking at Marci, "every year on October twenty-eighth."

"Happy Birthday to you. Happy Birthday to you." The slightly off-key sounds of Tommy's baritone and Lindsay's soprano accompanied the candlelit cake making its way from the kitchen to the table. Marci and Priscilla joined in. "Happy Birthday, dear B.J. Happy Birthday to you!"

B.J. stared at the cake. "All those sparkles, they sure drive home the point, don't they?"

"Need any help blowing them out, old man?"

B.J. took a deep breath, blew out all the candles, and then shot his grandson a cocky grin. "Guess I didn't."

Everyone laughed.

B.J. raised his champagne glass. "To the four key ingredients to my happiness," he began grandiosely. "To the young man who can make me laugh like no other, my handsome, wise-cracking, slam-dunking, touchdown-scoring grandson—"

Tommy grinned.

"Who happens to have a mighty good head on his shoulders too," B.J. went on, raising an eyebrow sternly. "And who, I have no doubt, will score even higher when he begins using *that* part of his body!"

The children giggled.

B.J.'s eyes softened as he lifted his glass toward Lindsay. "To my caring, thoughtful granddaughter, who knows from her report card that she is brilliant, and who, I have no doubt, will one day realize that she is breathtakingly beautiful as well."

Lindsay's cheeks flushed as she played with her napkin.

B.J. turned to Marci. "To the *only* business partner I have who gives me consistently sound advice, and the only one, I hasten to say, who is *not* on my payroll! My lovely, *regal* daughter-in-law. No," he corrected, staring deeply into Marci's eyes, *"daughter."*

He turned to Priscilla. "To the love of my life, who looks as young and fresh today as she did when I first caught sight of her forty-two years ago.

"And finally . . . finally, a toast to the person who links us all together." B.J. swallowed and gazed up at the ceiling. "To my son, Tom, the best offspring a mother and father could ever hope for . . ." His voice broke. He cleared his throat. "A proud and promising, loving young man who was stolen from us—from *all* of us—so very prematurely, whose memory binds us all together and lingers, cherished, in all our hearts." A tear streamed down B.J.'s cheek as Priscilla patted his hand.

Marci looked over at her children, who were wiping their eyes—*dry* eyes, she noted with a pang, *tearless* eyes. It was understandable, she told herself sadly. They had participated in this toasting ceremony for more years than they had known their father.

9

1968 "Hey, Hard-on," Sal Durone called over one Friday night in the locker room, "ain't the Vietnamese half and half? Half commies, half good guys?"

"Yup."

Durone sneered at Deke. "See, I told ya. Slime was right."

"That'sa whole point!" Slime shouted, slowly unbuttoning his workshirt. "You can't tell good from bad. They all look alike, and every night the commies load these rockets outside Saigon—rockets that are, like, set up on top of bamboo poles—and no one can see them, see? Even military planes, even from the air, they're invisible, these little commie people and their little rockets."

Slime chewed on his thumb nail as the guys waited, all ears. "And then in the morning, when the people in the city get up and walk outside, bing, bing, bing, bing. The rockets go off and a whole buncha innocent people, just, you know, goin' to work, goin' to school, they get exploded to bits. Just like that. All over the city."

"Who says?" sneered Cripple.

Slime turned on him. "NBC says. Right on the news. A guy had his head blowed off last night right while I was watching. Swear to God."

"But that's just Vietnams fighting Vietnams," Deke protested. "That ain't Americans."

"That's what the Americans are over there for, asshole!" shouted Con Man. "Helping the good Vietnam people kill the bad Vietnam people."

"But how can you tell which is which?" Deke persisted.

"The good guys have gold stars," howled Cripple, "and the bad guys have big Xs over their hearts and a sign that says 'Shoot here.'" He and Turd were laughing so hard they fell down on the bench.

Deke stared down at the floor frowning. "Yeah?"

"No, Shithead!"

"Dumb Greek!"

"That'sa problem," Slime went on, speaking slowly now as though addressing a very young child. "You don't know which is which. You never know. You go outa your mind. It's only like, if they kill you, then you know they're commies."

Silence.

"I don't even like the good ones, know what I mean?" Deke burped and sat down on the bench, his thick lips in a pout, with the lower one protruding, his large, hairy hand scratching his ample gut. "They're real little, kinda boney . . . all with the same face, those crooked eyes. Don't see breakin' my ass to save 'em."

"You don't do it for them, dickhead. You do it for America!" Cripple shouted. "That's why my dad went to the Pacific! For America. And we won the war and that's why we're the greatest."

"Not me, man." Deke's lips curled into a snarl. "I ain't riskin' my life for no slanty-eyed gooks."

"You just know you couldn't get into the service," Pimp snarled. "You couldn't pass the test! You never even passed ninth grade!"

"Don't hafta have no diploma to go die in Vietnam."

"Bullshit!" Pimp yelled. "Gotta be able to read! Gotta be able to add! Ask Slime, here, he flunked the test, and he finished tenth grade!"

Slime sighed. "Happiest day of my life, the day I flunked."

"That's a pile of crap." It was Sallie, who had been listening in uncharacteristic silence.

Slime's face turned red. "What do you know, big talker! You never passed that test!"

"Never took it," Sallie said smugly, pulling a can of deodorant

69

out of a brown bag. "I'd pass it if I took it. I'm just deferred is all."

"Deferred? How come?"

"Sole support of my mother." He opened the deodorant can.

"You really think you'd pass it?" Deke howled. "You're the guy who taught me how to sleep in eighth-grade math!"

"You woulda slept too if you was workin' the swing shift at Kelso 'n goin' to school at the same time." Sallie gave Deke a cocky look. "Us wops can hear even when we sleep. Not like you dumb Greeks."

"Sallie'd pass it," Lucky said reverently. "He's got the brains."

"Bet your ass." Sallie patted Lucky on the back. "I can pass any fuckin' test I wanna pass."

"You musta not wanted to pass a whole lot in high school," cackled Pimp.

The guys cracked up.

Durone stared Pimp down. "I can pass any test I wanna pass, Pimp," he bellowed.

It was as though a bomb had gone off. The gaiety subsided and all talk stopped.

"He's kidding, Sallie," Hard-on whispered.

"Yeah," Turd shouted nervously, "a joke, 'at's all."

" 'At right, Pimp?" Durone put his hands on his hips and shifted from foot to foot. "You was just kidding?" Pimp said nothing.

" '*At right*, Pimp?" Durone persisted.

"Yeah," Pimp said hoarsely. "Just kidding."

Never taking his two deadly eyes off Pimp, Sallie reached down, as though for a gun, picked up the deodorant can, and sprayed his left armpit. Then, again without shifting his gaze, he switched the can to his other hand and blasted his right armpit.

Total silence.

Durone's eyes surveyed the room, lingering momentarily on each face. Finally he bent down and put the can back in the paper bag. It was as though a bandit had been disarmed. Everyone relaxed and continued dressing.

"Gettin' dolled up for the big night, Sallie?" Lucky yelled out.

Durone snickered as he buttoned his shirt.

"New shirt!" cackled Cripple. "Must be a big night!"

"Who's the chick?"

"Miss Tits, 1968!" screeched Lucky.

Jaws dropped.

Poker-faced, Durone tucked in his shirt.

"Oooooooooooo Looooooooo," they started chanting.

Durone zipped up his fly, and then moved his crotch slowly back and forth.

"Bellllllllla Louellllllllla!"

"Oh, man, them tits," Durone moaned. "Hey, Lucky, 'member those balloons we used ta drop offa Hazel Bridge, down onto the highway? Them big round ones we bought at Mongon's 'n filled with water?"

"Yup." Lucky turned to the others. "They'd fall right on the car windshields, and the drivers'd think they been hit by a bomb or something, water would come bustin' out of 'em . . ."

All eyes returned to Durone. His eyes closed, Sallie held his hands out, palms up and slightly cupped, and began moving them around slowly in circles. "I'm bettin' that's what they're like . . ."

"What's like?"

"Louella's tits . . . just like them round balloons filled with water, rubbery and flowin' like, know what I mean? You push in a little here, and the balloon's rubber oozes out a little in this here direction. You kinda just rub real slow, 'round and 'round in circles, feeling the water inside kinda run back and forth . . ."

"Hate to break it to you," Slime howled. "But there ain't no water inside no chick's tits!"

"Yeah, and don't plan on touchin' Louella's!"

"Ain't nobody never has."

"Louella don't give boob feels."

"Not even tongue kisses!"

"Dick teases, 'at's all she gives out!"

Sallie laughed as he slicked his hair back. "All them years a teasin' musta made her hungry, don'tcha think?"

"Not for you," shouted Cripple.

"Bullshit. Just for me. She wants me, man, you can tell by how she acts."

"C'mon, man. Five bucks says you don't get nothin'."

Sal stared at Cripple. "Ten bucks says I do."

"How'll we know?"

"You'll just have to trust old Sallie."

"We'll know!" Lucky yelled out. "Chickie's been keepin' Louella pure for years now. If Sallie lays a hand on little sister, he'll show up black and blue at work Monday morning!"

Everyone laughed.

"Fuck," Sallie drawled as he cast an approving eye at himself in the mirror and headed for the locker-room door. "Chickie Parmacella don't scare me."

The guys followed Sallie out, teasing and taunting, leaving Hard-on and me alone in the locker room. "You have a date tonight too, Hard-on?" I asked.

"No time for dates." He slammed the door of his locker. "You date to mate. Not ready for that yet."

Hard-on was bland, blond, and deadly serious about increasing his productivity levels—a stark contrast to the hot-tempered Italian and Greek cut-ups who made up the bulk of Kelso's work force.

"Aren't you afraid all the good ones will be taken by the time you're ready?" I teased.

"The loose ones, maybe. The empty-headed ones." He stood up and tucked in his shirt. "Don't want that type. Gotta find one with a brain," he instructed me. "Otherwise you get dumb kids." He kept checking his watch.

"If you don't have a date," I asked, "why are you so worried about the time?"

"My dad's picking me up in a half hour for a job we have to do tonight." He glanced up at me. "Want to walk over to Mongon's with me? That's where he's picking me up."

I made a face. "That girl behind the counter, does she work Friday nights?"

"Sell? You scared of Sell?" He shook his head. "She barks but she doesn't bite. C'mon."

Mongon's was completely empty when we got there. Sell was sitting on a high stool behind the counter engrossed in a book. As we sat down, she stood up slowly and headed toward the counter, holding the book, her eyes darting down the page from line to line at a feverish pace.

"Sell's real out of it when she's reading," Hard-on snorted. "What's the name of this one?"

She held the cover up over her face. It was *Strong Poison* by

72

Dorothy Sayers. "Oh," she moaned, turning another page, "just when I started getting engrossed . . ."

"We hatta wait for floats while you engross?"

She put the book back on the stool and stared into space. "See, someone poisoned Philip Boyes, and Harriet Vane—his former girlfriend?—she's charged with murder, but Sir Peter Wimsey, he and I know she didn't do it."

"With Sell around you don't have to read," Hard-on grunted. "She does it for you, even summarizes."

She turned around smiling, but when she saw me, her eyes hardened. "Two root beer floats?"

"Sounds good to me."

She had a bright red scarf tied tightly around her head. Her long, straight dark hair hung down from the scarf curling up in a small "J" shape halfway down her back. She was wearing a red blouse that matched the scarf, and a white miniskirt. There was something wrong about the way she looked. Too much hair for her tiny body, maybe, or perhaps it was the excessive makeup. I couldn't figure out precisely what it was.

She slapped the floats down in front of us sullenly, and, to my relief, sat back down on the stool and picked up her book.

Hard-on and I drank in what had become our comfortable social milieu: total silence. A few weeks of toiling beside him on the loading dock had taught me this was one taciturn human being, not out of self-consciousness, like me, but rather, I had decided, out of an overwhelming sense of confidence. Hard-on seemed to feel most things just weren't worthy of comment.

After a while, I started thinking back to the guys' talk about Vietnam in the locker room. "How did you avoid getting drafted?" I asked.

"*Avoid?*" he asked angrily. "What's that supposed to mean?"

"Well, you know, you're not serving."

"Tried to. Went and enlisted the day after graduation." He took a few slurps on his float. "Wouldn't take me. Got two bum knees, see. The cartilage is all messed up from high-school football injuries." He drank some more. "Felt real bad about it too. Figure every man's got a duty to fight for his country."

I took in the square, clean lines of his face, the deep blue eyes, the solid, well-proportioned body without an ounce of excess flesh.

I felt as though I had just received a dressing-down from the army's poster boy.

Hard-on sank back into silence, but a restless one. He kept shifting his weight around on the stool and taking long, angry sucks on the straw. I had ruffled some feathers.

And not just Hard-on's. I heard a book slam shut over by the sink. "How about *you?*" I looked up to find Sell, off her stool and creeping over to the counter, a stalking tom cat, ready to pounce. "What's *your* story?"

"My, uh, my story?"

"You got it. Your story." She crept closer. "Don't you feel you owe your country something?"

A car horn honked outside. "My dad," Hard-on said, jumping up and plunking down some money on the counter. "See you Monday!"

The tension mounted with the slamming door. I was stuck with half a root beer float still to go and Uncle Sam's special enlistment officer bearing down on me.

"I'm deferred." I washed the words down with a gulp of root beer. "Student deferment . . . from, uh, from being in college. Means I'm not . . ." I cleared my throat again. "Not draftable until after I graduate."

"And then?" She moved closer still, so close I thought our heads would bump and mine would explode on impact. I took a deep breath. "Mr. Urquhart's cook did it!" I shouted, fighting her advance with the only weapon in my arsenal.

It worked. Her jaw dropped and she tottered backward a little. "You read *Strong Poison!* she gasped. "You *know?*"

"Yup." I sat up straighter.

"Liar!" she screeched, flailing her arms round. "Liar!"

"Philip Boyes was poisoned with arsenic!" I shouted, ducking to avoid the nail-polished daggers on the end of one of the flailing arms. "He'd just eaten a big meal at Mr. Urquhart's house!"

"How *could* you?" she wailed, grabbing the countertop, devastated. "How could you go and ruin the whole end of the book for me like that?"

I paused for a second, savoring the moment. "I couldn't," I announced, imbued with a sense of power I had never before felt. "Couldn't and wouldn't."

"What?"

"Everyone has standards," I went on grandly. "Patriotism works for some people. Me, I adhere rigidly to the mystery reader's oath."

"Which is?"

"Never, no matter how dire the consequences, never give away who did it."

"So the cook didn't—"

"Nope." I smiled.

"But you've limited the possibilities!"

"The cook wasn't even a suspect," I shouted, regaining the offensive. "Both men ate the same dinner together and then the maids finished it off afterward."

"So? How does that—"

"No one *else* got poisoned," I pointed out smugly, "so the arsenic couldn't have been planted in the food."

"True," she whispered, considering the possibility.

Oh, she was softening, softening at least for a witch-bitch. It elevated me to an unprecedented level of forthrightness. "You owe me," I declared.

"Huh?"

"For preserving your mystery. For not giving it away. You owe me."

"Owe you what?"

Her skin was caked with a thick layer of beige makeup that created an unpleasant ghostly aura at close range. I looked away. "An explanation for the other night. How did you know all those details about me?"

"Oh, I know everything." She shot me a cocky grin and started dancing around behind the counter. "I knew, for example, that Stavros Nunos was going to cheat on his wife before *he* even knew it," she said in singsong. "Simply because I knew Stavros Nunos better than he knew himself, and I saw the way he was eyeing Chrissy Ricci right here at my soda fountain counter . . ."

"But—"

"I knew who was going to win the All Saints Bingo Contest last winter before the contest even took place."

"How?"

"Because the contest was rigged, stupid!" She broke into giggles and held up a finger. "But I *knew* it was rigged. No one else did. Let me see now. What else. Oh, yes, I knew—"

"What about *me?*"

The laughter stopped. "I'm only trying to show you my credentials!" She sighed, suddenly deflated, and picked up the sponge. "My sister works the switchboard at the factory part-time." She started washing the counter. "My sister overheard the call from your uncle's friend."

"So everyone knew I was coming? Everyone knew—"

"Nah, just me. My sister's no talker, except to me, and then only when I pry things out of her."

"But *you're* a talker!"

She stopped sponging and put her hands on her hips. "Do any of the guys at the plant know about you?"

"Well, no. At least they don't seem to."

"There you go." She was back to sponging. "There's talking and there's telling, see? Quantity and quality. Real talkers—the pros like me—dole out the quantity, see, but keep the quality to themselves. I take in all I can, but keep the good stuff to myself."

"The other night you practically blabbed the whole thing out!"

"Yeah? And to whom? To a bunch of assholes I knew wouldn't pick up the vibes." She grinned. "That message was directed at an audience of one."

"Me."

"You got it."

"Why?"

She shrugged. "To attract your attention, maybe."

"Oh, great. Why didn't you just drop a bomb?"

"Not subtle enough."

"My BVDs," I gulped. "How'd you know I wear new BVDs?"

She shook her head and closed her eyes. "You let Mrs. Stompous do your wash, you leave yourself wide open."

"The letters to my sister?"

She put her hands out palms up. "You let Mrs. Stompous clean your room, you leave yourself wide open."

"The fact that I'm rich . . . which, by the way, I'm not."

"An educated guess. One you just confirmed." Her eyes sparkled. "Only rich people insist they're not rich."

I clenched my jaw and stared down at the counter.

"Definitions of 'rich' vary," she went on pointedly. "In Falls-ville, anyone who's earning a solid wage at the plant and still has a daddy who sends him a hundred dollars qualifies as 'rich.'

"Cash your checks at Piccini's," she went on in singsong, "and you leave yourself wide open!"

Once again I'd been run down by this verbal lawnmower. Once again I couldn't breathe. I reached into my pocket, counted out sixty-two cents, and headed for the door.

"Did you read *The Documents in the Case?*"

I whirled around. "My favorite Dorothy Sayers book!"

"Oh, thank God." She closed her eyes and took a deep breath. "I mean, it was my favorite too. Don't go. Please."

I was so confused I felt dizzy.

"I had a feeling, I mean, since you read this Sayers book . . . I just hoped, maybe, you liked that one even more. I did."

I hesitated at the door.

"I just come on like gangbusters at all the wrong moments," she claimed. "I wasn't trying to run you out. I was trying to impress you."

"Why?" As far as I knew, no one had ever tried to impress me before.

She shrugged. "Gets lonely in here."

"In here? Everyone comes to Mongon's!"

"No one . . . no one I can talk to."

"I . . . um . . . don't talk much," I said as I played with a display of greeting cards near the door, unwilling to commit myself.

"Do you know what it's like to know how to talk German and be surrounded by people who only talk Spanish?"

I picked a card off the rack and examined it. "I don't know German."

"Whatsamattah? You never studied literature? That was a *met-aphor*, jerko! By 'German' I meant 'educated'. All I was saying was—"

"I got it!" I yelled. "I got it the first time!" I winked at her. I had never winked at a girl before in my entire life, but I was feeling unusually sure of myself. "Where'd you learn to talk . . . uh . . . to think in a way superior to the natives?"

She took my empty glass over to the sink. "Three terrific teachers. No great accomplishment, that!" she offered parentheti-

77

cally over her shoulder as she turned on the water. "I mean, I've been in school eleven whole years and there have only been three good ones! And, well, I read every book I can get my hands on." She put the glass in the rack and returned to the counter drying her hands on the towel. "Sometimes when things get dull around here I translate what the guys say into my other language, just for kicks. Slime grunts 'S'hot!' and I think in my head, 'We're being victimized by unseasonably torrid climatic conditions.' "

I laughed.

"Here's one you can translate: 'Uh, he don't talk much,' " she grunted in a deep voice, " 'But uh, like, he pulls his own.' "

"I'm doing okay at the factory?" I asked hopefully.

"You got it." She grimaced and shook her head. "The muscled mighties putting in a hard day at the sucking plant. Crazy, huh?"

" 'The sucking plant?' " I frowned. "You lost me."

"Think," she instructed. "What do they make at Kelso?"

I didn't work the assembly line, so I hadn't seen it. I felt my face get hot, wondering for the first time what was in all those boxes I'd been toting on the loading dock. "I don't know," I confessed.

"You don't know? How could you—"

"Tell me."

She giggled into the palm of her hand. "Pacifiers!" she screeched.

"Pacifiers?"

"What they give babies to suck on! Fake nipples!"

It took a while for it to sink in, but when it did, I collapsed on the counter howling. "Fake nipples! That gang of toughies making fake nipples!"

"Oh," she gasped, in between giggles. "It's so wonderful to finally find someone else who thinks it's funny." Then she stopped abruptly. "Don't ever—*ever*—joke about that with Sallie Durone!"

"I don't joke with Sallie Durone, ever, about anything."

"Good." She smiled and just looked at me for a while. "I have to close up," she said apologetically. "Doc Mongon drives by sometimes just to make sure I turn the lights out on time. Actually, I'm late as it is. I was just hoping we could end friendlier than last time."

I opened the door.

"Will you come back?" she called out after me.

"I'll have to," I said over my shoulder. "How else will I find out what's new with me?"

Feeling unusually cocky, I ate a sandwich at the diner next door and then headed along on my usual shortcut through the woods to Mrs. Stompous's place. It was about nine o'clock, and the woods were getting dark. I had almost made it through them—I could see the little light Mrs. Stompous always kept lit out back glimmering beyond the trees—when I heard screams coming from someplace off to the left. I stopped and stood still, trying to figure out where it was coming from. Then I heard the screams again.

"No! No! Help!"

The cries were childlike. A kid, maybe, lost in the woods. Imbued with my new sense of self—Rodney Bingham a person to impress—I ran in the direction of the noise, entertaining notions of moving up a notch, to "Rodney Bingham as Clark Kent" perhaps. "It's okay," I'd tell the little girl, "darkness is nothing to be scared of. Just tell me where you live and I'll help you find your way home."

The screams were getting louder. More agonizing too. I picked up my pace. It sounded like an emergency situation.

"Hellllllp!"

I stood still to check the direction. Over to the right, in the clearing. I raced to the scene, moving so fast I almost collided with the big red pickup truck that was parked under the trees. The truck's flat back was jumping around on its springs. Some sort of struggle was going on, but the back slat was pulled up and I couldn't see anyone over its rim.

Superman turned back into Rodney Bingham. I backed off. Really backed off, hopping backward away from the truck. This was more complicated than I had anticipated.

"No! You *can't!*" came the childlike cries. "Help! Help! *Help!*"

I had to do something and do it fast to stop whatever was happening to that little girl. But what? And how? My rescuing instincts only went so far and I was beginning to see the red pickup truck as an artillery tank. I cringed.

"HELLLLLLLLLLLLLLLP!"

Every muscle, every nerve ending in my body was jumping, but it was strictly internal. The body itself was frozen still. I thought I was going to explode.

"Help! Help!" I shouted at the empty woods behind me. "Come! Help!" I screamed at the moss-covered hill. "Help! Help!" My exhortations seemed to soar up to the tops of the huge oak trees surrounding me and then fall back down around my feet, the noise thoroughly contained by the woods.

I gulped and stared at the truck. "Stop!" I hollered with all my might. "Stop!"

The bouncing stopped. At first there was dead calm, no noise, no movement, but then I saw a large male body bound up to a standing position in the back of the truck. It took a few seconds for my eyes to focus, and when they did, I begged for the opportunity to return to blurred vision.

Salvatore Durone stood before me, his muscles flexed.

I saw a girl stand up behind him suddenly in the back of the truck. With the back of her hand, she whisked a few errant strands of long auburn hair out of her eyes. I recognized the gesture and the long, painted fingernails. Bella Louella.

"What the fuck you want, Smarts?" Durone began moving toward me.

My body was paralyzed, but my mind began racing faster and faster. "Don't force her, Sallie," I said quickly. "For your own sake. I'm only thinking of you."

He jumped over the back of the truck and came at me.

"Doing it against her will like that, Sal, that's rape."

"*Rape?* What the fuck you talkin' 'bout, Golden Boy? Where you come off tellin' me how to act with a chick?"

"Not right to force her, Sal," I pleaded.

He kept coming, and I felt as though I were stuck in concrete, knowing I had to run for it, mentally even plotting the route I could take, but somehow unable to move. My feet had grown roots that extended deep into the soil. I stood there like an idiot, firing words at an approaching bomb. "Sal, I'm just saying—"

The punch was so fast I didn't even see his fist coming, just felt a whack on my jaw that sent my body flying backward. My forehead smashed against the tree as I fell. I looked up and saw the girl running off into the woods. And Durone coming at me again. I scrambled to my feet.

It was the wrong thing to do. I was rewarded with a blow to the stomach, delivered with the force of a cannon blast. It knocked all the air out of me and filled me with excruciating pain. I couldn't breathe, and I stopped trying. When I saw him coming toward me again, I actually hoped he'd finish the job, if only to stop the agony.

He made a valiant attempt. Pulling me up by my collar, he whomped me another one right in the gut, and then left me, crumpled up against the stump of the tree, clutching my stomach and shaking all over as strange strangulated moans came out of my mouth.

He ran after the girl. And I vomited, in convulsive motions that made my stomach ache so much I thought I'd die. I leaned back against the stump, whimpering, determined to just stay there until death came. But I knew Sallie Durone would be back to get his truck.

I scrambled to get up. I felt warm wet stuff trickling over my right eye, blinding my vision, and I realized in horror it had to be blood. My legs gave way and I fell backward into a lump on the ground.

I tried again. This time I made it up. Bent over, still clutching my stomach, which was now sending out shots of pain to all other parts of my body, I slowly made my way toward Mrs. Stompous's house, digging into the grassy slope with my fingers, crawling on hands and knees up the steep incline, and finally, making it into my room.

I went into the bathroom and looked in the mirror. The blood from the wound on my forehead had flowed down, caking over the entire right side of my face, leaving little red trickling marks on my shirt collar. The sight terrified me.

I fell down on the floor and got my head over the toilet bowl just in time. I vomited and vomited, and then began dry-heaving, certain that my guts were about to pour out, that all my insides would be gone soon and not caring. Each time I heaved, I felt something akin to a knife stabbing me inside my rib cage.

After a while, I crawled over to the bed on my hands and knees, and slowly, painfully, hoisted myself up on the mattress.

Unaccustomed to injury of any kind, I found the blood and pains terrifying. I knew I should do something to take care of myself, but I had no idea what to do. So I just lay there in a fetal position, hurting and whimpering, listening to my childlike hiccups and knowing only too well what my brothers would have done to Salvatore Durone, what my father would have done, what any

Bingham worth his salt would have done. I began shivering, shaking all over, and I wanted to die. Quickly.

"Rodney?" There was a knock on the door.

It sounded familiar, the female voice, the local accent. Mrs. Stompous? No, younger.

"Can I come in?"

It was Sell, Fallsville's information source. I writhed on the sheets. Things *could* get worse. Go away, I prayed, *oh, please go away*.

"Rodney?"

Knowing the door didn't have a lock, I put my face in the pillow to muffle the sounds of my chattering teeth. *Go away, witch-bitch. Goddamn it, go away!* I heard the door open, but I didn't move.

"Oh, geez," she whispered. I felt a hand on my shoulder.

"Go away!" I groaned.

"No."

She took the extra blanket from the foot of the bed and wrapped it tightly around me. Then she walked into the bathroom. I heard water running. She came back with a few steaming hot washclothes.

"Go away," I mumbled weakly as she began washing the blood off my face.

"Is this all from the gash in your forehead?" she asked. "Is that the only cut?"

"I think so." Comforted by the warm washcloth and the fact that someone else was taking over, I tuned out.

She frowned as she examined my forehead gash. "I'm really sorry." It wasn't a Sell voice. It was timid, all choked up. She cleared her throat. "Thank you for what you did."

What was this role switch? It was the last thing I expected to hear, and I guess my face radiated that fact.

"Louella's my sister," she said. "Didn't you know that?"

I shook my head, and immediately regretted the movement.

"She's all shook up, but she managed to make it home before Sallie Durone could catch up with her. She's just . . . Well, nothing, um nothing . . . you know . . . happened. So we're all—my whole family—is very grateful to you."

For what? I wanted to scream. For standing there like Salvatore

82

Durone's anemic punching bag? I closed my eyes, hoping she would go away.

"Can you get up?"

"Why?" I snarled.

"I think you should go to a hospital. The bleeding isn't stopping, and the cut is pretty deep. I think you need stitches."

"You bring an ambulance?"

She laughed a little. "No. But you have a car."

She said it the Fallsville way: "cah." Car, I wanted to scream, Car, car, carrrrr. I closed my eyes again.

"C'mon, I'll drive you."

Somehow the two of us managed to get me off the bed and into my VW bug. I have no idea how. The whole thing is a blur to me. All I remember is leaving the Orange County Hospital emergency room at one in the morning with ten stitches in my forehead, three severely bruised ribs, and no discernible skull fracture. I was told not to go to sleep for two hours, and Sell was told that if I suddenly lapsed into unconsciousness, she should call the emergency number immediately. The whole thing was surreal.

Back in my room at Mrs. Stompous's place, Sell propped me into a semi-sitting position on the bed with pillows, and then proceeded to keep me conscious and awake the only way she knew how—by nonstop talking. The girl had the stuff filibusters are made of.

Beginning with the first Parmacella ever to arrive in Fallsville, Massachusetts, she meandered verbally down every single branch of her family tree, nudging me each time my eyelids began drifting downward.

When the two hours were up, she told me I could go to sleep, and switched verbal gears. I drifted off to sleep hearing her tell me how very, very brave I had been. I felt like a child listening to a fairy tale.

10

Marci Courbienne was settling down to work after a business lunch when her intercom buzzed. "Yes, Cecilia?"

"There's a Mr. Durone here to see you . . . with a box."

A peculiar image flashed through Marci's head, an image of Salvatore Durone out in the law firm lobby—not *with* a box, but *in* a box. "What!"

She heard a male voice speaking quickly on the other end, and then Cecilia, back on the line. "He says his name is Frank Durone, Marci. He doesn't have an appointment, says he really doesn't need to see you. Just wants to drop off this, uh, box."

"Send Frank Durone in, Cecilia. *With* his box."

Impatiently, Marci ran her fingers through her short, dark hair, searching for a logical explanation for this unusual office visit.

The door opened and Frank Durone, attired in leathery black garb, his arms holding a large corregated box, leaned a shoulder against the door frame like some sort of nocturnal animal clinging to a rock for shelter from the daylight.

His eyes darted furtively around the office from one object to another, taking in the thick burgundy wall-to-wall carpeting, the high-gloss tables dotted with family pictures in silver frames. His face registered, first awe, then discomfort, then the seething contempt of the poor for the entrapments of wealth. "Big Daddy sure set you up real good," he drawled sarcastically.

Marci blinked, shocked by such brazen disrespect from a teenager she barely knew. "Big Daddy?"

Durone's upper lip curled malevolently. "Yah, you know, your old man, B.J."

"B. J. Courbienne is not my father," Marci corrected. "He is my father-in-law."

"Same thing. Right?" A glint appeared in Durone's eyes. "Same, like, you know, in terms of benefits."

"Not at all," Marci said icily. "B.J. is a real-estate developer. Ellsworth and Carver is a law firm. I am a lawyer. I am a partner here because I am a damn good lawyer, not because of my father-in-law's business holdings. B.J. is not even one of the firm's clients."

"Well, I just figured—"

"You figured being related to a rich person was the key to success." She stared him down. "That's a common theory in Fallsville. However, it is both incorrect and counterproductive. It tends to make people sit around waiting for luck to happen instead of working hard to succeed on their own."

Frank swallowed—uncomfortably, she noted with pleasure. She tilted her head coyly. "Now, Frank, did you come all the way over here to stand out in the hallway and listen to a career lecture?"

He trudged over and dropped the corregated box on her desk.

Marci peeked down at its opened top. The box was filled with packets of papers inside manila folders. She pulled out the folder lying on top of all the others, examined it, and then looked back up at Frank Durone with surprise.

He looked away. "Yeah. The bills."

"*You* stole them from that drawer in your father's room?"

"Wasn't stealing. Just took 'em." He shrugged. "Figured they're as much mine as hers."

"But why?"

"Felt like it." He scuffed his shoes around in the carpeting in front of her desk. "Just bothered me. Her goin' through his things like that."

"Your mother was just trying to take care of family business!"

"Says you." He cocked his head, causing his silver earring to jangle. "I call it snooping around in stuff that doesn't belong to her."

"Be practical, Frank. Someone has to keep paying the bills, now that your father's dead. Can *you* take on that responsibility?"

"Can *she?* Miss Airhead, 1989?"

The boy had a point, but it was one Marci was not about to concede. Francine might be an idiot, but she was also Frank Durone's sole surviving parent, and as such, her status had to be preserved, for his sake as much as hers.

Frank was pacing back and forth in front of her desk, his hands in fists, his jaw clenched, a bomb of hostile, raw energy waiting to be ignited by a verbal duel.

She moved in quickly to prevent an explosion. "Thank you for reconsidering, Frank," she said softly. "I appreciate your bringing me the bills."

"I did it for me, not you." He stood still and threw his shoulders back. "I want something in return."

"What?"

"That program she gave you—the one from the shopping center celebration."

Marci stared at him.

"You know, the Collier Chamber of Commerce thing, the program she found in my old man's pocket."

Surprised, Marci got up and walked over to a filing cabinet. She opened a drawer, searched for the file labeled "Salvatore Durone," pulled out the only item in the folder—the program Francine had given her, the "Collier Chamber of Commerce Salutes B. J. Courbienne." She scrutinized it quickly—searching for some sort of handwritten note, a clue she had missed, but there was nothing.

"Why?" she asked as she handed it to Frank Durone.

He shrugged. "I just know it meant something to him," Frank said softly, caressing the folds of wrinkled paper with a finger. "He was real sick, but, for some reason, he was hell-bent on going, and all by himself." He smiled at the program. " 'Your old man's a *genius,* Frankie.' That's what he told me when he got home."

"Why did he say that?"

"He wouldn't explain. Said it was too complicated." Frank Durone's eyes met hers and then looked away as he shifted his weight.

Something she saw in that split-second look into his dark brown eyes—anguish? pain? love?—moved her. She found herself

86

wanting to help, wanting to smooth away the anger and hurt she sensed fomenting inside him, but she couldn't figure out how. She sat back down at the desk and waited.

Gradually, in the silence, his pacing slowed. His shoulders began to droop a little. His chest deflated. "You, uh, you think you can find out who killed my dad?"

My dad. The words, and the way his voice sounded when he uttered them, told her the demon was just a child . . . a child bereft.

Marci played with the jade paperweight on her desk. "Were you close to your dad?"

"That's my business." He walked away from her.

"I just thought he might have told you something about his search for the person who killed him."

"Nope. Not a word."

She nodded silently at the paperweight.

"On purpose." Frank Durone stared at the tree branches outside her office window. "He said it was something he didn't want me to inherit from him—all the hate."

"Was he trying to track down the source of his cancer?"

"He said so." Frank whirled around, suddenly transformed from pensive back to angry. "What do *I* know? Maybe he just said it because he thought if he promised her money, she'd get off his back! That's all she cares about—*money!*"

The curtain was coming down. Marci rushed to get some more information before it closed completely. "Why did you change your mind and bring me the bills?"

"It wasn't my idea." He looked a little embarrassed, but then his whole demeanor seemed to change. "My therapist!" He laughed, carefully monitoring her reaction. "Whaddya think of that? It was my *therapist!*"

Marci's estimation of the high-school guidance department went up several notches. They had obviously taken some steps to get this boy help. Good for them. "I think it's great, Frank."

"Yah, even a dip like me from the wrong side of the county has himself a therapist," Frank Durone cackled. "What a great land we live in, hah?"

His face hardened as he looked at hers. Another mood swing. "You can call off your little boy scout, hear?" he said irritably. "I don't need no hand-outs. Don't need no Tommy Courbienne teaching me math." He walked out the door. "Take that message home with you!"

Marci stared into space.

Why, why on earth had Salvatore Durone gone out of his way to attend the Collier Chamber of Commerce's salute to B.J.? And gone home happy? It made no sense at all. She was certain Sal had never crossed paths with her father-in-law, and, as Francine had pointed out, Fallsvillians *never* came over to this part of the county, the "newcomers" part. Why, even her own mother acted as though she were entering enemy territory each time she came to dinner!

Marci's eyes drifted down to the folders inside the box. She pulled out the one marked "Telephone." The Durone family telephone bills were all arranged in neat order, month by month, with "paid" and a date scrawled across the bottom of each receipt. There were no long-distance calls for the first five months of the year, but sure enough, in June, the month Sal had discovered he had cancer, five long-distance calls had been made to the same number.

Impulsively, she picked up her telephone and dialed. It rang for a long time before someone picked up. "Labor Department, operator fifty-one, can I help you?"

Marci winced. "Operator, is this the general number? For the whole United States Labor Department?"

"For information. What party did you wish to be connected with, ma'am?"

Marci hung up and chastized herself. So much for playing detective. Obviously, the key information—like the name of the person he was calling—had been buried in Salvatore Durone's head. Nonetheless, this was all she had. She took out a pad and a telephone book and began listing the long-distance calls made in subsequent months, translating their area codes into cities. When she finished, she sat back and searched the list for a pattern. Two area codes stood out: Boston and Atlanta. Those were the numbers of the longest and most repeated calls, aside from those to the Labor Department in D.C.

She picked up the phone again and tapped out the Boston number. "You have reached Bill Blaine Associates," a man's voice stated. "Our office will be closed until Monday morning—" She hung up. One more try. She dialed the number in Atlanta. "Tapron Industries, Lydia speaking."

Marci grabbed a pencil. "How do you spell Tapron?"

"T-a-p-r-o-n."

Marci stared at it, begging the letters to trigger some sort of recognition. "What *is* Tapron Industries?"

"We're an American plastics firm," the voice purred, "with plants across the United States and in twenty-five countries around the world."

"Wonderful." She hung up and threw the telephone folder back in the box. Until she formulated a more coherent, intelligent plan of action, this exercise would yield her nothing but a huge phone bill.

Idly she flipped through some of the other files in the box. One labeled "Research" contained Xerox copies of newspaper articles about factories, and a sheet entitled "Contacts" with a list of names and telephone numbers, many of which were long distance.

A job hunt, was that what all the mysterious phone calls were about? Durone *was* constantly in and out of work.

A folder entitled "Diaries" contained a pack of hand-written entries on lined paper with dates at the top. She flipped through looking for a June entry that could shed some light on the mysterious form of cancer Francine had insisted he had. Ah-hah. "June tenth, 1989. The doctor says I got two choices: to live like a dying man, or to make the most of what time I got left. . . ." She flipped the page. "I'm hoping to keep writing." That was it—the last line, a diary that ended where she wanted it to begin.

A folder marked "Special" contained family memorabilia and military awards. And a picture—an ink sketch of a young Salvatore Durone, holding up a beer can, his head tilted back, his eyes merry. She looked at the bottom for a signature. "G.B."

Marci wondered who "G.B." was. A very creative artist, that was for sure. He had managed to create an appealingly sly, charming-looking Salvatore Durone.

To her shock, she found herself smiling back at the sketch.

11

🌹

1968 When I woke up, the sun was pouring in through the little window in my room, and she was gone. I began to wonder whether it had all been a bad dream. Until I moved.

With great discomfort, I got out of bed, walked into the bathroom, and looked in the mirror. I saw a blood-stained gauze bandage wrapped around my head, a blackened right eye, and a jaw that looked as though four wisdom teeth had been extracted by a bulldozer.

"Thanks, Dad," I said, staring at my reflection. "Thanks for my wonderful summer vacation." I stormed out of the bathroom, lowered my torso down slowly onto the bed, and stared at Mrs. Stompous's light bulb: a room with a view.

First I heard steps, then a knock at the door. "Rodney?"

I closed my eyes: humiliation Part Two, about to happen.

"Rodney, um, can I come in?"

Could I keep her out?

"How're you feeling this morning, Rodney? Better?"

I closed my eyes. "Yeah."

"Is that 'yeah' you feel better, or 'yeah' I can come in, or 'yeah' your name is Rodney?"

"Don't call me Rodney, okay? It sounds like my mother."

"Okay." Sell laughed as she opened the door. "What does your father call you?"

"Pansy" was what came immediately to mind. "Rod. Call me Rod."

She sat down on the bed. "So, how're you feeling, Rod?"

"Great." I kept my eyes closed. With a door that had no lock, it was my only means of keeping her out.

"Good enough to go on a picnic?"

A picnic? A guy on the critical list goes *picnicking?* The absurdity of the question made me open my eyes. I looked up into swirls of beige and pink and rose and black and aqua. It didn't look like a human face so much as one rendered on canvas by an artist using too-thick oils on a brush. "Makeup," I whispered, to myself as much as her.

"Like it?" Her frost-pink lips smiled excitedly around white teeth. "Let me tell you, it took me a long time to figure out how to do it just right! You've got to figure out what you want to highlight, see, and what you want to, well, kind of cover up. I don't know if you can tell," she said, pointing to an area just below her cheekbone, "but by using just a slightly darker skin-color shade right here, it kind of thins my face, lets the rosy glow applied to the upper levels stand out. And the dark liner and ebony-blue mascara? That makes my eyes appear even bigger. See, ah . . ." She shrugged sheepishly. "Let's just say I've been told my eyes are my best feature."

I squinted, trying to locate eyeballs in the mass of gloppy blackness. "How come you wear so much makeup?"

"How come, he asks!" She hopped off the bed and walked over to the window. "If you had a sister that looked like Louella, you'd wear all the makeup you could get your hands on!"

I laughed, not at the statement, but at the image before me. The scarf she had tied around her head was the same shade of pink as her lipstick and the ruffled miniskirted dress she was wearing. Her long straight hair was hanging down her back, and she was carrying a large picnic basket. It was Little Pink Riding Hood, but with the face of a whore.

"Well, whatcha know?" she giggled. "Mister Miserable has a funny bone after all!"

"Whose idea was the makeup?"

"Louella's been helping me. You know, so I can look like her.

91

Take my hair," she went on, holding up a clump. "You wouldn't believe it, but it's naturally curly—a real mess. Here, touch."

Obediently, I complied.

"See how nice and straight it is? That's a secret Louella taught me. You just iron it. That's all! And it's really easy. Every morning I just press my clothes for the day and then lean down, put my hair on the ironing board, and bingo! Ready to go!"

No girl had ever talked to me at this length before, let along about such topics. I could not figure out how I was supposed to react. So, I shut my eyes.

"Would you listen to me . . . giving away all my beauty tips! So? What do you say? It's an absolutely perfect day for a picnic."

I groaned.

"The kind of day when the heat of the sun and the cool of the breeze are wonderful enough to make anyone stop feeling sorry for himself." I opened my good eye, and she went on. "Don't get me wrong. You have every right to feel sorry for yourself. I just figured a picnic might cheer you up. And I know this gorgeous place by the river. No one ever goes there. We could take your car."

It was the last thing I wanted to do. But what was the alternative for a guy with a door that didn't lock?

In almost a month of meandering around Fallsville and environs, I had come to the conclusion that there was New England, and there was . . . this. I'd never seen a less attractive "rustic" area.

But she took me to a soft, lush, grassy embankment overlooking a rushing stream with water crashing gently against enormous, flat-topped rocks, creating gusts of white foam that sparkled in the bright sun.

"Are you a photographer?" she asked as she unfolded a blanket.

"No. Why?"

"Just the way you were checking out everything. My English teacher is a photographer, and she usually examines scenery the way you did. Searching for lines, trying to judge the best angle."

"I like to sketch," I said. "I guess instinctively I look for colors and textures . . . angles too."

"You're an artist!"

"I just like to sketch."

She unpacked the basket as I lowered my crippled remains onto the blanket. "This is for you," she said, handing me a can of beer. "The message is—Vincent and Charles Parmacella say 'thanks.'"

"For what?"

"For rescuing their kid sister, Louella."

The mortification of the night before came back to me. "And letting Durone off without a scratch?"

"They—uh—I believe they took care of that."

"What do you mean?"

"Welcome to the land of Italian ethics!" She sighed. "Fallsville, Mass., where everyone saves face by messing up someone else's. A stupid place," she grumbled, "filled with zombies."

"Your brothers are zombies?"

"One is. Charles, a.k.a. 'Chickie', Parmacella. He's just like Durone. And Vince goes along because Chickie makes him." She handed me a piece of fried chicken. It was still warm.

"Did you make this?"

"Nope. My mother made it for you. She's grateful too."

The "gratefulness" was wearing thin. Salt in the wounds. "Hey, let's cut the gratitude crap, okay?"

She looked at me seriously. "Messing up faces, *that's* crap. But the gratitude part, that's sincere. For a guy like you—"

"Meaning what? A weakling?"

"A slender, artistic type who's not used to using his fists."

"Artistic? That's what? A euphemism for—"

"Why can't you buy the truth? What you did was very brave!"

"Brave?" I screamed it. "I didn't do anything but act like an immobile punching bag for Sallie Durone!" I launched into a hysterical diatribe on exactly what had transpired in the woods, spitting out every cowardly thought I'd had, even adding some that had occurred to me in retrospect. My ribs ached, and my head was splitting, but I couldn't stop until all the venom had been released, the truth exposed. I yelled it all out, oblivious to her, just feeling this horrible need to own up to my wretched failings. When I finished, I collapsed on the blanket, spent.

I heard the sound of giggles, muffled at first, and then unmuffled. She, too, had fallen back on the blanket, but in gales of laughter.

I just looked at her.

"You are really funny! All those details! That is absolutely the most colorful description I have ever heard," she laughed. "What a sense of humor!"

"Pathos is a better word."

She scrambled up on an elbow. "It's the pathos that makes the humor, don't you see? Screaming 'Come help!' to the ferns and trees? I love it!" She roared even louder.

Maybe it *was* kind of funny. No it wasn't. "I was a complete coward," I whispered. "Don't you see?"

"No, I don't." She sat up. "Your gut reaction was very heroic. You could have run in the other direction when you heard the screams, you know."

"I *would* have, if I'd known what was waiting for me!"

"This guy is determined to make himself into a coward," she announced to a nearby bush. "Look, you heard screams, right? You ran to help, right? And you did help. You freed my sister and got made into mincemeat in the process."

"And came whimpering home like the most pathetic—"

"Hey, tell me something, would you? Where did a nice White Anglo-Saxon Protestant boy like you get infected with the Italian ethic? You're beginning to sound like Chickie!" Her eyes softened. "I almost died when I looked at you last night. It was awful what you went through. There's no reason to put yourself down like that."

I bit into the fried chicken. The partial transformation from coward to hero had made me suddenly very hungry. "Tell me about yourself," I said, anxious to move on to another topic.

"Trying to change the subject?" She grinned at me. "Okay, I'm seventeen, about to enter my senior year in high school, and I happen to be number one in the class."

"No kidding!"

"Yeah, well, no big deal when the class is at Fallsville High, believe me. It's sort of like being all dressed up with no place to go." She broke off a piece of chicken. "Anyway, what else? I am the youngest of four children, brought into this world by a breakdown in the rhythm method." She laughed a little. "And a lot of people say I've been kind of out of sync ever since."

"You were a mistake?"

"Can't really blame my folks for wanting to stop while they

were ahead. They already had all they needed—two strapping males and an American beauty rose."

The parallels with my own family were making me uncomfortable. "Is Sell your real name or your occupational category?"

She burst out laughing.

"I mean Sell, as in—"

"S-e-l-l, I knew what you meant. I'm not polished," she said, lowering her eyelids, "but I'm quick. Actually, it's worse than that. It's C-e-l and it's short for Marcella."

It took a while to register. "Marcella?" I asked, fighting to keep a straight face. "Marcella Parmacella? Marcella Parmacella, sister of Louella Parmacella?"

"My mother thought it was poetic."

I couldn't hold it back anymore. I began to laugh, really laugh. She joined in.

"I'm sorry," I said, trying to stop.

"No, it's a relief. Do you know what it's like to spend your whole life in a place where you're the *only* one who thinks being named Marcella and Louella Parmacella is funny?" She handed me another piece of chicken. "I've tried so hard to come up with a new name, or a decent nickname, even. In second grade I called myself Emily for a while, and then I tried names from books I'd read. Anastasia Parmacella. Scarlet Parmacella. Never found one that caught on, but I haven't given up." She looked at me. "What's your mother's name?"

"Althea." I couldn't remember when I'd been hungrier.

She wrinkled her nose. "No good, another 'a' at the end. You have a sister, right?"

I nodded. "Her name's Lindsay."

"Lindsay." She inhaled abruptly. "Oh, what a perfect name! Cute for a girl because of the 'y' sound at the end, but at the same time classy, you know, respect-commanding for a woman." She squinted into space. "I'll consider it. I'm still going over all the infinite possibilities."

"What are some of the others?"

"Infinite means 'endless.' "

"I know."

"I know *you* know!" she snapped. "I just wanted you to know *I* know, that this is one classy kid you're picnicking with!"

"I didn't for a moment think—"

"Actually, it doesn't matter that much because when I marry, I'll get a whole new last name." She looked at me slyly. "Marcella de Gaulle, maybe. How does that hit you? Oh, of course, you not knowing me that well and all, you'd have to call me Mrs. Charles de Gaulle."

"He's a little old for you, don't you think?"

"Okay, then, how about Mrs. Abba Eban? Or Mrs. Andrei Gromyko?"

"They're all too old!"

She looked crestfallen. "You're missing the point!"

"I am?"

"I happen to be about the only person in Fallsville who *knows* de Gaulle is President of France, Gromyko is the Soviet Foreign Minister, and Eban is Foreign Minister of Israel!"

I did not know what I was supposed to say.

"Well, you could be a little impressed, is all."

"I am. It's, uh, just—"

"Just that where you come from everyone knows, hah?" She shriveled up on the blanket, suddenly a very little girl. "I did it again," she whispered. "A steamroller. Vince says I gotta stop coming on like a steamroller."

"How, um, how *do* you know all those names?"

"From *The New York Times*."

"*The New York Times?*" I sat up with interest. "Where do they sell it around here? I've been looking—"

"They don't. Vince gave me a subscription for Christmas. 'For a bigger outlook', he said." She brightened. "It really worked. I read it every day. Try to learn all the names I can. Then Vince tests me on them. He says that's part of my ticket."

"Ticket?"

"Local expression," she laughed. "See, everyone in Fallsville's looking for a ticket—a ticket out of Fallsville. Vince and Chickie, their ticket is the military. They enlisted and they're due to go into the army in a few weeks. Vince says brains are my ticket out, but I've got to work on them."

"What's Durone's ticket?" I asked, intrigued by the idea.

"People like Sal don't *have* a ticket. That's the whole point.

They're the ones who stick around and make everyone else want to escape!"

I liked that. "What are you going to do for your ticket besides reading the *Times?*"

She lay back down on the blanket. "Try to get smarter, learn everything I can, and then wait for Vince to get home and figure out what I should do next." She watched the clouds float overhead. "I just hope Vince and I end up with tickets to the same place."

"He sounds—"

"The chairman of the SDS chapter at Columbia College!" she shouted. "What his name?"

"Mark Rudd."

"Damn you!" She flopped back down, but then eyed me slyly. "Okay, I got one. What does Mark Rudd's mother call him?"

"Markie?" I laughed.

"Wrong! 'My-son-the-revolutionary!' That's what!"

"Who says?"

"*New York Times!* Last week! Heh, heh, stumped you on that one at least." She began scraping the chicken bones into a container. "Time for dessert." She took some pastries out of the basket. "It's cannoli."

"Really? Did you make it?"

"Nah. I make lousy cannoli. Intentionally. It's a pain in the neck to prepare, and if you mess up, you don't get called in for cannoli duty."

I bit in. "It's good."

"Mmmm. Now, Louella, on the other hand, she's the cannoli champ. But then she's the all-around champ. I mean, the girl has to be every man's dream, that Louella. Who could ask for more? A body and a face Miss America would kill for, three years training as a varsity cheerleader, all the necessary kitchen skills, including a knack for whipping up the world's best cannoli."

I licked my fingers. "You jealous?"

"Who *wouldn't* be? Not bitter-jealous, though. Besides, see, we all work on our tickets. Hers is being sensational enough to marry herself out of Fallsville. Chickie is very grateful to you, see, for making sure the merchandise wasn't damaged last night."

I choked and began coughing.

"Is it me or the cannoli?"

97

"You!" I shouted between coughs. "Do all the Parmacellas say stuff like that out loud or is it just you?"

"Everyone does. You know how it is. Your family, that's the one place you can all relax and say whatever you want."

I went back to the cannoli.

"So what's your family like?"

I gave her the factual rundown: Thaddeus Bingham, fifty-eight, business executive; Althea Bingham, fifty-six, housewife; Thaddeus Junior, twenty-seven, naval officer; Todd Bingham, twenty-six, naval officer; Lindsay Bingham, twenty, college junior.

She waited. "I repeat," she said when nothing was forthcoming. "What's your family like?"

I shrugged. "Quiet."

"Quiet like what? Librarians? Everyone whispers?"

"No."

"So like what, then? No one talks?"

"Not if they don't have to."

"Well, like, at the dinner table . . . What do they say?"

" 'Please pass the salt.' 'Thank you.' 'Delicious meal.' "

"What are they? *Retarded?*"

"No." I chuckled. "Restrained."

"Oh, come on. Tell me one funny anecdote! There has to be at least one!"

I thought for a while and then recounted the scene with my father about the decision to send me to Kelso. I made it funnier, and her amusement made me burlesque it even more, acting out the dialogue with my father's voice a booming bass and mine a weak soprano.

"About the spy part," she said when we had stopped laughing. "You don't have to worry about being found out, or about the guys at the plant revolting. There've been rumors about Kelso closing for a while now." She sighed. "Happens all the time around here."

That brought me back to reality. "What about Monday morning?" I asked. "How am I going to face Durone?"

"A smart boy like you will be able to figure out how to handle it." She sat up and began packing up the picnic basket. "Just remember that no one knows what happened Friday night but you and Durone."

"Come on, now!"

"Eh. Am I the expert on this or what? It's back to the Italian ethic. My family would never tell, to protect Louella. And Durone would never tell, to protect himself. So, what you have to do is—"

"Duck!"

"No, dummy. Not duck, *think!* Size up the situation and decide how to handle it. And thinking is something you can pull off much better than Sallie Durone!"

We got back to her "names of the famous" in the car going home. "See, it's real easy to remember them," she told me, "if you just think up a gimmick. Take Nguyen Cao Ky, for example. 'Ky holds the key to Vietnam.' That's how I remember who he is."

I don't know what made me do it. Perhaps it was the emphasis she was putting on current events, or maybe I just wanted to show off a little myself, but I broke my cardinal rule: For the first time I brought up my private revolution, out loud, to another human being. "Who's the head of the Communist Party in Czechoslovakia?"

She thought for a while, trying, I could tell, to come up with the answer. And I entertained a new kind of dream: talking about Prague Spring with another person! I who had spent months in a silent dialogue with news publications actually contemplated enhancing the excitement through verbal communication. I would bring Prague Spring to Fallsville! I would educate her! I would transform her into an avid supporter like me. I was a smitten teenager about to intensify the pleasure of the romance by sharing its intimacy with a friend.

After a minute or two, her face lit up. "Alex . . . oh, gee, wait, give me a second . . . Alexander Du . . . Dubcek! *Alexander Dubcek!*"

"Right." I felt light-headed. Just hearing her come out with his name somehow validated his accomplishments and endeared her to me at the same time.

"I got it! I got it!" she shouted gleefully. But then, unfortunately, she elaborated. "See, once again, my memory trick paid off. I just tell myself, Alexander, you know, like Alexander the Great, 'cause this guy has to be great if he took over like that, right? And then the Dubcek part is easy. You just think 'Dumb Czech,' only like you have a cold—Dubcek—and you've got it!"

"Dumb Czech?" I screamed. "Boy, are you out of it! He happens to be one great human being!"

"Well, like I said, that's in the Alexander part—"

"Just memorizing names, that's what stupid people do," I raged. "You're not *reading* the *Times!* You're not absorbing the meaning of the news! You're just playing with it, to name-drop—to sound smart. And you know what? You *don't* sound smart. You don't sound the least bit smart. You sound like a real dope, if you ask me. An idiot, putting on airs." I bore down on the gas pedal.

"You, um, turn right over there," she said in a very little voice. I swerved around the corner and roared ahead.

"That's, uh, that's my house." She was pointing to a big old bungalow on a street that was a five-minute walk from Mrs. Stompous's place. She scrambled for the door handle.

I opened my mouth, but nothing came out.

"Bye." She slammed the car door and ran into the house.

It wasn't until hours later, after I'd finished reading a book in my room, that my head began to clear.

What is ingrained is ingrained, and the first pang of guilt I felt came under the heading "Bingham Manners." A proper Bingham does not raise his voice. A proper Bingham does not shout. A proper Bingham does not call another person "stupid," especially if that person *is* stupid.

I pled guilty to a behavioral lapse, and climbed into bed. The subject of common decency did not occur to me until some time in the middle of the night when I awoke from a dream, sweaty and cold and unable to just roll over and reenter oblivion. Then the voices came. "Who drove you to the hospital?" they hissed. "Who kept you awake to make sure you did not have a concussion?" and "Who took you to the most beautiful place in Fallsville and fed you and told you you were brave?" Who? Who? Who?

By three in the morning, Cel had entered the room—in audio. "A ticket out of Fallsville." "Marcella de Gaulle." "Gotta stop acting like a steamroller." "I'm not polished, but I'm quick."

I tossed and turned, hearing the words, seeing the funny face caked with makeup toss out a million different expressions—joy, commiseration, cockiness, anger, hurt, hurt, hurt, hurt.

By five-thirty, the sun was up and so was I, fully aware that I had awakened that day a new man—a total heel.

"Do the right thing," I heard my mother say, and I knew what the right thing was: apologize.

By noon, I was riding through nearby towns in search of an open flower shop and feeling much better. Translating guilt into etiquette made it less personal, easier. I ended up buying a bouquet at a store thirty miles away. The reflection in my car window of me standing on the sidewalk holding flowers made me cringe. What would I say? "I'm sorry for the way I acted." Then what?

That's enough, I assured myself. If this girl was good at anything, it was carrying on both sides of a conversation.

I drove by the house four times. On the fifth trip, I saw two guys a little older and infinitely more muscular than I walk out, get into a car, and drive off. The "zombies" were gone. I told myself the coast was as clear as it was ever going to be.

My knock was answered by a short, stocky, dark-haired woman. "Mrs. Parmacella?" I inquired with dancing-school manners.

"Yeah?"

"Hi, I'm Rodney Bingham. I—"

"Oh, yes!" She clasped her hands in front of her. "The hero! Thank you *so* much . . . Vito!" She yelled, turning around. "It's him! The boy that saved Louella!"

"Ask him in!" a deep voice ordered from a room upstairs.

"Come in!" she said, opening the screen door. "Please, come in. We're very grateful."

"I wondered," I said, stepping hesitantly over the threshold, "is Cel home?"

Mrs. Parmacella lost all her gusto. She put her hands to her mouth as though she were about to cry.

"Yes!" It was Louella's voice from a room off to the side. "G'wan, Mama, tell him yes."

"Glad to meet you!" shouted a plump, middle-aged man who was descending the stairs. He was carrying a tray full of food. He looked at Mrs. Parmacella and shrugged sadly. "She don't eat."

"Doesn't!" The word was screeched out from some place upstairs.

The two parents looked up nervously.

"What, Baby?" the man asked hopefully. "Whatcha say?"

"It's not don't, it's doesn't!" came the shrill reply.

"Yeah, yeah, sorry, Baby." The man closed his eyes and continued down the stairs, shaking his head. "She doesn't eat."

He practically bumped head-on into one of my irises. He looked from the bouquet to me to Mrs. Parmacella.

"He's here to see Baby," Mrs. Parmacella whispered, casting an anxious eye up the stairs.

The man shrugged. "So?"

"C'mere." It was Louella's voice from the side room.

"Could you please, maybe, excuse us for a minute?" Mrs. Parmacella asked, tugging the man into the side room.

I stood all by myself in the hallway listening to the discussion.

"She won't come down."

"How do you know?"

"I know, believe me."

"So? Let him go up."

"Are the beds made?"

"Yeah, yeah, the beds are made."

"A man in her bedroom?"

"What man? Just a boy!"

"With flowers?"

"A friend with flowers."

"Cheer her up, maybe."

"Yeah, cheer her up."

"If she can be cheered up."

"Who knows unless you try?"

"Try?"

"Try."

"Try!"

"Go, Mama, you tell him."

Mrs. Parmacella emerged from the powwow and nodded her head toward the staircase. "Second door to the right at the top of the stairs." She looked at me as though I were a cop hunting down an armed burglar. "Good luck."

I'm sorry for the way I acted. I'm sorry for the way I acted. I repeated the line to myself on each step as I climbed, but when I walked into the second room on the right, what I saw rendered me speechless.

Cel was sitting on the bed in shorts and a T-shirt, surrounded by cut-up newspapers. She was staring straight ahead through

102

swollen, red eyes. Her face was scrubbed clean, and her hair was short, very short—more than two feet shorter than it had been the day before—in a bob of curls around her face.

As usual, she found words first. "Welcome to the new me!" she sang out, hopping off the bed, holding out her arms and turning around and around and around. "Welcome to the new me!"

"I'm sorry for the way I acted." I hoped the prepared text might stop her spinning.

"No problem!" she sang. "Wheeeeeeee!" She went around a few more times. When she stopped, she collapsed dizzily on the bed. "No more put-ons!" she shouted, lying on her back and staring at the ceiling. "No more making believe I know about the world when I don't. No more trying to make myself look like Louella when I don't." She turned her head toward me, forcing a broad grin. "No more put-ons. It's as easy as that. Actually, I feel kind of free, you know?"

"Yeah. Sure. Free." I wondered if insanity was part of the freedom. "For you," I said, holding out the bouquet, anxious to get the formalities over as quickly as possible.

"Flowers!" she cooed. "Beautiful flowers!" She winked at me. "Mama just loves flowers. Give them to her on the way out, would you?"

Well, I'd tried, right? I had certainly done the right thing. Comforted that my slate was now clean, I headed for the bedroom door. I heard her scramble to her feet behind me. I looked over my shoulder.

"I know this will come as a shock to you," she said, standing up, hands on hips. "A real shock for a guy who mostly deals with, you know, 'Pass the salt,' . . . 'No, thank you,' . . . and 'Delicious meal' in the way of expression, but, um . . ."

Her chest was heaving, her lips trembling. A storm was coming, an explosion. I cringed, backing toward the door a little, in search of shelter.

She wrapped her arms around her torso, clamped her teeth down over her quivering lower lip, and stayed all tight and tied up like that for a moment, regaining her composure. *"You . . . hurt . . . my . . . feelings!"*

Each word was uttered in a breath of its own. When she

finished, she just stood there before me, clenched and rigid, her enormous brown eyes brimming over with tears.

Oh, I did not understand this crazy little girl, not one bit, but the emotion—the raw pain—*that* I understood. I felt a knot in my stomach, twisting and hurting and then the cramp moved up, into a choking feeling in my throat. I just stood there across the room from her, my eyes glued to hers, adopting her anguish as my own. I was back again, back to where I had been so many times before. I felt my face contort involuntarily, and then tears slither down my cheeks.

We stayed that way for a while, paralyzed in a standoff.

Then she whirled around and threw herself on the bed. "Shit! Shit! Shit!" she howled, pounding the pillow amid sobs.

"Cel?" I moved toward the bed cautiously, wiping my face with the back of my hand.

She sat up and looked at me. "You look so *gorgeous* when you cry!" she wailed, sobbing and laughing at the same time. "Oh, isn't it just my luck? To find a boy who cries prettier?"

Well, she was a complete nut, but for some reason, I took on the mood, snorting giggles and sniffling tears and even protesting.

"Such wonderful green eyes," she hiccuped. "It just tore me apart to see them get all sad and teary like that." And she looked up at me so sweetly, it made my eyes fill up all over again.

"I like the new you," I announced, pulling out a handkerchief and sitting down next to her on the bed.

"Ahh . . ."

"No, really, I like the look." I blew my nose and examined her, for the first time. I discovered—to my relief—that I really *did* like the look. "You have great cheekbones," I went on, honestly appraising the structure. "They don't need a dark dab of makeup for highlighting. If anything, they stand out more dramatically without it." I blew my nose again.

She shrugged and fidgeted with her fingers.

"And, believe me, it's a relief to see your eyes! All that black glop just covered them up." I took in the thick, lustrous dark brown curls of hair surrounding her face and found myself wanting to touch them. "And your hair, it's so soft and pretty this way . . ." I heard my voice catch a little. The sound and the words I had just uttered made me self-conscious. "I *hated* it all matted down and straight!" I shouted, hurrying to cover up the show of emotion. "It looked—fake!"

"And now?" She turned to me full-face. "What do I look like now?"

"Marci." I whispered it without thinking.

"Hah?"

I stared at her some more, and my head went up and down. "You look like your name should be Marci." She did. I didn't know why exactly. The soft darkness of the curly hair around the clear, glistening tan skin just made me come up with that that name. Soft and cuddly, I guess that's what the name conjured up for me.

"Do you know someone named Marci?"

"Nope."

"Marci," she whispered, trying it out.

"Come on, now, you mean to tell me, in all her searching, Marcella never came up with Marci as a possibility?"

She shook her head.

"You were so busy perusing *The New York Times* and your book lists, you didn't even think of looking inside your own name!" I smiled at her and she smiled back. "Marci," I repeated. "Yes, it fits."

She sighed. "I'll think about it."

I stood up but then turned around. "I understand how your mother probably likes flowers and all," I said, holding our my somewhat crumpled bouquet. "But I really brought these for you."

"They're beautiful," she said, taking them, her face radiant. "Thank you."

12

"Could Sal have been looking for a job, Francine?"

"A *job?*"

Marci pulled her kitchen telephone cord behind her as she walked over to the stove. "That's all I've been able to guess from the phone bills thus far—that maybe he was looking for a new job." With the phone clenched between her head and shoulder, she began dotting the chicken breasts in the casserole dish with butter.

"He *had* a job!" Francine's signature whine screeched through the receiver, accentuating Marci's headache. "A steady job!"

"Well, then, I'm probably wrong . . ."

"No, *I'm* probably wrong." Francine sniffed. "Jeez, Marci, nothin' surprises me no more. I swear, far as I knew, those months were the best time in our whole marriage. First time ever he was nice to me, y'know? No fights, no hollerin', just quiet, like. Peaceful. Then I find that bank statement and whatcha know? He was nice 'cause he was *cheatin'* on me!"

Marci grimaced as she turned on the oven. "Now, Francine, you don't know that. All you know is that he was taking money out of some bank account."

"And staying out late at night! My money! Blowing it on some two-bit—"

"You said it was his private account."

"Only 'cause he never told me about it! Who has private accounts when he's *married*, I'd like to know? Who goes around blowin' money like that? Money his family could use for better things?"

Marci heaved the casserole dish into the oven and checked the clock on the wall.

"And now it turns out he was job huntin' behind my back too! Probably planning on walkin' out, running off with that—"

"Francine!"

"Sorry." Francine sighed and then began sniffling little sobs. "I just get so upset. So upset, Marci. I don't know what to do."

"Look, I'm probably wrong about the job search. Why would he look for a job when he knew he was dying of cancer, for heaven's sake? It was a *guess*, that's all, a bad guess prompted by my inability to come up with anything else. I'll work on it some more, check some of the other calls, see what I can turn up."

"I'm in such a bind. I swear, Marci, I don't know *what* to do."

"In the meantime, I'll send the rest of the bill folders to school with Tommy. He can give them to Frank to bring home so you can use them to—"

"You'll be happy to know I didn't get on Frank's case," Francine reported. "I tried it your way. Just sayin' nothin'."

"Good, Francine. That's really the best thing to do. Frank's just upset too, you have to realize—"

"Just like his *father*." Francine spit the words out. "You know what a pain in the neck it is to be left with a rotten kid who's—"

"Give him time, Francine."

"The back of my hand, that's what I'd like to give him!"

"I have to go, Francine. Have to finish dinner. I'll let you know as soon as I find out anything."

"Sure. Fine." She sounded like a child scorned. "Fix dinner. Bye."

Marci opened her mouth to speak but heard a click and then a dial tone. She stood there listening to it for a few seconds, finding it a comforting replacement for Francine Durone's voice.

The front door opened and then slammed shut. "Hello."

"Hi, honey, I'm in the kitchen!"

Lindsay Courbienne trudged into the kitchen, her long, dark-

107

blond hair glistening, her tight purple slacks dramatizing the long legs and tiny butt underneath, her oversized white sweater camouflaging everything on top. She opened the oven door. "Yuk, chicken," she groaned, and then dumped her school bag on the kitchen table.

Bad day, Marci told herself silently.

"Bad day," Lindsay announced.

"Really? Why?"

"Mother, can't you see, I *don't* want to talk about it."

Marci put the potatoes into the toaster oven to bake and began making a salad. She eyed the forlorn silhouette who did not want to talk about it, but was obviously dying to be prodded. "How was the math quiz?"

"Fine."

"And the science test?"

"Easy."

"Did you get your English essay back?"

"No."

Comforted by the fact that the problem was not scholastic, Marci set about dicing the onion.

"I'm ugly. That has to be it."

Marci looked up. Lindsay was staring at her reflection in the pot Marci had taken out. Marci took in the nicely proportioned adolescent face adorned with enormous, almond-shaped brown eyes that were surrounded by an incredible set of long eyelashes, and decided it was wonderful how nature provided. In the seventh and eighth grades, when they really *were* ugly, girls never worried about it. It was only in the ninth grade, when they began looking so much better, that they became preoccupied with their faces. "Well, homeliness is just something you'll have to live with."

"Don't tell me I'm beautiful," Lindsay moaned. "I don't want to hear another of those lectures."

"Did I say you were beautiful? You weren't listening!" Marci threw the onions on top of the lettuce and went after the tomatoes. "You've convinced me. You're hopelessly marred physically, but beauty is only skin deep, right?"

"Very funny."

The vanity, the absurd vanity that came with the age! Marci's sharp knife dug into the tomato, cutting away at the vanity.

"I'm the only one in my whole group who hasn't been asked to the varsity dance." The tears began flowing down Lindsay's cheeks.

Marci's heart pounded, and her knife changed direction, cutting ridges into the faces of all the twerpy sons-of-bitches who had not asked her little girl to the varsity dance. "So? You can just go with a group of girls—like last year."

"*Seventh-* and *eighth-*grade girls go in groups," Lindsay said disdainfully. "Ninth-grade girls go with boys who ask them. The way I see it, this is just the beginning of a long and very lonely life."

Wanting to give Lindsay a hug, but knowing what the reaction would be, Marci sprinkled the tomatoes on the salad instead. "As I recall, Tommy never asked a girl to a dance when he was in ninth grade."

"Ninth-grade *boys* go in groups. Don't you see? That makes it all the better if you're a girl who gets asked! You've got millions of boys to dance with!"

"Honey, the mathematics just don't figure. If all the boys go in groups, who's left to ask out the girls?"

"It's my hair. It's just all this boring hair, hanging down next to a boring face. I just hate my face, and my body."

Marci threw down the green pepper and poured herself a Coke. "Lindsay, this is ridiculous. You have an absolutely lovely face—"

"I *told* you, I don't want another beauty lecture!"

"The boys will come, believe me," Marci shouted back. "I just think entirely too much time is being spent contemplating the packaging, and not enough time on what's inside."

"You think it's my personality?" The tears were now falling more plentifully. "You think that's the problem?"

"No! Oh, honey, it's just the *boys* that are the problem. They're too young and immature in the ninth grade to—"

"Yo *ho!*" It was a deep male voice coming from the hallway, accompanied by the sound of a slamming door.

In a green ski jacket and black cords, Tom Courbienne strutted into the kitchen, balancing a stack of books on his right hip. He opened the oven door, glanced inside, and then groaned. "Shit, it's chicken."

"Hi, honey," Marci said, sitting down next to Lindsay and putting her arm around her. "How was your day?"

"The guy's a creep, Mom." Tommy heaved his books on the kitchen table. "I'm telling you, this tutoring idea of yours is *not* going to work out." He opened the refrigerator, took out a wedge of cheddar cheese, broke off half, and stuffed it into his mouth.

"You have to give it time, Tom. People who need help are often not very receptive to getting it. They fight the idea. You just have to roll with the punches a little."

"Frank Durone hates his mother . . ." Tom shot Marci an evil grin. "Doesn't it scare you a little? Me hanging around with a guy who hates his mother? What if it's catching or something?"

Marci returned the look. "I'll just have to take my chances, I guess."

Tom broke off another wedge of cheese. "Can I ask you a question, Mom?" He chomped on the cheese and waved his hand in the air as though trying to formulate the question.

"Sure. What?" Marci raised the glass to her lips.

"Did Frank Durone's father try to rape Aunt Louella?"

Lindsay gasped, and Marci gagged on the Coke. She started coughing in violent spasms.

"Mommy!"

"Ma? You okay?"

"Fine. I'm fine," Marci croaked. She got up, went over to the kitchen sink, grabbed a glass, and filled it with water. She drank it all down, paused, and waited for her breathing to return to normal. "I'm fine. It was just . . ." She burst into giggles. "Quite a question!"

Tom and Lindsay laughed with her, relieved.

Marci turned to Tom. "How exactly did that come up?"

"Oh, real normally," Tom said sarcastically. "Just, like your average opening line. 'We're kinda related,' Frank Durone tells me in this loose, casual way. 'Oh, really?' I say. 'How?' He grins, his lids at half mast. 'My father tried to rape your Aunt Louella,' he tells me."

Lindsay and Marci stared at him dumbfounded.

"What did you say?" Marci asked.

"What *could* I say? 'Oh, yeah, Cousin Frank, welcome to the family?' " He walked over to the cabinet, took out a bag of Oreo cookies, and began shoving them into his mouth, by the handful.

110

"Well, what *did* you say?"

Tom shrugged as he chewed. "I said, 'You want to start with fractions or formulas?' "

"Well, that's probably the best way to deal with it." Marci got up and went back to the paring knife and the green pepper. "It's important to remember he's self-conscious about this tutoring. It's a defense mechanism of sorts. He's testing you—trying to put you off." She started slicing. "My guess is, once it gets underway, the two of you will get along better. He'll start seeing some progress. That will make him more interested in the whole thing."

Lindsay stood up. "I'm going upstairs to study," she said, picking up her books. "Call me when it's time to set the table. Until then"—she shot her mother a melodramatic look—"I'll be working on what's *underneath* the unimportant packaging!" She tossed her hair and exited.

"That kid's in a constant state of P.M.S.," groaned Tom.

"Huh?" Marci tossed some celery into the bowl.

"P.M.S.—premenstrual syndrome," he responded with a mouth full of cookies. "Females get all emotional around the time of the month when their period comes. High-strung?" He gave his mother a winning smile. "Surprised you haven't heard of it, you being a woman and all."

Marci grabbed the package of cookies. "That's enough, for God's sake."

"I'm starving, Mom! I had a huge workout at practice!"

"Then eat something healthy."

Tom grabbed one more cookie out of the pack before she closed it. "Let's just think of it as eating dessert before dinner, okay? I don't understand why you see it as such a big deal. It all ends up in the same place." Tom picked up his books, walked to the kitchen doorway, and checked to see no one was around. Then he turned back to Marci. "Mom?"

"What?"

"Did Frank Durone's father rape Aunt Louella?"

"No."

"Hey, Mom, the hysterical one is out of earshot. It's just you and me—the adults!"

Would the ghost of Salvatore Durone never stop rumbling?

111

"There was a time when Salvatore Durone and Aunt Louella were dating . . . and, well, he tried to go farther than she wanted."

"How far? Rape?"

"Oh, honey, they were just kids. The story's been blown out of proportion, I'm sure, after all these years."

"Is that what made Aunt Louella such a militant feminist?"

"No." Marci sighed. "Well, maybe. I don't know. But if so, it was just one of many contributing factors." She looked up at Tom. "Who . . . who told Frank Durone about his?"

Tom grinned wickedly. "I'll be sure and ask next week . . . in that awkward silence after we finish the first ten problems and before we go on to the second ten."

Lindsay walked back into the kitchen, her eyes red and swollen. "I wasn't up to homework." She sighed, pulling a long lock of hair out of her face.

"Well, if it isn't human tragedy, back in our midst!"

"That's *enough*, Tom," Marci snapped.

"Eh, I'm just reacting like any concerned older brother would. If you ask me, what you two need is a male perspective." Tom shifted his books to the other hip, and bent down with an exaggerated air of compassion. "Want to talk about it, Princess?"

"Tom." Marci shut her eyes and took a deep breath. "Surely you have someplace to go . . . someplace where you can drop off that heavy load of books and clean yourself up a little before dinner."

"P.M.S.," Tom muttered, shaking his head as he sauntered out. "Classic case."

"I'll set the table." Lindsay began pulling utensils out of the drawer. Then she moved toward her mother. "Tommy's upstairs now, Mom," she whispered. "It's just us women!"

Marci fortified herself for another emotional outpouring. "So?"

"So . . . what?" Marci asked, confused.

"So *tell* me," Lindsay demanded. "*Did* Frank Durone's father rape Aunt Louella?"

13

1968 "Jesus Christ, what happened to you?" Cripple shouted when I arrived for work Monday. Tooth and Hard-on, who were standing close by, just gaped.

"Car accident," I said.

"Holy shit," gasped Duke. "Just head injuries? Nothin' more?"

"Yeah," I said. "Head hit the windshield." Then I wondered how I was going to pull this off on the loading dock. "Some rib damage," I volunteered. "From the seat belt."

"Lucky you was wearin' a seat belt!" offered Lucky.

"Whose fault was it?" asked Hard-on.

"Mine," I said quickly—too quickly, I worried. "I, uh, was speeding."

"Who'd ya hit?"

"An old lady. An angry old lady, as it turned out."

The guys liked that. They guffawed and slapped me on the back. I grabbed a worksuit and went over to my locker, complimenting myself on the successful execution of the first item on my outline: entry. (I had arrived early.) Aware that the second item was completely in someone else's hands, I cowered in front of my locker.

"Shit, will ya take a look!" gasped Slime.

"Holy Mary," whispered Deke, and I knew Item Two had

begun. I turned my back on the group and began putting on the workpants.

"Sallie, baby!" Deke shouted. "You're the second guy to show up lookin' like dead meat today!"

"Yeah?"

"Yeah! Smarts was in a car accident."

(I ticked off Item Three.)

"He was, wazzee." It was uttered in a monotone.

"Sallie must've scored!" screeched Lucky. "Look at that face, boys, and tell me. Is that the masterful work of the Parmacella brothers, or what!"

"Looks like Chickie's punch to the right eye to me," squealed Slime. "I got one at the Elks Christmas party last year, and it looked just like that!"

"Goddamn woppo, you're somethin' else," Cripple said in awe. "How much I owe you? How much was our bet?"

"I don't need your money." Durone sneered.

"It must've been good!" Lucky yelled. "So good he don't need no money, even!"

"Okay, guys, let's get out on that floo-ah and build a beddah product!" Durone hollered.

"Will ya listen to him! Actin' like nothing even happened!" Slime laughed.

"Well, he's had the weekend to rest up after his big night!" said Lucky.

"On the floooo-ah!" yelled Durone.

My eyes down, I rushed past Sallie along with everyone else.

My planned agenda got a little difficult on the loading dock. My ribs hurt so much. Oh, God, how they hurt. "Trouble with seat belts?" Hard-on muttered after watching me for a while.

"Yeah." I grimaced as I lifted the cartons.

"Hey, Smarts!"

It was Deke, walking out onto the loading dock from inside the factory. "Sallie says he wants us to switch places. Go and fill in for me on the line."

"How come?"

"I dunno." Deke pouted. "He says he's mad at me for being so slow on Friday."

I had no idea what to do on the assembly line, but Pimp was

114

standing by ready to instruct me when I got there. It was tedious manual work but just that: strictly manual work. I was terribly relieved—both physically and mentally. I figured Durone and I had reached an understanding of sorts.

I definitely planned on going to Mongon's after work—I had been looking forward to it all day, as a matter of fact—but I wanted to get there after the rest of the group, so I took a long time changing.

Durone came back to the locker room late from his cleaning duties.

"Want us to wait for you, Sallie?" Slime asked when the rest were ready.

"Not goin' to Mongon's tonight. I got plans."

"Plans!" hooted Deke. "Listen to him! The guy has plans!"

"The brothers can mess up his face," gushed Lucky, "but they can't keep him from goin' back for more!"

The gang left, and soon Durone and I were the only ones in the locker room. We were sitting on benches at opposite ends.

I looked across at him, bent over his shoes. "Thank you for taking me off the loading dock," I said.

He lifted his head, and for the first time all day, I really looked at his face. One eye was swollen shut, his jaw all black and blue.

He nodded his head slowly, digesting my words. "Thanks, uh, for covering for me with the guys," he said gruffly.

I went back to my shoe-tying on a high: The plan had worked. A victory for the thinking man.

Then it hit me: the larger picture. For the first time in three days, my self-preoccupation gave way to a broader view, and I saw myself, not as victim turned winner, but rather as an accomplice in a darker scenario.

I heard Durone groan slightly as he walked across the locker room, a gigantic hairy hand extended my way. "Whatcha say, bygones is bygones," he grunted.

Still staring into space, I shook my head.

His hand wadded up into a fist. "Why not?"

"What about Louella?"

"Louella." He squeezed his eyes shut. "Promisin', teasin', makin' me want her so bad, just so's she could laugh in my face!"

115

His chest was heaving. "All them nights she's tellin' me I'm so great, 'n then turns out I ain't good enough. I'm scum."

"But the guys all think you scored with her, that she let you score. You and I together, we let them think that."

"So what?"

"So, our face-saving came at the expense of her reputation."

He limped away.

"In a town, Sal," I yelled after him, "where a reputation lasts a lifetime!"

"Bitch!" he screamed, heaving his workshirt into the dirty laundry pile and hobbling out of the locker room.

Cripple and Deke were leaving by the time I walked into Mongon's. "Lookee what's here!" Cripple called out to me. "A new Cel!"

"Only her hairdresser knows for sure!" chimed in Deke.

"She's got a new name too," offered Con Man. "Right, guys?"

"Mar-ci, Mar-ci," they chanted in unison, pounding their glasses on the counter.

"Ah, c'mon," begged the blushing object of their attention on the other side of the counter. "Cool it, eh?"

She did look good, and it wasn't just the cosmetic changes. Her cheeks were high in color, her eyes sparkling as though she felt beautiful. I sat down at the counter with the guys.

"Get you something?" she asked, her eyes not meeting mine.

"The usual."

She made my float, delivered it, and then hurried over to a group of girls sitting at the other end of the counter. I nursed my drink, watching and waiting.

The girls were the last to leave. "Louella comin' back to work tomorrow?" one called out from the door.

"Yeah. She just, you know, had a cold today."

"Okay."

She acted as though I wasn't there, silently carrying glasses over to the sink and rinsing them, her back to me.

"Mar-ci!" I called out playfully.

"Well, for now," she said over her shoulder. "Names come and go with me."

I told her how brilliantly I'd pulled things off with Durone at the plant. She nodded. Then I told her how I'd defended her sister's reputation when Durone wanted to make up. I figured I'd get extra credit for that one. Another nod. I played with my straw. "You hungry?"

She shrugged and kept rinsing.

"I was going to go over to the Friendly's by the highway. Want to come?"

"Nah." She dried her hands on a dish towel and walked back to retrieve some more glasses. "I've got homework."

"Homework?"

"Yah. *The New York Times.*" She was back at the sink, turning the water on again. "I've decided to really study them. To absorb the meaning instead of just memorizing names."

"I told you I was sorry," I protested. "I didn't mean what I said in the car."

"Well, you should have," she said over her shoulder. "You were right."

Her busy-ness and cold shoulder were getting to me. "It doesn't take all night to read *The New York Times!*"

"It does if you're rereading. I started with the first issue I got."

"Oh, great," I grunted. "What're you up to? February?"

"I'm not doing it paper by paper. I'm taking topics and following them through from day to day. One topic especially. I've put together a whole scrapbook about it."

"Yeah? What's the topic?"

She turned around and gave me a significant look. "Socialism with a human face."

I stared at her.

She avoided my stare, aggressively wiping down the countertop. "Alexander Dubcek is quite a guy."

"Look, I told you. I just flipped out in the car. See, the whole thing in Czechoslovakia, it's kind of special to me. I don't know why exactly, but—"

"You don't know why?" She looked at me from under lowered eyelids. "Gee, I do. Don't need a college education to figure out that one."

"Yeah? Why then?"

"The struggle is all about how the little guy can win out, if he's a thinker."

"Alexander Dubcek is hardly a little guy! He's—"

117

"Compared to Kosygin? Compared to the whole Communist bloc on the other side? I'd say he's a little guy. A dreamer."

I swallowed. "Okay, Okay." I was getting angry. "I thought your big plan was to better yourself," I snapped. "Not to borrow my preoccupation—"

"Your preoccupation? Since when do you own Alexander Dubcek?"

"Well, I brought him up in the first place."

"That doesn't mean he can't appeal to me too."

"What?" I demanded. "What's the appeal for you?"

She stopped sponging for a moment. "It sure flies in the face of Italian ethics," she cackled. "Alexander Dubcek is about as opposite to Chickie Parmacella as you can get!" She blushed a little and went back to scrubbing. "I guess I'm sounding dumb again, hah?"

"I don't know. Translate that for me."

"No explosions in Czechoslovakia. No 'Pow, right in the eye!' Instead you've got this man who's persistent, who's calm. He gets what he wants the quiet way, by pushing, pressuring. I like what he wants too. Must be nice to live in a place where people are dying to be free to read books. Sure beats this pisshole.

"Also—" She looked at me sheepishly. "Well, do you believe in fate?"

I shrugged.

"I do. And, see, Alexander Dubcek succeeded Antonin Novotny as the first secretary of the Communist Party on January fifth, right?"

"Right."

She beamed. "The very next day—January sixth? That's when my first issue of *The New York Times* arrived. Now, that's gotta be fate."

I felt an internal tug.

"And Novotny was forced to resign as President of Czechoslovakia on March twenty-second."

"That's right!"

Her eyes opened wide. "That's my birthday! I mean, that's pure—"

"Fate!" I shouted, delirious. She had pulled all the right strings. I was hers for the asking.

"We, um . . ." I played with the salt shaker. "We could stop by

118

your place and pick up your *New York Times* and take it with us to Friendly's, if you want."

She shrugged. "Okay."

"Here." I jumped off the stool. "I'll help you clean up." I carried my glass over to the sink.

"Oh, I almost forgot . . ." she said, following me. "My mother and father, they told me to invite you to our house this week for Sunday dinner."

Armed with the box of candy Marci had picked out for me the day before, I arrived at the Parmacellas' house at noon Sunday. The women quickly retreated to the kitchen, leaving me and Mr. Parmacella sitting together in the living room. He reminded me a little of Papa Bear—dark and hairy and soft all over, with a warm and comforting voice. "We're very grateful to you, Rod," he began. As he elaborated, I realized the show of gratitude was not for rescuing Louella. It was for preoccupying Baby.

"You understand what she says?" he whispered.

I nodded.

His face broke out in a look of relieved delight. "Then, please, talk to her. Talk her *out*, that's all I'm askin'." He closed his eyes and sighed. "See, she thinks all the time," he went on wearily. "She thinks, and then she gets way ahead a' you. It's like you're driving your car and you're just getting to Brown Street, and she's all the way up the hill over on Floral Avenue? And she says, 'The parade is ugly.' And you don't even know there *is* a parade, see, because you haven't made it over to Floral."

I nodded.

He winced. "And then she gets all upset—angry at you—because you don't say nothin', so she thinks you're disagreeing, but she's just drivin' too fast for you, that's all."

"I see." Not knowing the geography of Fallsville, I was at a disadvantage, but I grasped the underlying message.

All the smile wrinkles in his haggard face indented deeply. "It's good, real good, Rod, that she's found someone who can keep up with her. Makin' Baby happy, that's been the hardest thing." He closed his eyes as though to blot out vivid recollections. "But since you left here last Sunday—leaving off all them flowers?—I gotta tell you, Rod—Baby, she's been happy!"

119

The front door burst open and in walked the two thickest specimens of hairy masculinity I had ever encountered in my life. I knew one was two years older than the other, but they looked and walked like musclebound twins.

"This is Rod," Mr. Parmacella said cheerfully, standing and putting a hand on my shoulder. "Rod, meet Chickie and Vinnie." They nodded in stone-faced unison.

Mr. Parmacella headed for the kitchen. "Time to carve the meat." I yearned for the chance to assist him.

Chickie Parmacella's expressionless dark-brown eyes roamed slowly from my shoes to my slacks to my belt to my jacket and tie. The only sound in the room was the rhythmic cracking of his chewing gum. "You did good for Louella last Friday," he announced as his hand squeezed the life out of mine. He let go, turned, and walked out of the room.

"Tell me, big shot," Vince hissed as my hand slipped into his formidable grip. "Whatcha gonna do for our sister Louella next Friday? Hah?" His eyes squinted into scary little slits.

This was the lovable brother? I felt terror welling up inside. Then I saw something in his squinty eyes I had not seen in Chickie's—a light, way back there in the darkness, a sparkle. I noticed something else. Vince's jaw was pumping up and down just like his brother's, but there was no chewing gum inside his mouth.

I stared back, peering deep into his eyes, searching . . . hoping. Sure enough, the sparkle grew into a gleam, and two indentations appeared in the cheeks of his stony face: dimples!

Then some kind of strange, internal click occurred—a gut, nonverbal communication. We both cracked up at the same time and stood there in the living room, laughing and shaking our heads, as though we were childhood buddies who had just exchanged the secret handshake.

"I just love to out-Chickie Chickie!" Vince howled. "Besides, a guy powerful enough to get Baby to cut her hair, change her name, and talk about nothing but Czechoslovakia . . ." He went on grinning at me mischievously. "I figured he'd be strong enough to take the heat."

"Dinner's ready!" Mrs. Parmacella called out.

Sizzling platters of food were being heaped on the beige lacy tablecloth in the dining room. The walls of the room were cluttered with photos of the brothers in athletic uniforms, jumping and catching balls. There was a picture of Louella in a formal gown with a crown on her head accepting a bouquet of roses, and one of Marci in pigtails holding a trophy with a sign behind her that proclaimed FALLSVILLE SPELLING CHAMPION, 1962.

A family house, that's what it felt like to me, a magical place where children were the stars.

The dark coloring of my hosts, the spicy aromas, the clutter, the high energy levels . . . it was all so different from the staid silence of Bingham family dinners. I felt a little like a Peace Corps volunteer undergoing culture shock as he took in the customs of the natives.

Mrs. Parmacella assigned us seats, and Mr. Parmacella thanked God for blessing his household with health and happiness and the presence, this Sunday, of a special guest. Smiling back at the welcoming, upturned faces of my hosts, I found myself saying my own silent prayer of gratitude.

14

Saturday morning, after Tommy and Lindsay had left for the school football game, Marci Courbienne poured out a second cup of coffee and issued herself an order: Get *on* with it! You have a box filled with information and a free day to either uncover the Salvatore Durone mystery or put an end to Francine's fantasy.

Was he looking for a new job or wasn't he? Marci took out the folder marked "research" and turned to Durone's list of "contacts." She scanned the names: Joe Sallo (local), Angelo Pimpoli (Jacksonville, Florida). Her eyes moved faster down the list, ignoring those marked local. Sure enough, the telephone numbers with area codes matched the long-distance calls recorded on the Durones' July phone bill.

She picked up the telephone and tapped out the Jacksonville number. A woman answered after a few rings. "Hello?"

"Is there someone there by the name of Angelo Pimpoli?"

"Used to be. He don't live here no more."

"But he used to?" Marci persisted eagerly. "There *was* a man of that name at this telephone number?"

" 'Bout two years ago—yeah."

"Do you know where he is now? Where I could contact him?"

"If I did, I'd get him first," the lady grunted. "Left here owing me two weeks on his room."

"Could you tell me a little about Mr. Pimpoli? What did he do for a living?"

"Not a whole lot, lady, that's for sure."

"But did he—"

"Hey, look, honey. I got a house to run. I got no time for crank calls about drunks who don't pay their rent."

She heard a click, then a dial tone. Marci hung up and checked the phone bill. Salvatore Durone's call to the Jacksonville number on July second had lasted exactly one minute, five seconds. He had probably gotten the same response. She checked the records on the other long-distance calls. They were all equally short, which meant they were probably equally futile.

She pulled out the Orange County telephone book and began checking the names Durone had marked local. There were no listings for the first three names. She went for the fourth. *James Connomon* . . . Her hand ran down the page and stopped abruptly: "Connomon, James, 1503 Main, Daley." She started to dial the number, but then put the receiver back. Daley was just twenty minutes from her home in Collier.

She went downstairs to get her coat.

Fifteen-oh-three Main Street turned out to be a mobile home about a mile from the center of Daley, Massachusetts. There was a pickup truck parked outside.

A tall, balding man with a thick beard opened the door. The brown bathrobe he was wearing sagged over his sunken chest, bulged around a low-slung beer gut, and then stopped abruptly at a pair of hairy knees. He stared blankly at her through the glass of the closed storm door.

"Hello," Marci began quickly. "I'm looking for James Connomon . . ."

He nodded affably. "You got 'im!" His tone was folksy.

"I'm Marci Courbienne. I'm here on behalf of Salvatore Durone."

"Y'are?" The man smirked a little and opened the storm door a crack. "What'd Sallie be up to now?"

"You know him?" Marci's eyes expanded gratefully.

"Well, *knew* him. Been a long time."

"How long?"

He wrapped his arms around his robe. "Just after he got outta the service, 'round then was the last time I seen 'im. He, um, he come by here last summer though," Connomon offered.

"Really?"

"Yup. Wasn't here myself. Told my wife he'd be by again, but he never come back."

"Did he tell your wife *why* he'd come?" Marci asked hopefully.

"Didn't seem to have no reason. Only thing he asked was how I was feelin'." He chortled. "Got a kick outta that. Sallie showin' up after all these years just to ask about my health!"

Marci laughed and waited.

"My wife—she said she didn't wanna ask him how *he* was feelin'. Said he looked terrible."

"Yes, well, he was in bad shape." Marci cleared her throat. Time for the formal announcement. "He died last month—of cancer."

"Really?" His face registered surprise, but not grief. Yet another in the long list of Salvatore Durone's nonmourners.

"I was just finishing up some business for the family," Marci continued. "I found your name on a list. Can you think of any reason Sallie would try to contact you?"

"Not a one!" Connomon said brightly, and, Marci noted, without a morsel of curiosity.

She was getting cold, but not cold enough to request entrance. She reached into her purse and pulled out a business card. "Well, if you come up with any ideas, give me a call."

"Sure 'nough!" he said cheerfully, taking her card.

She smiled, waved good-bye, and walked back to her car.

Sure 'nough! The words stuck in her brain as she turned on the ignition and pulled away. Where did a Massachusetts native get such a funny expression? *Not a one. Sure 'nough.* There was something about the sluggish folksiness, the slow, sleepy tone of his drawl that sounded familiar.

Then a face came back. So clear . . . the big ears, the pointy chin. Her heart started pounding as it hit her.

She jammed on her brakes. A car honked angrily, but she ignored it. Of course! She had been so preoccupied with the man's speech, she had totally ignored the most obvious clue of all: his *name!* She drove back, ran back up the front steps, and rang the doorbell. When she saw him, she became uncertain all over again. "Con Man?"

He did a double take. "Who *are* you, lady?"

"You first!" she ordered. "You're Con Man, right?"

"Shoot, no one's called me that for—"

"But they did? Back at the factory? The Kelso plant?"

He closed his eyes and made a face. "Yup."

" 'Much obliged . . .' " she drawled in a deep voice, dragging the syllables out. "That's what you used to say when I asked if you wanted a root beer float!"

His eyes narrowed. "Mongon's . . ." he whispered. "Cel!"

"That's right. I was the girl behind the counter!" Marci laughed, "Your beard really threw me. It was the semi-Southern accent I recognized."

"Moved here from Texas when I was thirteen." He laughed and shook his head. "Nobody's called me Con Man in twenty years!"

"It was a high-school nickname?"

"Hell it was! It was a *Durone* nickname. Old bully gave us all these dumb names at the plant!" He shook his head. "I was Con Man for three long years. Alla time I worked at Kelso."

They were both shifting around uncomfortably. So much for nostalgia. She'd had nothing in common with Con Man then, and she had nothing in common with him now. "Durone's wife, she thinks someone murdered Sallie."

Connomon woke up a little. "Yeah?"

"That's why I'm contacting the people like you whose names I found on the list he had. That might be why he contacted you."

Connomon grinned at her. "You sayin' I'd better get an alibi?"

"No," Marci laughed. "Not at all. It's just . . . Well, keep thinking about why he might have wanted to talk to you." She started down the steps.

"Back when I knew him," Connomon shouted after her, "you woulda had a whole string of suspects!"

"Including me!" she shouted over her shoulder. "Hey . . ." She turned around. "Did you ever know anyone by the name of Angelo Pimpoli?"

He shook his head. "Can't say as I did."

She grinned up at him. "Good to see you again . . . Con Man!"

He put his hands over his ears and groaned.

In the car going home, Marci began adapting murder mystery plots to fit her evidence. A murderer in the old gang, maybe. Someone Sallie thought Con Man could finger. Or, Con Man as murderer!

But as she pulled into her driveway, she began wondering whether Salvatore Durone had left the murder accusation behind in a desperate attempt to add a touch of excitement to an otherwise drab, depressing life. A melodramatic exit line? She sighed and faced the truth: That explanation made the most sense.

15

1968   The morning after I turned down his "bygones is by-gones" handshake in the locker room, Durone put me back on the loading dock and then supervised me mercilessly to make sure my ribs were killing me as I moved it "fastah."

I managed to pull it off until Friday, the day the chemical truck arrived with its weekly supplies. On Fridays we unloaded metal cylinders in addition to loading cardboard boxes, and tanks of chemicals were infinitely heavier than boxes of fake nipples.

"We're specializing," Hard-on announced after observing me for a while. "You do the boxes. I do the tanks."

"That's not fair," I protested—mildly.

"That's the way I call it."

Instead of sharing the loading and the unloading, I ran boxes from the dock to the outgoing truck, while he toted the tanks off the incoming truck. The loaders on the other teams who shared space with us on the dock looked at Hard-on as though he was crazy. But the looks stopped when we started outpacing them.

Durone must have heard about it because he came running over halfway through the morning, but just as he started to protest, a supervisor came by and seemed pleased that "Sallie's boys" were setting new records for "fastah." So Durone walked away.

Durone no longer went to Mongon's. That was the only visible change precipitated by the skirmish with Louella. "Lousy floats," he'd sneer each time the suggestion came up.

I took his place, rapidly becoming the most regular of the regulars. When the rest of the gang left each night, I helped Marci clean up, and then the two of us would take her daily copy of *The New York Times* and head for either Friendlys or the Cozy Heart Diner, the area's two major night spots, where we'd have a three-hour dinner ingesting mostly newspaper stories on Czechoslovakia and each other's words.

It was the high point of my day—of my life, really. I was a monk, let out of the monastery, tasting the pleasures of companionship, discovering a new mental energy that knew no bounds and rewriting my autobiography in the process. In June of 1968, the Bingham family's black sheep turned into a witty raconteur, a Henry Higgins wallowing in the undivided attention of Eliza Doolittle.

Unfortunately, Eliza Doolittle's sister started complicating things. Perhaps because the guys at the factory thought she was "Durone's girl," for the first time in her life, Louella Parmacella was without male attention. After a week of withdrawal, like an addict willing to ingest a weaker substance to ease the craving, she moved in on me.

"How're you dooooing, Rod?" she began cooing each night, patting the stool next to hers, welcoming the gladiator who, by his show of heroics on her behalf, had been forced to endure another pain-racked workday. The greeting was the high point of our exchange. Louella was not very interesting—a reactor rather than a conversationalist—but for a very few magical moments, I enjoyed the company of Fallsville's very own geisha girl. It took a couple of nights for me to see through the happy haze. The scene, it turned out, was not playing well on the other side of the counter.

On the third night of geisha-ing me, Louella picked up her purse at the appointed hour and headed for the door along with the rest of the gang. "What time should I tell Mama you'll be home?" she asked her sister.

"About a half hour," Marci called out from the sink.

"How come so early?" Louella looked from me to Marci and then back to me.

"Because I'm tired, that's why!" Marci hollered. "I don't have

128

the cushy job you have, sitting all day at a switchboard! Because I wanna get some sleep, and if you have problems with that you can—"

"No problem! No problem!" Louella ran out the door.

"I'm sorry," I mumbled, picking up some glasses from the counter.

"Yah?" Marci wiped a strand of hair off her forehead with the back of a sudsy hand. "What're you sorry for?"

"Flirting with Louella."

She whirled around and stared at me, her mouth open.

"What are you acting so shocked about? That's what made you angry, wasn't it?"

"It's your admission that shocked me. I mean, if you'd said 'Louella was just driving me crazy,' or 'I was just being polite.'"

"'Bullshit,' you'd have screamed! You would have called me on it. You would have zeroed right in on the truth! You always do! That's what's so great about you."

"And what's so great about Louella?"

"Nothing." I closed my eyes. "I'm sorry."

"Then why were you flirting? You're the one who said flirting. Why were you flirting with her?"

"I was just being polite," I offered playfully.

She growled and headed back to the sink.

"Marci," I pleaded, "you're the best friend I've ever had in my life . . . the only real friend."

"Yeah, and isn't it nice your new best friend has a sister built like the Playmate of the Month?"

"She's—she's nothing to me. She's like . . . oh, cotton candy. You know, sweet going down, but of no real taste or nutritional value. You're, you're—"

"I'm what?" She turned off the water. "This I gotta hear."

"Sustenance. My real sustenance."

She turned the water back on. "Meet the Parmacella girls!" she shouted, throwing a soapy hand in the air. "Cotton candy and meat-and-potatoes."

"Come on now . . ."

"Once," she sighed, "once in my life, I'd like to be the cotton candy."

"You can't be serious."

"Get outta here."

"Marci—"

"Out!" She pointed to the door. "Friendly's! They'll give you sustenance!"

Marci was walking into Mongon's the next morning when I showed up. "I couldn't sleep last night until I'd crafted this written apology," I said, shoving an envelope into her hand. "I'm really sorry. I would have never acted that way if I'd thought it would upset you."

She shrugged and looked down at the envelope.

"Could we go out tonight?" I asked hopefully. "After you close up?"

"Here's all you really need," she said, handing me the newspaper she was carrying. "Take *The New York Times* to dinner."

I put it back in her arms. "I need *you!*"

She blinked and looked up at me in surprise.

I took a breath. "Please?"

She hesitated.

"Yes?" I squinted at her. "I sense a yes deep down there, moving slowly to the surface, but it's moving so slowly . . ."

She laughed, pushing me in the direction of the factory. "Go on. You'll be late for work."

"Then I'll be late." I held my ground. "I have to know. I'm not moving until—"

"Yes!"

It was Friday, another chemical tank delivery day, and Hard-on once again rose to my aid. "You're a helluva nice guy to help me like this," I told him.

He kept unloading.

"Thank you," I persisted.

" 'S good for me," he grunted as he heaved a load. He seemed to be lifting with a peculiar new body movement.

"You okay?"

"Rrrrnnnnffff!" It was a common Hard-on emission, one that translated out as "Yes," "Sure," "Okay," or "Whatever you want," depending upon the question that had provoked it. But the more I watched him, the more concerned I got. He was picking up the metal cylinders, carrying them across the dock, but then suddenly, straining visibly, he would make a big dip down in front of the dolly, then stand up erect and release the tank.

"What are you doing?" I asked finally.

He stopped and wiped his brow. "Training the muscles."

"Training? For what?"

"Me and my dad're gonna do a big excavation project come September. I'm getting my digging muscles in shape." He walked back to the truck and picked up another tank. "See here?" he grunted as he once again pirouetted slightly with the metal container. "See how I'm acting like I'm shoveling a little?" His legs began trembling as he held the stance so I could inspect. "See, the weight is kind of like the weight of the dirt and rock I'm gonna have on my shovel. . . ."

His face was getting purple from the strain. "By stooping this way, I build up the muscles I'm gonna need in the back of my thighs and my buttocks for the shoveling." When lowered the tank, his whole body practically went onto the dolly along with it.

"You okay? *Hard-on!*"

He was wavering a little. I raced over and grabbed onto him. His body was drenched and quivering involuntarily. "Jesus, Hard-on, you're going to die if you keep pushing yourself like this!"

I was entertaining my own plans on the loading dock that afternoon. They stimulated the formation of a two-pronged solution: a way to get myself out of a jam and express my gratitude to my loading-dock partner at the same time.

"How'd it go today?" Louella murmured sympathetically when I walked into Mongon's, her velvety brown eyes intent on sucking the misery out of mine.

"Terrific!" I sighed gratefully. "Thanks to Hard-on."

She turned her head to the guy silently mounting the stool on the other side of hers. "Hard-on?"

He shrugged off the attention, Lone Ranger style.

"Hard-on's the one who's been covering for me at work," I confessed. "Doing my work and his at the same time. You wouldn't believe how strong the guy is. I'd be dead if it weren't for Hard-on."

"Gee, that's real nice of you," Louella purred at him.

"Marci!" I called out, getting a little carried away. "Make it

131

three root beer floats! One for me and two for Hard-on. He's gotta be plenty thirsty!"

"But the metal tanks, they're the heaviest part," Louella was moaning.

My float was served up swiftly, gently, and with a look of affection. I downed it with a view of Louella's back, listening to bits and pieces of the dullest monologue going . . . a detailed account of which muscles did what and the father-son construction business.

My plan worked too well. When Marci and I left Mongon's, it was on a double date with Louella and Hard-on. At the Cozy Heart Diner, Marci's *Times* lay unopened on the bench, while the three of us listened to Louella's account of how incredibly strong Hard-on was, and which muscle did which physical chore.

Marci and I joked about it in the car the next day as we drove to what had become our traditional weekend hangout, the embankment over the river. I acted out Louella going on and on, and Marci played Hard-on, interrupting with a one-word correction when Louella got the name of a muscle wrong. And we laughed, relishing the sense of shared superiority that came from being a twosome, a unified force.

We spread the blanket and discussed the day's news as we ate lunch. When we finished, she picked up the picnic basket, which I had placed on the blanket between us, set it on her other side, and moved closer to me. My heart started pounding.

"Your wound's healing nicely," she whispered, running her fingers over the gash in my forehead.

The touch caused dizzying chills to radiate out from my head to my chest to my hands and even my feet, momentarily curtailing all respiratory functions.

"Does it hurt when I touch it?" she asked with concern.

Unable to find words, I shook my head in quick, frenetic jerks, grabbed my book, and rolled over on my stomach, away from her.

"Reading time," she said in a whisper, almost to herself. She picked up her book an opened it.

It was going to happen. Right now. She was going to say something, and then what would I do? The truth was, in the two intimate weeks I had spent with Marci, I had never kissed her, never hugged her, never even reached out and squeezed her hand. It was

132

not that I did not want to. It was just that, for some painful, inexplicable reason, I had been unable to.

I not only lacked sexual experience. I lacked physical experience. I had grown up in a family that did not hug or kiss or even straighten out each other's neckties for that matter—a family that, quite frankly, did not touch. And now, here I was, feeling powerful tugs to transform the emotions I felt for Marci into some sort of physical expression. But the more I wanted to, the more I couldn't.

I stared at the page without even noticing the words in front of me, scared and confused, waiting for the dream to explode. For two glorious weeks I had been brilliant, witty, in charge, superior. These two weeks had been heady enough to make me even believe I had turned into something special. It was back to reality time, back to being Rodney Bingham, half a man. Not even half.

Marci rolled over on her back, and my stomach churned.

I stared at the printed page, as I heard the exhortations my father had given me all my life about kicking the ball or catching the ball or throwing the ball. "You can do it, Rod! Everybody can do it!"

Well, I could not do it. I'd proven that to my father, and now, in this very different sports arena, once again I wasn't scoring. Worse—I was making the most special person I had ever known feel as though she were some sort of untouchable.

She put her hand on my arm, and I registered the powerful conflicting pang that always occurred when a part of her body made contact with mine. Mentally, I was dying to touch back. Physically, I was rendered immobile.

"Want to go for a swim?" she asked.

"I didn't bring my suit." I never brought my suit to the embankment. A bathing suit meant near-nudity, and hence a double whammy: heightened self-consciousness and more of her not to touch.

"Well, I did."

I buried my head in my book. I heard clothes rustling as she scrambled out of her shorts and T-shirt. Then she stood up, I assumed, clad only in a bathing suit. My stomach ached. I went on reading.

She strutted about on the blanket. "How do you like my new suit?" she asked.

With a feeling akin to terror, I looked up. She was wearing a bright yellow bikini that clung to the curves of her body as though it were part of the smooth dark skin it caressed.

"Stop chewing your lower lip," I instructed.

"Hah?"

"You always do that when you're nervous." It was the artistic-proportions expert, back at work. "No matter what you wear, if you stand there gnawing on your lip, it ruins the effect."

She stopped and lifted her chin up. "Sort of the way you chew on the inside of your cheek when you're nervous?" she asked. "There, you're doing it right now."

I ran my tongue along the inside of my cheek, searching for proof of her incorrect call. It felt like a pasture a thousand cows had been working on daily. "*You're* the one who's worried about looking beautiful, not me," I retorted. "I don't care how I look."

She shrugged. "Guess it doesn't matter if you never put on a bathing suit."

I felt my face get hot. "Marci, you look beautiful."

The vision of her before me confirmed both the accuracy of my statement and the underhanded way it had been delivered. She looked like an insecure, self-conscious little girl in a perfect body.

She ran down the slope and went for a swim—alone.

That night, all by myself in my bed at Mrs. Stompous's, I mustered the courage to approach her. There in the darkness, I crept closer, first burying my face in her hair, enjoying its curly softness, then rubbing my lips back and forth gently against hers, feeling hers part, tasting their pleasures.

I ran my hands along the finely chiseled curves of her compact body, enchanted by the softness of her skin, the round, firm flesh of her hips . . . and her body responded to my touch, writhing, pulling me closer until our stomachs were slithering against each other, lubricated by suntan oil.

Her eyes begged me, and I unhooked the top of her yellow bikini, unleashing her breasts from their restrictive cloth. She moaned a little in relief as they flowed before my eyes, round and sensitive, paler than the tanned skin above and below, needing my caress. And she made whimpering sounds of pleasure as I felt them and kneaded them gently and then buried my face in them, kissing, lost in sensuous pleasure, both sated and yearning for more.

Four times that night, all by myself in my room, I made love to Marcella Parmacella.

But when I awoke the next morning, my arms were holding a cold white pillow, and the mere thought of reaching out and touching any part of her body frightened me. I scrambled out of bed, rushed into the bathroom, and turned the water in the bath tub on full force, desperate to drown out the accusations reverberating in my mind.

Nature provided. An unseasonal rain spell made bathing-suited privacy on the embankment an impossibility for the next two weekends. That meant two more weeks separated by a table at Friendly's and the Cozy Heart Diner, two more weeks of my being brilliant, witty, in charge, and superior. I rose majestically to the occasion.

The fare at the Cozy Heart Diner was barely edible, but it was my favorite place for supper. It was a dark, small room with a green linoleum floor and greasy, silver-speckled white Formica tabletops, but each table had a little candle in the center That's what made it my favorite place, the candles. I loved the way the candles' flickering flares highlighted the soft lines of Marci's smooth, round face and the lushness of her hair. And then there was that special prize—the moments when something I said made her eyes radiate sparkles from within that danced in happy unison with the sparkles emanating from the candles. For a boy too timid to touch, the view was a sensual high.

The sparkles were plentiful, and they were changing my entire outlook. Life was no longer something to get through. It was a rich and varied tapestry I examined closely each day, searching, always searching, for cherished morsels I could bring back to Marci.

I was in the middle of a vivid description of a feud between Pimp and Cripple one night when Marci interrupted me. "Write this stuff down." I made a face, but she said, "I mean it." Her eyes were sparkling in my favorite way. "You'd be a terrific writer."

"I can't write," I protested. "I just like to tell."

"But telling is what writing is, silly! It's just telling on paper! And you're the most wonderful teller in the world."

The words enveloped me in a dreamy warmth.

"You pick up all these funny details no one else would ever notice, and then turn them into clues kinda, clues that make those dimwits interesting, just like book characters."

"Naw . . ."

"You've even got a central character!" She played with the melting wax around the candle. "Who eases Tooth through each work day? Who can break up locker-room brawls with one loud command? Who's always putting big-shot Con Man down in order to get more work out of him?" She leaned across the table and looked up at me through lowered eyelids. "Who scares *you* into working double time?"

"Durone?"

She shrugged. "He's sure coming off as your invisible central character—the guy behind the scenes who gets everyone to do what he wants."

"The orchestrator," I mumbled. "The manipulator." I looked up at her. "You're right!"

"Well, if he is, then *you're* right, not me. To me Sallie Durone is a total ass. This other view, that's what I'm getting from your stories." The sparkles were there again. "You're very convincing. Write it down!"

"But it's the telling I like," I confessed to her. "Only reason I notice all this stuff is so I can tell you. That's the pleasure."

Her face softened and her dark-brown eyes became moister, larger, offering me a look of such sweet tenderness, I felt drunk with longing.

I began writing letters to her, in my room every night after I dropped her off—but only on the condition that she write to me too. Every morning, before work, we exchanged envelopes in front of Mongon's.

The correspondence was significant. Marci wrote about her feelings—her family, her place in her family, her self-doubts. Willingly, anxiously even, she opened herself up for us both to explore. Her letters were an introspective look at a girl who had tried all her life to fit into a world in which she did not fit, and who had suddenly—happily—discovered a new world, with me, in which she could be herself.

Mine were observations—about the guys in the plant, about

Marci's feelings, about Mrs. Stompous's mannerisms and hair styles. They added up to a definitive chronicle on "Life in Fallsville in June 1968"—not exactly a subject the rest of the world was craving.

But they were important in two ways: in what they left out (the inner turmoil I was experiencing, which I was not about to explore), and in the pattern they set. I was developing a shrewd investigative eye and working hard, scribbling on my bed each night, to translate my observations into fascinating prose for my prized audience. What is more, I was consumed by the process. I did not realize it then, but I think those letters layed the groundwork. That was when I became a writer.

16

1968 At the end of June, Chickie and Vince Parmacella entered military service. The night before they left, the Parmacellas had a huge send-off for the boys, to which the entire community had been invited.

Louella waved to me excitedly from the front porch as I walked up. She was standing next to a large American flag in a painstakingly coordinated outfit. The headband in her long, flowing, silky hair was navy blue with white stars. Her dress, lipstick, and nail polish all matched Old Glory's red stripes. To this ultimate patriotic statement, she had added her own little erotic flare. The dress ended high on the thigh and had a neckline that plunged practically to her waist.

On her left, a poker-faced Hard-on was surveying the crowd, his eyes taking an occasional side trip down Louella's front. Behind them stood Chickie Parmacella, his arms folded across his mammoth chest, attentively keeping his eye on Hard-on's eyes. When Chickie saw me he grinned, reached out, and shook my hand.

"Lookit that tent of ours!" he hollered, nodding toward the huge structure that was covering the whole front yard. "Rod, here, he spent the whole weekend with me and Vinnie and my dad putting up the tent," Chickie informed Hard-on coldly. ("Make tents, not my sister," the underlying message.)

"Can you *believe* all these people?" Louella squealed in delight, pointing to the cars that were unloading huge numbers of casserole-carrying guests in front of the house.

I could not believe the crowd—not its size, so much, as its mood. Half the men trudging up the Parmacellas' steps had come attired in their old military uniforms—from World War II and the Korean War—and most of the children were wearing red, white, and blue. In my almost two months of residence, I had gotten accustomed to the fact that Fallsville, Massachusetts, marched to a different tune than the parts of the United States I knew, but it was a shock, nonetheless.

It was, after all, the summer of 1968, a time when young men throughout America were burning their draft cards and trampling Old Glory. And here an entire town was rushing to this house for a highly charged patriotic celebration of the Parmacella boys' enlistment in Uncle Sam's glorious service.

"Baby!"

"Will ya look at her!"

"Baby!"

"Oh, how gorgeous!"

"I ask you, Sam. Is she a doll or what?"

I followed the cries through the entryway and into the living room, arriving in time to hear a short, fat bald man I assumed was Sam make his pronouncement. "A doll, that's what she is!"

And I had to agree. In a tiny, high-collared sleeveless white linen dress that clung to her in all the right places, Marci was being happily pummeled as she cried out appellations like "Aunt Steffie! . . . Uncle Victor! . . . Aunt Bella! . . . Uncle Sam!"

When she spied me standing alone across the room, she waved me over. "This," she announced breathlessly, taking my hand, "this is my friend, Rod." She giggled a little between "my" and "friend," thereby insinuating the presence of "boy," and the relatives were quick on the uptake. The aunts cooed and the uncles gave me the once-over, thereby offering me the excuse I needed to move my hand out of Marci's and begin shaking theirs.

"He's working at Kelso this summer," Marci was explaining. "A college boy from out of town."

("No, really?" . . . "A what?" . . . "A *college* boy, she said" . . . "Nice to meet you, Rod.")

"Oh, my God, it's Lucille!" Mrs. Parmacella screamed from deep in the living room, rushing toward the front door.

"Lucille!" Mrs. Parmacella gasped, throwing her arms around the new arrival.

"Lucille!" the crowd roared.

The face I saw looking over Mrs. Parmacella's shoulder was middle-aged and heavily made-up. The woman's lipstick had been carefully applied in a way that extended outside the edges of her lips. She looked like someone who had downed a glass of tomato juice to quench a ravenous thirst, but had not wiped off the residue.

"Lucille has come!" Mrs. Parmacella announced breathlessly. "All the way from Bedford, too!" She said it the way my mother would have announced a guest from Paris.

"You think I'd miss an occasion like this?" Lucille belted out. "To see my favorite nephews answer the call?"

Mrs. Parmacella blushed.

"Where are they?" Lucille demanded. "Where are my boys?"

"Chickie?" . . . "Vinnie?" the crowd called out, looking around, "Chickie?" "Vinnie?" The hushed whispers turned into cheers as the two all-stars materialized from the sidelines.

"Chickie! . . . Vinnie!" Lucille screamed, squooshing the cheeks presented to her before tattooing each with a lipstick imprint. "Imogene," she sighed to Mrs. Parmacella. "Such fantastic men you have created for the girls of America!"

"And Uncle Sam!" one uniformed guest shouted out.

"Uncle Sam first!" Lucille proclaimed, holding up a clenched fist. "Then the women of America!"

"So, where's Abe?" a woman shouted.

"Aah, making money." Lucille dismissed the question with a wave of her hand. "That's all he has time for, making money." The men scowled and the women heaved jealous sighs.

As Lucille carried on at center stage, whispered Lucille stories were circulating around the room. "Lucille Romero, the hottest thing in Fallsville," one uniformed "uncle" whispered wistfully. "Until Abe Goldfarb, the Jewish door-to-door salesman from Bedford, showed up selling gloves . . ."

"And the fit was perfect!" Six tired brown eyes roamed back to center stage. "For her *every* fit was perfect." The men nodded sadly.

140

Marci was called by her mother for food duty, and I roamed around the room, meeting tired uncles in military garb that no longer fit.

"Best years of my life," intoned Uncle Zack, an arm hooked around the shoulders of Vincent Parmacella, the seams of his navy uniform's sleeves straining at the gesture. "Go for it, boy. It's gonna be the best years of your life."

That, I gathered after a while, was the theme of the party: over-the-hill men passing on the gauntlet to a younger generation, their tired old eyes gleaming in envy, promising the two young recruits "the best years of your life."

Once again, the differences between the two Parmacella boys were evident: Vince, the party boy, was working the crowd with funny jokes, smiles, and back slaps, while Chickie was circulating with a swagger, already, it seemed, searching for Viet Cong.

The war stories being dispensed by the elders matched the brothers' personalities. Chickie heard bloody tales of combat. Vince got an earful of anecdotes about all-night boozing and screwing in ports around the world. But the themes were essentially the same. Less than two months after listening to Harvard choruses of "Hell no, I won't go!" I was listening to middle-aged Fallsvillians proclaim: "Goddamn, I'd do it again!"

Marci and I were standing in a corner of the dining room talking later when I felt a hand on my shoulder. "Hide me, hide me!" someone hissed into my collar. I whirled around, and then stuck out my hand. "Vince!"

He closed his eyes and smiled serenely. "Oh, please, say it again."

"Vince!"

He reached out and shook my hand warmly. "One more time . . ."

"Vince?" I looked at Marci in total confusion.

"I don't know if you've noticed," she giggled, "but you and I are the only ones who call him that."

"Minnie-vinnie-quickie-chickie," Vince muttered disgustedly. He turned to Marci. "How'd I ever get the name Vinnie? When did it start?"

"Before I was born." She shrugged. "But when you were in

141

kindergarten, I remember, that's when you decided to call yourself Vince."

"Yah, well, as you can see," he said, looking around the room, "it caught on like wild fire."

"What's the difference?" I asked.

"Funny you should ask, Roddie!"

"Okay, I get the point!"

"Remember that big campaign we launched when you were ten," Marci asked, "to try to convince Chickie he wanted to be Charles? 'Sticky, icky, Chickie!' we marched around the house singing."

"Yup. See, Chickie's always been the enforcer," Vince explained to me. "We knew if he bought the idea of Vince and Charles, he'd make sure the rest of the town adhered to it."

"What happened?"

Marci smirked.

"He liked it," Vince moaned. "Went in and told all the kids at school to call him 'Sticky-icky-Chickie.' "

"And they did!" Marci nudged her brother. "Shows what forcefulness produces! They called him that for about a year, until he decided it was too long a name."

The two of them began regaling me with whispered anecdotes about the cast of characters milling around us. Like Marci, Vince was more an amused, drole observer of what was going on than a participant. But he shared his sister's affection for the group. "They are crazy," they both seemed to be telling me. "But they are family."

Vince and Marci teased each other mercilessly, but the teasing was obviously based on a profound closeness. The more I became aware of that closeness, however, the more I started feeling the pangs return. I began to witness the scene—the three of us—from the outside. I, the boyfriend, was standing there passively, hands at my sides, as Vince Parmacella hugged his kid sister, pushing her and squeezing her arm and cradling her face in his hands.

I gave myself silent pep talks: *You can do it! Just pat her on the back or chuck her under the chin! Show her you're not made of cardboard!* But the orders only made my blood turn to ice, freezing my flesh into a statuelike mold. Before I knew it, my hands were no longer at my sides. They were buried irretrievably in my pants pockets, clenched into fists and quivering a little.

When a distant cousin came by and began reminiscing with Marci and Vince, I excused myself. "Think I'll check out the tent," I told Marci. "See if those Christmas lights we strung up are working."

They were working out all right, casting eerie red and green hues upon the group cavorting around the tent area to the scratchy strains of Italian folk music coming from the record player in the corner. The sound was alien to me, and so were the crooning dancers, who were jiggling and whirling and clapping their hands: adults oozing sweat as they pranced around the floor with children in their arms; men squeezing women, and women squeezing back; twelve-year-olds sneaking kisses as they trotted to the music.

"Gypsies." I imagined the word uttered condescendingly in my mother's voice. I pictured the parties that had gone on in my parents' home, where the only sounds were low murmurs and clinking ice cubes. Ice cubes, that was it, the background music of my childhood. And that was what my hands felt like in my pants pockets, melting ice cubes surrounded by gradually increasing pools of water. The red and green lights, the lips, the flesh, the smell of wine and sweat . . . It was making me dizzy. I headed over to the food table.

A major mistake, it turned out. Like a guy on a park bench with a bag of bread crumbs, the pigeons began descending upon me from all directions, only the situation was reversed. The pigeons were aunts, and they weren't interested in my bread crumbs. They were begging me to sample theirs.

"I'm Aunt Gussie," a woman in an apron holding a serving spoon on the other side of the table announced. "Yah hungry?"

"He's a boy!" shrieked the tiny lady standing next to me. "Ah coahse he's hungry!" She put her arm around me as high as she could reach, which was waist level. "Bones," she whined, squeezing. "He's ahl bones!"

The hands on my flesh—the little lady at my rib cage and Aunt Emma at shoulder level—reverberated throughout my body like an electric shock, jolting me, making me perspire, tensing my muscles. How could I appease *any* of these pigeons when I couldn't even pull my hands out of my pockets?

I had to be alone. I had to find an empty room where I could calm down. "One minute!" I told the aunts and headed for the bathroom.

I actually fantasized about it a little en route . . . that green soap in the dish on the sink that smelled so nice and matched the leaves on the wallpaper . . . those pretty little guest towels Mrs. Parmacella always had hanging in there . . . the emptiness . . . the peace . . . the silence.

I grabbed the door handle in relief. The door opened easily, but, it turned out, that was because the occupants had forgotten to lock it. As I walked in I came face-to-face with Hard-on sitting on the toilet seat, Louella on his lap, a messy lipstick smear at the corner of Hard-on's mouth.

"Sorry!" I croaked, backing out, carefully reshutting the bathroom door. Then, trancelike, I continued backing my way down the hall, stunned, dazed, disturbed.

In the kitchen, Mr. and Mrs. Parmacella had their heads over the sink, their backs to me. I made a beeline for the back door, closing it tenderly behind me so it would not slam. I tiptoed down the back steps. With most of the partying going on in the house and under the tent out front, the backyard was dark and silent. The sky was clear and filled with bright stars. I took a deep breath of the cool moist air.

A small group of people was sitting on chairs talking quietly over to the right. But there was no one on the left . . . just cool, damp grass. I headed in that direction, through the circular clump of bushes, casting anxious glances over my shoulder back at the house. I was halfway through the shrubs, right next to Mr. Parmacella's prized rose garden, when my foot got stuck. Still concentrating on the back door, I tried to lift it, but it would not budge. I looked down. My foot was being held to the ground by two enormous hairy hands.

A head shot out of the bushes at ground level. It was looking up at me and laughing.

"Vince!"

"Scared the shit outa you, didn't I?" he cackled, sitting up and brushing leaves off his sports jacket.

"What're you doing here?"

"Same thing as you. It's just a little harder to slip out and head home when the party's *in* your home." He patted the ground beside him and held up a bottle. "Have a seat. No fun drinking alone."

I sat down but cast another anxious look at the back door.

"Hey, man, you're in Vince Parmacella's childhood foxhole! No one'll see us here." He handed me the bottle. I took a swig, as though it were beer, but it wasn't beer. A fiery heat swept through my mouth, and then burned its way down my throat and chest, transforming my digestive tract into a clearly discernible route of passage. Somewhere in the pit of my stomach, the radioactive substance burned itself out, leaving me with a warm buzz and a mouth that felt as though it had been rinsed in a powerful disinfectant. "You certain no one will see us?" I only uttered the words to make sure my voice box was still functioning.

"Yup, this is the place I always chose when Chickie 'n me'd play hide and seek."

"Always?"

"Yah. The big tree over there was home, see, so soon as Chickie walked around to the front yard, I'd just hop up, run over, and shout 'Home free all!' He beamed at me proudly. "I always won."

I raised an eyebrow. "Didn't Chickie catch on after a while?"

"Nope." He said it with a straight face, but then began laughing. "Hard to believe, isn't it? That the guy would miss the *same* hiding spot every single time we played?"

"Well, but each time you won—"

"That was the best part!" Vince began kicking his feet into the ground, as close to dancing as you could get in a seated position. "A *classic* case of Vince and Chickie!"

"What do you mean?"

"He'd look at me, standing victoriously over there by Home Free All, see, and his face would pucker up mad and all, and then he'd say, 'I just didn't think you were *dumb* enough to hide in the same place!' "

I don't know whether it was the craziness of the anecdote or the booze finding its way to my head, but I fell back on the grass giggling as if it were the funniest thing I had ever heard.

"Classic case," Vince muttered quietly, caressing the bottle in his arms. "Classic in the result it had." He looked at me and began laughing. "I always ended up feeling dumb!"

145

"Louella?" It was Mrs. Parmacella standing at the back door. I scrambled up to see, but Vince pulled me back down to his level, so I was hidden by the shrubbery. "Shh!" He peered attentively through the bush branches.

"Louella?" Mrs. Parmacella called out again. "Are you out there?"

Silence.

"She's not over here with us, Imogene!" someone shouted from the other side of the backyard.

Mrs. Parmacella turned around on the top step. "Chickie!" she yelled as she reentered the house. "Go find Louella. I need her."

I groaned from my foxhole position.

"No problem," Vince whispered. "My mom went back in. Chickie'll find Louella."

"Yeah? And believe me, we'll know when he does," I whispered back. "She's necking with Hard-on in the bathroom!"

"Is *that* what they're doing in there?" Vince snorted. "I saw the two of 'em heading in that direction about an hour ago. . . ."

"Well, what did you think they were going in the bathroom together for?"

The dimples indented merrily. "Figured maybe Hard-on just wanted to take a leak without straining his fly-zipping muscles."

I cracked up.

"Keep your eye on that Hard-on," Vince said, molding his facial muscles into Hard-on's expressionless signature. "He's headed for success."

"How so?"

"Anyone with that little humor and emotion will get what he wants outa life." He took a swig. "Tunnel vision," he continued, in perfect imitation of one of my work partner's tiresome, deadpan explanations. "It makes you keep plodding straight ahead toward your goal without the distractions that bother us more creative types. Unfortunately, it also makes you real dull."

Breaking character, Vince jabbed me playfully in the ribs and handed me the bottle. I was careful to ingest a much smaller amount this time and it didn't hurt at all.

"Orion," Vince announced, pointing to a group of stars to the right.

I leaned back and looked up. The star-filled sky was breathtakingly clear. "Yup. That's Orion."

"The warrior," Vince whispered. He stared at it some more. "Whatcha think, Rod, does he look like me?"

I examined the starry outline—the shoulders, the legs, the sword. "Naw, you're tougher."

Vince nodded soberly. "Uncle Zack says the army's gonna make a man out of me," he said, taking another swig. "Uncle Victor, he says I'm gonna have a ball. Chickie, well, he seems to think the two of us, working together, we're gonna wipe the enemy out and make Vietnam safe for democracy."

"Chickie said that?"

"Well," Vince laughed, "more or less. 'Kill the gooks' was how he put it."

"That sounds more like it!"

"But me . . . Oh geez, I don't know, I keep wondering all these crazy things . . ."

"Like what?"

He shrugged uncomfortably, his eyes on the sky. "What's the mythology?" He nodded toward the constellation. "How did Orion die?"

It made me uneasy. "Actually, I'm not sure he was a warrior," I hedged. "A hunter, that's what I think he was."

"Warrior, hunter, the same thing."

"Not really. A hun—"

"So? How did he die?"

My cloudy brain searched back to Miss Schneider, my fourth-grade teacher, pointing to dots on the blackboard. "A scorpion," I said slowly. "I think he was stung by a scorpion sent by Apollo." It comforted me. I knew it wasn't scorpions Vince was afraid of in Vietnam. "Actually, come to think of it, the scorpion's supposed to be up there some place," I said, twisting my head and looking around. "If I remember correctly, it's a constellation too."

"Doesn't matter."

I stopped looking.

"Gonna see the world, that's for sure." Vince leaned back on his elbows. "Cousin of mine, Elaine? She married a newcomer. That's what they're called in Fallsville, people who're born someplace else. Well, he was from Boston, and when he died, there was a family plot reserved for him in Boston. Cousin Elaine was broke—couldn't figure out, you know, how to get his body there. Me and Chickie and my dad, we had to put old Robert's remains in the truck back and get it to Boston."

I winced, preparing myself for a grizzly tale, but Vince's eyes lit up excitedly. "Ended up spending two days and three nights in Boston! Fell in love with the city! Only place I'd ever slept outside Fallsville."

"You're kidding!"

"Nah." He shrugged sheepishly. "Us Fallsville types, we don't travel much." He took another swig. "Anyway," he said, handing me the bottle and lying back on the grass, his hands behind his head, "that's where I'm heading—to Boston."

"You've lost me."

"Guess I *am* taking a kind of roundabout route!" he cackled. "Boston may be an hour's drive from here, see, but the only way I can get there is by way of Vietnam." He smiled at the stars. "Boston has jobs, and Uncle Sam has a whole bunch of programs that train you for jobs. For Chickie, joining the army is an end in itself." He chortled. "It kind of gives him a license to do what he does best, beat up on people. For me . . ." He took a deep breath and let it out dreamily. "For me the army's a ticket to Boston."

I lay down on the grass next to him and stared up at the stars, unable to think of anything to say.

"The ticket comes with a steep price tag, that's what you're thinking, hah? But see, that way I'll feel I earned it . . . you know, by serving my country."

I begged Orion for inspiration. "What, uh, what are you going to do with your ticket? When you get out?"

"Get an education. College maybe. My teachers—all the ones who yelled at me for not studying? They kept insisting I was some kind of genius. Might as well see if they were right."

"You've got what it takes, Vince."

He closed his eyes and sighed serenely. "A wife, some kids I can coach in football, a good job . . . and Boston. That's what I want. Don't even care what I end up doing, if you want to know the truth. I just want a job I can go to every day wearing a suit and tie." He bounced up into a sitting position and grinned at me. "No Parmacella *ever* has had a job that required a suit and tie!

148

"To Boston!" He tugged the bottle out of my hands, guzzled some more booze, and handed it back to me.

"To suits and ties!" I shouted, taking a swig. I was feeling good, really good. It was the very first time I had ever been high, and it was also the first experience I had ever had in man-to-man companionship. Nothing was more gratifying than feeling mildly shit-faced, sharing a foxhole with Vince Parmacella . . . especially when the foxhole was on a serene, grassy lawn next to a rose garden. This was *my* kind of military combat, and I rose, macho-style, to the occasion.

"Anything you want me to do for you while you're away?" I asked with a swagger.

His face sobered as he contemplated the offer. Mine did, too, in sudden terror of the request that might be forthcoming.

"Baby . . . uh, Marci? . . . She's top in her class, you know . . ." he said slowly.

"Yeah, she told me."

He was shaking his head. "But she's not going to *do* anything about it, that's what pisses me. See, on the one hand, there's no money for her to go to college, but at the same time, there's enough for her not to have to get a job right out of high school. My dad's plumbing business is doing okay and Louella's working. See what I'm saying?"

"If she could get a scholarship . . ."

"Yeah. I don't know how to find out about things like that."

"I do." Hot-shot Rod Bingham to the rescue. I felt invincible. "And I will."

He patted me on the back. "That's all I want. She's really smart, and it just kills me to think she might just waste away here." He was playing with a blade of grass. "See, I've always been around to push her, take care of her, kind of, and it scares me a little to leave her all alone."

I nodded.

"That's a crock of shit." He closed his eyes. He sat very still for a while, and then opened his eyes and grunted a laugh. "I've just spent too much time listening to the uncles tonight. I'm starting to sound like them!" He began pulling out whole clumps of grass. "Truth is, I'm scared for me, not her . . . scared a little about what it might be like not having her around. Scared I might never—" His

Adam's apple bulged a little as he swallowed uncomfortably. "Just . . . gonna miss her a whole lot, is what it is."

I put my hand on his sleeve, and we sat in silence for a while. Then he turned to me. "You got a sister too, right?"

"Yeah."

"Then you understand how I feel."

An image came to me, that of Lindsay Bingham languishing atop her frilly bedspread rereading newspaper accounts of debutante balls. "I understand how you feel, but well, my sister doesn't hold a candle to yours." My choked voice surprised me.

We stared at each other, and I felt as though our eyes were transmitting all kinds of abstract thoughts—youthful male fears and confusions and longings—thoughts too complicated to tell each other in words. After a while he lifted the bottle to his lips, drank some more, and started giggling.

"What's so funny?"

"Just . . . just the vision of Baby going to work every day in a suit and tie!"

"The Departure" was the big conversation topic at Mongon's the next night. The gang from the plant was plying Marci and Louella with questions: What did the brothers take with them? Where's their boot camp? How soon before they get sent out? What did they say when they walked out the door?

Enjoying their new roles as public-relations honchos for the Big Shots, the sisters were offering up whole paragraphs for each and every inquiry, especially Louella, who spent a good ten minutes at one juncture itemizing each morsel of food the heroes had consumed at breakfast.

"I'd give anything to be doing what they're doing." Hard-on grunted wistfully, taking a slug of his float.

Ever the cheerleader, Louella began assuring him the rotten knee cartilage that had made him 4F was the result of his being a football hero—"Just a different kind of hero!"

That's when I tuned out, happily returning to my own dreams of grandeur. I had spent the whole day with bleary eyes and a heavy head, and I had relished every moment of it. It was my very first hangover, and I saw it as a trophy, a symbol of a rite of passage that had yielded me my first honest-to-God buddy and an altered sense

150

of self. I was Vince Parmacella's secret drinking partner, and that made me impressive in ways I had never even contemplated. Each throbbing sensation inside my forehead was proof that it had really happened, that I had held my own as "one of the guys" in a very select fraternity.

"I'm so proud of them," Marci gushed. "Vince says the army will train him to do just about *anything* he wants! Can you imagine?"

There was something about the pitch of Marci's voice that caught my attention. It was higher than usual. I watched her more closely. She was laughing uproariously at things that were not funny. And the glasses were shaking a little bit in her hands as she carried them over to the sink.

My hangover high evaporated, and a chilly reality set in. I began worrying about my new buddy, and feeling a profound tenderness for his little sister who was making such a valiant attempt to mask her real feelings.

Gradually, as they did every night, the gang filtered out, leaving Mongon's two-person clean-up crew alone at last. But that made it worse, not better. I couldn't think of anything to say to help. As we washed the dishes and cleaned up, Marci kept chirping a string of happy homilies, and I racked my brain for the right words. "Vince knows what he's doing." . . . "He'll be fine." . . . "He's not worried, why should you be?" But it was all, in the immortal words of Vincent Parmacella, "a crock of shit." And she would know that.

A glass tumbled out of her hands and came shattering down on the floor, splattering into tiny pieces. "Would you look at me?" she sang out. "Too charged up by all the festivities, I guess."

I picked up the dustpan.

"Oh, here, let me do that!" She was fluttering all over the place. "No problem, I'll just—" The dustpan crashed to the floor.

And I grabbed her. I grabbed her without thinking, out of this all-consuming need I had to snuff out the turbulence inside her the only way left—with my hands.

"C'mon, stop it . . ." She pushed me away, but I wouldn't let go.

"Relax," I whispered. "Please? You don't have to put on a show for me."

She kept resisting, rearing back, turning away from me, but then her body gave in. She buried her head in my chest and clung back. I felt little sobs erupting against me, and I tightened my hold. "Good." I whispered softly. "Just let go."

She cried harder.

"What if something happens to Vince?" she wailed into my shirt. "Oh, Rod, I couldn't take it if they killed Vince!"

"You're just assuming the worst." I closed my eyes and rubbed my cheek against her hair. "Millions of people go into the military and come back fine."

"I just think I should be prepared for the worst."

"You who's always yelling at me for worrying?" I shouted. "You who spend all your time preparing only for the *best* for everyone you care about? Why switch gears now?"

She looked up at me, her brown eyes both grateful and vulnerable. Her face was streaked with tears, her lips trembling.

I had to stop the tremble. I put my hand under her chin and lifted her lips up to mine and I kissed them, to calm her, to wipe away the sadness. And then I kissed them again, this time for a very long time because, to tell the truth, I couldn't stop. I was lost in the kiss, every single part of me was lost in that kiss.

She rested her head back down against my chest when I finished, snuggling up in my arms. Her breathing become slower, relaxed, and I felt comforted by my ability to comfort her.

I shut my eyes tightly and I prayed to whoever would listen, prayed that Vincent Parmacella return from war safely, because he was a truly wonderful human being. I prayed for him because I was crazy about him, and then I prayed for him for Marci's sake, and then I prayed again, this time out of a strange feeling of gratitude. For, as I ran my hands up and down along Marci's back, and felt her heart beating against me, I was acutely aware that, indirectly, Vincent Parmacella's departure had transformed my life.

17

Marci Courbienne sat alone in her living room reminding herself that this sisterly reunion had been her idea. She tried to recall the feelings of warmth that had precipitated it, but instead her mind kept replaying vivid recollections of nightmarish Louella–Marci scenes from the past.

When the doorbell rang, she took a final gulp of red wine, put the glass down on the fireplace mantel, and gazed pleadingly at the ceiling, as though offering a last prayer up to some private deity lurking amid the overhanging beams. Then she headed for the front door.

Louella Parmacella, in an enormous ankle-length black poncho, stood grinning broadly on the front steps, waving a champagne bottle at Marci through the window in the door, her face a tiny flesh-colored speck overwhelmed by large wire-rimmed glasses, wildly frizzed hair, and long, heavy silver earrings.

"My God, champagne!" Marci gasped as they hugged. "This *must* be a major occasion!"

"You said you wanted to talk, but I told you *I* was coming to celebrate!" Louella released her sister and raised an eyebrow. "Red wine," she announced. "You smell like red wine."

"Damn you."

Louella beamed victoriously. *"Definitely* red wine . . . and the high-class spread. Not the four-dollars-a-jug peasant stuff I drink."

"It's been a long night."

Louella looked at her watch. "Nine o'clock! How can it *already* have been a long night?"

"It's been an hour since I dropped my daughter off at the varsity dance."

"Of course! How could I forget?" Louella handed over her poncho. Her sizable girth was draped in a long black skirt and a hand-embroidered lavender peasant overblouse Marci was certain had been crafted by some Latin American Indian tribe that had been exploited by either American or South American fascists.

"Pretty color on you," Marci mumbled, heading quickly to the closet with the poncho in hopes of avoiding the sociopolitical details.

"Well," Louella demanded, hands on hips, "what was the final decision? Did Lindsay wear the peach-colored silky number that might be too dressy or the turtle neck/skirt combination that might not be dressy enough?"

"When did you talk to Lindsay?"

"Last night. I called you to see if our talk session was still on and was told Mom was out on a date." Louella grinned. "So? What did she choose?"

"The peach." Marci sighed, heading for the dining-room cabinet where the glasses were kept. "Not that it mattered," she called over her shoulder. "I dropped off a perfectly proportioned child in a dress that dramatized all those nice proportions, and you know what? She looked terrible—shoulders rounded, backbone hunched, a forlorn expression on her face that proclaimed for all the world to see: 'Anyone who would ask *me* to dance has to be a total creep.' "

"You *have* had a long night." Louella nodded sympathetically.

"The brave smile, that's what did it." Marci was staring at the cabinet door. "Her melodramatic ramblings, they just make me angry, fill me with this maddening desire to turn off the sound. And the raging adolescent inconsistencies, they move me to fight back. You know, to point out the illogic." She took two champagne glasses out of the cabinet and headed back. "But that brave smile, that public show of fake cheerfulness she flashed at me when she got out of the car in front of the school, this solo arrival against a backdrop of girls trekking up the steps with dates and corsages and—" Her voice caught. "It turned me to total mush."

"It's a stage. Honey, the kid's fourteen years old."

"Okay, so that's one problem—"

"Problem, *hell!*" Louella shouted. "In social work school they teach you. 'A fourteen-year-old girl is not a symptom, it's a diagnosis'! Look, I spent a good hour on the phone with Lindsay last night, and she's a textbook case."

Marci's eyes opened wide in horror. "Of what?"

Louella giggled at the response. "Of being a fourteen-year-old girl! You *have* to go through all the stuff she's going through! It's part of the normal development process."

It was so much easier to be a professional therapist than a mother, Marci thought, forcing a smile. "What are we celebrating?" she asked.

"You first." Louella put the bottle down on a table, plopped into a chair, and pulled a pack of cigarettes out of her huge canvas bag. "After all, you are the one who called this meeting. The celebration part, that came later."

Why on earth *had* she called this meeting? Marci folded her arms across her chest and walked around in circles, trying to figure out how to begin her prepared speech. "It's just . . . been a funny period for me. I keep finding myself going back, realizing all these things I've buried."

Louella registered the impersonal approval of a seasoned social worker. Marci stared at the floor. "It started a couple of weeks ago, at Sallie Durone's funeral?"

Louella's face froze.

"Well, I only went because Mama made me. You know, a show of support for Cousin Francine during her moment of duress?" A sardonic gleam appeared in Louella's eyes, one that translated roughly as "cut the crap," and filled Marci with sisterly warmth.

"I dare you to say that again with a straight face," Louella ordered, and they both exploded in laughter the way they had as children, over a shared intimacy. "*Cousin* Francine?" Louella hooted, and the giggles started all over again.

"Anyway," Marci went on, once they had both calmed down, "that started it. Not the funeral so much as just being back in St.

Mary's Church again. It brought back this crazy rush of childhood memories."

"You got in touch with your feelings."

The corny psychologist's cliché dumped ice on the warmth of their renewed intimacy. Marci shut her eyes and continued quickly. "I guess, for me, that started the process of going back, or remembering, of wanting to—"

"Mama says you've been working with Francine . . . trying to help her legally?" Louella interrupted.

Now they were all the way back, back to the older sister's directing the conversation. "Oh, that's not important," Marci muttered irritably.

Louella raised an eyebrow.

"It seems Sal Durone thought someone gave him his cancer!" Marci laughed.

Louella did not laugh back. Instead she stared at Marci, waiting for more. "Well, no matter," Marci went on uncomfortably. "As it turns out, that's hit a dead end right now . . ."

"How come?"

"I'm a lawyer, not a private eye. I'm just having trouble trying to figure it out!"

Louella leaned back in the chair and lit a cigarette. "Lennie Lucinski died yesterday." She exhaled significantly. "Mama says he had the same kind of cancer Sal had."

"I know. I tried to get information from him," Marci continued, wondering why she felt this need to defend herself. "I visited him in the hospital when Francine told me that, but he wasn't conscious. Believe me, I felt like a total idiot, bending over this half-dead stranger, trying to—"

"Stranger?" Louella shook her head. "Lennie Lucinski was hardly a stranger!"

"Louella, I never knew Lennie Lucinski."

"Sure you did." The statement came out in a clump of smoke. "He moved to Lovell about ten years ago, but he grew up in Fallsville. He was short . . . kind of fat? Sal Durone's best friend in high school! Come on, you remember! He always worshiped Sal."

A blurry vision passed through Marci's head of a squat, pimply sidekick playing Pancho to Sal Durone's Don Quixote. "Lucky." She murmured it without thinking.

"Yeah! That's the one! They used to call him Lucky. I *told* you you knew him!" Louella smiled smugly. She reached to the right for an ashtray, but then stopped and inhaled abruptly. Her hand trembled a little as she picked up the picture of Vince Parmacella in his army uniform from the oval table next to her. "Oh, my," she whispered, caressing the glass with her fingers. "Oh, honey, I'm so sorry."

"For what?"

"For going on like that." Louella stared at the picture for a long time, smiling back at it. Then her eyes filled with tears. "This, um, this was what you were building up to, wasn't it? Your punchline."

"Yes."

"When did you—"

"A few weeks ago. It was all this going-back stuff that did it." She shrugged. "Crazy, isn't it? How something like Salvatore Durone's death could be the pivotal point, the impetus for bringing Vince back to life . . . or at least allowing the memories of Vince back into my life?"

Tears filled Louella's eyes. "No. Not crazy at all. Kind of wonderful."

"That's how it's been! Before, the only memories I had were ones I wanted to wipe out—memories of his death—coming home from school, seeing that car with out-of-state tags in front of the house. Then going in and finding that dreadful military priest in the living room . . ."

"And now? Since you brought this picture out of mothballs?"

"Oh, it's made me remember good times, the fun we had. The things he said. You wouldn't believe how vividly they're all coming back! The pronouncements of Vince Parmacella, even after all these years! I've started talking about him nonstop to the kids. They think I'm a little crazy. I mean, they always knew he existed, but all they knew was that they had two uncles who were killed in the Vietnam War before they were born. And they knew that the way they knew their great-grandfather had a vegetable market. Big deal. Ancient family history. Dead history. Now—"

"What do you tell them to explain—"

Marci scrunched down in the chair. "I've told them that having two members of one family killed off suddenly like that jars the whole family in ways that take years to recover." Her eyes began overflowing. "That the parents never really get over it, that sisters compensate in funny ways—one by acting out her anger—flagrantly, demonstratively—the other by rigidly repressing it. Both reactions, I've told them, inhibit the healing process for everyone." Marci's lips drew up into a puckered rigidity. Clumsily, she wiped the tears off her face with the palms of her hands. "Oh, the truth is, even though I've pretended not to notice, Vince Parmacella has been alive and living with me here for sixteen years now in the person of my son."

"Amen!" Louella proclaimed to the rafters. "That's what's been so funny! All the characteristics that have driven you crazy about Tommy—the cockiness, the will-of-his-own, the major intelligence quotient that is not channeling itself adequately into academic endeavors—they're all Vince! And *now* I can say what I've wanted to say at least a hundred times!" She leaned forward in her chair and grinned wickedly. "Isn't it a helluva lot more pleasant to be Vince Parmacella's prized kid sister than it is to be his mother?"

"I bet you've shared that little insight with Mama, haven't you?"

"Frequently."

"Do you . . ." Marci fidgeted. "Do you have a picture of Chickie I could—"

"Yup."

"Thinking of Vince has made me think of Chickie. Oh, mostly hostile thoughts, mind you, the many ways he tormented me. But . . ." she played with the seam of her pants. "Vince loved him and you loved him and, well, increasingly I've come to feel that in a hateful way I might have loved him a little too. I've certainly never . . ." Her voice trailed off. "By the time we heard about Chickie, I was a total zombie. No feelings left."

"Why?" Louella was scrutinizing her.

"You know . . . Vince's death."

"Nothing else?" Louella leaned forward attentively. "Wasn't there maybe something that, say, made you a bit of an emotional zombie, back there in the fall of 'sixty-eight? Before we even heard about Vince? Something that happened at the end of that summer?"

"Oh, Louella," Marci sighed. "Let's not search for *more* skeletons! Don't we have enough right at hand to work with? Isn't it better—"

"To live with that handy little capsule summary of yours? 'One sister acted out her anger. The other repressed it.' " Louella stabbed out her cigarette. "It's easier, that's for sure. But it's not entirely valid."

Marci leaned forward irritably. "In what way?"

"*Both* sisters acted out their anger, Marci. I screamed and flailed and went into therapy. You clenched your teeth, threw out your old life, and climbed up here into this new one."

"That's not so different from what I—"

"The causes of our anger were not the same. Mine was the dissolution of the family."

"And mine wasn't?" Marci gasped. "Losing Vince—"

"Filled you with sorrow. Profound, almost incapacitating sorrow, sorrow that you could not bear to deal with, as you've already said. But I think you couldn't deal with it because it came right on the heels of something else—a different kind of loss, and that first one, *that* was where all the anger came from, the anger that propelled you to make it in this different world."

Marci sighed wearily. "What are you talking about?"

Louella shook her head. "That answer has to come from you." She stared at Marci for a while, waiting for something, but then gave up. "Another time . . ." She sighed. "Rome was not built in a day."

"What is *that* supposed to mean?"

"One breakthrough at a time. Tonight we rejoice at the reentry of Vince Parmacella into your life. Tomorrow?" She winked. "Who knows what might show up."

"Louella!"

"It's champagne time!" Louella announced, picking up the bottle. "And, oh, Baby, we are really celebrating!" She reached out and squeezed Marci's hand. "I came here prepared with my unilateral declaration, see, only to discover you had one too." She flopped back in her chair, shaking her head. "It's incredible . . . the way . . . the way . . ." Her voice stopped suddenly, and her eyes filled with tears all over again.

"The way what, Louella?"

The cork popped out, hit the ceiling, and went bouncing across the room. "All *right!*" Louella filled the two champagne glasses and held one up. "To the fact that I'm about to stop being a financial burden!" Louella leaned forward excitedly. "I'm leaving the low pay at the Women's Shelter and taking a job with a fancy-schmancy private counseling group." She laughed. "Your sister the radical is about to become your sister the yuppie!"

Marci frowned. "Are you sure this is what you want?

"It's what I want. Rich people need help too. And it's a terrific place. I decided the time had come to try, and to my surprise they actually wanted me!"

Marci clicked her glass against Louella's happily and drank up. "Well, if Salvatore Durone's demise was the cause for me, what was the cause for *your*, um, turnaround?"

Louella seemed agitated once again. "A . . . well, a love affair, you could say."

Marci looked up with surprise. Louella rarely dated.

"One that's over!" Her lips smiled but her eyes did not. "A disastrous love affair, but one that left me with new resolve."

Marci studied Louella for a long time. "Why do I have this gut feeling that a profound sadness lurks underneath your chirpy cheerfulness?"

Louella leaned over and kissed her on the cheek. "Because you're my sister, and you still know me better than anyone else." She bit her lip and refilled Marci's glass. "Drink up!"

After Louella left, Marci sat dreamily in the big armchair in front of the fireplace, allowing the Parmacella family scrapbook to play itself out in her head. She saw plump round faces with missing front teeth . . . four children catching fireflies in the backyard on hot summer nights . . . a pigtailed Louella selling Girl Scout cookies . . . Vince sorting out his baseball cards . . . Chickie, on a dare, managing to make it all the way up to the very top of the oak tree behind the school, but then getting so carried away with his feat he let go of the branch and ended up with a humiliating thud on the ground.

She giggled. "Trees are for monkys." She could still see the words printed out on Chickie's leg cast in her precise second-grade penmanship, just as she could still hear Vince dancing around her singing, "Spelled it wrong! Spelled it wrong!"

Teases and taunts. Sibling talk. Film clips of later years began floating by, cameo shots of bodies and faces maturing . . . Louella holding her painted fingernails out to dry . . . Chickie carving up his

160

face with a razor in search of a beard . . . Vince at the wheel of a sputtering car as her father screamed from the sidelines, "Clutch! Clutch!"

Then another, later, image came to her, this one circa 1970: Louella, the former beauty queen, in drab clothes and combat boots snarling, "You *forced* me to live out my life imprisoned in a stereotype!" as Mama and Papa Parmacella, trembling on their ragged, overstuffed sofa, asked weakly, "Louella, sweetie, what's a stereotype?"

That one had been nightmarish at the time, but now it seemed terribly funny. *"Sweetie, what's a stereotype?"*

She and Louella had spent a good twenty years frozen into a painfully polite formality, consciously sidestepping around each other to avoid the landmines. Tonight had been a return to old times. It was the familiarity that had felt so good, the bickering, even the bitchiness. It was as though the receptivity they had developed for each other early in life had been preserved—underground—all these years, waiting for a time when they were both willing to return to it.

Marci stared at the fire. She was willing to return, dying to return, to tell the truth. For two decades now she had been discarding the past as unwieldy baggage, pushing herself, goading herself on to new goals that were totally future-oriented.

An empty trek. "The past is prologue." How could she ever have expected to go on to the future as a whole person without it?

She heard familiar sounds—the key in the lock, the front door opening, and then shutting.

"Louella! Damn, I smell Aunt Louella's cigarettes!" Tom Courbienne sniffed exaggeratedly as he walked into the living room. He was wearing a tie and white shirt, and carrying his sports jacket over his shoulder.

"Ahh, a nose Sherlock Holmes would be proud of!" Marci laughed, taking him in with pleasure. "Have fun at the dance?"

"It was okay."

"Just okay?"

"No. More than okay, I guess." He swaggered a little. "Word is, Sue Lehrer's mine for the asking."

"Whose word? Sue Lehrer's?"

"Nah . . . just, you know, the guys. Danced with her a couple

161

of times and they said she looked like she was dying for me to ask her out." He flashed her a cocky look.

Marci frowned. "But what about your date? Sarah what's-her-name? Did you jilt her?"

"Her name's Sarah Chambers, and there you go again, Mom, always worrying about the girls! Believe me, Sarah was plenty busy dancing with Jake every time I danced with Sue." He looked at his watch. "What're you doing up so late?"

"Just . . . thinking. Louella stayed until about an hour ago."

"Gotta tell her to stop smoking, Mom," Tom muttered, heading for the stairs. "Bad for her lungs . . . bad for my nose!"

"Tom?" He turned around before Marci had time to think of a subtle way to phrase the question. "Did you see Lindsay at the dance?"

"Yeah."

"Well?" Marci pushed nervously. "How did she look? Did . . . did she seem to be having fun?"

"Guess so." He shrugged. "Didn't she tell you?"

"She didn't come home. Had a slumber party at Lilah's right after the dance, remember?"

"That's right. I forgot."

"So? Fill me in!"

"I only saw her dancing with one guy."

Marci's face fell. "Just one dance? All night long?"

"Nah, a lotta dances . . . just all with the same guy."

"*Who*, Tom?" Marci shook her head irritably. "What do I have to do to drag it out of you?"

Tom grinned and sauntered about, obviously relishing the information he was about to impart. "Why, none other than our newfound Cousin Frank, Mom!"

Marci's body tensed. She leaned forward attentively. "He asked her to dance?"

"Wrong again!" Tom hooted. "She asked *him*, at least the first time. Now, see, here's the scene—Lindsay and all her friends are standing around together, just like everyone else. You know, everyone's hanging around in gangs. With one exception, that is. Durone, he's soloing it. All by himself over in this empty corner of the gym. And then, dum-dee-dum dum! They call a girl's choice. And our sweet, compassionate Lindsay walks over to that lonely corner, that

162

corner where all other mortals fear to tread, and she asks Durone to dance!" He buried his eyes in his hands, feigning tears. "Really, it was so beautiful, the gesture, the little care-about-other-people's-feelings kid, going out of her way . . ."

"Why was the boy standing alone in the corner?" Marci demanded.

"Hey!" Tom's eyes opened angrily. "Don't get after me! I invited him to come over to where we were all standing! He didn't want to. See, my friends are all a year older 'n he is. And he doesn't have any friends of his own." He smiled mischievously at his mother. "Didn't have any friends of his own. He definitely has one now!"

"What do you mean?" Her voice squeaked slightly.

"They danced together for the rest of the evening. Danced, and, well, you know, just stood there together, talking? Looking at each other kind of funny."

Marci's jaw clenched.

"Well, hell, Mom, it's your fault! You know how Lindsay is about feelings—Miss Supersensitive! And you've been going on and on about how poor, friendless Frank Durone needs—"

"To you!" Marci shouted. "Only to you!"

Tom tilted his head, his eyes twinkling. "Well, well, well . . . do we have a double standard operating here?" he asked. "It's okay for your son to tutor a school reject, but you wouldn't want your daughter to marry one?"

"Don't be ridiculous!" Marci stormed.

"I hit a nerve with that one!" Tom said, heading for the stairs.

She admitted it. She *was* being silly. Here she wanted to kill her son, and for what? For aptly underscoring her own hypocrisy? It was all right for Tommy to help Frank Durone, but wrong for Lindsay to like the boy? What kind of condescending garbage was that? Besides, if Frank Durone had succeeded in transforming the miserable waif she'd dropped off into someone who felt like the belle of the ball, then she owed the boy her utmost gratitude. "You're right," she announced to her son's back. "I apologize for being so silly."

Tom turned around. "Look," he said, walking affably back into the room. "The truth is, you were right about Durone. He's not a bad person. We've started hitting it off pretty good in the tutoring."

" 'Well,' " Marci groaned. "Not 'good,' 'well.' "

163

"Whatever." He laughed a little. "Know what he calls me?" Tom strutted around, shoulders back, chest out, chin in the air.

Marci watched the demonstration with a smile. "What does Frank Durone call you, dear?"

"Smarts." He shot back a crafty grin.

The color drained from Marci's cheeks. "What?" she gasped, *"What* does he call you?"

Tom shrugged, startled by her reaction. "Smarts."

"Why?" Her eyes were enormous. *"Why* does he call you that?"

"Because it fits, I guess." Tom beamed, but then stopped when he saw her expression. "Mom? You okay?"

Marci turned back to the fire. "I'm fine, honey. You just go on upstairs. It's late."

"Hey, what is it? What's the matter with having Smarts as a nickname?"

Marci squeezed her hands into fists on the arms of the chair. "Nothing," she whispered.

Tom watched her for a while. Then, when he got no response, he shook his head and went on up the stairs.

Marci stared into the embers, searching for some reassurance, but all she got was an ominous feeling.

Smarts. She felt a different series of snapshots, pressuring for entry to her mental scrapbook, but she fought them off. No. Never. Her eyes opened wide reflecting the flames in the fireplace. And then they filled with tears.

There was therapeutic nostalgia, and there were remembrances that tore you apart: two different categories. Certain memories were best left buried.

18

1968   "Ovah heee-ah!" Sal Durone howled, in the whine yell we knew as his Supervisor Voice. "Everybody ovah heee-ah on the double!"

Knowing the assembly-line gang had been messing up again, we formed a circle around him, anticipating another pep talk.

"I been hearin' things," Durone said, staring out over our heads. "I been hearin' talk, and I think there was, uh, a mis-un-dah-stan-din'." He punctuated each syllable with a shake of his head. The fidgeting stopped. Everyone stood at attention.

Durone shifted his weight around, then planted each foot firmly on the floor and put his hands on his hips. "It's about Louella Parmacella," he went on gruffly. " 'Bout me and her."

I shot a look at Hard-on. His face was blank.

"It's, uh, it's been brought to my attention that some of you guys think I, ah, made it with the broad—that that's why her brothers beat me up."

Never had the group been so silent. Everyone gaped at Durone, who seemed to be addressing his remarks to a spot on the ceiling. "It ain't true. Let the record show, it ain't true."

Lucky started hopping about. "Jeez, Sal—"

"Chickie and Vinnie Parmacella worked Sallie Durone oh-vah

for *wantin'* they'ah sistah!" he bellowed to the rafters. "Just for the wantin', not for gettin' nothin'."

"So what?"

"Who the hell cares?"

"What's the big—"

"Sallie Durone can make it with any chick he wants," Durone roared. "Sallie Durone don't need no *fake* reputation!"

"What the fuck—"

"Out on the floooah!" Durone yelled. "Everybody out on the floooah!"

Obediently, the shift scampered out. As I rushed past Durone, I felt a heavy hand on the back of my neck. I kept moving, but the fingers dug deeper into my flesh, until I felt like an immobilized puppy being lifted off the ground by its collar.

"You owe me, Smarts," Durone hissed in my ear. "You owe me now!"

When the hand let go, I hurried out to the loading dock, wondering what exactly did I owe him? And when would he try to collect?

Durone was standing next to the locker-room door when Hard-on and I walked out that night. Hard-on rambled on about some construction job he and his dad had landed as we headed outside. I wasn't listening. Aware that Durone had walked out directly behind us, I was concentrating on getting my body over to Mongon's—the Durone-free zone—before I felt another hand on my collar.

"Eh, Smarts!" It was the command I had been dreading.

We turned around.

"C'mere a minute!"

"Tell him you got plans," Hard-on coached.

"Can't tonight, Sal!" I shouted back. "Me and Hard-on, we've got plans."

"Tonight, Smarts." It was an order. "The plans can wait a few minutes."

Something imbued me with confidence at that moment, although I have no idea what it was. Perhaps I was just aware of the fact that I still had a lot of weeks at Kelso ahead of me. Best to get it over with.

"It's okay," I told Hard-on. "Just tell Marci I'll be late."

166

"You sure?"

"I got a choice?"

His eyes turned serious, earnest. "Yeah, you got a choice. I can stick around. Be happy to."

"Naw," I said, beginning to believe the fairy-tale image of courageous Rod building in my head. "I'll be okay."

"In the truck!" Durone ordered when I reached him. I climbed into his red pickup truck, and we drove off. In the side mirror, I saw Hard-on getting smaller and smaller as he stared after us.

Durone clamped down on the gas pedal and the truck vroomed, up hills, around corners, snarling and squealing in the night. Holding one hand on the door handle—for quick escape—I watched carefully, memorizing the route, fully expecting to have to make it back on foot. What did he want? Hadn't his destructive impulses been sated by our last encounter?

He turned off the road and pulled the truck up on a steep incline, stopping when it hit a bush head-on. He turned off the ignition, lit a cigarette, and looked out the window, surveying the woodsy, hilly area. "My property," he grunted, nodding his head at what lay outside. "This here's all my property. About three acres' worth."

"Nice," I gulped, my eyes touring a dense thicket. "Lotta, you know, foliage."

"I own a whole buncha property 'round Fallsville," Durone boasted. "Shocks you, don't it? Poor-boy Sallie, a landowner?"

"Where, um, where's the other land you own?"

"All over the county. One plot's near where they're gonna put an interstate." He shot me a crafty grin. "You know that four-lane connecter route they're gonna put in just outside Fallsville?"

"Hey, yeah!" At last I'd found some common ground. "I read about it in the local paper!"

"Own ten acres a pastureland right next to it," he cackled, pounding the steering wheel. "That's gonna be my gold mine!"

I had not followed the newspaper articles that closely, but it seemed to me the planned interstate was mired in controversy. A wealthy recluse whose estate was nearby had objected to the site, and the local politician was on his side. "Is it definite?"

"Almost." Durone's face sobered. "This rich asshole—Sam Pritchard's his name—he's tryin' to stop it, but he won't."

"But the State Senator—Berlanti?"

"Frankie Berlanti." Durone nodded, screwing his lips up malevolently into a sneer that almost touched his overhanging nose. "Grew up in Fallsville. Knew my dad. He owns land up near the interstate too."

"But he's on Prichard's side, isn't he?" I asked. "It seemed to me from what I read in the papers that Berlanti—"

"Don't believe all ya read, kid." Durone fixed me with a deadly look. "Berlanti's about to change his mind. I'm, uh, workin' on somethin' that's gonna convince him."

"Well, I guess if Berlanti owns land there, he stands to make something from the interstate too," I ventured hopefully. "Is that your pitch?"

He grinned darkly. "Part of it."

I squirmed around in the front seat. Well, we'd had our little talk, hadn't we? "It's, um, getting kind of late, Sallie. I—"

"Jeez," Durone snorted. "Got so caught up in property talk, I forgot why we're here!" Durone reached down beside the driver's seat and pulled out a few pieces of of paper. "Gettin' too dark in here," he muttered. "C'mon." He climbed out, pulled a kerosene lantern out of the truck back, and lit it. "This way."

With both trepidation and discomfort, I followed him through hissing mosquitoes and clinging brambles to a small clearing where a weathered wooden picnic table stood with two cut-down tree stumps placed around it as chairs.

"Have a seat," Durone ordered, putting the lantern down and hurling one of the pieces of paper my way. "Read it."

Obediently, I read it. And then I read it again, certain I had to be missing something. "$X + 2 = 14$, $X = 14 - 2$, $X = 12$." That's all that was written on the sheet.

"Well?" Sal's eyes flashed at me. "Is the goddamn answer right?"

I jumped. "Yes."

He threw me another piece of paper. "How about this one?" It read: "$2X = 40$, $X = 40 - 2$, $X = 38$."

"Are you taking some kind of math test?" I asked incredulously.

"None a your goddamn business!" he shouted. "All I wanna know is one thing—is it right?"

168

"No," I said slowly, dreading the consequences. "This one is wrong."

"Yeah?" He sat down on the tree stump across from me and leaned forward suspiciously. "How come?"

I explained the difference between 2X and X + 2, the difference between multiplication and addition in figuring equations. I did a few problems for him to demonstrate.

His lips puckered out into a big fleshy wad, an expression I hoped meant he was finally catching on. Not wanting to lose the thread, I quickly wrote out a page of problems and handed the paper and pencil back to him.

So there we sat in our lantern-lit tutorial hideaway, Durone sweating out elementary math, as the mosquitoes made a feast out of me. I got up and walked around the table, missing Marci, wondering why Durone suddenly needed to know math. When I glanced over at him, he had put the pencil down, and, seemingly oblivious to the cigarette smoke wafting up from his lips to his eyes, he was staring down at his hands, attempting, it seemed, to separate his fingers into groups of seven. I walked behind him and glanced over his shoulder. The third problem—7X = 35—was apparently the stumper.

"What's two times seven, Sallie?"

"Fourteen!" He sneered.

"What's four times seven?"

His eyes drifted down to his fingers.

Goliath could not multiply. "Gotta review the multiplication tables, Sal. You could buy a set of cards at that store over in—"

"Ain't buying no math cards!" he stormed. "You tell me the answers, and I'll learn 'em! Ain't buying nothing' where someone'll see me!"

At the rate this was going, it would be past Marci's ten o'clock curfew by the time we returned. I scratched my arm and my fingers came up with a string of huge welts. Twenty minutes more in the outdoor tutorial chamber and I'd be eaten alive. "Tell you what, I'll write out the tables tonight in my room and give them to you at work tomorrow . . ."

"Someone'll see you." He shook his head. "No one's tuh know—"

"I'll put them in your truck when no one's looking. Under the front seat."

He contemplated that. I plunged forward, taking advantage of his indecision. "That way you could study them by yourself, and we could get together again when you feel you know them!" I assured myself that mental challenge would take Durone at least two months. By that time, I'd be back in my college dormitory.

"Yeah," he grunted, picking up the lantern. "Okay."

As the truck chugged along the road, I reviewed "tough guy-ism à la Fallsville." I was coming up with a lot of form and little substance. Swaggering as kingpin of a nipple factory that was about to close. Kidnapping for the solution to fourth-grade math problems. The truth was, the only time Salvatore Durone had used brute force was when I had caught him in the midst of a humiliating failure. I thought back to his confession earlier in the day, this time with some tenderness. The fact that it had taken him three weeks to build up the strength to make the speech—and that it had been motivated by the need to figure out a simple equation—made the confession both profound and pathetic. I turned to him with a sudden feeling of sympathy and power. Power first.

"I don't owe you anything," I said curtly.

"Yeah?" He shot me an angry look. "What's 'at s'posed to mean?"

"I will help you study for this . . . this . . . test, whatever it is." I went on. "But we do it on my terms. We do it out of friendship. A friend helping a friend. Not as a debt. Not as a threat. Out of friendship."

"Friendship." He sneered, shaking his head.

"Friendship." I repeated. "I like math, and I'm pretty good at it. But I'll do it only on those terms."

He stared at the road. "You, uh, gonna put those times tables in my truck tomorrow?"

"Yup."

He growled.

"And then you tell me when you're ready, Sal, and we'll go over them again."

The lights were out in Mongon's, but I saw a timid-looking figure standing out front, biting her nails as we arrived.

170

She'd waited for me. I was so excited I opened the door before the truck came to a stop.

Durone grabbed my arm. "That chick a yours got the biggest mouth in Fallsville. You tell her and I'll—"

"Friendship!" I reminded, scrambling out. "Friendship!" I slammed the door and ran over to Marci.

She backed fearfully into Mongon's doorway. "You okay?"

"Yes!" I danced around victoriously, arms in the air. "All in one piece! One hundred percent okay!"

Her moist, dewey eyes hardened into beady slits as she squinted and put her hands on her hips. "Where have you been?"

"You will never guess." I giggled, pulling her into my arms, hungry for the feel of her. "Never in a million years." She pushed me away. "What's the matter?"

"What's the *matter*? I've been waiting for you for two hours!"

"Didn't Hard-on tell you—"

"That Sallie took you away! Yah, he told me! A great piece of news, that was! It gave me a whole lot to think about as I paced! You, half dead and bleeding on a hillside someplace, that's what I had to think about!"

The sight of her red, puffy eyes shocked me into speechlessness.

"Two minutes more!" she screamed. "Just two minutes, and I swear I was gonna go call the police!"

My throat tightened. "Thank you."

She tossed her head angrily. "For what, exactly?"

I shrugged. "For worrying about me."

"Now you make me feel dumb," she whimpered, pressing her forehead against my chest. "What did he want?"

"Help with algebra."

"*What?*"

"Swear to God," I laughed, "that was it. Elementary algebra."

"Why?"

"Beats me." I nudged her. "You're the one who's supposed to know everything going on around here. You tell me!"

"I'll find out . . ."

"Hey, Marci, now don't go telling anyone—"

"You don't trust me! You honestly think I would go out and—"

"I trust you."

"That's all he wanted, help with . . . algebra?"

I closed my eyes and shook my head. "That and a financial consultation on his real-estate holdings."

"Oh . . ." she groaned. "Not his property! That is something I *do* know about. Something everybody knows about." She made a face. "Sallie Durone keeps buying up all these little pieces of totally useless land, and then brags to everyone about how he's gonna make a killing some day."

"Well, you never know with land."

She looked at me deadpan. "With the land he's bought, you know, believe me. Most of it has gone down in value since he bought it! It's the joke of the town. Papa always says, 'You know your property isn't worth a nickel when Durone offers you a dime for it!' "

"Still, he says he owns a plot near where they may put in the interstate. If they—"

"No way they're gonna put it there! Old Man Pritchard says, 'I don't want it near my property,' and everyone does what Old Man Pritchard says. He's the only rich person around here!"

"But the State Senator—Berlanti?"

"Earns more on the side from Pritchard than he earns as State Senator! No way he's gonna do anything the 'big man' doesn't like!"

We were standing in front of her house. "Your father's not out on the front porch yet." I took her hand. "Tell me something to wipe away the taste of Durone."

"Almost forgot! A news story out of Moscow quotes Pravda as saying that 'hostile forces are seeking to separate Czechoslovakia from the socialist community.' Here." She pulled a piece of newspaper out of her purse and stuffed it in my pants pocket. "I clipped it from the paper for you."

"Did you have dinner?"

She shrugged.

"You mean you were standing there in front of Mongon's waiting for me all night?"

"Dumb, huh?" Her eyes searched mine terrified of finding confirmation.

I pulled my faithful worrier and newspaper-clipper closer and kissed her. For the first time in my life I felt I really belonged to

172

someone, and it comforted me and warmed me and made me feel like crying, all at the same time. The kiss lasted so long it left us both breathless.

"So? Maybe it wasn't so dumb!" She giggled, hugging me.

"Baby? You out there?" It was Mr. Parmacella on the porch.

"Coming, Papa!" She gave me a peck on the cheek and ran up the steps.

"Marci!" I whisper-shouted, running after her. "Marci!"

She turned around.

"Do you . . ." I raced up the steps. "Do you have a pair of scissors I could borrow? I told Durone I'd make him multiplication cards and sneak them under the seat of his truck tomorrow morning before work."

I could hear her laughter echoing throughout the house. "Do me a favor," she said as she came back with the scissors. "Don't go buying real estate on your new pal's advice, okay?"

The next morning, when I was pretty sure all the guys had already entered the plant, I snuck around to Durone's truck and shoved the flash cards I'd made under the front seat.

"Whatcha doin'?" a voice asked from behind. I whirled around and, with enormous relief, discovered it was just Hard-on.

"Just leaving Sal some money I owed him."

Hard-on did not ask me how I had come to owe Durone money nor, for that matter, how I had managed to escape bodily harm the night before. He just yawned and nodded.

"Let's get out onto that floooooah," Durone was howling as we walked into the locker room. "Gotta get out they-ah and build a beddah product!"

19

1968   I closed my eyes and rubbed my face against the soft flannel blanket. The smell of Coppertone had taken on intoxicating dimensions.

Marci's fingers caressed my shoulders, then the backs of my arms and hands, stroking, lingering. "Time to do the front," she whispered in my ear.

"Uh-uh." I groaned into the blanket. "Can't move."

She tickled me in the ribs. I flinched, and then gave in. Rays of sunlight fluttered against my closed eyelids as her suntan lotion—spreading hands danced along my legs, awakening my flesh.

My body, which for nineteen long years had been an unmitigated embarrassment, the central cause of my many inadequacies, had been miraculously transformed in just a few days into a remarkable source of pleasure.

Her hands roamed to my stomach and chest, moving in circles. I opened my eyes and watched my fingers caress the soft insides of her arms and then her taut bronze tummy. The same sun that attacked my pale skin seemed to bathe Marci's in benevolent rays, warming it, darkening its color into a glistening deep-brown hue. In her snug yellow bikini, nature's girl was mine, all mine. I was a little confused by this sudden stroke of good fortune. "What do you see in me?" I asked her.

She tilted her head, surprised, and then her eyes got larger and larger. "Wait!" She held up her hand and stared into space, as though she were attempting to put some complicated concept into words. Finally, she turned back to me, her chin up, her lips tightly pursed. "Oh, but my dahling," she proclaimed, "I was attracted to you from the outset."

I did a double take. "Huh?"

She collapsed on the blanket, her eyes closed. "Unbelievable. I actually got the chance to say it."

"To say what?"

She hugged herself. "I spent most of the summer after eighth grade reading these mushy romance novels. And there was one . . . I can't even remember the name of it. All I remember is the heroine—this fancy, rich British lady—says to the hero, 'Oh, but my darling, I was attracted to you from the outset.' "

She opened her eyes and smiled at the clear blue skies. "I remember reading that in the hammock in the backyard and day-dreaming about someday finding myself in a situation where I'd have a chance to say that to someone. It, oh, you know, it just sounded so classy." She kissed me on the cheek and snuggled up next to me. "And now I've done it!"

I folded my arms across my chest, moping.

"What's the matter?"

"You didn't answer my question."

"Do you think I'd say something I didn't mean?" she cried.

"Then when exactly was the outset?" I challenged. "Was it April, when your sister came home and told you she'd overheard that a college boy was coming?"

"Yup." She stared happily into space. "That did it."

"Then it wasn't me you were attracted to! It was—anyone! Any college boy!"

"No, it was you."

"Yeah? Name one thing you knew about me personally!"

" 'Needs to put some hair on his chest.' " She giggled. "That's what your uncle told the Kelso plant manager."

I groaned.

"For a girl who's spent her whole life surrounded by hairy apes, that was a real turn-on, I'm telling you!" She sat up and hugged

175

herself. "A regular dream come true—a college boy without hair on his chest!"

I burst out laughing and pulled her down on top of me. "You're crazy," I mumbled, kissing her hair. "Absolutely crazy."

She studied me. "Once I saw you, it was the eyes that got me," she said softly, running her finger along the outlines of my face. "Such amazing, deep-green eyes. At first they looked so hurt, I was willing to do anything, absolutely anything, to make them stop hurting." Her own eyes sparkled. "And then I discovered that when they get happy, they get lighter and liquidy, magical almost . . . and warm . . . so warm they warm me up, just looking at them."

I picked up my head and kissed her lips, to stop the words, because they were embarrassing me. And then I kissed her cheek and her neck and her chest and the cleavage in between her breasts at the edge of her bikini top, happily assuming my new identity, the much coveted college boy with the magical, warming green eyes. I felt hungry, dizzy with the feeling.

We lay there for a long time, our mouths passionately engaged, our hands moving slowly over each other's bodies—seeking, touching, rubbing, caressing—until the heat from the sun and the heat from within combined into an overwhelming force. She sat up first, slippery with sweat. "Water," she croaked.

"Water," I concurred. I stood up and pulled her to her feet. She swayed and flopped against me, slithering against my chest.

Holding hands, we walked over to the cliff and then down the steep slope to the riverbed. We maneuvered our way over the small jagged rocks until we got out into the main stream, where the gurgling rivulets merged, forming deep pools of water between huge, flat rock plateaus. We climbed on top of one of the rocks.

"Water!" I shouted, diving into the dark pool on the other side. She staggered over to the edge and flopped in on top of me, and we went down, way down, our bodies entwined. We kissed underwater, then giggled and made our way through the pocket of little air bubbles back up to the surface.

"Wonderful!" she shouted, turning a somersault in the water. "Wonderful!" she shouted again when she came up for air. We swam around for a while performing acrobatic feats in unsuccessful attempts to keep afloat and clutch each other at the same time. Finally she stopped at a low-lying rock. Floating on her back, she leaned her head on the ledge as though it were a pillow. I put my head next to hers. It felt so nice, floating there beside her, staring upstream at the mountain of rocks and cascading water. "It's like a dream, this place."

She smiled at me. "The funny thing is, I never thought of it that way before. It was just, you know—"

"The place where the Parmacella kids spent their summers?"

"Yup. Cave dwelling and rock climbing."

"Cave dwelling?" I looked around. "Where?"

"Oh, up the hill. Chickie transformed a cave into a hide-out." She grimaced. "Chickie's big project. 'Gotta have a place in case it rains,' he insisted. So he found one. There was a big rock that hung out over a cliff in a way that formed a natural cave, about three feet high."

"If nature created it, how did it become Chickie's project?"

"Leave it to Chickie to go and improve on nature. And force poor Vince to help him! They came down here with shovels when we were all, oh, I don't know, around elementary-school age, and, for a whole summer, while Louella and I swam and played around, they were digging, sweating, excavating."

"Did it work?"

"Yes and no. The project was successful. The end result was a cave five feet high." She laughed. "But Vince and Chickie were so sick of it by the time they finished, they never went inside again!"

"How about you and Louella?"

"We came . . . for a while. Used to smuggle cigarettes in every now and then, until we got old enough to admit to each other that we hated smoking, that we were only doing it because we loved our secret hideaway and couldn't think of any other reason to go there."

I looked around at the cliffs above. "Where is it?"

She shook her head resolutely, kicking her feet around in the water. "Can't tell."

"Why?"

She let go of the ledge and swam out into the deep part. "I took a sisterly vow. Louella and I promised each other we would never, ever tell anyone where our secret cave was." She laughed, treading water. "Blood oath! Serious stuff!"

"I'll force it out of you!" I went after her. We chased around in circles, over rocks, underwater, across the water's surface, until I finally trapped her in a corner where I could touch bottom but she couldn't.

She melted against me, wrapping her limbs around my body, kissing my shoulders and my neck, and it started all over again, the internal longings, the dizzy head.

"You win!" I gasped, hungrily kissing her eyes, her nose, any place I could get to. "I don't care about the cave. Just . . . Just . . ."

"Just what?"

"Just stay like this for a minute." We swayed back and forth in the water, our hands slowly stroking each other. We stayed that way for more than a minute, long enough for us both to start shivering. She stretched out in the water, floating on her back, her legs around my waist.

"Cold?"

She nodded.

"We'd better go back to the blanket."

She nodded again, but didn't move.

I stared happily down at her.

"What're you thinking?" she asked after a while.

"I'm not thinking. I'm memorizing."

"Memorizing?"

"Uh-huh. You said you have to go to a family funeral all day tomorrow."

"What does that have to do with memorizing?" she asked.

"A whole Sunday by myself." I shrugged. "If I memorize how you look, see, then I can play it back in my head tomorrow when I'm lonely and missing you."

She seemed pleased at first, then worried. "How, um, how do I look?"

I bent over and kissed her belly button. "Beautiful. But you'll freeze to death if we don't get out of the water!" We climbed out and headed up the cliff.

When we got to the top, she stretched out on the blanket and raised her hands up to the sky. "I . . . feel . . . so . . . *Czechoslovakian!*" she screamed.

Lying down next to her, on my stomach, I looked at her as though she'd gone batty.

She rolled over on her side. "You know that long article you gave me the other night? The one about what Prague Spring had

178

really meant? About how this totally repressed society had suddenly started opening up, painting, writing, loving, making movies, tasting freedom? Enjoying that delicious first taste?"

I chuckled a little, grasping her message.

"I swear, that's exactly how I feel! It's like I've spent my whole life in this gloomy, dark, miserable shell and now, suddenly, this whole new world is opening up to me, and it all tastes so incredibly *delicious!*" She stopped suddenly and looked at me nervously. "Know what I mean?"

I knew exactly what she meant. I felt the same way, after all. But I couldn't get the words out. They were the kind of words I could never get out, and my throat constricted as I tried this time. "Yes." I tried again. "I feel . . ."

She nodded anxiously. "Czechoslovakian?"

She looked so cute and hopeful I couldn't stand it. I played with her hand, pulling her fingers apart. It was easier to tell her hand the truth than to tell it to her eyes. "I feel as though you're my personal Alexander Dubcek, freeing me to be someone I've never been able to be before." I couldn't believe I had actually managed to get the line out.

She gaped at me, equally shocked. "Thank you."

I shook my head, and this time I looked directly into her eyes. "No, thank *you.*"

She was fidgeting. "You . . . um . . ." She nodded at the picnic basket. "You want something to eat?"

I told myself I was on a streak: Go for boldness. I rolled over on my back and put my hands under my head. "Know what I really want?"

She leaned down beside me. "What?"

"I want to unhook the top of your bikini."

"What?"

"You heard me," I chortled. "I mean, I'll take a peanut butter and jelly sandwich, but if you want to know what—"

"You want to unhook the top of Alexander Dubcek's bikini?"

"Shocking, huh?"

"Shocking!" She sat very still for a while. Then she stood and picked up the picnic basket. "Grab the blanket," she ordered over her shoulder.

She headed toward the cliff, but far to the left of the path we always took when we went for a swim, toward one of the many gray rock formations at the edge of the cliff. I picked up the blanket and turned to follow her, but when I looked up again, she was gone.

I walked over to where she had been, and when I stepped down the cliff, around the rock, I found her, sitting on the floor of a cave. It was about five feet in height, and roughly the width of a king-size bed. I sat down next to her and faced forward, taking in a spectacular view of the riverbed below. The cave was deep and dark. Soft breezes were blowing in through the large open front. I turned to Marci. "Great ventilation."

"There's even an exit hole," she said, pointing to an opening in the ceiling rock at the back.

"Did Chickie drill it?"

"Nope. Mother Nature provided it." She made a face. "Chickie, of course, took credit." She got up on her knees. "C'mon, let's spread out the blanket. It's softer than the dirt floor."

We spread the blanket, and then sat back down on it. I leaned over and kissed her. "Are you sure you want—"

"Yes." She put her head on my shoulder and ran her hand across my chest and then down to my stomach. "As much as you."

"What about the blood oath?"

She laughed. "If Louella finds out, I'll just say I broke it for a special occasion."

"Really?" I unhooked her bikini top and gazed at the first breasts I had ever seen in my life. They were full and round. I sat there mesmerized.

She lay back down on the blanket.

I lay down next to her. "What's the special occasion?" My voice was raspy.

"Prague Summer," she whispered as I kissed her bare breasts. "Prague Summer."

Rod Bingham took his hands off the keyboard and stretched his arms out, smiling at the screen of his word processor. He picked up the cup next to him, took a sip of coffee, and then leaned back in the swivel chair, way back, shutting his eyes.

He jumped when the telephone rang on the desk beside him. "Hello."

"Hear you have seventy-eight degrees and sunny skies, you

180

bastard!" Stanley Kurtz roared by way of salutation. "What are you doing?"

Rod sighed. "Fantasizing about adolescent sex."

There was a long pause. "Yeah?"

Rod laughed, picturing the expression on the face at the other end of the telephone.

"How's, uh, how's that Brandy Devine girl?" Kurtz asked suspiciously.

"Too old for adolescent sex, Stan. Stop sweating it. It isn't the cleaning lady. It's what I'm writing that got me started."

"Now you're talking! How's my book coming?"

"It's not a book. I told you before, it's a therapeutic exercise. I'm trying to relive something that . . . Oh, shit, Stan, I don't know . . ."

" 'An experience that changed your life.' That's what you told me last week. I remember, even if you've lost track."

"Maybe." Rod leaned back in the chair and gazed up at the ceiling. "The assignment, as I recall, was to live like a monk and find something that meant something to me."

"Adolescent sex? You had to go that far back to find something?"

"Guess so."

"Still," Kurtz began again hopefully. "You're writing, right? Hell, a book's a book. Won't it be publishable?"

"Not this one . . ." Rod swept his hand affectionately against the computer screen. "But maybe it'll lead to something that is."

"All *right!* My obsessive writer back on the job. That's enough for now." Kurtz paused and Rod could feel the wheels turning in his agent's head. "You said it was autobiographical?"

"I said an autobiographical *exercise,* Stan. I thought I was supposed to be finding myself down here, not coming up with *Gone With the Wind.*"

"You're right, you're right. Still, I mean, as long as the old juices are flowing again, I was thinking Eastern Europe might give you more fuel for thought than Miami. Looks like it's gonna become the 'Revolution of Nineteen Eighty-nine' over there, doesn't it? All the headlines lately about Communism's big fall. Solidarity taking over Poland, thousands of East Germans streaming across the borders to the west every day?"

"Mmm," Rod muttered, not knowing what Kurtz was talking about, and not caring. "I'm sort of writing about Eastern Europe," he said, smiling at the last line on his word processor screen, "Czechoslovakia."

"*Czechoslovakia?* What's happening in—"

"Forget it. A joke. Look, Stan, let's hold this discussion on Eastern Europe until I come back, huh?"

"Okay, but just think about the possibility of going over there, will you? I mean, nothing much seems to be happening right now in Czechoslovakia, compared to Poland and Germany, but if that's where you—"

"Sure, Stan. Sure." Rod Bingham hung up and grabbed a pad of handwritten notes lying next to the word processor. He leaned back in his chair, reading them. After a while he sat up and started writing again.

I was inordinately happy when I walked home from Marci's house that night, so distracted that I didn't even notice the red pickup truck parked out in front of Mrs. Stompous's place. "Eh, Smarts," a familiar voice called out as I walked by.

"Sal?"

"Yeah, 's me. I'm ready for you, Smarts."

"For me?"

"Whatcha think, I got the hots for Ole Lady Stompous or somethin'? I'm here to see you!"

"How, um, how did you know I'd—"

"Parmacella girls get locked up every night at ten. Everyone knows 'at. Figured you'd be comin' by soon enough."

"But, what do you want?"

"The times tables, asshole! I know 'em cold! Hop in and we'll go out to my place so's I can show you."

The idea of another night in mosquito land did not appeal to me. "You're here, Sal. Why don't we just go over them in my room?" I realized I was inviting the wolf into Little Red Riding Hood's grandmother's house, but Durone seemed unusually nonlethal—chipper, even—and I was off in my own happy dream world.

Once inside, Durone smacked the multiplication cards down on the table next to the bed, sat down on the only chair in the room, and folded his arms across his chest. "Shoot, Golden Boy!"

I sat down on the bed and began holding up cards, checking his responses with the answers on the other side. We went through the whole pack in record time, and then again, just to be sure.

The fighter had obviously prepared for the bout. "You know them cold, Sallie," I said finally with admiration. I extended my hand.

He slapped it away, his eyes gleaming. "Not yet, Smarts." He took the cards out of my hand, turned the pack around, and gave them back to me. "Let's try it backward, kid."

"Backward?"

"Yeah." He grinned. "Just show me the answers this time. I'll tell you the questions!"

Obediently, I began holding the cards up, and once again, his performance was flawless.

I held up the last card: 24.

"Huh, huh! Heh, heh! Ho, ho! Bet you think you're gonna get ole Sallie, don'tcha?" he hooted. He slammed his fist down on the arm of the chair and leaned toward me. "Either two times twelve or three times eight!" He applauded himself.

"Or?" I asked, still holding the card.

His eyes squinted malevolently, then opened up, gleaming. "Four times six," he whispered.

It was a side of Durone I'd never seen before—playful, light-hearted, a pal instead of a punisher. Feeling like his partner in victory, I walked over and smacked him on the shoulder.

"Brought us a little somethin' to celebrate with," he said, dragging a six-pack out of the brown paper bag he'd carried in from the truck. He opened his can and handed the opener to me.

"This mathematics stuff is for what, Sal, some kind of test?" He winked mysteriously.

"Come on," I prodded, enjoying my new role as partner. "If you tell me, then maybe I can help you prepare."

"Like how?"

"Well, if it is a test, do you have samples of it?" I opened my can.

He took a long draw on his beer. "Not s'posed to," he said smugly. "But Danny Vasiliades got so pissed when he couldn't do the problems, he tore off some sheets and wadded 'em up into a ball." Durone guffawed. "He was still fistin' 'em when come out!" He

183

pulled a few tattered pieces of paper out of his pocket and handed them to me.

I looked over the math problems, and then my eyes wandered up to the top of the page. "Selective Service," I read out loud. I looked at him. "This is the draft test," I gasped. *"That's* what you're trying to pass?"

Durone drank some more.

"I thought you were deferred!" I protested. " 'Sole support of my mother'—that's what you said that day in the locker room!"

"Yeah, well, I am," Durone said softly. "Or I *would* be, if I wanted to be deferred." He laughed. "Fact is, my name's never come up. I never been called."

"And you're actually thinking of enlisting?" I asked incredulously.

His jaw clenched. "You got problems with that?"

"No." I gulped down some beer, then gulped down some more. "Why do you want to?" I asked when I finally got up the nerve.

He lit a cigarette. "Started workin' at Kelso summers when I's just a kid," he said slowly. "My uncle, he worked there, 'n' he helped me get the job. 'Good money for life, boy!' 'At's what he told me. 'You're good, Sal. You're one strong ox!' Pritchett—the foreman?—'at's what he kep' sayin'." Durone drank some more. "Worked the swing shift—eight hours—whiles I was still in school."

He stuck the cigarette in his mouth and stared at me through a cloud of smoke. "I'm not just a supervisor, y'know. I'm a *cleaner*, Smarts. Know what that means?"

"No, not the details."

His beady eyes bore a line into mine. "Means I got the hardest, most skilled job in the plant, Golden Boy. Job 'at comes with Kelso's fattest pay check, outsida management!"

"We never get to see what the cleaners—"

"No one gets to see, 'cept us guys 'at do it. Two guys per crew, six in all. Just six, see, for the whole plant. I clean every other morning, gettin' to the plant two hours before you chumps show up, 'n then I do it again a half hour before closin' time every day. Us cleaners gotta jump into 'at tub and scrub it clean, break our asses to get all the crusty stuff off, get that tub into top shape, and do it

184

fast, real fast. 'S hard work—work for people who know what they're doin'."

"You and Lucky are both—"

"Taught him everything he knows. Just ask 'im. He'll tell ya. He'll tell ya he learned from the best. 'Best cleaner we ever had!' 'At's what they been tellin' me ever since I started. 'Best cleaner we ever had.' " He stared off into space, oblivious to the smoke that was wafting up from his mouth to his eyes.

"And now?"

"Now . . ." He sighed and sat still for a while. Then he leaned forward conspiratorially. "You're not s'posed to know this. No one is. Kelso's closin' down, movin' the plant come September. Way I figure, all that stuff about bein' strong and bein' best don't mean shit if there's no place around to get a job."

"But there are other—"

"Not 'at pay as good as Kelso." His face was lost in a haze of smoke. "Orange County, see, it's filled with towns like Fallsville. Plants come and go. Whole lotta guys on the shift at Kelso now, they come from Dale City, Darby, Lovell, all them other towns. We gotta plant, see. Theirs is all closed."

He took a long swig and leaned back in his chair. "Always been like that 'round here. Used to be, mosta the factories was over in Collier. My old man, he worked there. Used to drive over every day. First he worked makin' shoes. Then it closed, 'n' he worked makin' shirts. Then it closed too."

He drank some more. "Ain't no plants in Collier now, just a buncha out-a-work people. Oh, they got some new stuff too, stuff 'at's come up from Boston. But it ain't like the stuff 'at used to come up, see. It's just, like, y'know, scientists workin' in a buncha new buildings. Don't make nothin', the scientists."

I laughed at his contempt. "Well, they must make *something*, Sallie!

"Research, 'at's what they make! I know—called lookin' for a job last week! 'Research,' they told me." He snarled. " 'At's nothin' a guy like me can put together! Can't go haulin' research off in a truck, y'know!"

"But in this whole area, Sal, there must be something."

"Listen, fightin's what I do best." He shot me a sly grin. "Might even put you down as a reference!" He slapped his thigh over that.

185

I drank some beer. "You're not the least bit scared?"

"Scared about passin' the fuckin' test, yah! 'Bout that I'm plenty scared!" He threw his empty can in the wastepaper basket and took out another. "Scared about fightin' a war? Nah. I'm good at that, man! I'll kill me a whole bunch of gooks before it's over!"

"And maybe die in the process."

"In a blaze o' glory! With medals sent home for all Fallsville to see! We still got a buncha my Uncle Hank's medals from Korea. An', lemme tell ya, they're somethin' to look at!" He took a swig. "No glory in stayin' round here, that's for sure."

"What if you flunk the test?"

" 'At's your problem," he drawled. "Ain't gonna enlist 'til you're sure I'll pass the test!"

I felt little pellets of sweat trickling down from my armpits. I looked at the sheets of math problems in front of me. "But these are just a few pages of the test," I protested.

" 'At'sa only pages Vasiliades couldn't do." Durone smiled. "If he could do the rest, I can. " 'E's dumb, even for a Greek."

"It's, uh, just math? Isn't there a reading part too?"

"Hell, I can read, for Chrissakes! Been reading since first grade!"

"Still, though, maybe you should practice a little."

"Bullshit."

Sobered by this new responsibility, I worked out a strategy: I would make up math worksheets, based on the test samples, and put them under the front seat of Durone's truck every morning. He would do them, timing himself, and then place the finished sheet back in the truck for me to correct. After a while—when I thought he was ready—I'd give him a trial test. He thought that sounded like a good idea.

I leaned back on the bed and looked at him. "Say you survive in Vietnam, Sal, say you even come back a hero. What're you going to do to support yourself then? I mean, service only lasts a couple of years."

"Figure I'll have a kinda investment goin' by then." He gave me his wolf-grin. "Gonna take care a that tomorrow. Gonna see my State Senator. Get him to change his mind 'bout the freeway."

"Ahh, you mean your property?"

"Yeah. See, if he puts the freeway near where my property is, it'll go way up in value." He gulped some more beer and swaggered

186

around. "Even got plans for other ways to make the property better." He leaned his head back against the chair top and looked at me from under lowered eyelids. "You ever hear a shopping centers, Smarts?"

He said it as though he were talking about some new scientific discovery. "Big money in shopping centers. Big money."

"But, um, exactly how are you going to convince Senator Berlanti?" I remembered what Marci had told me. "Isn't he dead-set against putting the freeway near where your property is?"

He reached into his hip pocket, pulled out a packet of snap-shots, and threw it onto the bed.

I opened it and looked at the pictures. There was one of a middle-aged man and a young girl dancing, a couple of pictures of the two of them kissing in what looked like a restaurant, and then several snapshots in which they were standing in front of a door numbered 105. "I—I don't get it, Sal."

" 'At's Berlanti . . . Berlanti and his girlfriend, Annabelle Vetere." He leered at me. "*Now* you get it?"

"No . . ."

"Berlanti's married, see. Married to a lady whose daddy's a big shot in the party . . . got Berlanti elected in the first place. Big Daddy's not gonna be happy to find out his son-in-law's carryin' on with Annabelle there."

"You're going to show these pictures to her father?"

"Smarts, you don't know politics worth shit! Not gonna show 'em to Big Daddy! Not gonna *have* to! Just gonna let Berlanti see what I got on him. 'At'll be enough."

"You're sure?"

"Eh." He stared me dead in the eye. "Sallie is sure. Sallie's never been surer of anything!" He stood up. "You got any books?" he asked, nodding at the stack on my windowsill.

"Yes. Why?"

He shrugged. "Thought maybe I'd borrow a couple, y' know, to get ready for the test. Tolstoy?" he asked, picking up one. "He a good writer?"

I decided *War and Peace* would be a little heavy as a starter. "He's Russian, Sal."

Durone made an ugly face and heaved the book back on the windowsill. "How about this book?"

He was holding a paperback whodunit. "That's a mystery story, Sal. You might like it . . . lots of suspense."

"Lotta spaces between the sentences," Durone guffawed, shifting through the pages. "My kinda book!" He tucked it inside his shirt, headed for the door, and then stopped. "One thing," he said, pointing a finger at me. "Big Mouth, she can't know nothin' 'bout all this, hear? Nothin' 'bout Berlanti, nothin' 'bout the military, nothin' 'bout you and me workin' for the test . . ." He squinted at me. "Okay?"

I nodded, knowing I would tell Marci, and feeling infinitely more guilty for not defending her against the unfair reputation as "Big Mouth" than for lying to Durone.

20

"LEONARD LUCINSKI, TRUCK DRIVER," it said in bold letters in the obituary column of the *Orange County Sentinel.* The picture above the caption bore no resemblance to the hairless, jaundiced near-corpse Marci had tried to communicate with in the hospital a few weeks before.

It was, however, unmistakably "Lucky." He had the same sad, smiling eyes, expectant, timid, so anxious not to displease. The cheeks were still round, the adolescent acne condition memorialized in crater-textured facial skin.

Marci searched the face, looking for hidden clues, the way she always did in newspaper accounts of tragedy, seeking the similarities that would enable her to empathize with the emotions of the bereft, while at the same time hoping to find the difference, the factual abnormality, that would distance her, that would prove this wouldn't, couldn't happen to "us."

The circular line of a dark T-shirt cut across at the bottom of his neck. A snapshot, she guessed, plucked from a page in a scrapbook. The picture had been taken at a family outing—a picnic, maybe—snapped impulsively by a happy chronicler of life, never dreaming it would become the final representation of Leonard Lucinski.

Marci's eyes dropped down to the end paragraph: "He leaves his wife of eighteen years, Carol; four children, Salvatore, Leonard Jr., Michael, and Susan; his parents, Ray and—"

Marci's eyes shot back to the children's names. "Salvatore." Leonard Lucinski had named his first-born male offspring after Salvatore Durone. Sallie first, Lucky second, an adolescent pattern carried on into adulthood.

The shrill ring of the telephone startled her. Who could be calling so early on a Sunday morning? She got up from the kitchen table, tugging her bathrobe around her as she picked up the receiver. "Hello."

"Is this, um, Marci Cour . . . uh . . . Cour-beeeen?"

Close enough. "Yes."

"Hi, Jim Connomon here . . . You know, uh, Con Man?"

"Yes!" she shouted, recognizing the deep, drawling speech pattern. "What's up?"

"Well, uh, you seen the obituary in the county paper yet?"

"Lucky."

"Oh, Lord. I was right, then? It *is* Lucky—from the Kelso plant?"

"Yes."

"Oh, hey! Gave me the creeps, seein' it thatta way. Never knew Lucky's real name, see, but I'm tellin' you, just lookin' at that mugshot this mornin', bells kinda went off in my head. Set me to thinkin' about that name you asked me if I knew—Angelo Pimpoli? You said Durone had written his name down along with mine."

"Yes. But I don't—"

"*Pimp!*" Connomon screamed. "I bet Angelo Pimpoli's the guy at Kelso we called Pimp!"

Another recollection worked its way into Marci's head, this one of a chunky teenager with a thick, curly head of hair and a vile vocabulary. Nothing quite like wandering down memory lane clutching the Sunday obituaries.

"That started me and the wife talkin', see, 'n she reminded me that Jake Simmons died three years ago. Now Jake, he worked at Kelso too, a couple of years before we all did."

"What did he die of?" Marci's voice was hoarse.

"Liver gave out. That's all I heard. Jake lived near me here in Dale City. It all just set me to wonderin' . . ."

190

"Wondering what?"

"Jake's dead. Lucky's dead. Durone's dead. Durone thinks someone killed him and he's trying to find me—outta the blue, after all these years—and he's looking for a guy whose name sounds like he could be Pimp."

Marci bit her thumbnail.

"You think, uh—" Connomon cleared his throat. "You think maybe, someone's out to kill all the guys who worked at Kelso?"

"No." That was enough to snap her back. "No, Jim," she said calmly, quickly, "I *don't* think so. More likely, Sallie Durone got cancer and, being Sallie Durone, he was unwilling to just accept that fact the way other normal people do. He had to make a big deal out of it. He had to transform bad luck—fate—into some kind of conspiracy!"

"But what about Jake Simmons?"

"Happenstance," Marci snapped. "Coincidence. Look, Jim, I feel very guilty for getting you all worked up this way. The truth is, I sought you out—"

"Because *my* name was on Durone's list! The death list!"

"It wasn't a death list. It was just a list! I was checking out all the names, if you must know, just to convince Sallie's wife, Francine, that there was nothing to this conspiracy idea!"

"You really think—"

"I think Durone wanted to go out in a blaze of glory. That's what I think! He'd tried unsuccessfully to live gloriously, and this was his last hope, a gloriously mysterious death. That's all it is."

"It's just, you know, looking at that obit—"

"Perfectly understandable, under the circumstances—at least the circumstances I dropped off at your front door. And that's my fault. Completely my fault. Listen, let me check around some more so that I can assure you you have nothing to worry about. I'll call you some time this week and let you know what I've found out."

"Well, it would be a relief if there's nothing to worry about!"

"I'm *sure* there's nothing to worry about! I'll call you in a few days."

"Much obliged."

Marci slammed the telephone into the wall receiver and paced angrily around the kitchen. Durone's revenge, that's what it was! In death, Old Sallie had managed to do what he'd never been able to

191

accomplish in life. He'd sucked everyone else into his peculiar brand of paranoia! Francine, Marci . . . even poor Jim Connomon.

She began unloading the dishwasher, hurling the clean silverware into a drawer. But then her eyes shot back to the obituary page, and gradually, her rage switched directions—from Durone to herself.

Lennie Lucinski, the man she had steadfastly insisted she had never known, had turned out to be Lucky, another presence from her past. The files in that corregated box upstairs were the product of a responsible, organized man, not the Salvatore Durone she insisted upon remembering. Had she let prejudice cloud this investigation?

Her body chilled. *What* investigation? She had set out to prove there was no need to investigate, hadn't she? Sneering at the idea of a "cancer pill" while ignoring the facts?

The facts: Two men who had worked at Kelso were dead—three, if Jim Connomon was right. She pulled a clean plate out of the dishwasher and headed for the cabinet. *Three men with a shared employment history had died prematurely.*

If a new client had entered her office with that information, what would she have done? She stopped suddenly, clutching the plate, fully aware of what her course of action would have been, had the assignment come from a different source.

Her mind went back to the corregated box upstairs, taking inventory: the phone bills; the useless diary that ended too soon; "Research." She saw the word scrawled across the top of the folder in Durone's handwriting. *Research.*

Her eyes opened wide as she contemplated a painful possibility: *Salvatore Durone had done all the work for her!* She put the plate down on the counter and headed upstairs—to the corregated box.

Six hours later, Marci Courbienne's car screeched around a corner and bounded into the parking lot next to the small townhouse that headquartered the regional office of the National Brotherhood of Chemical and Electrical Workers.

She found the familiar automobile and parked next to it. "Aha! Just as I thought!"

She hopped out of her car, ran up the front steps of the townhouse, and held her finger down on the doorbell. "C'mon, Jack!

192

I know you're in there!" she shouted, banging on the door with her free hand. "Open up!"

After about a minute Jack Whelan opened the door and gaped at her, hands on hips, bifocals halfway down his nose, a mystified expression on his face. "What the bejesus—"

"Why didn't you answer your phone?" She screamed, "Damn, I've been calling and calling!"

"Turned the phones off so I could get some work done."

"That's what I figured," she said breathlessly, jumping around on the top step. "That's why I came. Oh, Jack, it's incredible!"

His eyes wandered lethargically down from her makeup-less face and uncombed hair to her stained sweatshirt and tattered jeans. "Sure seems that way."

"Sorry!" she laughed. "You probably think I'm nuts, barging in on you like this!"

"The thought did cross my mind."

"Busy?"

"Naw . . ." he mumbled to her back as she raced across the threshold past him. "I just came down here 'cause I had nothing better to do." He closed the door and followed as she raced up the stairs toward his office. "Of course I *am* going into week-long contract negotiations tomorrow that could mean life or death to a local chapter of the union, but hey, I mean—"

"I promise," she announced, plopping down in the chair on the other side of his desk, "it will only take a minute."

The room was sparsely furnished—a desk, desk chair, and two large chairs for visitors. The walls were a mélange of snapshots of Whelan's children and grandchildren and posters proclaiming UNION, YES!

"Oh, Jack, I think I've got it figured out!" She put her elbows on his desktop and leaned across. "The Salvatore Durone murder mystery! I've been working on it all day, and, well, I just need your help in finding the last piece of the puzzle!"

"*My* help?" he protested, collapsing in his desk chair. "I'm no detective."

"Don't need a detective. Need a specialist."

His tired, crinkly face offered up a look of calm indulgence, like an affectionate father intent on channeling a teenage outburst into rational dialogue. "I take it the Durone telephone bills turned up."

"Yes. Yes, they did. I—"

"Ahh . . . and the floosie did it?" His eyes sparkled mischievously. "Remember? The bank withdrawals—one hundred dollars one week, seventy-five the next? Come on, now, Marci! The statements you were pondering the last time I saw you!"

"Oh, Jack . . ." She cupped her hands over her mouth and dropped back against the chair.

"What's the matter?"

"I guess in all my excitement I had forgotten the last time I saw you." She looked up at him. "Here you come to my house and tell me you don't want to be just a friend . . . and walk out, slamming the door behind you, and then the first time *I* need a friend, I—"

"A friend?" He tilted his head. "I thought you said you needed a specialist."

She smiled appreciatively. "Yes, that's what I need!"

"Go on, then."

She took a deep breath. "I think Salvatore Durone's murderer wasn't a person. It was a job. I think he died of workplace exposure to a hazardous substance." She smiled at him smugly. "Now, are you the right man for this quest or not?"

Whelan threw back his shoulders and puffed out his chest. "A specialist!"

She leaned back in her chair. "Salvatore Durone died of angiosarcoma of the liver."

Whelan squinted over the tops of his bifocals. "Who says?"

"A highly reputable cancer expert at Boston Hospital, reached by me via telephone three hours ago in Sweden, where he's presently teaching for six months."

"Angiosarcoma . . ." Whelan stared into space. "That's the disease they've linked to—"

"No!" She held her hand up. "Let *me* tell *you*. See if I got it right." She took a deep breath. "Angiosarcoma is a very, very rare form of liver cancer, one that cannot be diagnosed until it is too late, until it's incurable. And unlike other workplace-related illnesses, where the cause-effect link is hazy, a fairly clear causal link has been established between angiosarcoma and workplace contact with the gas vinyl chloride."

Whelan nodded slowly. "Yeah, that's it. Vinyl chloride. That came out in those hearings back in the—"

"C'mon now, it's *my* murder mystery!"

"Go on," Whelan chuckled." By all means, go on."

"Vinyl chloride is the basic ingredient used in making polyvinyl chloride, which is used to make everything from flooring to shoe soles to plastic utensils. Now, they didn't discover vinyl chloride was dangerous until the early seventies, or at least the danger was not public knowledge. As a result of that discovery, worker exposure to vinyl chloride today is regulated by government standards that restrict exposure levels. But that exposure standard did not go into effect until 1974."

"I think it was 'seventy-five, actually," Whelan interrupted. "It seems to me the plastics manufacturers filed a lawsuit—"

"Whatever. Doesn't matter. It takes more than fifteen years for exposure to vinyl chloride to result in angiosarcoma, so by the time the standards went into effect, the damage had been done to Salvadore Durone."

"If he had, in fact, worked in a place where—"

"He did. I'm sure he did. Matter of fact, I think I know the name of the company he was working for when he came in contact with vinyl chloride."

"You only *think* you know?"

"Tapron Industries."

"Tapron, Tapron . . ." Whelan ran a hand through his thinning hair. "The big conglomerate in Atlanta?"

Marci rested her elbows on Whelan's desk. "Tapron's been making polyvinyl plastic from vinyl chloride for about fifty years now. At first the firm produced things like fireproof covering for electric wiring in ships. Then, back when polyvinyl products began to take off, Tapron branched out into other areas—phonograph records, shower curtains, containers, that kind of thing."

"But I thought Durone was a home-town boy—a Fallsville native. When did he work in Atlanta?"

"Tapron branched out geographically, too, with the onset of polyvinyl products. The firm set up plants all over the country. The company had an intricate network going, see. Some plants produced the vinyl chloride, others used the vinyl chloride to produce consumer items, some did both." Marci sighed and shook her head. "Unfortunately for me, only the Atlanta headquarters bore the name

'Tapron.' All the regional plants were Tapron-owned, but operated under other names."

"Why is that a problem?"

"I haven't been able to verify a Tapron link to the local plant Durone worked at."

"But you know for a fact that Durone worked in a Tapron-owned plant?"

"Yes." She stood up and began walking around the office. "I have Durone's notes. I have Durone's phone bills. I have an educated guess. I'm missing a direct link—the information Durone had in his head."

"No great loss there," Whelan bellowed. "From what you've told me, the big oaf had mighty little in his head."

Marci shook her head resolutely. "I was wrong, Jack. Very, very wrong."

"On the basis of *what*, exactly, have you come to this conclusion?"

"His files." She walked back and leaned over Jack Whelan's desk. "Oh, Jack, you wouldn't believe them. Tucked in there with all the family bills was this folder labeled 'Research.' It was filled with feature articles on plastics plants, news clippings on the vinyl-chloride hearings, a big public-relations packet on Tapron's national and international network, Xeroxed pages of books he found in the library . . ."

"But how can you—"

"Bill Blaine—"

Whelan's eyes lit up hopefully. "Bill's involved in this, is he?"

"You know him?"

"Sure I know him! One of the best occupational health specialists around! He testifies for me all the time on stuff like this. Has a consultant firm in Boston."

"Bill Blaine Associates." Marci nodded. "Durone was referred to him by someone at the Labor Department in Washington." She grinned. "You'll be happy to know that like you, Bill Blaine is working today too. Unlike you, however, he had his phones turned on."

"So, how does Bill Blaine figure in this?"

"The doctor at Boston Hospital told Durone about the known link between angiosarcoma and exposure to vinyl chloride. But

196

Durone had worked in chemical plants most of his life . . . since he was twelve years old. Bill Blaine's name was given to him as someone who might be able to help him figure out at *which* job he had been exposed to it."

"Since he was twelve?" Whelan howled. "Come off it! The law forbids any child under the age of eighteen from working in a chemical plant!"

"Not if you're big for your age and have family connections— chemical plant worker relatives anxious to turn you into a bread-winner, and local management only too happy to look the other way."

"Nice family!" Whelan growled.

"Blaine said Sal had no idea what chemicals he'd worked with. He only knew what he'd made—the finished product. He went over the products and procedures with Blaine on the telephone, and Blaine said there was one plant—only *one*—that fit the vinyl chloride scenario to a 'T.' 'A classic case,' that's what Blaine remembers about the conversation."

"And what was the name of the plant?"

She made a face. "That is . . . uncertain."

Whelan looked surprised. "A guy like Bill Blaine didn't think to ask?"

"Yeah, he asked." She sighed. "Durone wouldn't tell him."

"*What?*"

"Look, the guy was paranoid, Jack. He was always certain—"

Whelan yawned and scratched his belly. "So, in truth, Marci, what we have here is an admittedly paranoid man who's wanting to finger a former employer for his cancer, and out of all the many places he worked in his lifetime, only one is even a remote possibility."

"No, listen." Marci folded her arms across her chest. "Durone told Bill Blaine he had ways of figuring out what had happened to the plant, who owned it. Blaine didn't hear from him for more than a month. When Durone called back, he told Blaine the name of the parent company was Tapron Industries—that, in fact, when asked outright on the telephone, Tapron Industries said yes, they had operated a plant of that name in Fallsville."

"*What* name?"

"Blaine told him he'd find him a lawyer. But when Blaine called back a week later, with a legal referral, Durone was in the hospital." She shrugged. "Then he died."

"And Durone, this dying man," Whelan said dramatically to an invisible audience, "he didn't think that maybe it might be a good idea to write down the details—the name of the regional plant, the specific links between that plant and Tapron—before his fast-approaching day of reckoning?"

"He died of complications from pneumonia. He thought he had longer to live!" She played with the clasp on her purse. "See, my problem is that Sal knew the name of the plant and worked forward from that. We have to work in reverse. We have to start with Tapron and work backward."

"We?"

"Jack, look, at some time in the last thirty years, Tapron owned a plant in the region." She stared him down. "I need proof. I need an official Tapron admission of ownership . . . and an official company description of what the workers at the plant it operated did."

"So? Call the company and ask!"

"And put them on the defensive? Why? When with your help I could—"

"My help?"

"According to one of the clippings in Durone's file, Tapron is a union shop."

He put his hands over his eyes.

"Your union, as a matter of fact." She beamed at the backs of his fingers. "I just thought that through your connections, you could secretly get a list of plants Tapron operated around here and their procedures."

He growled. "I still think the floosie did it!"

Marci got a gleam in her eye. She opened her mouth to speak, but then closed it firmly.

"What?" Whelan looked at her suspiciously. "What's that look about?"

She played with a pen lying on his desk. "Just . . . well, there was one folder marked 'Diaries.' It was filled with papers, each one with a date at the top."

"Ah-hah. Now you've come up with something interesting! What do they say?"

"Sweet stuff." Marci stared into space. "Simple stuff. The one

I read was about how good it was to talk to 'her.' How she made him feel 'multidimensional.' " Marci frowned. "She must have been an educated person."

"What makes you say that?"

"Muhl-dee-duh-men-shun-ull." She said it slowly, in a deep voice and then giggled. "That word wasn't in Durone's vocabulary, believe me!" Her face clouded. "Now I feel kind of guilty," she said softly. "The passage I read was so . . ." She looked up at Whelan sadly. "They were obviously deeply felt sentiments he was expressing."

"And what did the others say?"

"I only glanced at one!" she protested indignantly. "I didn't think it was fair to read them. They were personal."

"Oh, then I suppose you returned them to his wife."

"The hell I did! They were personal!"

Whelan raised an eyebrow. "So you threw them out? Preserving his secret forever?"

Marci smoothed out the bottom of her sweatshirt.

"Well?"

"No," she admitted. "I saved them. Put them away." Her eyes got fiery. "He has children, Jack. I thought some day, when they are older, it might be meaningful for them to read—"

"To read love letters by their father to another woman?"

"No! Just . . . to . . . to read his heartfelt sentiments!" She stood up and put a hand on her hip. "We're getting off-track, Jack. Are you going to check this plant out for me or not?"

"Yup." He leaned back in his chair and put his hands behind his head. "But not on the basis of what you've told me. Rather, on the basis of what you *haven't* told me. You know what the name of the Fallsville plant was."

"Well, I have a—"

"*More* than a hunch." His eyes dared her to disagree.

She fingered with the sleeve of her dirty sweatshirt gingerly, as though it were made of velvet. "Prove me right, Jack." She headed for the door.

"Marci?" he called out after her. "Were they all on Wednesdays?"

She turned around. "Were *what* on Wednesdays?"

"Durone's lovelorn entries. You said they were dated, and you

199

also told me, if I recall, that his wife told you that for a while there, he was coming home late every Wednesday."

"Such a smartie!" She giggled coquettishly, walking quickly out the door and closing it behind her. "All on Wednesdays, Jack." He heard her giggle as her shoes clattered down the steps. "All on Wednesdays!"

21

1968   Marci's fingers brushed against mine as she put down
my root beer float, setting off a charge someplace deep inside that
made me yearn for closing time.

"How was Kelso?"

"Same as always." I played with my glass. "Except Durone
called in sick. Apparently he got beaten up over the weekend."

It took a second for that to register. "You told me he was
going to—"

"I guess maybe he did."

She put a hand over her mouth. "You think Berlanti did it?
When he showed him those pictures?"

"I don't know. The plant manager said he might be out all
week. And according to the guys, he's never missed a day of work
before. I've been worrying about him all day. Isn't that crazy? Me
worrying about Sal Durone?"

"Yeah, that's crazy all right." She ran her index finger over
mine, setting off another charge. "But kind of sweet, too."

I growled. "Sweet!"

She gave me a loving look. "You made him sound almost
human in the stuff you wrote for me this morning."

"Human or pathetic? This great big oaf all charged up over the multiplication tables? Planning on raising his property's value by blackmailing a politician?"

"Sallie's not at home," Lucky announced, as the door slammed behind him. He climbed up on a stool. "Gimme a float, Marci, okay?"

"Where is he?" the guys called out.

"In the hospital?"

"Nah." Lucky strummed his fingers on the counter. "His mother said he just went out in his truck someplace. She said he wasn't beat up so bad. She was real pissed . . . about how he's not workin' and all."

Marci served Lucky his float and then came back to my end of the counter. "Think Sal went after Berlanti's thugs?"

I winced.

"You're chewing on the inside of your cheek," she said pointedly. "That's always a bad sign."

"And you're biting your lower lip."

"I only do it when you chew your cheek." She continued nibbling. "Look, even Sal's not dumb enough to get himself beaten up all over again." She waited for me to say something. "Oh, he probably just went off to get out of the house. Believe me," she confided in a whisper, "if you had a mother like his, you wouldn't spend much time at home!" When I didn't respond, she took out a sponge and started wiping the counter. "He's probably getting drunk up at that bramble patch he took you to."

I looked at her in disbelief. "Why would anyone go there?"

"That's where he always goes," she said. "It's Sal Durone's dream property. That's where Chickie and Vince set out to look for him the night he attacked Louella." She threw the sponge in the bowl of cleanser. "And we all know they found him that night, don't we?"

I pushed the glass around on the counter. "I should have told him it was a dumb idea."

"Yeah?" Her eyes got larger. "And gotten your head knocked off!"

"No, Marci, he really wasn't like that Saturday night. He was all . . . friendly."

"Only friend Sallie's ever had is Lucky, and that's because Lucky applauds all the time. A friend who says no doesn't last long."

202

She leaned across the counter on her elbows. "And it was a nasty idea! Thinking he could blackmail—"

"But resourceful! That's what gets me!"

"Shh!" She indicated the guys a few seats away.

I lowered my voice. "He finds out the plant's closing after all the time and energy he's put in working there. Just finding out is pretty resourceful in itself. No one else knows that yet! . . . He's backed into a corner—"

"And he comes out fighting!"

"But with a *plan* this time, not with his fists! Don't you see, he figures out a way to make things work for him!"

"By blackmail!" she scowled. "Why are you impressed by that?"

I shrugged. "I would've just stayed in the corner. Feeling hopeless." I sat there playing with the glass. Then, all of a sudden, I stood up. "I'm . . . I'm just going to see if he is out at that bramble patch."

Durone's truck was parked just where it was the night he'd driven me out to "his property"—up on the hill, front first into a big bush. It was empty. I climbed out of my car, tiptoed around the truck, opened the door, and stuck the math problems under the driver's seat. My hand brushed against a pamphlet. I pulled it out. "SHOPPING CENTERS OF THE UNITED STATES" was written in big letters across the front. I thought I heard a noise, and shoved the pamphlet back under the seat along with the math problems.

When I got to the clearing, there was Durone, lying lifelessly on his back on top of the picnic table, his mouth open, his body surrounded by crushed beer cans. It looked bizarre—as though his body had been laid out in a casket and the cans were flowers.

I tiptoed closer, all the way over to the table, and shuddered as I gazed down at the corpse. His right eye was swollen, and so were his lips. A huge, red-blue gash carved a circular path from his left eye to the side of his mouth. His chin was a mass of small cuts. His chest was rising and falling rhythmically as a snoring sound buzzed from his open mouth.

The corpse was alive. The fact both relieved me and terrified me. "Sal?"

He opened his eyes. One eye, to be exact. The swollen right lid just fluttered a little. "Sal? You okay?"

He groaned, staring up at me. "Smarts." It was uttered as a declarative sentence.

"Yeah, it's me".

"Whatchoo doin' 'eer?" His face was expressionless.

"Just wondered how you were is all."

The eye closed. "Go 'way."

I stood there, tempted by the suggestion.

"Getta fuck outta 'ere."

"You . . ." I surveyed the beer cans. "Are you, um, drunk? Or are you hurt?"

"No."

"Did Berlanti beat you up?"

"His boys beat me up."

"Are you okay?"

"Yeah. Let me sleep."

"Come on, Sal. You have to get up! You have to come back to work, keep earning money while you figure out what you're going to do next. You'll figure out something!" No response.

"I put the math problems under the front seat of your truck, Sal." Nothing.

"You know, just because the Berlanti idea fell through, that doesn't mean it's the end of the world or anything! You can still take the selective service test! You can pass it too . . . go off and become a war hero, just like you said."

He did not move. I gave up. He was alive. He had been fit enough to drive himself to the bramble patch. He could drive himself home as well, once he sobered up. I headed for the path.

"Smarts."

I turned around. He had propped himself up on his elbow on the table.

"Yeah, Sal?"

"Why d'you come?"

"To . . . you know, to see if you were okay." I walked back toward him.

"Who gives a shit?"

"The guys, Sal! They were all wondering where you were. 'Sallie never misses work,' they were saying. 'Something must be

204

really wrong.' Lucky, he even went over to your house looking for you!"

I sat down on the tree stump next to the table. "Management, I'm sure they missed you too. Deke was screwing around. Pimp got the assembly line all messed up. Hard-on and I were relaxing . . . you know, moving slow." I laughed nervously. "Without you there, believe me, everyone got away with murder!"

He was staring into space.

"Who knows, Sal, maybe in the end they *will* put the freeway there."

He lay back down. "Not gonna be where I want it. Decision's made."

"How do you know for sure?"

"Got contacts. I know."

"Well, if you have contacts, then maybe you can find out where they will be putting it! Find out ahead of time, you know? Before anyone else! You could sell the land you own and use the money to buy some where the freeway's going to be."

He closed his good eye.

I felt like a blabbering idiot, Mr. Put-on-a-Happy-Face. I sat very still, staring at my fingers. Finally, I started talking to them. "You were something the other night in my room, Sal, figuring out all those ways to make things happen for you . . . all your plans. I thought about that a whole lot today." I picked at my fingernails. "See, I'm not good at that at all. I always throw in the towel. As soon as something goes wrong, I just crawl off into a corner and give up.

"But you—you find out the plant's closing, and you come up with a whole bunch of ways you can make it without the plant! I respected that a lot. I guess, well, I guess I just came to find you because I hoped you'd keep trying. I was afraid—your not showing up for work like that—I was afraid you'd started acting like me." I swallowed hard. "Like a loser."

He remained immobile.

I sat there fidgeting some more, wondering whether we were going to spend the whole night this way, me running off at the mouth, him catatonic. Suddenly I heard a thud, and looked up. He had whirled his legs off the table and onto the ground. Groaning, he pulled himself to his feet and began walking slowly toward the path, very slowly, as though each step took enormous effort. "Gotta go home." Painfully, he made his way. "Gotta sleep."

"Sure you can drive?" I asked.

"Made it here," he grunted, folding himself into his truck. "C'n make it home."

I slammed the truck door and stood there with my hand on the window ledge.

"I'll be in tomorrow," he announced, turning his opened eye in my direction. "Can't have 'em all fuckin' up on the job that way."

He patted my hand with one hairy paw and turned on the ignition with the other.

I got into my car and followed him, just to be sure he made it. Durone's "home" turned out to be a tiny dilapidated hut.

Marci was sitting on the front steps of her house when I got there, reading the newspaper. She looked up and then back down at the paper.

I sat down next to her on the step. "Sorry."

She turned the page. "Did you find him?"

"Yes. You were right. He was out at his bramble patch. Whew, he was a real mess."

"Good. Serves him right." She turned the page.

"I, uh, I think he'll be all right."

"I thought heroes were supposed to slay dragons." She sneered. "Just my luck to find one who goes out and saves 'em!"

I laughed and hugged her. "Let's go for a walk or something."

"Can't. It's almost curfew time."

"Come on," I begged, prodding her with my shoulder. "Please? I've got something to tell you."

Begrudgingly, she stood up and walked with me down the front walk. She stopped when we got to the gate. "What?"

"I love you."

She looked up at me, and her eyes filled with tears. "How could you say something like that for the very first time—something so special—just to get yourself out of a jam? How could you ruin it! Ruin the meaning!" She was crying.

"Well, because I just realized it. It came to me, kind of, in the car."

"I'll bet it did!" She sobbed. "You were sitting there thinking

206

'Uh-oh. How am I going to keep Marci from being mad at me for choosing slimey Durone over her?' And then it just came to you: 'I'll tell her I love her!' "

"That wasn't it at all." I leaned on the fence. "I was sitting in the car thinking about how I'd dreamed about spending tonight with you all day yesterday and all day today, and I was asking myself why. How come I messed up my own plans that way."

"And?"

"Not why had I messed them up for Durone. Why had I messed them up for anyone? It's not like me, what I did tonight. I swear, I've never worried about anyone but myself. Then I realized it's because I've fallen in love with you. Being in love with you has made me happy for the first time in my life. And it's also, well, spread all over the place, kind of, opened me up, made me notice other people's feelings, made me care."

Her sniffles subsided slightly.

"Then I realized I hadn't ever really told you—not in those three words—how I felt." I turned to her. "I guess it was bad timing."

She shrugged.

I picked up her hands and kissed them. "I promise I'll tell you again, in a better place, at a better time." I pulled her close and put my arms around her. "There will be a whole lot of other chances, see, because I don't plan on ever stopping." I felt her arms closing around me. I buried my face in her hair. "I love you, Marci."

Some time in mid-July, I went into heat. I could not be near Marci without needing to be nearer. I could not be alone with her without touching. I was a magnet, unable to let go.

Fortunately, I had a conducive partner. Although neither of us noticed out loud, our routine changed accordingly. Instead of talking by candlelight at the Cozy Heart Diner on weekday nights after we closed up at Mongon's, we began taking sandwiches, along with a flashlight, to the cave, where our conversations took on a decidedly different pattern.

"Ohh."

"Here?"

"No . . ."

"Here?"

"Yes. Oh, yes . . . Oh . . . Oh . . ."

We did not have intercourse. That was the rule of the cave. Marci was convinced that "doing it" endowed the participants with new physical traits that would become immediately apparent. Everyone would know. Her parents would be devastated, her sister shocked, and the message would be powerful enough to transmit itself through unknown wave lengths to her brothers' boot camp, delivering a blow that would in some way render them incapable of combating the Viet Cong. She could not do that to her family.

I did not push. A wide-eyed virgin myself, I was unsure precisely what it was I would be pushing. I knew I wanted more— always wanted more—but I also knew that what I was getting was remarkable.

We lay in the cave for hours that summer, verbally deprecating the act. Still, for some reason neither of us put into words, the intercourse discussions always evolved into passionate moaning sessions afterward in which we frantically and furiously pursued the pleasures we allowed ourselves.

"Oh, yes . . . yes . . .

"Can you—"

"Don't stop. Oh, please, don't stop."

The crowd was filtering out of Mongon's one night, and I felt the pleasant ache building in my groin as I eyed the sandwich bag and flashlight on the counter and mentally undressed the girl working behind it. It had become one of my favorite moments of the day. Anticipating. In exactly forty-five minutes, we would be in the cave. All my sensory nerves and vital organs seemed to be waking up, twitching happily, pumping the blood faster and faster as my mind meandered over memories of past pleasures and dreams of future ones.

"Surprise!" It was a mood-shattering trill. I turned around to find Louella and Hard-on rushing to the counter with a huge pizza box. "A celebration!" Louella proclaimed. "We've brought you a party!"

"A party?" Marci clapped her hands with an enthusiasm that irritated me. "What are we celebrating?"

"The job!" Louella hugged herself and smiled at her sister.

"You got it?" Marci stared at Louella for one second before

208

answering her own question. "You got it!" She began jumping around behind the counter. "She got it!" she shouted at me. "The job in the accountant's office over in Darby!" She reached over and squeezed Louella's hands. "My sister, the receptionist!"

"Pays even better than I thought." Louella smiled smugly. "Fifty cents an hour more than Kelso."

"Oh, my God!"

"And it only takes about fifteen minutes to drive there. Papa says I can use the car."

"I don't believe it!"

Louella and Hard-on were wearing bright matching yellow shorts, yellow-and-white striped T-shirts, and iridescent yellow baseball caps. The sight raised my hopes. Softball was the only recreation Hard-on allowed himself. (Undoubtedly he'd figured out swinging a bat developed some hidden brick-laying muscles.) "Listen," I said, nodding at the uniforms. "Don't you two have a softball game tonight?"

"Not till eight!" Louella squealed. "Plenty of time to celebrate first."

As we ate the victory pizza, the substance of the conversation began bothering me even more than the intrusion. Louella and Hard-on were talking about how they'd "made it." Just two months after they had graduated from high school, they were set for life—she with her low-paying dead-end job as a receptionist and he with his plans for scratching out a living in construction.

I was used to a social milieu where the passage from youth to maturity lasted a decade or more, and came with boundless possibilities. Here these two kids—people a year younger than I—were not only making decisions, but eagerly accepting life-limiting options.

That saddened me, but it was Marci's reaction that was sending out alarm sirens. She was telling them how lucky they were, reacting, it seemed to me, with an awe bordering on jealousy. What would happen to someone as gifted as Marci in this place of limited horizons? Surely she had loftier dreams. Would she give them up when the time came?

I became anxious. I had to get her out, and as soon as possible. As the three of them talked, I made plans: We'd go to Boston on Saturday. I'd show her some of the colleges. My head began spinning with ideas. She'd love the museums. She'd go crazy when I showed her the Harvard library. We'd take in a concert.

"Boston?" she gasped when they left and I brought up the idea. "Why go all the way to Boston?"

"It's only about an hour's drive."

She giggled. "Why drive an hour when the cave is only three minutes away?"

"Because there aren't any colleges where the cave is."

She stopped drying the glass and looked up at me, frightened. "Colleges?"

"You'll be graduating in less than a year. I think it's time for you to start thinking about college."

"Yeah?" She put the glass on the rack and picked up a plate. "A job, that's what I think I have to start thinking about."

"Why not college?"

"No money."

"You could get a scholarship." I put my hand on her shoulder. "You're number one in your class, after all."

"Number one in a class with no class." She pulled her shoulder out from under my hand and walked away. "Doesn't mean much, being number one at Fallsville High."

"It does so!" I stared at her back. "Are you telling me you haven't even thought about going to college?"

"Some day, maybe . . ." She shrugged. "After I earn enough money."

"Have you taken the college board exam?" The question came out like an accusation.

"No. I told you—"

"You've got to take it." I was pacing back and forth, suddenly panicked. "There's still time. Senior year's not too late. You could take it in the fall, I think. Yeah, they give them in the fall, right after school starts."

"Why?"

"Because it's a helluva lot easier to get into college with a full scholarship right after high school than it is after you've been out for a few years, that's why!" The outburst startled both of us. I tried to calm down. "Where were you planning on going to college?" I added quickly, "I mean, you said some day . . ."

210

She played with the dish towel. "There's a place called Bointon about fifteen minutes from here."

"Why go there?"

She shrugged. "It's the only college I've heard of."

"That's not true. You've heard of Harvard. Surely, you've heard—"

"As a *possibility!* For me!"

"Why is Bointon a possibility?"

"It's . . . close." She was on the verge of tears.

"You have to make plans, Marci," I said softly. "Otherwise you'll end up like Louella—"

"And what's the matter with Louella?" Her eyes scrunched into tiny slits. "She's not good enough for you, huh?"

"It's not a question of being good enough. It has nothing to do with that."

"Hah!"

"Be practical! You've very smart! You'd go nuts stuck in this dumpy little town all your—"

"Dumpy little town?" She was outraged. "It's sure been good enough for you this summer, hasn't it? Or was all that a lie too? All the talk about how happy you've been? About how great my parents are. How you love spending time with—"

"No, no, that was the truth." I put my arms around her. "I love you," I whispered into her hair. "You're misunderstanding. Look, why don't we just finish up here and go talk about this someplace where we can—"

"We've talked enough, far as I'm concerned." She pulled away from me. "I'll finish up here alone. You go home."

"But Marci—"

"Good night, Rod."

It was the first time I had been accused of being better than anyone, and I rose to the occasion, basking in my newly acquired privileged status. By the time I got to my room, the sense of superiority had inspired a condescending benevolence. I was right and she was wrong, but, because I loved her, I was willing to go out of my way to convince her, for her own good.

I knew just how to do it, too. I would invoke God—at least her personal deity. "If Vince had been the one telling you to aim for college tonight, your reaction would have been totally different," my letter began. It went on to spell out how her reaction (not my suggestion) was steeped in prejudice, and why she should—and could—go on to college right after high school.

In conclusion, I threw out my ace: "I brought the subject up because the pizza celebration made me concerned about your future," I wrote. "However, the idea of steering you toward college was your brother's. Vince asked me to do it just before he left."

I read it over and over, patting myself on the back each time, and then sealed the envelope and fell into a deep and satisfied sleep.

With a taciturn coolness we exchanged missives as usual at Mongon's the next morning. I made the mistake of reading hers on my way to work.

> *You're not the first college boy who's worked a summer at Kelso. The others, they've each blessed a local girl with attention and then vanished forever on Labor Day. I knew what I was getting into. But it's been worth it—a once-in-a-lifetime moment.*

I slumped down on a bench outside the factory and kept reading.

> *You're different from me. . . . You started out different. You are going to end up different. I've always known that, and if you haven't, then you haven't been thinking. Fallsville's a place the Rodney Binghams only visit once and the Marcella Parmacellas never leave.*
>
> *Don't you see? Our paths have crossed for this one short period. For a few months, we've had the chance to be the same and to share it. What we've found has been magical. Don't ruin it by pressuring me with thoughts of college, by pretending you could ever become a part of my world or I yours.*
>
> *Marci*

In a daze, I walked back to Mrs. Stompous's house, borrowed her telephone, and called in sick at the plant. I then went to my room and sat down on the bed, feeling my foundation crumble. She was right. I hadn't been thinking—not even about the obvious fact that the summer would end.

Why?

Because then *I* would end—at least this new me I had convinced everyone I was. I would have to go back to them—the tormenters.

No, even now I could not bear to think about that. I shook my head and pushed the thought away, out of my mind. I felt pain welling up inside. Was that all I was to Marci, I asked the overhead light bulb, the summer "college boy"?

In the end, it was Vince Parmacella who gave me the strength to rise from the ashes. I had made a commitment. I had promised him. I would fulfill that promise. I got up, got into my car, and drove out of town in search of a bookstore.

I bought an *SAT College Board Directory* and sat down to read it, searching for colleges in the vicinity. It did not surprise me that Bointon College, the one Marci had mentioned, was not accredited, but it pleased me greatly.

By eight o'clock that night, I had visited four nearby institutions of higher learning, inquired as to available scholarships, and determined which one Marcella Parmacella would be attending.

The lights were on when I got to Mongon's. Marci was sitting on a chair by the sink staring into space. She jumped up when she saw me and rushed over to the counter. "They said you called in sick."

"Yup."

"How come?"

"I had work to do." I clomped all the materials I had picked up on top of the counter and sat down on a stool.

She put her hand on mine. "I'm sorry. What you said in your letter about Vince—you were right."

"This is the college entrance examination book." I pulled my hand away and held up the tome. "It has samples of questions from college board exams so you can test yourself, get prepared."

Her eyes searched my face. "I hurt your feelings. That stuff in my letter about how—"

"It has samples of vocabulary words too. Your vocabulary is pretty strong—from all your reading—but you should check the list, learn the words you don't know."

213

"I knew as soon as I read your letter I shouldn't have written mine. It was just . . . You made me feel like such a hick."

I pulled out a pamphlet. "This is Seaton College."

"I went to the plant at lunchbreak, to tell you not to read the letter, and when they said you'd called in sick, I—"

"Can I tell you about Seaton College?"

She nodded.

"It's brand-new, only two years old. It's over in Collier, just a twenty-minute drive from here. It's been endowed heavily by a few corporations that have set up nearby. The corporations are interested in developing a local research facility, see, and the college is already benefiting from that. It has a broad curriculum, what seems to be a strong staff, and . . ." I looked at her smugly. "They're interested in having you."

She raised an eyebrow. "Who says?"

"The director of admissions. I talked to him."

"You talked to him? Just like that?"

"Yup. His name is Kirk Dorchester. He's a really nice guy. He said he went to college with a teacher at Fallsville High . . ." I checked my notes. "Emily Samson."

"Miss Samson," she gasped. "My English teacher!"

"He says a recommendation from her would mean a lot."

She stood there hugging herself, excited but hesitant.

"They not only have scholarships at Seaton," I pushed. "Several of the faculty members offer room and board to students in return for baby-sitting. That way, see, if you wanted to, you could stay there during the week and come home for weekends."

She started perusing the Seaton pamphlet.

"I could take you there to see for yourself," I said, and she dropped the pamphlet. "Okay, okay. Just say you'll think about it."

"I'll think about it." She looked at me lovingly. "Thank you. My letter . . . I'm sorry. Really I am. I think I was just trying to prepare myself, you know."

My jaw clenched. I swallowed. "I am not walking out of your life in September, Marci."

"You don't have to pretend." She was trembling. "I'm just saying I can take it. I'm strong."

"Well, I'm not strong. I—" They were all there bubbling up, ready to come out, all the words that would let her know, in detail, what a messed-up creep I was. I clamped my mouth shut, certain that if I let the words out, I'd lose her. My eyes filled with tears. I slammed them shut too.

I felt her hands cradling my face. "Oh, Rod, I'm so sorry," she whispered. She kissed my eyelids. "Forget what I wrote. Please?" I could tell by her voice that she was crying. "Could you just forget it?"

I nodded my head, and I forgot it—just like that. I pushed it out of my mind, and locked it away, off-limits, along with all the other mental baggage I could not bear to contemplate.

22

Everyone called B. J. Courbienne "B.J."—everyone at his company, from the day laborers and typists and coffee girls up to the salesmen and engineers. No matter that he was the chief executive officer of Courbienne Enterprises, the biggest development firm in the county, he found "mister" out of the question, "sir" downright blasphemous.

The appellation extended beyond company headquarters. All of Collier, Massachusetts, from its elected officials down to its common citizenry—business leaders and garbage men, long-time friends and total strangers—everyone who knew the man walked right up to him and addressed him as "B.J."

"The doctor can see you now, B.J." . . . "Your car's ready, B.J." . . . "You don't know me, B.J., but I live over on Cranberry Street and . . ."

"I like the democratizing effect it has," B. J. Courbienne had once confided pompously to his daughter-in-law.

"Not to mention the celebrity status," Marci had retorted.

"That too!" he had guffawed, happily letting out all the pretension. "That too!"

Anonymity was anathema to B. J. Courbienne.

Thus, when B.J. suggested, for a "change of pace," they bypass his regular haunt and meet for lunch instead at La Petite Fontaine, Collier's brand-new French restaurant, Marci guessed it was so B.J. could make himself known to the newest entrepreneur in town. And when she arrived and found the owner, Jacques Soulanger, waiting for her at the door, anxious to direct her personally to "Monsieur Bee Shay's table," she was not the least surprised.

Nor was she surprised at the table's location: front and center in the large main room. B.J. loved to see and be seen, and welcomed casual drop-bys during the meal. He was chatting with Frank Simmons, the president of Collier's main bank, when Jacques Soulanger and Marci arrived at the table.

"How're ya doin', darlin'?" B.J. asked as he hugged her. He was wearing a handsome gray worsted suit and white pinpoint oxford shirt (Priscilla dressed him exquisitely) with an outrageously loud red-and-white checked tie (he always added a touch of his own). "Frank, you know my beautiful daughter-in-law."

"Sure do!" Simmons pumped her hand. "Nice to see you, Marci."

"See you've met Jock, here," B.J. stage-whispered, acknowledging Marci's personal escort. "He's sure turned this into a beautiful place, hasn't he? Beautiful place!"

"*Ah, merci.*" Jacques bowed grandly as he pulled out a chair for Marci. "*Soyez les bienvenus, Monsieur Bee Shay!*"

"Yeah, well, thank you, Jock." B.J. sat back down in his chair. "Thanks a lot."

"*Bon appetit!*"

"I hate it when they spout out all that French stuff," B.J. grumbled sotto voce, opening his menu.

"Be fair," Marci laughed. "It *is* a French restaurant!"

"Located in the U S of A," B.J. said pointedly. " 'S one thing to feed you French. Another to talk to you in French."

"He probably thinks you understood," Marci offered. "Courbienne is, after all, a French name."

"Was." B.J. leaned across the table. "Truth is, only Courbienne I knew who spoke French was my great-grandmother, and we were never sure if she was talking or just hallucinating!" He bellowed out a laugh as he signaled a waiter. "How about a glass of white wine, Marci?"

"Fine."

"One white wine, one scotch on the rocks," he told the waiter.

There were a few more drop-bys before the drinks came: two subcontractors, B.J.'s dentist, and a jeweler who owned one of the stores in B.J.'s shopping center.

Marci and B.J. had lunch together every other Tuesday and the lunches had, over the years, developed a consistent pattern. First there was what Marci called the reception period: short chitchats at tableside with familiar faces. Then came the family agenda. B.J. kept in close telephone contact with his grandchildren and those conversations inspired either funny anecdotes or topics of concern, which he shared with Marci. Today's subject fit into the concern category. Tommy had gotten a speeding ticket.

"Didn't need police verification," B.J. grumbled into his scotch on the rocks. "Just riding with him a couple of times was enough for me, Marci. The kid drives like a bat out of hell!"

Sometimes she soothed away B.J.'s concerns, but in cases like this one—when she felt the concern was not only justified, but one she shared—she welcomed his input. He was the "other parent" in her children's lives, the only person as intricately involved in their ups and downs as she, and she welcomed—counted on—his participation. They decided B.J. would have a long talk with Tommy.

That brought them to her favorite part of the lunch, the let-it-all-hang out period, when all the formalities were finished and B.J. had imbibed enough scotch to loosen up and let go with whatever was on his mind.

Sometimes they ended up fighting ferociously. Sometimes they had long, serious discussions on problems one of them was facing. Sometimes they just had a good laugh. But the outcome was almost always satisfying to Marci because it was the only time her father-in-law let his public and family personas fade and his real feelings show.

"I'm gonna have this sausage-pasta thing," he told the waiter, closing the menu.

"I'll have the luncheon salad," Marci said.

"Now remember—" B.J. began, leaning forward.

"I know, I know," Marci laughed. "If Priscilla asks, I'll tell her *you* had the salad and *I* had the sausage!"

"Not that it matters." B.J. sighed. "Swear to God, honey, all my sins are catching up with me. Got a cholesterol level higher than

218

Tommy's S.A.T. scores! Got a weight a Sumo wrestler'd envy, and I'm sure my liver is down there just begging for relief."

His blue eyes gleamed, energized by her laughter.

"Way I figure, all my organs are engaging in this internal dialogue, see, fighting over which one gets to go first. 'C'mon, let me kill him!' pleads my heart. 'He's done me wrong for decades now!' 'Naw, let me give out first,' screeches my lungs. 'Ole asshole still sneaks cigars whenever Priscilla's not around.' " He waved his hand in the air dramatically and then stopped suddenly, cringing. "Bursitis has been killin' me all week too," he mumbled, rubbing his shoulder. "I'm a mess."

"No," Marci said softly. "You're just going through a little period of adjustment."

"Meaning?"

"You're upset about turning seventy." She reached over and squeezed his hand. "It's perfectly normal."

"Says Miss Expert!" he snarled, pulling his hand away. "Miss Thirty-Eight-Year-Old Expert at that! You're telling me—what?— I'm going through a midlife crisis all over again?"

"In a way."

"*End*-of-life crisis, then! You got it! And what follows this one, honey? The great abyss?"

"Not for a long time," Marci laughed. "Once you get over the crisis-feeling part, chances are you'll have plenty of end-of-life productive years left."

B.J. laughed. Then he sipped his scotch and jiggled the ice cubes around for a while. He ran his tongue along the inside of his cheek.

Marci watched him with a growing uneasiness. Something was coming, something important.

He looked up at her suddenly. "Would you have married Tom if I hadn't offered to pay for your college?"

Marci shook her head in jerky motions, as though she were trying to get rid of something rattling around inside. "Why, B.J.? Why, all of a sudden, are you bringing up something like that?"

"Turning seventy." He shrugged. "Oh, you're right, just facing the birthday and all, it gives you pause, makes you think. Find yourself going back over all the twists and turns that've happened in your life. Your entrance into my family, that was one hell of a pivotal change. Something I'm so grateful for—"

"Then why are you acting as though I were an investment? As though what we have between us is some kind of financial return?" She felt her face get hot. "I married your son. I wasn't *bought!*"

B.J. leaned across the table. "Would you have married Tom if I hadn't offered to pay for your college?"

"I had a full scholarship to college," Marci corrected. "What you paid for was the income I needed at that time to help my family out financially so I could continue *going* to college."

"You're avoiding the question!"

"And the offer was broader." Marci lifted her wineglass with a trembling hand. "It was for the last two years of college—then law school."

"Old fart's prerogative—the right to forget details. Your answer?"

She took a sip of wine. "I would have waited. Would have finished college first."

"With what? Your dad had lost his job. Your family—"

"I would have found a way." She shrugged. "Millions of people work their way through college."

"Would have taken you a long time. You might have found someone else to marry by the time you were finished."

"That's not giving your son much credit in the girl-winning department!"

His eyes were bearing down on her. "I give my son all kinds of credit. He was one hell of an operator. Bright. Hard-working. Driven, verging on ruthless. But I'm not sure he had as much going for him in the girl-winning department."

Marci looked around at the other tables, as though she were searching for help. "I can't believe we're having this conversation." She turned on B.J., her eyes flashing. "Whose idea was the financial offer? Yours or your son's?"

"His. Tom wanted you. Always wanted you. And he was mighty good at figuring out how to get what he wanted."

Her eyes filled with tears. "Why now, B.J.? Why bring it up now? After all these years?"

He reached out and squeezed her arm. "Not to stick a wedge between us, that's for sure." His eyes radiated alarm. "Because I love

220

you, love you like my own child. Because you're the only person in the world I am completely honest with. Because, oh, well, maybe because turning seventy and all, I wanted to clear up a few things—to have that question answered."

She played with her napkin. "I still haven't answered it."

"Yes, you have, darlin'." B.J. leaned back in his chair and sighed sadly. "Yes, you have."

23

1968   Durone sauntered over to my locker while I was changing for the morning shift. "Don't tell me the end," he whispered. "Just tell me one thing, okay?"

The line was delivered in Duronesque fashion: It filtered over his shoulder from the corner of his mouth. His back was to me, his eyes darting around the room like a man with a gun surveying the group he was holding at bay to make sure none of them had a concealed weapon.

"The end of what, Sallie?"

"Shh! The book you lent me, asshole! All I wanna know is—does the green vase figure in the murder?"

I devoured cheap murder mysteries much the way I devoured hamburgers and fries: They went down pleasantly, but left me with few lingering memories. "The green vase? Gee, Sallie, I don't remember."

He looked at me aghast. "How the fuck c'n you read a book and not remember?"

The next day he ambled up all smiles. "Green vase was the big clue! Old Sallie guessed it right away!" He whomped me on the back and handed me my book. "Got any more? Mysteries, man. Like them mysteries."

Within a week, he had gone through my small windowsill collection of sleazy mystery stories, and I was borrowing books from Marci, just to keep him supplied.

Sallie Durone was a talker. He sat at lunch break each day going on and on in a rambling monologue as his gang of regulars—Lucky, Slime, Cripple, and Tooth—sat around him, eating and breaking into his scenario every so often with such poignant remarks as " 'At right, Sallie?"

Now, suddenly, the subject matter changed, from broads and trucks, his old favorites, to books. "This cat Sam Sloan, he's a private detective, see, real cool. Drives a fancy car, has loadsa chicks hangin' all over 'im."

" 'At right, Sallie?"

Score one for leadership potential. Durone started to prefer reading at lunch to listening to himself talk, and soon there was no talk at all. Lucky, Slime, Cripple, and Tooth were sitting at Durone's side eating their sandwiches and pouring laboriously through pages of books retrieved from my windowsill collection and "lent" to them by Sallie Durone. The rule was, they only got books he had finished. Durone didn't want his boys getting ahead of him. As a result, it took a while before there were enough books to go around. Then the ready supply increased faster than demand. Durone kept reading and reading, but I don't think any of his boys ever made it through their first attempt.

The message went out loud and clear, though: Sallie Durone liked book talk even more than he liked to hear the boys tell him how strong and sharp he was. The lunch break banter changed accordingly.

"I like this guy, Vic Thomas," Cripple would say, glancing up at Durone from page three.

"Keep readin', Crip," Durone would respond with his wolflike grin. "Betcha change yah mind!"

Hard-on and I sat off to the side, as we always did, taking in the scene: five neanderthals reading books, four of them silently mouthing the words as their eyes plodded down the page.

Hard-on and I always sat together. We talked while we ate—usually about me. Asking questions came easier to Hard-on than answering, and he kept the dialogue going through the ten minutes it took each day to consume our sandwiches with such exciting repartee as "Why?" "When?" "How?"

It was amazing how much he managed to pull out of me about myself with this technique. Five straight "Why?"'s and before I knew it, I was going on and on about current events or dormitory life at Harvard. Talking to Hard-on was rather like talking to myself, and I'd done that all my life.

His attention span only lasted as long as his sandwich. After that, Hard-on went back into training. He usually brought a tennis ball in his lunch box, along with a manual on some scintillating subject like "pipes," or "handling concrete slabs." As soon as the food was eaten, he began reading—one hand holding the book, the other squeezing the tennis ball, and then he'd switch after a while. I have no idea what squeezing the tennis ball did for which muscles, although I'm certain he explained it to me at length. I was not as good a listener as he.

I could tell Hard-on got as much of a kick out of the emerging Durone literary circle as I did, although it was not from anything he said. Hard-on and I communicated mostly by exchanging significant glances at appropriate moments. His eyes bespoke his intelligence, sending me signals that he understood a subtlety that was lost on the others. Communication was not his strong suit, but he was a thinker. Every so often he would come out with a remark—six words maximum—that made me realize he had been astutely observing all that was going on.

The best way to describe Hard-on was "positively passive." To be honest, I guess my reaction to him was largely an ego response: I liked him because he seemed to like me. But I liked him a lot.

The "bookworm" was diligently forging ahead in arithmetic too. Every morning before work I snuck around to Durone's truck, removed the previous day's completed assignment, and put a new sheet of math problems under the front seat. Each sheet came back a hundred percent accurate, and, according to the time calculations he put in the upper-right-hand corner, he was completing the assignments in less and less time. Einstein was ready for the big pretest exam.

We stopped to pick up some cold beer ("Gotta feelin' we gonna be celebratin', Golden Boy!") and drove off in his truck, but Sal headed in a new direction. "Gonna check out some property," he explained.

We pulled off the road I'd taken on my education-exploration trip for Marci and parked at the base of a steep incline of rocks and bushes.

"Bigger Hill," he announced, staring up the incline. " 'At's what we always called it." He picked up the brown paper bag and began climbing. "Bigger 'n what, I dunno," he mumbled to himself.

Grabbing my book and the four pages of math problems I'd worked out, I followed him up, over rocks and through dense vegetation to a clearing near the crest of the hill. I couldn't tell whether my breathing difficulties came from the strenuous trek or the suffocatingly damp, earthy pungency of the air.

He slumped down on a rock when we got to the top and pulled out a pencil. "Hit me with it, Smarts! I'm ready!"

I read my book while he worked on the test. He whipped though it all in record time and tossed the pages in my direction. He was beaming when I finished checking his answers. "All right—right?"

"Right."

Cheering himself loudly, he pulled out two cans of beer, handed me one, and raised his. "To Smarts—from Gettin' Smarter!"

I looked at him in shock. "That's clever, Sallie!"

"Ain't it?" He cackled, savoring his brilliance. Lying down on his back, he stared contentedly up into the trees.

Still amused by the witty toast, I reminded myself that Durone was filled with surprises. "Sal, how come you have a book on shopping centers in your truck?"

He frowned suspiciously.

"It's right there under the front seat where I've been leaving the math problems. Couldn't help but see it!"

The frown disappeared and he got a dreamy expression on his face. "Saw this shopping center when I had to take my ole lady to Beardsley last year. Amazing." He sat up. "See, what they did is, they put all these stores, together like, with a huge parking lot all 'round 'em. Gotta place you c'd see a movie, even. Liquor store, candy store, groceries, clothes, *everything*, all put together out in the open like that, so's everything you want's in one place!"

It was as though he had just visited NASA's space center and

225

was marveling over the technology. I bit my lip to keep from laughing.

He seemed to intuit my lack of enthusiasm. "Yah, well, 'at's why I got me a book." He lay back down.

"How come we're up here, Sal?"

He sat up again. "Got a cousin, works on roads. He says his supervisor been told to figure costs for five different places in Orange County to put the freeway." His eyes squinted as they roamed to the right. "Over there's one of the places."

"Why would they put it there?"

"This town's Collier. Used to be the biggest town in Orange County. Now it's the poorest. Justa buncha down-'n-outers. Ain't no one in alla Orange County wants a freeway, but folks in Collier, I figure they got less say, see?"

I took another swig of beer. "Why build a freeway if no one wants one?"

"Boston people want one. They want a four-lane truck route up to New England."

The name Collier registered. I realized Durone's down-and-out Collier was Seaton College's up-and-coming Collier, and that the corporations endowing Marci's college-to-be were probably the new scientific facilities Durone had complained about the night he'd come to my room. "There's another reason to put it through Collier, Sallie. Those research facilities—the ones you said had no jobs for you? I bet they'd be interested in a fast route down to Boston."

He gurgled a laugh. "Ole Smarts, *he's* gettin' smarter too!" His eyes roamed through the trees to the flat farmland down on the other side of Route 190, the road we had arrived on. " 'At's what I wanna buy. Farmer's name is Fio Marconi. He 'n his wife'r pretty old, farmin' the land alone, since their kids left a long time ago. You can see jus' by lookin', place's a mess. All dried out, not many crops. Figure they're gettin' tired a farmin'." He turned to me. "Whatcha think?"

"Do you know them?"

He stared down at the land with an intensity that made me glad I wasn't Fio Marconi. "Gonna *get* to know 'em."

The game plan was to sell off all his small land holdings around Orange County and offer the money to Fio Marconi in return for the ten acres of Marconi's farm that faced Route 190. Durone was sure he could get the deal signed before he went to Vietnam, and then come home a hero—with a substantial real-estate investment.

"Then what?" I asked. "Say your hunch pays off and they do put the freeway up there, what will you do with the land? Sell it off to the highest bidder?"

His eyes were darting around the farmland, like an interior decorator plotting a room layout—the sofa here, the coffee table there, the armchair over in the corner. I gazed down at the land trying to figure out what he was doing. Finally it came to me. "A shopping center!" I whispered. "You want to put a shopping center down there!"

It was the first time I'd ever seen Durone embarrassed. He looked like a child with a dream, unwilling to share it for fear of being ridiculed.

"Why not, Sal? I mean, you'll have all these newcomer types— the research facility people. And you have that freeway up there, bringing in—"

"An area of population growth with a high per-capita expenditure rate and proximity to a major highway." He said it like a student who'd memorized a difficult passage in Latin. He shifted from foot to foot. " 'At's what the shoppin' center book says you gotta have." He turned to me. " 'At 'per-capita' shit, it means rich people, right?"

"Right."

His eyes gleamed. "A feeder road. Says you gotta have a feeder road too." His eyes caressed Route 190. He opened a new can of beer and sighed as he looked at the land across the road. "A waterfall." He smiled. "I'm seein' a waterfall."

"A what?"

"At the Beardsley one, right in the middle of the shopping center was a fountain with water shootin' outa it, shootin' real high, and then fallin' down." He drank some beer. "Don't think I ever seen nothin' that nice. Real classy."

We were both thoroughly soused by the time we got back into the truck, laughing and rolling with the curves, which Durone was riding at high speed.

When we got to Mrs. Stompous's he became serious. "You

227

can't go tellin' Big Mouth, Smarts. Fio Marconi's her mother's cousin. She'll blow the whole thing!"

"*Marci*, Sallie. Call her Marci!"

He fixed his eyes on mine. "Don't tell Marci."

"I won't."

He tapped his knuckles against the steering wheel. "Y'always say that, but y'always tell her."

I whirled around.

"Smarts, the guys all know about the tutorin'."

"How?"

"From her! How else? Word I got is she told 'em!" His eyes beseeched mine. "The broad can't keep her mouth shut, never could! All her life, she never could! I been tellin' you that all this time, but you don't listen."

I felt suddenly sober.

"Hey, kid, look, I know, I told you before I'd beat you up if you told her. Well, 'at was before. Ain't gonna beat you up. Never. Hell, you're . . . you're my *buddy*. Just . . . Fuck, man, she'd blow it for me!"

"I won't tell her. I give you my word I won't." I got out and slammed the door, but then leaned through the opened window. "I want to do one thing, though."

"Whazzat?"

"I told her about the tutoring only because I tell her everything. I, um, I'm in love with her." It was more like an apology for an affliction than a statement. "All I'm saying is, if she did tell the guys, then she betrayed me too. I'd like to confront her—tell her what you just told me. Have it out with her. Is that okay?"

"Yeah."

After Sal left, I wrote a long and angrily accusing letter to Marci. I taped it to the front door of Mongon's the next morning, before she got to work.

She ignored me when I arrived at Mongon's that night. I buried my face in a newspaper. The Soviet Union and East Germany were both increasing tanks and aircraft on their Czech borders, and a confrontation between the Soviet and Czech Communist parties was scheduled to take place at the end of the week in the Czech city of Cierna.

As the gang started filing out, I sensed my own "Cierna confrontation" was about to happen.

She came at me, her cheeks inflamed, her mouth hardened and distorted. "I *told* you I would not tell anyone," she said through clenched teeth as she slapped her hand down on the counter in front of me. "How dare you take the word of that creep over mine? When I tell you something, I mean it!"

"But—"

"Nothing!" Her arms flailed out in all directions. "To anyone! Ever!" She whirled around and began frenetically performing make-do work at the sink, rerinsing glasses she had already placed on the drying rack.

I wanted to bow out, to forget it, but we'd always been completely honest with each other. "How did they all find out, then?"

"That's not the issue," she told the sink. "The issue is trust. If you can't trust me, what have we got?"

It was a point I'd tried to make in my letter to her, but the way she said it was so final it scared me.

"The issue is your trusting me," she went on. "Believing in me! Standing up for me enough to place my promise not to tell above Sallie's accusation!"

Well, that was the issue, all right. Absolutely. The problem was, I was still pretty certain she'd blabbed it out. I felt both guilty about not defending her, and guilty about still distrusting her.

"How many days have the two of you been exchanging math papers under the front seat of Durone's truck?" she asked the sink. "In the parking lot, which is in clear view from inside the factory, from the windows in the locker room, for example."

"Sixteen, seventeen days, I guess."

She whirled around. "And isn't it just possible that in those sixteen days of secret exchanges, the other guys noticed?" She was strutting toward me, her hands on her hips, her words carefully measured out to match the pace of her steps. "Isn't it just *possible* that they noticed enough to perk up their curiosity? That one of them maybe went out to Durone's truck during a break and looked?"

"And what did he find?" I demanded, anxious for a show of strength. "A paper filled with math problems! How would he have been able to figure out from that what Durone was studying for?"

She stared deep into my eyes and I despaired, terrified of her proven discerning capabilities. Then she squinted. "Did Durone say they knew about the draft test?" she asked. "Or just the tutoring?"

I didn't remember.

"I mean, he didn't say, 'Cripple told me' or 'Slime said.' He didn't even mention my accuser by name! It was very general. 'The word I got,' he said. That means it was secondhand, thirdhand, or—worse yet—Sal Durone's interpretation of some rumor going around the locker room!" Her eyes were brimming with tears.

I felt a pang, a need to make her feel better. "Well, maybe—"

"And that little hint," she cried, "that . . . that suggestion. That was all it took for you to take his side against me!"

I started to defend myself, but then stopped. What the hell was I doing? This was, I reminded myself, an argument I did not want to win—one, in fact, I desperately wanted to lose. "I'm sorry."

"Sorry, but not convinced." She stood before me, dripping tears, hand on hip.

I cursed myself for writing the stupid letter. "Oh, Marci . . ." I reached out for her, but she backed away.

"Convinced!" I shouted, an octave higher than I'd intended. I cleared my throat. "Convinced," I repeated, this time sounding more like a man in control, but feeling less and less like one. "It was just—oh, you know Durone. I guess he kind of bullied me into it." I picked up my glass and raced to the other side of the counter, anxious to get clean-up done as quickly as possible, wanting her back, wanting "us" back.

I was greeted at the sink by sympathetic, velvety brown eyes. "Sallie Durone's just a big bully, Rod." Her fingers stroked my cheek. I nibbled on them when they meandered on down to my lips. "There's no reason for you to fear him the way you do."

For fifteen minutes, she dumped on Sal Durone and I concurred, even trashing my brand-new friend a little on my own in my desire to smooth things over. A serious conscience check might have revealed both guilt over doing him in and the conviction—still—that Durone, not Marci, was telling the truth, but the heat flashing through my body put off all thoughts of a conscience check. Durone's "final exam" had made me lose out on one whole night in the cave. I was an addict, overwhelmed by my craving.

Besides, who cared whether she'd kept the tutoring a secret? Calling her on it had undoubtedly set things straight. She would not betray my confidence again.

Eastern Europe gradually edged out Durone as our conversation topic. What would happen when the entire Politburo of the Soviet Communist Party took on the Presidium of the Czechoslovak Communist Party in Cierna? We pondered the possibilities. Would Dubcek give in at Cierna? Would he stand firm and be blasted away by Soviet troops? Was it possible he could convince the Russians to leave him alone?

It was a strange scene: political talk with strange electric undercurrents. Marci seemed to be feeling it too. We began drying dishes with the same towel, so our hands would touch . . . reaching around each other to put things away, and rubbing a little in the process. When I picked up a napkin from the floor by her foot, I dragged my hand against the back of her leg, and we held the same glass under the warm water, our fingers entwined.

As a result, clean-up took a very long time, and when it ended, I was explosive, filled with a lust that was driving me crazy. When I looked at my watch and realized how late it was, I went bananas.

We never made it to the cave. I pulled off the road about two blocks from Mongon's. "Come here," I moaned, moving over to her side of the front seat," right now. Oh, please, Marci, right now."

"Yes," she begged back, pulling me down on top of her, running her hands up under my shirt.

We scrambled around my car, first in the front seat, then in the backseat, unable to find enough space in either location, unzipping, unbuttoning . . . then groping and groaning, whispering "I'm sorry"s along the way, impassioned but frantic—more than frantic: out and out desperate. There was simply not enough time.

We were still breathing heavily when I drove her home. Our clothes were rumpled, our bodies drenched in sweat, unsatisfied. We clung to each other in the car in front of her house, kissing, fondling, burning hotter and hotter, until we heard the familiar curfew cough from her father on the front porch.

"Coming, Papa!" she shouted casually, but she turned back to me instead of getting out of the car. We kissed and it went on and on and on, this hungry mixture of sucking and rubbing and wanting . . . until her father coughed again, and, whimpering a little, she hopped out of the car and ran up the front steps.

I yearned. I ached. I felt as though I was about to self-destruct. I parked my car and sprinted a lap around the block, hoping to dissipate some of the longing.

24

Marci Courbienne stared into space, seeing herself thirty years younger, her hair in pigtails, standing in front of her house, waiting for the most exciting thing that happened on Friday mornings in Fallsville in those days, the arrival of the big silver bullet of a truck with the name TONIKKER scrawled in huge black letters across the top.

She smiled as the image faded, pulled the folder marked "Salvatore Durone" out of the second drawer, and carried it back to her desk. The folder had become very thick in recent days.

She sat down and began going through the papers inside—the retainer agreement that would soon bear Francine's signature, the list of medical experts who could document the proven link between exposure to vinyl chloride and angiosarcoma of the liver, the former coworkers who could describe the details of Durone's job, the occupational health specialists to explain the exposure levels that came with that job.

Marci had done her homework. She was ready, a primed athlete rechecking the game plan as she awaited the nod from the coach that would send her out onto the field. The athletic image made her laugh a little.

"What's so funny?" It was Jack Whelan standing in the doorway.

"My, my," she clucked. "You didn't waste any time, did you?"

"Let's just say I was concerned about your well-being." He walked in and closed the door. "You sounded as if you'd pop a blood vessel if I took more than five minutes!" He sat down on the chair across from her.

"So?" Whelan put his hands firmly on her desktop and leaned toward her, conspirator-to-conspirator. *"Kelso."*

She fell back in her chair and exhaled, closing her eyes. "Yes."

Whelan put on his bifocals and pulled a piece of paper out of his coat pocket. "In Nineteen fifty-five, Tapron Industries set up a factory in Fallsville, Massachusetts, to produce infant pacifiers from polyvinyl-chloride plastic," he read. "The Fallsville plant was called Kelso after Tapron's executive director, James Kelsey. Kelsey's son, Sean, managed the Fallsville plant."

She shot him a look of unbridled affection. "Viva organized labor!"

"The Kelso plant not only produced pacifiers from polyvinyl-chloride plastic," Whelan continued matter-of-factly. "It also made the plastic in the first place."

"I thought so, but I wasn't sure!" She said, jumping out of her chair and walking around the room.

"To produce polyvinyl-chloride, vinyl-chloride gas is piped into large reactor vessels, where it is agitated together with a liquid and catalysts. The process causes something they call 'polymerization.' " He looked up from the paper. "It links together the molecules of the gas into long chains that give the plastic its strength."

"Where'd you get that information?"

"Company records. Tapron's process and procedures manuals go way back. My boys did a little clandestine research. This is a page Xeroxed from a company book and faxed to me." He handed it to her.

She kissed the paper and placed it inside the Durone folder.

He leaned toward her. "Baby, from what the union steward in Atlanta tells me, if Durone was one of the guys that cleaned out the reactor, you got it made."

She bent down. "Baby," she whispered in his ear, "we got it made!"

"No shit! He was a cleaner?"

"For *twelve* years he was a cleaner. Started when he was only

233

twelve. Told them he was eighteen and they believed him, or at least pretended to believe him."

"Why?"

"It was a dirty job. They had trouble finding people who wanted to do it. Also, according to one of his foremen, Durone was the best cleaner they ever had. Real fast, that's what the foreman said."

"Not fast enough." Whelan sighed. "You know what they did? The cleaners?"

Marci shrugged. "Cleaned the tubs, that's all I know."

"That's on the sheet too. They crawled inside the reactors after each batch of polyvinyl-chloride was drained off and chipped away at the congealed stuff." He winced. "According to the guys in Atlanta, they inhaled fumes that were *five hundred* times the limits finally set for worker exposure fifteen years ago, after the government found out how lethal the stuff was." Whelan pointed a finger at her. "Even with those limits, employers gotta tell vinyl-chloride workers today that they're working with a potential cancer-causer! Didn't have to then."

Marci walked around the room. "Was Tapron under any obligation to inform prior employees," she asked, "after the medical details came out?"

"Nope. The labor movement tried to get a law through Congress a few years ago that would have made such warnings for past exposure mandatory, but it didn't pass."

"What about your boys?" she asked skeptically. "Where was the union when Durone was inhaling potent whiffs of vinyl chloride?"

"Locked out, that's where! We only succeeded in organizing Tapron two years ago. The company insists it has no employee rosters before Nineteen seventy-five, the year the standards went into effect. All the plants Tapron operates today are carefully monitored for exposure."

"Pacifiers." She shook her head slowly as she looked out the window. "Who would think babies' pacifiers could prove lethal?"

"The final product wasn't dangerous. Just the process. And even then, it takes fifteen to twenty years for the cancer to develop." He turned to Marci. "When exactly did Durone work at Kelso?"

"Nineteen fifty-six to Nineteen sixty-eight."

234

"Twelve years' exposure, more than twenty years ago." Whelan nodded. "The timing's right!"

"Legally, I'm afraid I'm a little over my head on this one. I haven't had much experience in toxic tort litigation. It requires putting on medical expert testimony, cross-examining, proving causation. To do it right, I'd need to to gain access to some of the large data bases so I could get familiar with the epidemiological studies . . ."

"So you're saying what?" Whelan interrupted irritably. "You're not going to do it?"

"No! I've just decided I'd like to work with Jake Dworcek on this case. What do you think?"

"Perfect." Whelan relaxed. "I was going to suggest him. He's the best."

"I have a lunch date set up with Jake tomorrow to discuss it."

"How many people are involved?"

"Don't know for sure. There's Leonard Lucinski, Durone's friend. Lucinski was a cleaner too, and he died of the same illness." She held up a hand. "Supposedly. I haven't checked it out yet. Plus there's at least one other cleaner I've heard about who died a few years ago of 'liver disease.' "

"Sounds suspicious."

"Yes, but I've got to get it all nailed down. A quick hit, that's what I'm aiming for. As much as I can get for the Durones as swiftly as possible."

"Dworcek should be a real help. He's up on the case law and has all kinds of computerized data on this stuff right at his fingertips."

She nodded, jotting down a few notes.

"Tapron's gonna go nuts when you sue them," he cackled. "From what I hear—"

"We're not going to sue Tapron." She kept scribbling.

"But then why was I asked to check out Tapron? To discover the link between Tapron and Kelso?"

"You did more than discover the link! You did what I thought you would—come up with the details of the process that suggest Kelso was where Durone got his cancer. Do you realize that no one I've interviewed who worked at Kelso had any idea what they were working with? 'We pumped the stuff in,' a former foreman told me,

235

'mixed it with the stuff in the vats, tested it, worked it into bricks, and took it down to the machine room.'

" 'What stuff?' I asked. 'Dunno.' "

Whelan frowned. "Durone knew, didn't he?"

"The doctor told him about vinyl chloride. But it wasn't until he went over his employment history with your friend Bill Blaine that he figured out where he'd worked with it. From the articles in his files on vinyl chloride, I suspected it was probably Kelso, but I needed you to make sure."

"You're sure Kelso was the only place?"

"Yes. I've since gotten a list of his other jobs. None had anything to do with vinyl chloride."

"But you said Durone fingered Tapron. All those phone calls, all the information. Don't you think Durone planned on suing Tapron?"

She gave Whelan a haughty look. "Only because he hadn't consulted a lawyer. If we sued Tapron all we could hope to recover is workman's compensation benefits. I want more. I wasn't sure until you confirmed the fact that there were two processes in operation at the plant—that they made the plastic, and then used it to produce pacifiers."

He waited patiently for the punchline and then gave up when none was forthcoming. "You lost me, sweetheart. I repeat: *Who* are you going to sue?"

"The company that provided the vinyl-chloride gas! *That* was the raw material. *That* was the toxic substance. Under strict liability, the supplier is responsible for what his product does, not the company that uses it for manufacture."

Whelan slumped in his chair, confused.

Marci went on enthusiastically, "I've done some checking around. You know, looking over similar toxic injury cases? In asbestos cases, plant workers injured by contact with asbestos who were employed by companies making asbestos-containing insulation have been successful in pursuing claims against the companies that mined raw asbestos—the companies who supplied the fiber the workers turned into finished products."

"Listen to her! Some 'total novice'!" He beamed. "So, what's the plan? You're going to get Tapron to give you the name of the vinyl-chloride supplier, as part of discovery?"

She closed her eyes, calling up the image of herself in pigtails watching a great big silver bullet of a truck driving over the hill near her house en route to the Kelso plant. "I don't need to. Tonikker," she said. "It's T-o-n-i-k-k-e-r."

25

1968   I was awakened from a deep sleep by a cold finger pressed against my lips. "Shh," she whispered.

I jumped and then scrambled up on my elbow, blinking. The room was night-dark. "Marci?"

"Nah." She giggled, kissing my nose. "It's Mrs. Stompous."

"What's wrong?" It came out in a squeak-whisper.

"Nothing," she whispered back. "Everything's right! That's what I came to tell you!"

I sat up in bed, rubbing my eyes. "But it's the middle of the night!"

"It's five A.M.," she whispered. "I've been up since four, cooking and cleaning for Mama's birthday party."

"How'd you get away?"

"I told Louella I was going to watch the sunrise."

"But how come—"

"I had to tell you, soon as I heard it on the radio." She plopped down on the edge of the bed. "Czechoslovakia won! They said so on the news!"

"In the Cierna meeting with the Russians?"

"Uh-huh. The official Soviet communiqué says it was a 'comradely exchange of opinions in an atmosphere of frankness and sincerity.' " Her voice was breathy. "That means they're going to let Czechoslovakia alone, right?"

"Maybe." I leaned back against the pillow, chewing on a fingernail. "It could just be talk. They could be pretending. You know, distracting everyone with friendly words while they build up their troops on the Czech border."

"No! That's just it! The Soviets announced they're removing their troops from the Czech border next week!" She squeezed my hand. Hers felt icy. "The news report said the Soviet and East German press have stopped criticizing Czechoslovakia."

"You're kidding!"

"Oh, Rod, it all worked out—and without him giving in! Dubcek said on TV last night, 'We kept our promise to stand fast.' "

We threw our arms around each other, laughing, jiggling around in jubilation.

"Soon as I heard it, I knew I just had to come."

"I'm glad you did," I whispered, closing my eyes and hugging her. "Can't think of a nicer way to wake up." Her whole body was shaking. "You're shivering," I said with concern, rubbing my hands along her arms.

"Try sitting on the back steps peeling potatoes at four o'clock in the morning. You'd shiver too!"

I rubbed her shoulders and then her back, to defrost her.

"Louella," she groaned. "She's on one of her perfect-daughter binges. 'We have to do all the work so Mama can relax on her birthday,' she tells me and the next thing I know I'm stuck peeling potatoes, playing the drone to Madam Queen Bee!"

I wrapped my hands around hers. I felt like a hothouse enveloping an ice cube. "What's the Queen Bee doing to help?"

"Creative stuff. She plans, I just follow orders. When it comes to cooking, she's the champ." Her teeth were chattering. "I just wish she didn't keep reminding me of it so much!"

"Here, put a blanket around you." I reached for the one at the foot of the bed.

"Can't stay." She stood up. "I told Louella—"

"But the sun hasn't risen yet. We can celebrate Dubcek's victory by watching it together from here."

"Can't see the sunrise from that dinky little window you have!"

"No," I chuckled. "But we can tell when it's happening. C'mon." I pulled back the covers. "Get in and I'll warm you up."

"In your bed?" Her voice quivered.

"Why not?"

"I, um . . ." She was shifting from foot to foot. "I didn't bring a nightgown or anything . . ."

That cracked me up. "You don't need a nightgown to crawl under the covers!"

"Yeah?" She was edging nervously toward the door. "You're wearing pajamas."

"No," I said, speedily unbuttoning my pajama top. "Not any-more."

"Don't!" she cried. "You'll be naked!"

I stopped and stared at her. All I could make out was a silhouette. "But we're naked all the time at the cave."

"That's the cave!"

"What's the difference?"

"This is . . . is . . . sleeping together."

"We're not going to sleep," I protested. "Just, you know, feel cozy . . . warm you up." I squinted, trying to make out her face, so I could read it.

"But what if—"

"Can't get pregnant from lying in a bed together," I offered, trying to figure out the obstacles and knock them down.

She still did not move.

"Mrs. Stompous isn't going to walk in at five in the morning," I whispered, trying a different tact. "Here," I said finally, rebuttoning my pajamas. "I'll keep them on. And you keep on your clothes."

She didn't move.

"I promise, nothing's going to happen," I begged. "I just want to, you know, be together . . . hold you."

I heard her kick off her shoes, and my heart started pumping faster. I moved over to make room and lifted the covers.

She crawled in next to me. I spread the covers over her and moved closer. She was wearing a sleeveless blouse and shorts. I pulled her against me, welcoming her, wanting her, trying not to show how much.

"Oh, you're warm," she whimpered, snuggling against me. "So wonderfully, wonderfully warm."

240

I covered her feet with mine, and wrapped my arms around her. Closing my eyes, I took a deep breath and let it out, telling myself I was holding a fully clad iceberg, wondering why it felt so satisfying. "I will always remember Dubcek's victory at Cierna in a special way," I sighed.

Marci laughed, and I felt the iceberg melting, relaxing with the thaw. Her cheek brushed back and forth on my chest under my chin. Her hand moved up my arm and then down my side. "So cozy," she murmured.

"I have dreams about your being here in bed with me," I confided. "All the time I dream about it."

"Daydreams or night dreams?"

"Daydreams . . . but, um, at night."

Her hand roamed up under my pajama top. "What do we do . . . in your dreams?"

My mind churned over all the details, madly censoring. "Uh . . . well, we usually end up like this."

"Oh . . ." She looked up at me forlornly. "I'm sorry I'm being such a total—"

I kissed her, to stop the sound, and then we rolled over on our sides, facing each other, our lips and noses almost touching. "There are a whole lot of ways to make love," I whispered, stroking her cheek. "One is sneaking out of the house at five in the morning and into my room, and then into my bed—breaking all the Parmacella rules—just to make me happy."

"It makes me happy too."

I smiled at her. "Then it's really lovemaking."

She threw her arms around me and we held onto each other, whispering and snuggling and kissing and laughing until the rays of light beaming through the window forced us to accept the painful fact: The sun had risen.

I returned from Mrs. Parmacella's birthday party at ten o'clock that night to find Sallie Durone waiting for me. I was not surprised. For more than a week Durone had been showing up regularly at my place around Marci's curfew time, just to "chew the shit."

He was sitting in my only chair, his nose in a book. "Just got back from a church social in Collier," he announced, smiling. "Met a real nice farmer and his wife."

241

"You made contact with Fio Marconi?"

The smile intensified and funny words began coming out of his mouth, words I did not understand uttered in uncharacteristically dulcet tones. He kept talking, smoothly, comfortably, sounding more articulate than he ever had before, which was ironic, considering I had no idea what he was saying. It was in a language that I didn't know. "Italian?" I guessed after a while.

"You got it, Smarts!" He smacked his hand on his thigh and leaned forward in the chair. "First off, see, it wasn't workin'. I mean, I'm standin' there, makin' talk, 'n ole Fio's hardly even answerin' me, like 'ee's wonderin'—you know—'How come this guy who don't even belong to the church's standin' here trying to put the make on me?'

"So I back off a little, see?" He leaned back in the chair and held his hands up, palms out. "Try sizin' things up. I check out this ole fart. 'He ain't just ole,' I tell myself. 'He's ole country—wearin' these baggy, dirt-stained pants held up by funny suspenders 'n all.' Only place I seen someone lookin' like him 's in pictures o' my old man's family back in Italy.

"So I say to myself, 'This guy, maybe he's been here mosta his life, but it don't show. Looks like he's still back there!' So, on a hunch, I walk up to him. 'Where'd ya grow up, Mr. Marconi?' I ask in Italian. 'Where your people from?' "

Durone folded his arms across his chest. "Whole new ball game, Golden Boy! He's warmin' up, tellin' as how he's from Locri, 'n I tell him my people are from Bovalino Marina, 'n he blows a gasket right there! 'His people's from Bovalino Marina!' he shouts at his wife in Italian, 'n fore I know it, we're goin' back 'n forth, the three a us now, me tryin' to dig up all the ole country stories I c'n find in my head.

" 'You speak real good Italian," his wife tells me, and I tell her I learned from my ole man, how he always said, 'Wanna talk to me, gotta do it in Italian.'

"They're moanin' 'bout how their sons don't know Italian, 'n I'm tellin' em how my old man come here when he was thirteen 'n never much liked America. Man, they grooved on that! Seems like Fio never liked it here it a whole lot neither. I throw in how my old man died when I was fourteen, 'n all, you know, makin' 'em feel for me. Then I start askin' where they live—all in Italian, see. Whole

242

conversation's in Italian. 'N they tell me. Well, more'n just tell me."
He winked at me. "Got the big invite, Smarts! Goin' over their place
for Sunday dinner tomorrow."

"What are you going to do?" I was beginning to worry about
the two old-world innocents.

He was staring dreamily at the ceiling, his hands behind his
head. "Bring 'em flowers, maybe. Whatcha think? Flowers a good
idea?"

"No, I mean once you win them over."

"Already won," he cackled. "Already won 'em, if ya ask me!"

"What's the game plan, Sal?" I asked impatiently. "It doesn't
seem right to me, sneaking up on them like that, lying to them—"

"Who's *lyin'*?" he shouted. "My old man's family, honest-to-
God, they come from Bovalina Marina!" He frowned, thinking.
"Leastways, I know his cousin did . . ."

"No, I mean acting innocent when you really have this grand
plan all mapped out."

His eyes froze. "They're sittin' on acres 'n acres a dead land
that ain't worth a damn."

"But if your guess about the highway is right, it's going to be
worth more than you plan to give them."

"Not much more." He grinned at me. "Not till my shopping
center goes in. Way I see it, I'm takin' a lotta risk. I'm gonna pay
'em good money 'n I'm gonna leave 'em plenty a land. All I want
is what's frontin' on highway one-ninety. Th' whole thing could fall
through, Smarts!"

"But—"

"I could end up land poor livin' next to a crazy ole farmer who
wants to talk Italian all day!"

I leaned back on the bed. "How did you learn Italian, Sal?"

"From my old man! What, you think I'm a liar or somethin'?
Just like I tole 'em. He made me talk to him in Italian."

"All the time?"

"Uh-huh." He smiled a little. "My old lady, she's born here, 'n
her people, they never taught her Italian. Tried to forget it, is what
they did." The smile turned into a snicker. "Think that's why he
made me learn it. Him 'n me, see, we'd go on 'n on, 'n my ole lady,
she'd go nuts. Couldn't understand what we's talkin' about!"

" 'This here property, son,' " I said, mimicking the gruff way

Durone had sounded, " 'this here's all gonna be your inheritance.' Say that for me in Italian."

He sat back in the chair and sweet, soft sounds came out of his mouth. It sounded so much better in Italian.

26

"BULGARIA AND EAST GERMANY—NEXT TO FALL?"

Marci's eyes darted from the banner splattered across the morning newspaper down to the subheadings—"Rigid Hardliner Resigns as Bulgaria's President" . . . "200,000 Rally for Democracy in Leipzig" . . . "Three Million Cross Berlin Wall in One Week"— and then the copy: "East Germany and Bulgaria appear ready to join Poland and Hungary in radical liberalization . . ."

The wind howled outside, slapping rain against the kitchen window panes, duplicating the winds of rage rocking Eastern Europe.

"Unbelievable," she whispered in awe, tugging her bathrobe around her. She got no reaction from the two deadbeats sitting across the table. Tommy, in a T-shirt and BVDs, was pouring over the sports section. Lindsay bit into a strawberry-jellied English muffin as she pondered the daily horoscope.

"Unbelievable!" Marci exclaimed, louder this time.

Still no reaction.

She gave up and went back to the newspaper, getting more and more excited as she devoured the stories. It was happening. One by one. All fall down. Never the same again.

Her eyes caught a tiny headline in the lower left-hand corner of the front page: "Czechoslovakia Eases Travel Restrictions."

"Oh, my God," she gasped, reading the article. *"Czechoslovakia is joining in!"* she shouted, slamming the paper down on the table.

Tom looked up, his expression more polite than interested. "Huh?"

"Czechoslovakia." She giggled giddily. "After all these years of repression! After rounding up the prominent dissidents and clubbing student demonstrators just one week ago, Czechoslovakia is giving in too! Look." She pointed at the headline.

"Big deal." Tom yawned. "So now they can travel." His eyes beat a path back to the sports section.

"Don't you see? That's just the first step . . . a sign of crumbling, caving in!"

"Get this, Mom!" Lindsay looked up excitedly. "According to your horoscope for today—"

"Are you two aware that a revolution is sweeping Eastern Europe?" Her eyes moved accusingly from one to the other.

"Uh-huh." Tom turned the page. "The Communist Bloc is crumbling."

"I'm aware," Lindsay said brightly. "Got an 'A' on the test!" She took a deep breath and closed her eyes. "June fourth, Nineteen eighty-nine, voters in Poland give the Solidarity trade union overwhelming support . . . September eleventh, exodus of East Germans to the West begins . . . October seventh, Hungarian Communist Party switches from Marxism to Democratic Socialism . . . October twelth, Poland's Solidarity-led government details program to create free market economy—"

"But what does it *mean?*" Marci cut in impatiently.

"Means the old order's falling apart." Tom elbowed his sister in the ribs. "I did pretty well on my test too, y'know." He turned to his mother. "Like I wrote on the essay question, Mom—"

"*As* I wrote—"

"*As* I wrote. I think the crumbling means more to the older generation—you know, your age group." He offered up a kindly smile as though trying to calm a mental patient. "I mean, see, we've spent our whole lives living with the Cold War. To my age group, it's just another part of current events. Not that big a deal. Know what I mean?"

"No," she said icily. "Not really."

"Mrs. Grant did." He grinned. "She wrote 'good point' in the margin next to my answer."

"When I was your age, there was a revolution in Czechoslovakia," Marci stormed. "*I* cared then. Cared plenty!" (Too much, she admitted to herself. Much too much.)

Tom shrugged apologetically. "People are different."

Marci went back to the newspaper.

"Aries is going to have a change of heart today, Mom," Lindsay chirped excitedly. "That's what it says here, you're going to have a change of heart!"

The doorbell rang and Marci blessed outside intervention.

"I'll get it!" Lindsay jumped up and ran out of the kitchen.

Marci and Tom continued reading in steely silence.

"Oh, wow!" They heard Lindsay scream from the front hall. "He did it! I can't believe it! He really did it!"

"Holy shit," Tom gasped, hopping up. "It must be Frank Durone!" He ran out of the kitchen.

Marci frowned and sat very still in the chair, her arms folded across the front of her bathrobe, listening. The front door opened and then slammed shut.

"Oh, you're absolutely soaked," Lindsay cooed. "We've got to get you dry clothes!"

"Water rat!" bellowed Tom with a touch of awe in his voice.

"Well, it's kind of wet out there," Frank agreed with a chuckle. "Didn't think I'd make it, eh, Smarts?"

The appellation made Marci's stomach churn. She sat very still in the chair for a moment, her lips pursed, her fists clenched. When she had regained her composure, she got up and walked out to the front hallway.

"Mom! Mom! Frank won his bet with Tommy!" Lindsay's cheeks were flushed, her eyes sparkling.

"I'll get you some dry clothes!" Tom shouted, racing up the stairs.

"I can't believe you did it," Lindsay purred. "And on such an awful day!"

Marci's eyes traveled to the center of attention, the thin, dark-haired boy in a sweatshirt, jeans, and a blue jacket, all of which were dripping water on her floor. Water rat, she decided silently, had been an apt description.

247

"Sorry about the mess, Mrs. Courbienne," Frank Durone said nervously stepping back onto the doormat.

The tone was diffident, quite a contrast to the belligerent snarl he'd used on his visit to her office.

"I'll try not to track up your house." He began taking off his shoes and socks.

Marci noted Frank Durone's earring was gone and so was the black-leather garb. His hair was cut short. She raised an eyebrow. The teenage thug was masquerading as nice-boy-next-door. "What exactly was the bet?" she asked.

"Frank said he could make it all the way over here from Fallsville, just by hitchhiking." Lindsay sighed worshipfully.

"These should fit. They're all a little small on me!" Tom bounded down the steps with a stack of clothes. "I stuck in a towel too. You can just change right in here." He opened the door to the powder room.

Frank Durone lined his wet shoes and socks up neatly next to the front door. "Thanks." He grabbed the clothes and went in.

"How long did it take you?" Tom shouted through the closed door.

"Two hours. I was fine once I got on the highway, but I waited for hours around Fallsville. There were just no cars."

"Two hours," Tom said, shaking his head in admiration. "Hey, Durone, what's the matter? You never heard of an umbrella?"

"That wasn't part of the bargain."

"Two hours in the pouring rain without even an umbrella!" moaned Lindsay.

Marci picked up the soggy shoes and socks, went into the kitchen, and hauled them all into the dryer. "What was your part of the bet, Tom?" She asked as she walked back.

"Video games."

Durone walked out in Tom's sweater and jeans. The clothes fit loosely, but not too loosely. "Yeah, he said he'd take me to the video-game place at the mall."

"You look better than Tommy in those!" Lindsay gushed.

Durone eyed Tom's BVDs in deadpan. "You gonna go like that?"

Tom laughed a little, and then returned the dead-eyed look. "You got a problem with that?"

248

"Oh, can I come?" Lindsay begged. "Please?"

Durone smiled at her. "That was part of the bargain."

"You might want to remove the strawberry jam from your upper lip first," Tom said.

Lindsay dashed up the steps wiping her upper lip. "I'll get dressed and be right down!"

Tom headed up after her. "Think I will change," he laughed. "It's kind of cold out for just underwear."

"Good thinking," Durone yelled after him. "That's why I call you Smarts!"

Marci's heart pounded. He'd said it again. What message was Frank Durone trying to send her? "Why do you call Tommy Smarts?"

Frank looked down at his hands. "My dad was once tutored kind of like Tom's tutoring me," he said softly. "He told me he called his tutor Smarts."

Marci nodded. "When did this tutoring take place?"

"Long time ago. Really long. Before my dad went to Vietnam, even."

"And that's *all* your father told you? That he was tutored by a man he called Smarts?"

"No, um . . . It's a compliment," Frank blurted out, nervously tugging on the cuff of the sweater. "Oh . . . uh . . . Tom, he doesn't know that, but it is. See, my dad said Smarts was the first real friend he ever had." His face was red. "He said Smarts was not only smart, see, he was, well, special. He, like, understood my dad, kinda helped him figure things out."

"When did your father tell you that?" she asked.

"When we would talk . . . in the . . . in the weeks before he died."

"Calling Tommy Smarts," she continued, determined to pursue this to the end, regardless. "Weren't you doing that for another reason too? Weren't you—just possibly—sending *me* a message?"

"You?" Durone's voice squeaked. He shook his head in confusion. "What does the name Smarts have to do with you?"

"Your father never told you I knew him too?"

Frank Durone's eyes lit up. "*You* knew Smarts?"

"Yes."

"Really!" He looked at her expectantly. "Hey, if it wouldn't be

249

too much trouble, sometime I'd, well, I'd really like it if you could tell me more about him. My dad talked about him so much, see . . . I'd love to find out more about him."

"I'm ready!" Lindsay bounced down the stairs.

Marci tugged her bathrobe around her.

"The video champ has arrived!" Tommy strode down fully dressed, waving and bowing majestically to an invisible audience of admirers. "Thank you . . . Thank you!"

"You're crazy," Frank laughed.

Marci noted a hero-worship look in his eyes.

"*I'm* rooting for the challenger!" Lindsay proclaimed.

Marci cringed at the hero-worship look in her daughter's eyes.

Tommy rattled the car keys. "Be back around four, Mom, depending on whether Frank's as good as he says!"

"Frank—" Marci called out. "Did your father ever see Smarts again? After he tutored him?"

Frank Durone shook his head. "My dad said he thought he'd hear from him when he got back from the service but he never did. He said it was like Smarts just disappeared off the face of the earth."

The kids returned late in the afternoon, exuberant and filled with play-by-play accounts of their video-game mastery. Watching the three of them laugh together, Marci had to admit Frank Durone had accomplished something she had tried—unsuccessfully—to do for years: He had brought her two children together as friends.

Without really thinking it out, Marci walked upstairs to the study, took two paperbacks off the third shelf, and reached behind them for the hardback book hidden in a corner. She pulled the book out, took it downstairs, and handed it to Frank.

"*Jeremiah Pruitt?*" Durone read the title out loud and looked up at her inquiringly.

"I thought you might enjoy borrowing it," she said. "Smarts grew up to be a writer. That book won a big journalism prize."

"Thanks!" Frank flipped to the back flap and looked at the picture of the author. "Golden Boy," he whispered reverently. "That's what my dad said he called him. He sure looks like a golden boy, doesn't he? Blond hair and all?" He frowned a little. "Rodney Bingham?" He turned to Marci. "That's his name?"

250

"Who's Rodney Bingham?" Lindsay asked, looking over Frank's shoulder.

"An old friend of Frank's father," Marci said.

"A graduate of Harvard College," Frank Durone read aloud, "Reporter-writer Rodney Bingham lives in New York City with his wife." He smiled up at Marci, but she was staring out the window.

27

1968 "Why do you look so happy?" Pimp growled at Slime.

" 'Gunsmoke.' " Slime got a distant look in his eyes. "It's on TV tonight."

Pimp shook his head and walked away.

" 'Gunsmoke's my favorite show," Slime sighed as his fingers fumbled with the buttons on his workshirt. "Just love the way, you know, they all get along so nice, real friends and all. Matt and Kitty stand there leanin' on the bar, talkin' 'n foolin', and then old Chester comes hobblin' in . . ."

Turd and Con Man were arguing about the Red Sox.

Tooth was applauding Lucky's animated melodic rendition of "Talk to the Animals." Nasty and Fatso were having a shoelace fight in front of their lockers, hooting and yelping as they belted each other with the stringy whips.

"O-vah he-ah!" Durone bellowed from the far corner of the locker room. "Everybody ov-ah he-ahhhh!"

Though Durone loved to give pep talks in the morning—especially those mornings when he'd come in two hours before us to clean the tub and had all that extra time to think—he rarely gave pep talks at the end of the workday. Obediently, but a little surprised, we all walked over and sat down on the benches before him.

Sallie was standing with his left foot up on the top of the bench, his elbow resting on his left leg, and a cigarette dangling from the corner of his mouth. He looked unusually grim. He waited until all the talking stopped. "The plant's closin,' " he announced. "Kelso's shuttin' down in a month 'n a half."

Jaws fell open room-wide. Pimp finally broke the silence. "How come?"

"Gonna move the plant to Tennessee." Durone took a long drag on his cigarette. "Workers work for less pay there. Supplies're cheaper."

"Where 'bouts is Tenysee?"

"Too far, Tooth," Durone said softly. " 'At's all ya gotta know."

The growling began. "Buncha fuckers!" "Lousy sonsabitches!" "Shitheads!"

"Burn 'em down!" shouted Deke, standing up and looking around. "I say we burn 'em down!"

"Me too." Nasty rose to his feet.

"I'm with ya," Con Man joined in.

"Count me in!" shouted Pimp.

Soon everyone was standing up and shouting except Hard-on and me.

"Whatcha think, Sallie?" Lucky asked.

Sallie stamped out his cigarette. "Burn 'em down 'n we all lose six weeks' pay."

"Nah. We wait six weeks, then torch 'em!"

"Yeah. Wait till the end!"

"Then blow this plant outta the ground!"

"Just like they done at Beacon Mills six years ago!"

They were all jumping around, animatedly making plans.

Sallie lit another cigarette.

Lucky was the first to step out of the plan-making circle. He sat back down on the bench and stared up at Sallie. Pimp followed Lucky. Then Nasty and Fatso sat down too. After a while, everyone was sitting back down, very still. "Whatcha think, Sal?" Deke asked finally.

Durone took a long drag and watched the smoke curl up to the ceiling. "How you guys feel when you pass the ole Beacon Mills plant?"

"Like they put it to 'em!" shrieked Turd.

"Showed them!" chortled Slime.

"Yah?" Sallie's eyes roamed from person to person. "I feel like Beacon Mills got a fresh start someplace else—enjoyin' a whole lotta extra insurance money on accounta the fire—an' we got left with a dried-up piece a burnt tin that tells alla other companies 'Don't build a plant 'round here.' "

"So? What*choo* wanna do, fancy talker?" Deke demanded.

"Gonna work my tail off next six weeks." Durone flicked ashes on the locker-room floor. "Gonna show 'em what a mistake 'ey're makin'—leavin' a buncha workers like we got."

"And then?"

"Yeah. When they still choose to go?"

"Gonna leave this factory standin', clean 'n shiny so's someone else'll come in, maybe. An' if no one comes, leastways I c'n lookit the place 'n say, 'Worked my ass off for Kelso, 'n I'm prouda all I done.' " His eyes roamed from man to man. "Ain't no one worked harder for this here plant 'n Sallie Durone."

"How's that gonna help you make your truck payments, Sal?"

"Yeah, how you gonna buy food?"

Durone shrugged. "Gonna be buildin' a new interstate in Orange County soon. Gonna be lotta road jobs for the askin.' "

"Soon?" screeched Turd. "Ain't no one figured out where to put the dumb road yet!"

"Gonna be somewhere in Orange County," Sal protested. "Know that much. Probably we'll know where too, 'fore Kelso closes down."

"You gonna wait, Sallie? You willin' to hope like that?"

Durone pulled a piece of graph paper out of his pants pocket. He unfolded it and held it up before the group.

It was a very complicated drawing of a huge rectangle with a series of contiguous squares and smaller rectangles running along three of its sides. The drawing was filled with messy erasure marks. I couldn't figure out what it was until I saw two lines running parallel to the fourth side. "Route 190" was written inside the lines. I smiled.

Deke studied the drawing and made a face. "Whazzat?"

"A shoppin' center," Durone announced with the pride of a man who had just discovered a cure for cancer.

254

"A what?"

Durone walked over to his locker and pulled out his *Shopping Centers U.S.A.* book. He passed it around. "Shoppin' centers is this new thing that's startin' to pop up all over the country," he explained. "I seen one in Beardsley, just outta Boston last winter. Real nice." He held up the drawing. "See, these squares 'n all, they're s'posed to be stores—whole buncha diff'rent kinda stores, alla kinds there is, see, 'n they're all in one place, with a parkin' lot out front so's everyone c'n pull up, see, 'n then buy a coupla shirts in the shirt store . . ." He pointed to one square. "Buy shoes here in this here one . . ." He pointed to another square. "Buy food in a big grocery store. Everythin', see, all at one place."

Total silence.

"You gone crazy or somethin'?" demanded Slime, voicing the room-wide opinion.

"Ain't gonna pay off your truck with all them li'l squares!"

"Yeah! So what? You gotta pitchah!"

"I got a dream," Sallie corrected. "A dream . . . and a hunch. A wild guess, maybe 'at's all. See, I think they're gonna put the interstate in over in Collier. I think the land right 'cross from Bigger Hill'd be a perfect place for puttin' in this here shoppin' center."

"You own that land?" asked Hard-on.

Durone shot him a cocky grin. "Aim to. Workin' on buyin' it right now."

"With what you gonna buy it?" Pimp sneered.

"Gonna sell off alla land I own, just for that li'l piece. Go into hock, maybe, if'n I gotta."

"You gone nuts?"

"Maybe." Durone shrugged. "All I'm sayin' is, you gotta have a dream. Otherways, you don't got nothin'. Whatcha gonna do after you burn Kelso to the ground? Hah? Fire's gonna only lasta coupla hours. Then what?"

"What's this funny circle here?" asked Slime, pointing to something in the front of the drawing.

Sallie looked a little embarrassed. "Didn't know how to draw it right, see 'cause none a the plans in my book had one in 'em." He smiled affectionately down at the circle. "That there's my fountain. Gonna be beautiful, just like-a one I seen at a shopping center in

255

Beardsley, outside-a Boston. Water just gushin' up outta the center alla time."

The guys wrinkled their noses at the circle, and then looked back at Sallie, shaking their heads. "You nuts, Sal."

"You gone outta your mind."

"A little, maybe." Sallie laughed and took some tape out of his pocket and taped the drawing up on his locker door.

I was happier than I'd ever been in my life during those early weeks of August 1968. I had a spectacular girl friend whose loving Italian parents had come to consider me one of their own. I had a rather remarkable new pal who showed up every night at 10 P.M. to "chew the shit" and kept me talking and laughing into the early hours of the morning. I'd begun feeling like "one of the guys" at the plant, teasing, joking, joining in the pranks.

Even my old David and Goliath fantasy was coming true: Soviet press criticism of Czechoslovakia had subsided, and Yugoslavia's President Tito, on a visit to Prague, had pledged his support of Dubcek's efforts toward liberalization.

It was an unusual state for me—out-and-out happiness—and I was responding in an unusual way: lapping it all up without a care in the world.

"*Thaddeus* Bingham?" Sallie Durone hooted as I walked in at curfew time one night. "You honest-to-God got 'n ole man name a Thaddeus?" He was staring at the return address on an envelope Mrs. Stompous had left on my bed.

"So what was *your* old man's name, big shot?"

"Frank," he declared self-righteously. "A normal name. Frank."

"Yeah? The folks over in Bovalina Marina came up with Frank?"

"Nah. He did," Durone began drolly. " 'At's what he said his name was when he come through Immigration. See, the guy 'at checked him in was Italian-American. Looked all-American, far as my old man was concerned. Had a name tag on his jacket 'n all. ' 'At's what I wanna look like,' my ole man thinks to himself. So he just takes the guy's name. Alla it. Bought the whole name tag: Frank Durone."

"Durone wasn't his real name either?"

"Nope."

"What was it, then?"

"Never tole me! All them nights he's sittin' there, soused outta his mind, 'n I'm askin' 'n askin' . . . Never tole me!"

"Couldn't you check back yourself?"

"Maybe." Durone shrugged. "Not real hot to try. Knowin' my old man, I figure he mighta had a real good reason for forgettin' his name . . . like there could be a couple unfriendly types from the ole country lookin' for him." He grinned at me. "Feel kinda comfortable havin' a name that can be traced back to a nice, clean, good-lookin' immigration officer!"

I laughed.

"Now, see, now I got another reason not to check. It could turn out to be somethin' sickly like Thaddeus!" He held out the envelope. "You got a letter from your ole man."

"Look again." I folded my arms over my chest. "He never writes. Even when he sends me a check, my mother addresses it. A dollar says the return address is Mrs. Thaddeus Bingham."

He examined the envelope closely, and then beamed. "Hand over the money, Golden Boy!"

I grabbed the envelope. "Thaddeus Bingham," it said, not only in letters, but in the bold, unmistakable script on the back of the envelope. My hand started trembling. I pulled out a dollar, handed it to Durone, and threw the letter on the table.

"Not gonna open it?"

"No. Not until I have to. When my father writes, it's never good news." I stared nervously at the letter, sure it was a time bomb, wanting to postpone the explosion.

Sal shrugged and, pulling a piece of graph paper out of his pocket, he asked, " 'Ey, whatcha think?"

It was the draft of his shopping center dream—a bunch of squares and rectangles and erasure marks. I examined it closely, thinking I was supposed to notice something new he had added this time, but it looked just like the drawing he had posted on the outside of his locker. I shook my head in confusion. "It looks the same."

"Good. I was afraid I mighta missed something. Took me a long time to draw it the first time."

"How come you drew it again?"

"First one got stole! Some shithead ripped it offa my locker," he snarled. "Think it mighta been Deke. 'E's the only one still hasn't got a new job lined up."

My eyes zeroed in on the circle front and center. I took out a pencil and sat down at the table.

"Don't go ruinin' it, now!" he shouted nervously.

"I'm just doing it in pencil. You can erase it if you want."

I sketched in a tiny replica of a real fountain, spritzing water up into the air, as Sallie stood off in the corner, shifting from foot to foot and grumbling about how many hours it had taken him to redraw the diagram, and here I was messing up his work. But his face lit up when I handed it to him. Then he eyed me suspiciously. "You sure you never saw the one in Beardsley?"

"No. I heard you talk about it enough to know, Sal."

"Holy shit!" He was dancing around as he headed toward the door. "I'm glad some asshole stole th' other!" He opened the door and walked out. "Willya lookit this!" I heard his voice shouting in the late-night silence. "A real fountain!"

A few seconds later he was back at my door. He nodded at the envelope from my father on the table. "You gonna be okay?"

"I'll be fine, Sal." I think we both knew it was a lie.

The letter was an order all right, an order from high command that I leave Fallsville more than two weeks ahead of schedule to attend a cousin's wedding on August twenty-first in Newport, Rhode Island. I had planned to drive right from Fallsville to Harvard, where I was supposed to report for classes on September fourth.

My "good life" came crumbling down. Happiness would soon be a memory.

I threw the letter back on the table and got ready for bed, trying not to think about the way my father's words had knocked the air out of me, just as they always did. In bed, I stared at the shadows on the ceiling, trembling and twitching, preparing for the family reunion by unraveling before I even got there. Finally I fell into a fitful sleep.

The next morning, I felt the letter burning a hole in my pocket as I sat stoically for interminable hours in the gnat-infested Fallsville stands with Marci and Louella, watching Hard-on star in the local softball game.

* * *

258

"Don't mind the amorphous shape of the sandwiches," Marci said, unpacking the basket, after we'd climbed inside the cave. "In my desire to assuage our hunger, I fear I was somewhat less than abstemious, assiduously augmenting each sandwich."

She had been studying the college board vocabulary list. I unwrapped the sandwich she gave me. "I take it you haven't made it out of the A's yet."

"Your conjecture is fallacious. I frankly believe you are trying to vilify my prodigious attempt to master the language!"

" 'Vilify' means slander," I said. "You meant 'minimize.' That's different from 'slander.' "

"Why are you being so truculent today?"

Because I was sitting there, watching her fiddle while Rome burned. Life as we knew it was on the verge of disappearing, and she was playfully showing off her new vocabulary skills.

We ate in silence.

"What's the matter with you?" she asked finally, throwing her sandwich back in the basket.

I reached into my pocket, pulled out the letter, and threw it at her.

She gasped when she got to the date of departure. As she read the letter a second time, she seemed to be working on maintaining her composure. "So?" she said finally, tossing it back to me. "It's a shame you have to go so early, but I told you I was prepared for the end."

It was happening. A few lines from my father had turned us into strangers. I couldn't breathe. "And I told you—"

"Not a bad place to exit to, is it?" She stared out the cave opening. "Sure sounds posh to me."

Posh? I was being summoned to a war zone, and that's all she could come up with? "What exactly sounds posh?" I demanded angrily.

"A big hunky-dory estate, right on the water?" She sighed dreamily. "A mansion with maids and cooks . . . gigantic weeping willow trees surrounding a long, rolling front lawn. I call that posh."

Another one of her book fantasies. "Where exactly does it say that in this letter?" I yelled, shaking it in her face.

She kept staring down at the riverbed. " 'The wedding's at the summer house. Uncle Brad says he can put us all up there, along with the wedding party,'" she quoted in monotone. "I just read between the lines."

The fact that, in her embellishment, she had come up with a fairly accurate description of Uncle Bradley Bingham's summer home only fueled my anger. "Aren't you missing the point?"

"Am I?" She kept looking away.

I grabbed her shoulders and turned her around, facing me. "I live in a great big penthouse apartment—six bedrooms, heirloom furniture, servants' quarters, the works!" I said through clenched teeth. "Posh to the hilt! And you know what? I can't think of one moment in my life—*one moment*—when I've been happy to be there!"

"A penthouse?" She gasped. "Is that a kind of—"

"Forget it!" I let go of her shoulders.

She frowned as she examined me. "Why does it make you unhappy?"

"My family's not . . . much fun."

"So?" she countered impatiently. "What family is? I mean my parents, they drive me crazy half the time, and Louella—"

"You don't understand."

"How am I supposed to understand if you won't tell me anything?" she demanded.

I shifted around uncomfortably.

"C'mon," she nudged playfully. "Act out your father . . . You know, the way you always do the guys at the plant."

We were back to fun and games. I inhaled deeply, puffing out my chest, held out my arms with my fists clenched, and worked my face into a bulldog snarl.

"Big and mean," she gasped, feigning terror. "Two hundred pounds of iron and steel!"

"One hundred ninety pounds." I laughed, exhaling. "Otherwise, you're right on the nose."

She applauded herself. "Now do your mother!"

I thought for a second and then held my hands in front of me, palms down, and stuck my fingers out so they were stiff and separated.

She leaned forward and studied my hands intently, searching for clues. "This is your mother?"

"Uh-huh." I chuckled over the brilliance of the presentation.

260

She backed off, frustrated. "I give up."

"This is the view of my mother I am most accustomed to
. . . resting on her bed in a robe, waiting for her nails to dry so she
can draw up a list."

She blinked. "What kind of list?"

"All kinds." I laughed. "Guest lists, shopping lists for the cook,
packing lists, cleaning lists for the maid, lists of clothes to be put into
storage, clothes to be taken out."

Marci frowned. "Is she, you know, motherly?"

"Definitely. Well, In a pad-and-pencil kind of way. She makes
lists of which child needs what and who should buy it, lists of her
offspring's doctor's appointments, dental appointments—"

"Does she hug?" Marci broke in impatiently.

I shook my head. "Bad for the nails."

"Close your eyes, and think of your mother, the way she was
when you were little," she ordered. "Picture . . . oh . . . picture
suppertime."

I closed my eyes. "Okay."

"Now . . . what do you smell?"

"Perfume."

"That's what supper smelled like at your house?"

"No," I laughed. "That's what my *mother* smelled like."

She growled. "Well, what do you hear, then?"

"Jingling. Ice cubes . . . bracelets."

"What's she wearing?"

"A fur coat."

"In the kitchen? What's she doing in a fur coat in the kitchen?"

"She's saying good night to us. She's going out with my
father."

"Well, what do they all talk about, then?"

"Nobody talks much."

She raised an eyebrow.

"Well, not like your family. Not lighthearted personal talk.
Everyone talks themes."

"Themes?"

"Uh-huh. My dad talks he-man stuff. He was a naval officer and
a football hero, obviously at very impressionable ages. Whether he's
eating, socializing, or just taking a crap, he does it in a military/
football-hero mode."

261

She giggled.

I went on, enjoying the drole sarcasm of my presentation. "My brothers are former football heroes, presently naval officers. They've both been preparing for the stage all their lives at my father's knee. They're big and strong and stiff, just like him. Have no trouble scoring touchdowns or destroying the enemy, but they don't bend real easily, know what I mean?"

She nodded eagerly, waiting for more.

"My sister and my mother talk female talk—who are the prettiest debutantes this season, who didn't get invited to what party and for what reason, whether dresses are getting longer or shorter, and whether this suitor or that one would make an appropriate husband for my sister. The female subject matter has changed over the years as my sister has gotten older, but it has been consistently fatuous." I pointed a finger at her. *"Fatuous."*

"Fatuous," she announced, sitting up straighter. " 'Complacently foolish, silly, inane.' " She played with the picnic basket. "They sound kind of stuffy, but . . . well, harmless."

I forced a smile. Rod-the-raconteur had done it again, translated angst into entertainment. I stared down at the riverbed sadly. I would not only miss Fallsville—I would miss the colorful, endearing cast of fictional characters I had created that summer in my stories for Marci.

"Are there, like, chandeliers hanging from the ceiling in your apartment?" she asked. "The kind that glisten and reflect the lights?"

I nodded. "Crystal. Three of them."

"Must be just awful," she scoffed. "Having to go back to living in splendor!"

My blood turned to ice. "You missed the point."

"Yeah?" she said angrily. "Well, I sure wouldn't mind spending time in your fancy penthouse!"

She was waving a red flag in front of me. I charged. "You wouldn't be invited."

The color drained from her face. "What?"

"As a rule, tradesmen's daughters aren't allowed," I said brutally. "The air in the penthouse is quite rarified. Italians and Negroes make deliveries at the back door. Jews sometimes appear on invitation lists, but their names are erased as soon as their background is

262

verified. Guineas, blackies, kikes . . . That's how my father explains the rejectees."

She moved away, crawling backward on her hands and knees over to the wall on the other side of the cave.

"Now you're starting to understand what it feels like."

"To be a guinea?" Her voice quivered.

"No, to be rejected." I cracked my knuckles, the way Durone always did when he was edgy. "Believe me, my father has a few choice names for me too. I'm only admitted because of the accident of birth."

"Yeah? What's that supposed to mean?"

Total honesty was so complicated. "Rodney talk!" I said brightly, "That's another conversation topic in my family! Rodney talk is usually kicked off by a maternal sigh and a paternal clench of the fist." I held up an index finger. "Those are the signals to the other kids that it's time to leave the room."

I fidgeted a little. "Rodney talk usually starts with a fatherly question, like 'Why the hell did you fail us again?' and then degenerates into two simultaneous monologues. My father roams the room slamming his fist on any surface available, wondering what he, Thad Bingham, Father of the Year, could have done to create this disastrous offspring. And my mother, dabbing her eyes with a handkerchief, defends me by saying, 'Rod was always the weak one, the delicate one, the unpopular one.' "

She leaned forward. "And how does this Rodney talk make you feel?"

"Hopeless. Pathetic." I looked up at her. "How the hell would *you* feel?"

"Furious!"

Another comparison lost. I yearned for her strength. I started folding my father's letter into little squares.

"All these years, you've accepted their estimate?"

I shrugged. "It's true."

" 'The unpopular one'?" she quoted, outraged. "With all those soccer team buddies you hung around with in prep school?"

"I lied about that. They were real, but . . . Well, I mean, the guys I told you about, they were on the soccer team and all. I wasn't." The squares were getting smaller and smaller. "I never even

263

tried out. They, uh, the guys on the team, they used to bully me all the time . . . thought I was a total creep."

"But your college roommates sure sounded—"

"I have a single."

She stared at me as though she were looking at a stranger. "All those funny stories you told me about Zack-the-boozer and Charlie-the-wacko-philosophy-major and Jake—"

"They lived down the hall." The letter was now a tiny paper ball. "They don't even know I exist. No one in my dorm does."

"What?"

"I'm a loner. Total loner. Recluse, really. Never had any friends at all until I came to Fallsville."

She made a face. "You thought . . . what? That I'd only fall for you if you were this hot-shot soccer player? A boy with room-mates?"

I had never thought about it. Intentionally. "No. I didn't lie to you to get you. Not to keep you, either. It all, well, it just fit in with the person I'd become."

"Which was?"

I chewed on my thumb nail. "A guy with a girl friend . . . and a family that cared about him, even if it wasn't his own family." I shrugged. "A guy with friends. A strong person. Funny. Clever. Nice. Caring, kind of. I never cared about anyone else before. Never. Worrying about me was a full-time job."

I heard her crawling across the cave, back beside me.

I focused on the river, afraid to look at her. "This summer . . . has given me more than I've ever had, see? But it's just a summer. The Rodney talk, that's the truth. That's what I really am."

"But different people are good at different things! You're good at—"

"All the *wrong* things! Don't you see?" The tightness in my throat made the words scratchy. "Writing and drawing and study-ing, that's for girls—"

"Who said?"

"My father." I swallowed hard. "He has a way with words."

"Guinea! Kike!" She spit them out. "Yeah, he sure has a way with words! What words does your father use for you?"

"The story I told you about, when my buddies and I went out

264

whoring? Never happened. Never had intercourse in my life." The breaths were coming faster and faster. "All my former girl friends? Abigail? Cynthia? They were lies too. Lies. Never had a girl friend. Never even touched—"

"What does that have to do with what your father calls you?"

I clenched my jaw and gazed bravely down at the riverbed. " 'Faggot,' I said. "That's what my father calls me! 'Pansy' . . . 'Faggot' . . . 'Queer.' " I shrugged, my eyes never leaving the scene below. "Never 'homosexual.' It's like Italian and guinea. He always goes for nasty instead of factual."

She squeezed my hand.

The river blurred before me. "It started off as a family joke when I was little. Whenever we got in the car, he'd have my brothers sit up with him and he'd put me and my sister in the back. 'Boys in the front, girls in the back!' That's what he'd say. Everyone would laugh. Big family joke."

My heart was pounding. I felt as though I were doing a crossword puzzle, and the answers were coming so fast, I was having trouble getting the letters into the right squares in time. "The ugly words, they came later, whenever I didn't measure up. And, see, I never did . . . Always failed all his manly tests. I was ten when I found out the words meant something more specific than 'shithead' or 'asshole.' "

Suddenly I was seeing it all so clearly. "Then I realized he was was telling me that, as far as he was concerned, I was the worst thing a person could be. First I hurt, then I hated. Half of me almost wanted to have it be true, just to rub it in his face, mortify him, let the whole damn world see that he, Thaddeus Bingham—starting quarterback! Naval Commander! CEO—could have raised this, this *worst* of all possible things!"

"Did you think it was true?"

My head jerked up and down as a wailing sound came out of my mouth.

"Just because he said so?"

"He didn't say so. He *says* so, all the time, over and over again, not so much with words anymore, but with looks, with disgust, with disapproval, with—"

I squeezed my eyes closed. "I felt like a person with a conta-

gious disease. Afraid to make friends, like it might be an uncontrolla-
ble thing. So scared . . . scared of everyone, not just boys . . . terrified
of having a girl look at me and know—just by looking—there was
something wrong with me. Oh, I knew I was all messed up. I hated
my body. It felt like a prison. I couldn't even stand to look at it. It
never worked the way it was supposed to. Never came through for
me . . . until . . . until . . ."

The words stopped. I stared at the riverbed, panting and
sweating and begging for reassurance. Was that it? The explanation
for all those years of abstract pain?

I felt her hands turning my face toward hers. There were tears
streaming down her cheeks. She kissed me and put her arms around
me.

I burrowed my face into her shoulder and held on to her with
trembling arms. "You think I'm going crazy?"

"It's your *father* who's crazy," she whispered. "Just him." Lying
back down on the blanket, she pulled me on top of her.

It was so comforting, having her hold me like that, I let go and
started crying. "I can't go back," I sobbed. "It's going to start all
over again!"

"Nah." Her hands moved slowly up and down my back. "Once
you learn to walk, you never forget how. You're going back a
different person."

I thought about that, relaxing a little as I let myself believe it.
After a while, the crying stopped, and we lay there holding each
other, kissing.

"One thing for sure," she said. "You've killed my taste for
crystal chandeliers!"

I laughed and climbed up on my elbows, looking down at her.
Her blouse was wet from my tears, her face streaked with her own.
"I love you."

"I love you too." She played with my shirt, avoiding my eyes.
There was something she was not telling me.

I realized I'd probably ruined everything, carrying on the way
I had. "Marci?" I asked nervously. "What are you thinking?"

She shrugged uncomfortably.

"What?"

"Just . . . it scared me when you started coming out with all the stuff about lies. I thought maybe you were going to tell me something worse."

"What could be worse than what I told you?"

"That—" A fresh set of tears flooded her eyes. "That you had a steady girl back home."

28

They start coming up inside me, these awful pains, squeezing me, kind of. They're not pain-pains. They're thoughts in my head, confusions, fears, but I swear they hurt more than any bellyache or broken bone I ever had.

Marci's eyes strained as she worked at discerning the hard-to-read scrawl of Salvatore Durone's diaries.

They always start in the car when I'm driving to pick her up . . . like I know it's okay to have them then because she'll help me take care of them. And what's crazy is, she always does. No matter how bad it is, I'm always calmed down after we talk.

Marci retranslated the handwriting one more time, to make sure she'd gotten the words right. Mental anguish erupting inside Salvatore Durone? Sal Durone, seeking the healing balm of a mental geisha girl? She checked the date at the top of the page—February 24th—against her 1989 desk calendar. February 24th was a Wednesday. Francine had said Durone had started staying out late Wednesday nights. There *was* another woman. "She," that's all

Durone called her in this diary of laboriously filled lined notebook pages. But "she" sounded more like a friend—a very close friend—than the "floosie" Francine had insisted her husband was blowing his secret savings on.

Marci pulled out the bank withdrawal slips Francine had found tucked away in the glove compartment of Sal's truck. Sure enough, on February 24th, Durone had withdrawn a hundred dollars.

Her eyes scanned the statement. One hundred dollars one Wednesday, seventy-five dollars the next, a consistent pattern lasting through February, March, April, and May. What did "she" provide for a charge? And what on earth accounted for the twenty-five-dollar week-to-week discrepancy?

She turned over a few pages and randomly stopped at another entry: March 16th.

> *Tonight we laughed, oh, man, how we laughed, just let go, like, and went with it. We laughed at all the crazy people in our lives, and how they'd figured in making us crazy. Time to blame them, we decided. Time to lay off ourselves and finger the guilties. She can make me laugh like nobody else can. It's like she crawls inside me and knows where all the ticklish parts is.*

Marci smiled fondly at the simile, and then chastised herself. This was the highly personal diary of a man extending the pleasure of his Wednesday-night experiences by recording them. It was not meant for someone else's eyes. She was certain of that. Had Salvatore Durone known, when he went into the hospital with pneumonia that he would never make it out alive, he would probably have ripped up these pages.

Since it did not bear on the Durone legal case, she had no right to be reading it. She was an uninvited voyeur. But even though she felt guilty, she flipped a few pages and began reading again, unable to stop, hungry for information.

> *She don't make me hot like other women. Warm, that's how she makes me. Warm all over, it feels good. Tender, comfortable, that kind of thing. We been staying out longer and longer. Tonight they practically closed the place down around us, it was so late. But I never want to go. I think it's*

because I know, soon as I leave her, the chill's gonna come back. Love, that's the word I got to use to explain how I feel about her. Out and out love. The best in my life, the only kind, ever, that made me happy. All the others, they made me miserable. I don't tell her about the love. I don't tell her about warm neither. It's funny. I tell her everything else—all the terrible things—I admit them out loud, and that don't bother me. The one good thing I got going, what she does for me, that I can't get the strength to tell her.

Marci stared down at the page, surprised at how the words had moved her. What happened, she wondered, feverishly turning pages to get to the end of the love story. Did he ever confess? She pulled out the last entry, in June. She skimmed the paragraph she had read before—the medical diagnosis, the proclamation to "make the best of it,"—and read what followed.

I was real strong when I told the family, and I stayed that way at first when I told her. But then she took hold of my hand. We been touching only in words, all this time, and her reaching out like that, it did me in. I started crying. Bawling like a baby. She put her arms around me and held me and we cried together.

I hardly ever cried in front of anyone before in my life, never in a woman's arms, but maybe that was because there was never the right arms. "Never going to see my girls grow up," I'm crying. "What's going to happen to Frankie?" and she's holding me and it's so relieving, the holding, and all the time, she's helping me figure things out.

But she couldn't help me on one thing because I couldn't think how to tell her. We could of made it work, the two of us. That's what I wanted to tell her. It was going so good and it would of gotten better and better, I'm sure of it. All it needed was more time. And now there's hardly any.

Marci's eyes filled with tears as they read the last line on the page.

I'm hoping to still keep writing.

270

29

1968 The night before I left Fallsville, Marci and I lay in the cave, clinging to each other, two scared kids, insisting there was nothing to worry about. The big line of the night was: "It's just the end of the beginning." I was the one who had come up with it, but it was not original. I'd plagiarized it from one of the speeches at my prep-school graduation.

We itemized the ways we'd each grown that summer, prospered from being together, and we made plans. I would call, and she would come, and I would visit and then, next summer . . . They felt good going down, the plans, but for some reason, the comfort they created was as ephemeral as the breezes drifting in and out of the cave.

I was the big plan-maker. She was enthusiastic about each of my ideas, but I had a funny feeling she didn't believe me. I figured it had something to do with her crazy conviction that summer college boys never returned. She behaved that night like a patient who knew she was terminally ill but was pretending—for her boyfriend's sake—that she'd be better soon.

Both of us were feeling terribly fragile. The truth was, our fantasy summer was over, and we knew it.

When we got back to her house, Marci started to get out of the car. I pulled her back. "Not so fast."

"Aren't you coming in to say good-bye?"

"In a minute." I pulled two presents out from under the front seat.

Her eyes registered trepidation. "Farewell gifts?"

"No," I laughed. "I'll-be-back-soon gifts. Open the big box first."

It was a picture (ripped, when no one was looking, from a library magazine) of Dubcek and Kosygin holding carnations and waving from a balcony after the Cierna meeting.

She laughed and threw her arms around me. "I will always remember that when this picture was taken I was watching a glorious sunrise from your bedroom window!"

"There's a caption, but it's on the back of the picture."

She opened the frame. " 'Yours and His forever, Rod,' " she read. "A capital 'H,' " she gasped. "That's *blasphemous!* Mama will—"

"That's why it's on the inside."

"You're crazy," she said lovingly.

"Open the little box."

It was a delicate gold pendant—a beautifully crafted flower that hung from a gold chain—the result of a day-long search that had taken me to every jewelry store in a thirty-mile radius and cost most of my August wages from the plant. As soon as I saw it, I knew it was perfect. Suddenly, I wasn't so sure. I looked away nervously as she opened the box.

Nothing. No sound at all. I chewed on the inside of my mouth and studied the tree outside the car window, suffering second thoughts. Finally I turned around. "You don't like it?"

She was holding it in her hand, staring down at it, and crying. "I love it," she sniffed. "I absolutely love it. I've never had anything so beautiful. It's like it's . . . a dream."

"It's gold—"

"Real gold?" She looked up in terror. "Oh, my God, I never—"

"That means you can wear it all the time, and it won't tarnish."

"I will! Oh, I will!"

"You'd better," I teased. I took it from her hand and fixed the chain around her neck. "I'm going to drop in on you every so often without telling you, just to check."

The present got a louder reaction inside. *"Gorgeous!"* shouted Mrs. Parmacella. "Is that gorgeous, or what?"

"A beautiful necklace for a beautiful neck!" Mr. Parmacella announced, kissing the bride.

"Yah hungry?" It was Mrs Parmacella's eternal question.

"No. I'm fine." I smiled at her affectionately. "But I'm sure going to miss hearing you say that."

"Ya need anything, Roddy?" Mr. Parmacella said. "Help loading?"

"No. That shouldn't take too long."

"Anything we can do for you?"

"You could adopt me," I suggested.

"Done!" said Mrs. Parmacella, throwing her arms around me and planting a big kiss on my cheek.

"Our home is yours," Mr. Parmacella said softly. "You know that."

"I do. Thank you for . . . everything." I was getting all choked up, and they sensed it.

"Don't be a stranger!"

"Have a safe trip!"

"We're gonna miss you!"

"Won't be the same without you, Roddy, won't be the same."

"I'll be back before you know it," I whispered as Marci and I clung tightly to each other on the Parmacellas' front porch. "I love you. Oh, I love you."

I stopped dead when I found Durone waiting for me in my room. "I thought you were going to come by at the crack of dawn instead," I said. "For the big send-off!"

"Changed my mind. What's a send-off without beer, I says to myself." He grinned slyly. "Beer don't go down right at five A.M."

"Sal, when I turn twenty-one, the first thing I'm gonna do is grab my I.D., come up here, and treat you to a whole summer of beers!" I laughed. "Hell, I owe you!"

" 'At'd be when? Two years from now?" He shot me his crafty look. "I should be back by then."

"Back from—" My eyes lit up. "You did it! You enlisted!"

He handed me a beer. "I'm takin' the test Saturday."

I clanked my can against his. "You're gonna pass, Sallie."

"You bet your ass I'm gonna pass."

There was a knock on my door.

We looked at each other, startled.

"Come in," I called out.

The door opened slowly, and Hard-on stood faltering self-consciously in the doorway. "I, uh, just stopped by to say good-bye."

Gestures of friendship did not come easily to Hard-on. The fact that he was willing to "break training"—to forsake an hour or so of sleep on the eve of another pick-and-shovel day with his old man—just to drop by for a final farewell really touched me. "Hey, thanks, Hard-on," I said. "C'mon in and have one of Sallie's beers."

Durone held out a can.

"You missed curfew!" I teased, pointing a finger at him.

Hard-on's boyish face reddened. "Well, just by about five minutes," he said sheepishly.

"You guys gotta be crazy," snorted Durone. "Datin' th' only two girls in Fallsville with curfews!"

A discussion on the curfew-less women in Fallsville evolved, with Durone, the only expert in the room, doing most of the talking. After he finished, Sallie stood up to go.

"Wait, I've got something for you," I announced, going over to the dresser. "I was going to give it to you tomorrow morning, but since you came by tonight instead . . ." I found it in the top drawer under my socks. "Here. A souvenir."

It was an ink sketch I'd drawn of Durone the way I'd come to know him best: leaning back on my bed, tilting a beer can up to his mouth. I'd worked hard on it, determined to capture the cagey smile.

He took it and just stood there staring at it. "Holy shit," he whispered. When his eyes met mine, they were filled with something I'd never seen before: unmitigated respect. "You draw this?"

"Yeah."

He gazed back at the sketch. "It's me!" he shouted giddily. "Holy shit! Looka here, Hard-on! It's me!"

Hard-on looked blankly at the paper thrust in his face. "Hmm." His eyes frowned as they zeroed in on the signature at the bottom. "G. B.?" He asked, looking from one of us to the other, "What's 'G. B.' stand for?"

"*Golden Boy*, asshole!" Sallie bellowed, jumping around the room. "Him! Golden boy! It'sa pitcha by him, 'bout me!" He took the sketch back and smiled at it narcissistically. "Really looks like me, don't it?"

"That's what I was aiming for, Sal."

"Well, yah done good, Golden Boy, real good." He pounded my shoulder. It was, I figured, Sallie Durone's way of hugging. "Gonna be here with alla beer y'owe me when I get back, right?"

"Back from where?" Hard-on asked.

Durone waved him away. "Whole 'nother story." He turned to me. "Well?"

"I'll be here. Good luck Saturday."

"Don't need it." He pounded my shoulder some more. "Thanks ta you." He stopped when he got to the door. "I like ya, Smarts," he said softly. "Like ya a lot." He growled a little and shook his head. "Sure never figured I would, back in May."

"Ditto on both counts, Sallie!" I shouted to the closing door.

After he left, Hard-on and I talked a while—the way we usually did. He asked terse questions and I supplied verbose answers. Where was I going? When did school start? When would I be coming back?

I was still really warmed by the fact that shy old Hard-on had gone out of his way to come by, but, truthfully, it was getting a little boring, just sitting there listening to myself answer questions. And for some reason, he didn't show any signs of leaving. I decided that, unaccustomed as he was to social overtures, he couldn't figure out how to execute an exit line.

I thought about how little I really knew about the guy. All those hours we'd spent together, and I still didn't know him at all. "Do you realize," I asked incredulously, "I don't even know your name? I mean, I've got a funny feeling your mother didn't name you Hard-on!"

"No," he groaned. "Sallie did. I made the mistake of signing on at the plant with my whole name—first, middle, and last. Sallie got the Hard-on from my middle name. It came from my mother. You know, her maiden name."

"Hey," I said. "My middle name's my mother's maiden name too!" (At last, something in common with Hard-on.) I stood up. "How do you do." I bowed formally." My name's Rodney Everett Bingham."

He stood up and held out his hand. "Glad to meet you, Rodney. My name's Thomas Hardon Core-bean." We shook hands.

"Core-bean?" I repeated. "How do you spell that?"

"C-o-u-r-b-i-e-n-n-e."

"The spelling . . . it's a French name, isn't it?"

"I guess. My dad's family was French-Canadian."

" 'Good-hearted,' that would be the rough translation," I said, pulling him casually toward my door. "It fits."

He shifted awkwardly from one foot to the other.

"Well, I've got bad news for you, Thomas Hardon Courbienne," I laughed, ushering him out. "I'm afraid after all this time, you'll always be Hard-on to me!"

"You're sure cheerful," he said abruptly.

I blinked. "Well, I'm leaving, but I plan to come back. No reason not to be cheerful."

He nodded, staring down into his beer. "I just heard you were upset."

"Who told you that?"

"Oh, no matter." He put the beer can down and stretched. "I better be heading home."

"Thanks for stopping by." I really meant it.

He seemed nervous as he headed for the door. "Listen," he blurted out, turning back suddenly. "Do you really think you're, you know, a fairy?"

It was like a blow to the head. I froze. "A what?"

"A, you know . . ." He couldn't get the word out, and I was not about to help him.

"A homosexual," he said finally. "Don't . . . don't worry about it, really don't." He shrugged. "You sure seem okay to me."

Ice. My whole body was chilled and immobile.

"You can tell the real ones," he reassured. "They dress funny and act, you know, different. Real weird." He shifted around uncomfortably in front of the door. "It sounds like your family, um, they kind of scared you into believing it."

"Where—" I gasped, groping at the air. "How . . . how did you—"

"Hey, don't take it out on her," he said softly, his hand on my arm. "Marci, she just worries about people, you know. She's got a big heart to go with her big mouth."

I don't remember what else was said. He made some other well-intentioned assurances about my mental and sexual health, and then ventured out into the night.

At first my mind went into high speed, desperately trying to figure out a way to alter the facts, frantic to find a logical explanation—*any* explanation—other than the one that was glaring me in the face.

But there was none. Only Marci. "What name does your father call you?" . . . "How did that make you feel?" . . . "What name, what name, what name . . ."

I heard her voice saying the words, and I felt her squeezing my hand, putting her arms around me, getting me to say things I had not dared even think to myself. My love. My confidante. My everything. Who else could it be but Marci? I'd never even understood it myself until I told her.

I don't know how long I stood there, rigid, my feet stuck to the floor, everything out of focus. I just know that when I came out of the trancelike state, I felt exposed in a way more devastating than anything I had ever experienced before.

I was naked—physically and mentally naked—and the whole town was gaping. My loving adopted family, the Parmacellas, my very first intimate friend, Sallie Durone . . . What had they been told about me behind my back? What did they know? What would they know, once the coast was clear? If she had told someone as distant to her as Hard-on, she would tell everyone soon enough.

It was them versus me, all over again, just like prep school, only this time the guys had figured out a really clever way to suck me in. Fallsville, Massachusetts, my cozy, nurturing paradise had been transformed into a large gathering of "them," pointing their fingers and laughing at me as Big Mouth, the town crier, divulged secrets so painful I had spent a lifetime pretending they did not exist.

I seized the escape route that had been handed me. She had, after all, already written me out of the script. Why was I lingering?

In a complete daze, I packed the car. It seemed to take hours—hours spent in slow motion—and I drove off, not feeling anything but a dull pain that both tormented me and dulled my senses at the same time. I knew my life was over—my good life. But I didn't think about any of the specifics. I just turned the classical music up real loud on the radio, pressed down on the gas pedal, and set out on the highway.

I drove. Head up, eyes forward, body tense, mind turned off, I drove. I was outside Boston when I heard an announcer's voice break into the broadcast.

"Armed forces of the Soviet Union, East Germany, Poland, Hungary, and Bulgaria invaded Czechoslovakia tonight in a swift military action."

"No!" I screamed it out.

"Reports are the invaders have occupied the country and several leading members of the government, including Czechoslovak Communist Party First Secretary, Alexander Dubcek, have been flown to Moscow."

My body began trembling violently.

"The Czech Communist Party Central Committee is warning Czechoslovak citizens not to resist. There are reports of scattered violence in several cities, but in general, the invasion is being met with little resistance."

I swerved my car off the highway, onto the nearest shoulder, threw my arms around the steering wheel, and loud, shrill cries of anguish spilled out of my mouth. I cried until there was nothing left inside, nothing left to come out.

The sun began rising. Daybreak, August 21st, 1968. All the dreams were over.

30

"I can't put the book down," Frank Durone confessed as Marci turned off the highway at the Fallsville sign. "I swear, it's like I spend the whole day waiting to sneak off and read *Jeremiah Pruitt.*"

"I felt the same way," she sighed, "the first time I read it."

"It must have taken years to prove the murder, don't you think? To get all those local people to open up to him that way?"

"Yes." She smiled dreamily at the road ahead. "The author had to build up a lot of trust."

"Thanks for lending it to me." Frank fidgeted with his school books. "Thanks for . . . well, your whole family's been so great to me." His eyes were sweet, doelike. "You, Tommy, Lindsay, Louella . . ."

"Louella?" Marci said, her eyes jumping from Frank to the road ahead and then back again. "What does Louella have to do with it?"

"I thought you knew," he said apologetically. "I've been going to her twice a week since my dad died for counseling."

"Louella's your counselor?"

"Yeah," he said brightly. "She's really great. And what's more, she'd doing it for free."

Marci grit her teeth. Fallsville, the place where your aunt married your second cousin, where your uncle was also your half-sister's stepbrother, and where your sister ended up counseling her former rapist's son. And for free, no less! Oh, it made perfect sense, given what you had to begin with: a whole town filled with incessantly intermingling wacko people!

A flowing green velour robe hung loosely over Louella's frame. "My, what a nice surprise!" Her cheeks scrunched up lifting her lips into a perfect half circle. "C'mon in!"

"My, what a nice surprise!" Marci mimicked her sister's chirpy voice. "You *knew* I was coming," she accused. "You expected me."

Louella's face reddened. "Frank *did* call—"

"To warn you?"

Louella stared her down, a teacher waiting for silence in an unruly classroom. "The kid just called to apologize for assuming I'd told my sister about the therapy sessions." She took Marci's jacket and hung it up in the closet. "Knowing you, I admit I thought possibly—"

"Remarkable, isn't it?" Marci snapped. "The fact that you know me so much better than I know you."

"Surely you're not angry at me for not telling you about my confidential relationship with the boy . . ." She stood erect, the embodiment of professionalism.

Marci forced a statesmanlike smile. "I think it's wonderful what you've done for Frank."

"Now, don't minimize the important role *you*'ve played," Louella said. "I think it's wonderful what we've both done, or at least helped him do for himself."

Marci dug her hands into her jean pockets and straightened her shoulders. "Louella," she announced, "I'm ready to talk."

"About what?"

"Anything." The heels of her boots made little clicking sounds as she paced around the wooden flooring. "Anything and everything. A horrible thought occurred to me in the car just now— privacy works both ways!"

Louella giggled.

"Laugh if you want to!" Marci approached her menacingly. "But Rip Van Winkle woke up, and she wants to be filled in."

Louella raised an eyebrow. "Would she like some wine to ease the transition?"

"Wine would be fine."

Louella headed toward her kitchen. "For starters," Marci yelled after her, "when did you and Salvatore Durone become buddies?"

"Frank told you that?"

"Yup."

"About a year ago." Louella returned with a big jug of red wine and two glasses. "I bumped into him one day when he came to the women's center for help."

Another insanity masquerading in the guise of a declarative sentence. "Salvatore Durone, wife-beater, went to the Center for Battered Women to get help for his problem." Marci nodded solemnly. "Makes perfect sense."

"Oh, poor baby." Louella poured out the wine. "It was just typical Durone—right intentions, but a misguided sense about how to go about fulfilling them." She chuckled. "Thank God *I* spotted him when he walked in. Had he gone to one of our more militant social workers, he might have been even more psychologically damaged before the afternoon was over."

"Thank God?" Marci shook her head. "I must be missing something."

"Well, you know, the center's designed to help battered women, not men who abuse their wives. I just meant—"

"Hold it," Marci ordered, raising a hand. "You're telling me that *you*—a person Salvatore Durone had once tried to rape—were in a better position to counsel—"

"That, uh, that incident . . . well, it was was a bit overblown." Louella sighed, shaking her head. "Fallsville folklore."

Marci squinted. "Come again?"

"The great attempted rape." She laughed, shaking her head. "Truth is, Sallie just tried to unbutton my blouse that night in his truck. Well, I mean, in fairness to *me*, we had quite a struggle. He broke three of my fingernails! He had a problem with violence even then."

"But you came home that night screaming that Sallie Durone had tried to rape you," Marci insisted. "I was there!"

"I had plenty of reason, believe me. Chickie would have *killed* me if I had told the truth. See, it was my idea, the date with Durone. Can you imagine how mad Chickie would have been?"

"But what about poor Salvatore Durone, for heaven's sake? He—"

"Forgave me. Even found the anecdote useful as an example of forgive and forget. He told Frank about it to demonstrate how memories fade."

Marci just stared at her.

"Oh, Fallsville standards." Louella groaned, handing Marci a glass of wine. "Teasing girls and violent boys. Such an unhealthy environment for both sexes! Sallie and I understood each other's problems pretty well because they had such similar roots."

"Yeah. Sure." Marci took an enormous gulp of wine. "Must have been a nice ice-breaker."

"You knew he beat Francine?"

"Yes."

"How did you know?"

"Professional ethics prevent me from disclosing."

Louella gave her the finger. They both broke out laughing.

"Francine's been coming to me for advice for years." Marci played with the glass. "Correction—she *came* to me. She never followed any of my advice." She looked at her sister. "I take it Sal was a better advice-follower than Francine."

"Much better." Louella settled down on the shag rug and lit a cigarette. "I sent him to a social worker friend of mine, and he went religiously. Every single Wednesday night. Never missed a session."

Marci leaned forward attentively. "Every *Wednesday* night? Starting how long ago, Louella?"

Louella thought for a moment. "Last February. That's when he started."

"How much did the therapist charge?" Marci pushed. "Do you know?"

"Seventy-five dollars." Louella shrugged. "That's the going rate."

Marci relaxed on the sofa savoring the facts, enjoying the logic: A man married to Francine needed a therapist even more than a floosie! One mystery solved, or at least one part of the mystery. There was still that other twenty-five-dollar withdrawal every other week to account for. And the woman in the diary. Had Sal fallen for his therapist? Was the money for some sort of medication?

"It was tragic when Sallie got sick. For the first time in his life, it was all coming together for him." Louella was watching the cigarette smoke curl up to the ceiling. "And then he died so suddenly. I was out of town, remember? At that conference in Hartford? When I came back and found out . . ." She shook her head slowly. "So sad."

"*That*'s why you pushed me to keep working on finding out who killed him!"

"Yes."

"But didn't he tell you anything about his suspicions? It sure would have helped to know I was looking for a chemical murderer and not a human being!"

"He just told me what he told everyone else, that someone was going to pay for what they did. He was all excited about how he was going to give everyone a big surprise. He would have divulged more if he'd known he could die at any minute. But he was certain he had a good three months left—more, he figured, because he'd had chemotherapy." She squeezed Marci's arm. "I knew you'd be smart enough to figure it out. Mama says you're going to get some money for them."

"Too early to tell. We've filed the papers. We're waiting for a response from the company. But it's a very good case."

"Frank's so bright, Marci. The kid should go to college. You think there'll be enough money?"

"Frank will go to college."

"Not on B.J.'s money!" Louella shouted. "Sallie—" She stopped suddenly and turned away. "Will there be enough in the settlement to send him to college?"

Marci squinted at her. "Why would Sal object to B.J.'s money?"

Louella stared into her wineglass.

Marci leaned forward. "Louella, why did Sal go to the big Chamber of Commerce celebration for B.J.'s shopping center? I didn't think he even *knew* B.J. But Frank says Sal insisted upon going, all alone, and then he came back from the celebration happy, declaring that he—Sal Durone—was a genius!"

"A long story . . ." Louella patted Marci's hand. "For another time."

"Why can't you tell me now?"

"Why did you break up with Rod Bingham?"

283

Marci collapsed against the sofa. "How's *that* for a non sequitur!"

"You walked in here telling me you were ready to talk—about anything and everything. Seems to me you've been doing a lot of asking and no answering!"

"Rodney Bingham is ancient history."

"Ancient history is often relevant. You've never fallen for anyone as hard as you fell for him." She snickered. "Never saw anything like it, if you want to know the truth. It was a little sick, you know, the two of you lying there together, making out and reciting poetry at the same time."

"That's just because you're evaluating it from an adult perspective." Marci laughed. "It was a teenage romance . . . Two kids, madly in love for three months." She shook her head slowly. "How can it be relevant when it happened half a lifetime ago? It has nothing to do with today."

"Don't be so sure." Louella took a long drag on her cigarette, tossed her head back, and exhaled dramatically. "Rod Bingham drove a wedge between us. That was the beginning. That's when we stopped talking. Oh, things got worse after Vince and Chickie died, but our real parting of ways came before—during that summer."

Marci got a distant look in her eyes. "I guess I felt it was a special, private thing, what he and I had. I didn't want to share it with anyone." She glared at her sister. "Only in the *Parmacella* household would privacy be considered a sin!"

"There's privacy and there's suppression. Two different things."

"Don't start social-working me, Louella."

"Dom Pascale came back to Fallsville for a visit about a month ago." Louella stood up and started pacing around the room. "We all had dinner together at Mama's house. It was the first time I'd seen old man Pascale since he closed his store and moved away. We had a great time listening to Dom tell all these funny anecdotes about the four crazy Parmacella kids, all their antics." She paused and shot her sister a significant look.

Marci bristled. "*Another* non sequitur . . ."

Louella went back to her pacing. "One of the stories intrigued me. Dom said he was climbing into his truck one morning, getting ready to make one of his regular runs into Boston to pick up supplies for the store, and he found *you* there waiting for him . . . all dressed up in your Sunday best. You'd skipped school?"

Marci looked away.

"You begged him to take you with him to Boston. He said it was only a week after we'd heard about Vince, and you seemed so troubled, so desperate to go, he was afraid if he didn't take you, you would try getting there on your own." Louella looked at her again.

Marci drank some wine.

"Then, of course, Mama started up. 'That musta been when she broke up with Rod,' Mama wails, going into her spiel about how that was the stupidest thing you'd ever done in your life, such a nice boy Roddy, and Baby had to go and end it—"

"Louella, is there a point to all this?"

"Yeah. It started me thinking about your big break-up with Rod Bingham, see, how he called and called all the time, and then you announced you were sick of him and you were going to end it." Louella groaned. "What an awful time . . . Mama and Papa shouting, 'Don't do it! Don't do it!' You screaming, 'I'll do what I want to do!' "

"Down memory lane . . . Family fun at the Parmacellas."

"That's when it hit me—no one was ever *home* when Rod called you. Funny coincidence, don't you think, that he always happened to call when you were in the house alone?"

"So?" Marci shrugged. "I lied. Big deal. Supersensitive Rod Bingham turned out to be a total shit. He left Fallsville, and I never heard from him again. It was easier for me to handle it the way I did." She bowed down formally from her seat on the couch. "I confess, Big Sister, I stole the cookies from the cookie jar!"

"What happened when you went to Harvard?"

"Nothing particularly traumatic."

"How can you say that? You'd been horribly rejected by this kid who'd promised he'd be right back. You were devastated by your brothers' death. You went searching for some kind of relief, and it sounds like you didn't find it."

"Ancient hurt." Marci sighed. "Forgotten history."

"So? All the easier to divulge then."

Marci watched her fingers as they outlined the floral pattern on the slip cover. "I got his room number at the administration building. The steps of his dormitory were crowded with all these

285

disheveled-looking kids. The boys had long hair, and they were unshaven, and everybody—girls and boys alike—were all in torn jeans and ripped shirts."

Marci winced. "I suddenly realized how completely stupid I looked, all dolled up in my heels and hose and prim, proper dress. The lower class, trying feebly to look upper, when the real 'uppers' had so much inbred status they could walk about like vagabonds! I knew right there on the spot why he had discarded me."

Louella put her hand on Marci's sleeve.

Marci pulled her arm away. "So, I saved face." She shrugged. "It's as simple as that. I ran back down the steps and back to Dominick Pascale's pickup truck." She turned to her sister. "I apologize for not telling you all the little details, Louella, but frankly, it was the best thing that ever happened to me. *That* was the day I declared Rodney Bingham dead. Just like Vince." She sat up very straight, her eyes defiant. "And *that* was the day I realized I would *not* die . . . that I could make it. I could survive with the two most important people in my life gone forever."

"As long as you blocked them both out. As long as you—"

"I not only made it." Marci's voice got stronger. "Hatred for Rod Bingham fueled me to go on to college, and then law school. Just so some day I could meet him and say, 'I'm as good as you are now.' "

Marci got up and walked over to the wine jug. "A whole lot of people get what they want without filing law suits, Louella. It's bad for my business, but I've learned to live with it. Maybe it's time for *you* to face the fact that some people can figure things out for themselves without indulging in melodramatic confessions." She refilled her glass with wine.

"Hatred left smouldering—"

"Well, as I said, it turned out to be very energizing!"

"Frank says you lent him a book Rod Bingham wrote."

"Big deal, so I read his books!" Marci snapped over her shoulder. "Minor relapses. In every other way I erased him from my life."

"Why don't you look him up?" Louella asked.

"Why?" Marci walked back to the sofa. "What *is* it with you and all this nostalgia?"

"Gotta face the past to be rid of it."

"I'm rid of it! Have been for years! You're the one having problems."

Louella stomped out her cigarette. "Look how Rod Bingham messed up your life! 'Fueled you to go on to college and then law school'" she quoted in disgust. "Forced you to marry Tom just so you could get the financial backing to stay enrolled, that's what he did!"

Marci looked at her in outrage. "You're saying my drive to better myself made me into a coldhearted opportunist?"

"Wish it had." Louella said sadly. "In fact, it made you into a victim. *Tom* was the opportunist. He spent years searching for a way to get you. You gave him one."

"That's not fair to Tom. He was very sweet, very loving . . ."

"Oh, he was in love with you allright. That's one of the reasons I broke up with him. He only dated me to get near you. He got what he wanted. You got—"

"Two terrific kids. A very thoughtful husband—"

"A very boring marriage." Louella lit another cigarette. "That's the other reason I broke up with old Hard-on. He was downright boring."

Marci swirled the wine around in the glass. "Tom Courbienne lived the way he made houses—with careful forethought, assiduous research, and astute planning. The end result was a life that was as structurally sound as the best four-bedroom split-level on the market."

"Like I said, boring!"

"No, *giving*." Marci shook her head resolutely. "He gave me more than I paid for—just like the people who bought his houses. More than I deserved. He was a much better husband than I was a wife."

"You would have suffocated in that marriage."

"He let me off the hook, didn't he? At great personal expense."

"*Are* you off the hook?" Louella raised an eyebrow. "You've certainly gone out of your way all these years to avoid romantic commitment. They left you with a double whammy, Rod and Tom. One showed you how much love could hurt. The other made you feel guilty for not loving back."

"Such tiring armchair psychology, Louella."

Louella exhaled smoke. "Want a second opinion on your angel husband? According to Sallie—"

"No!"

"Why?"

"Because I'm tired of going over it all. Over and over and over. Can't we go on? Can't we stop going back?"

"Sure that's the *only* reason?" Louella snarled. "Sure you're not dismissing the story because it came from Sal Durone, mean, nasty, wife-beating Sal Durone?"

"I'm sure." Marci sighed sadly. "I've changed my opinion rather dramatically lately about Sal Durone."

"How come?"

Marci played with her hair. "Just . . . just going through all his papers for the legal case, I've learned a lot. A soul," she whispered, almost to herself. "Sal Durone had a soul, a soft, sensitive side to him that I never realized existed."

"Yes, he did."

The choked tone of the delivery made Marci look up. "Louella," she began gingerly, "your relationship with Sallie, was it . . . professional?"

"Oh, no. Not at all. I wasn't treating him. It's just, well, therapy can very disturbing. You're left at the end of the session with a whole lot of raised but unresolved issues." She shrugged. "It scared him. The first time he went to the therapist, he showed up on my doorstep . . . confused, very emotional. We went out for dinner, to talk about it."

Louella leaned back against a big pillow on the floor and smiled dreamily. "He took me to this little Italian restaurant over in Dobbs-ville, Luselli's it's called. We walk in, and the next thing I know, Sallie's talking Italian to Mama Luselli! Crazy, the feelings it brought out in me . . . the smells, the sounds . . . I don't remember any Italian. Hadn't even heard Italian since Grandma died. But just the sound of it brought back all these memories . . . comfort, coziness, heavy food, heavy love."

Louella twirled a lock of hair around her finger. "Sallie'd known the Lusellis for years. They're real old, in their eighties, still operat-ing this tiny restaurant." She grunted a laugh. "Anyway, Sal—big spender Durone? He plunks down twenty-five dollars on the table, and he says, 'Give us the best you got, Mama.' And damned if she didn't! A five-course meal—wine, dessert, the works! You wouldn't *believe* what twenty-five dollars can get you at Luselli's! It became our hangout, our special place. We had such wonderful times, some of our dinners lasted past midnight!"

Marci recalled the hand-written diary entries.

Tonight they practically closed the place down around us, it was so late. But I never wanted to go. I think it's because I know, soon as I leave her, the chill's gonna come back.

Marci leaned forward. "And you kept going back?" she asked eagerly. "After his therapy sessions?"

"Every single Wednesday night," Louella proclaimed happily. "We had a big fight about the bill, Sallie and I. I insisted on paying. I mean, he was forking over seventy-five dollars a week to the therapist, and that was a lot of a money for him."

"So you compromised!" Marci shouted excitedly. "He let you pay every *other* Wednesday night?"

Louella frowned. "How did you know?"

"Social workers don't have the intuition market cornered completely," Marci scoffed.

"The most delicious food in the world, and, oh, damn, the best wine I ever tasted." Louella's cheeks were getting flushed. "And God, the talk. I mean, Marci, you gotta envision this—the wife-beater and the radical feminist, two wounded warriors of the modern world, being lulled back into the sweetness and simplicity of childhood by the dialect and food of our grandmothers . . ." She laughed. "A trip and a half, that's what it was!"

"But more than that," Marci prodded. "More than just a crazy night out every week."

"A lot more." Louella smiled serenely. "The peace, you simply can't imagine how soothing it was, talking and talking and talking late into the night. The best times . . . They were the very best times."

Slowly, the smile faded. "We stopped going out when he got sick. I visited him at home instead." Louella shrugged. "Francine, she was happy to have someone come in to entertain him. I mean, she knew she didn't have to worry about competition from big fat me, know what I mean?"

"No."

"One time I went, he was in a lot of pain. It was some new medication he was on. And he said, 'Hold my hand. Please, hold my hand.'" Her eyes got watery. "I did. All afternoon. We sat there talking, and holding hands, connected kind of, both of us needing the connection. And I felt this . . . this . . . funny feeling."

Love, that's the word I got to use to explain how I feel about her. Out and out love. The best in my life, the only kind, ever, that made me happy.

Tears came to Marci's eyes. "I've got a present for you, Louella. I'll bring it by tomorrow."

"What kind of present?"

"A, um, a diary Sal kept . . . It was stuck in with the family bills Frank brought to my office. I kept it. I don't know why exactly. I just knew it wasn't something he'd written for Francine."

"What does it say?"

It was going so good and it would of gotten better and better, I'm sure of it. All it needed was more time, and now there's hardly any.

"I just skimmed it." Marci wiped her eyes with the back of her hand. "You read it. You decide."

Louella squinted suspiciously. "How come you're crying?"

"It was . . . very moving, the diary."

"Who would have thought it," Louella sighed. *"You,* moved to tears by something Sallie Durone wrote!"

"Yeah. Well. Who would have thought Sallie Durone was soft at the center, huh?"

Louella stared into space, lost in some reverie.

Marci sat back on the sofa, holding her wineglass on her chest, thinking about Durone and Louella, and then moving back—back to ancient history. She remembered green eyes, constantly changing color as the blues and yellows fought each other for dominance. Oh, how they could chill, freeze to the cold hardness of malachite when he was despondent. But happiness had made them liquefy, effervesce with such luminous energy she'd felt she was basking in them, basking in her own private sunshine.

"Louella?" she asked after a while. "How did you know Rod and I made out and recited poetry at the same time? You weren't there, and I never told you anything about it."

"The cave." Louella groaned, rolling over on the floor. "You did it in the cave!" She began to laugh. "One thing none of us knew about the cave in our secret Parmacella family hideout days was that it functioned a bit like an amphitheater, booming the voices from the inside out! I think it was that crack in the rock at the very back, you know, the part Vince called the ventilator?

"One night I led Tom down there, filled with anticipation about this romantic evening together, and what do we hear when we get there? These two familiar voices . . . One's panting, 'Oh yes, oh yes!' and the other's going on in verse." She raised an eyebrow. "*You* were the poet, as I recall."

Marci's face reddened, and then she burst out laughing.

"That's when I knew." Louella took a long gulp of wine. "That night was when I realized *you* were Tom's real love. He absolutely did not want to leave. He couldn't hear enough . . . he just sat there, listening to everything you two said." She thought for a while. "I think he went back other times too. Without me. Just to listen."

Marci winced. "What?"

Louella nodded. "A couple of times he'd let something slip, something he knew about your plans, what the two of you were going to do, that sort of thing—the type of thing he'd have to have found out by eavesdropping."

Marci stopped sipping her wine.

"A bit disconcerting?" Louella winked at her slyly. "Your future husband listening to you carry on with your teenage lover?"

"I guess it would have been, had I known about it then." Marci's eyes traveled up and down Louella's macrame wall hanging. "Now it seems so remote. Irrelevant, really."

Wet hair, sun-hot skin . . . she could feel it, just as she could see those translucent green eyes dreamily examining her body as though it were a priceless sculpture . . . and then his hands, following his eyes, exploring, exciting, until the painfully self-conscious girl felt transformed, beautiful—more beautiful, even, than all those fictional heroines she had read about—intoxicating and intoxicated, lost in the pleasures of their intimacy.

Marci sat very still on the floor in the far corner of her attic swaying back and forth. She opened her eyes. "Received at Mongon's, 1968," it said on the tattered shoebox on the floor beside her. The box's contents was spilled out across her lap—letters, drawings, poems, trinkets.

She stared down at the evenly spaced lines of rounded script in blue fountain pen ink, noting how the smoothness of the penmanship camouflaged the intensity of the outpouring. These were letters of love, but filled with ideas as well, pondering shared curiosities, open, honest, unguarded in a way that shocked her.

Babes in the woods. No antibodies, no defenses. Young love. First love. Last love?

Twenty-one years of feeling rejected had made her forget the most important part. For three glorious months she had been a love object, a source of strength, an intellectual inspiration. It was all coming back to her, those electric charges of energy, the warmth of his adoration. How unbelievably wonderful it had felt!

And now? Now she felt listless, repressed, suffocating in maturity. The dazzling star had turned into a plodding director—mother, lawyer, daughter—working tirelessly behind the scenes to make sure everyone else's production went off smashingly. She found herself yearning to return to that spotlight—oh, the pleasures of feeling like a sex symbol *and* a brain trust all rolled into one! She wondered, just for one moment she let herself wonder, whether any of that old chemistry would resurface if Rod Bingham, noted author, and Marci Courbienne, damned good lawyer, were to come face to face again.

The yearning embarrassed her, the wondering mortified her. She quickly refolded the letters and other memorabilia and stuffed them back into the box. She placed a rubber band around the box and pushed it back into its chronological resting place: on top of the high-school scrapbooks, but underneath the wedding photos and college and law-school awards. Just one of many mementos.

She stood up and groped her way around the storage bags and trunks to the attic stairs. Time to do something useful.

She paused on the landing, wondering if Rodney Bingham had children. None had ever been mentioned on the book jackets she'd studied so intensely. He was a famous writer now, no doubt understandably unwilling to let the public invade his privacy. It was most interesting, however, that he had never dedicated any of his books to his wife. That she knew for a fact. No one had studied the credits in the front of Rodney Bingham's books more thoroughly than she.

Who cared? What did it matter? Back to reality. Time to make dinner. She took out a jar of spaghetti sauce, and then changed her mind. *Real* spaghetti sauce, for a change, the kind her mother made. She began pulling ingredients out of the refrigerator and cabinets, and then plunged in, mincing, chopping, frying, stirring.

Suddenly she threw the wooden spoon into the sink. Wiping her hands on a dish towel, she picked up the telephone, and tapped out New York City Information.

31

On the desk, next to the word processor, the wheel of the printer darted back and forth across the pages, aggressively spitting out text. Then it stopped. Another chapter, printed.

Put your feet on the floor, Rod Bingham silently commanded himself. *Sit up. Stand up. Walk over to the word processor. Program it to print out the next chapter. Then you can come back to the sofa.*

But his pajama-clad body remained immobile as he stared at the white stucco ceiling of Stanley's condo living room, soothed by the sudden silence, exhausted by the idea of moving.

Where had all the energy gone? The man who had spent more than a month steadily increasing his jogging mileage and speed, riding ocean waves, holding to a strenuous daily schedule of drawing, thinking, and writing had turned into a lethargic lump. He often felt this way after he finished a book—empty, listless, the literary equivalent of postpartum depression. However, this was more severe, and this wasn't a book. It was a small project that had consumed him for a tiny period of time.

Consumed him. An apt description. Eaten him up. Depleted him. Perhaps because it was different. This wasn't someone else's story he'd painstakingly ferreted out. Nor were these fictional characters he'd given life and breath to in his head. These were real people—his own story, dug up and resurrected after more than two decades of burial.

Why had he fallen back in love with them all, with the Fallsvillians? Had they been special? Or had he just come upon them at an unusually vulnerable time?

In contrast to that summer, the rest of his life seemed colorless, inconsequential, twenty-one years that could be summed up in a few paragraphs, an afterthought. *Then write the postscript*, he ordered himself.

It was easier than lifting his heavy limbs off the sofa.

The immediate aftermath was easy to recall. He'd been a mess. "Treading water" was the best way to describe it. He'd been embroiled in a continuous battle to keep his head above the wave's crest, ferociously and tirelessly fighting the unrelenting currents he'd felt pulling him under. It was the first real fight he'd ever put up, and he'd won.

Then he had been swept up in the national revolution taking over the country. The ready supply of marijuana at Harvard had fostered campus-wide "dropping out." Sex was free and emotion was considered an unnecessary investment. He'd learned to give pleasure and get pleasure without feeling he had to give or get anything else.

At home, he was no longer the runt of the proud Bingham litter. He was a student during a new period of omnipotent, militant students, and therefore a potential bomb-throwing barricade-stormer. Instead of upbraiding him for the things he could *not* do, his father had started applauding him for all the terrible things he wasn't doing.

He closed his eyes. That was it—the behavior pattern that had set the trend for the rest of his Teflon-coated life.

Had that one adolescent betrayal in Fallsville so many years ago caused him to shy away, instinctively, from intimacy? Was it possible that in actively suppressing the experience, steadfastly rubbing out all the memories, he had rendered himself incapable of all personal involvement? Was that why the characters in his books—real and fictional—were the only people he'd cared about in his adult life?

If so, there was a bright side. This—whatever it was, this concentrated effort at recalling—would have positive long-range effects. He understood things now, understood himself. He was certainly a different person from the Rod Bingham who had left New York City in October. He was . . .

Depressed. That's all that came to mind: acute physical-mental depression. That and a thoroughly irrational desire to climb into bed with little Marcella Parmacella.

He decided to settle for partial fulfillment: bed.

He had no idea how long he'd been sleeping when the telephone rang. He found it on the floor under a stack of clothes. "Hello?"

"Happy day-before-Thanksgiving!"

The boom in Stanley Kurtz's voice pained him. "Hi, Stan."

"Geez, you sound lousy."

"Mmm. I'm just printing out the . . . uh . . . what I wrote, Stan."

"Great. That's why I called. What do you think about my Eastern Europe idea now? Unbelievable, isn't it? And every day it gets more unbelievable! First the Berlin Wall, now even *your* country seems to be joining in!"

His country? Had there been a time in recent history when they had discussed an idea and he'd had a country? Rod's mind clumped along feebly trying to recall. "What country, Stan?"

"Czechoslovakia!"

The shock of the name short-circuited his thinking process. He closed his eyes. "I should be back in a day or so."

"Okay, at least think about going to Eastern Europe, will ya?"

A murky but easy assignment. "Sure."

"You want your telephone messages?"

He didn't but it seemed like an easier conversation topic than Eastern Europe. "Yes."

"Your sister called. She wants to know whether January fifteenth would be a good date for the big anniversary party for your parents. Your dentist says you're due. And an odd one—you ever work at a place called Kelso?"

It was back again, this strange anachronistic mix of past and present. "Yes."

"Well, seems there's a lawsuit, something about workers who were hurt by a chemical they used at the plant."

"I never came near any chemicals."

"So we can skip the message?"

296

"We can skip the message."

"Fine with me," Kurtz growled. "She was a real pisser, the lady lawyer who called, enraged that I wouldn't give her your telephone number."

Bingham kept his eyes closed. "They're all pissers, lady lawyers."

"Well, for some reason, this one was hot under the collar, insisting that I at least tell you the name of the worker who died. You know, the one whose death triggered the class-action lawsuit?"

An electrical charge went off in his head. His mind cleared. His body chilled with a sense of dread. Rod opened his eyes, and sat up in bed. "What was his name?"

The rattling and shifting of papers seemed to go on forever, as visions of vulnerable young men—buddies—passed before Rod's eyes. "Here it is—Sallie Durone. That's the name. Mean something to you?"

"Yes." His voice was hoarse. "Listen, Stan, I'll call when I get back." He hung up.

In a trance, Rodney Bingham stood up and walked into the extra bedroom. He sifted through the stack of sketches on the desk and pulled out the one he'd done of Sallie Durone—the very first one he'd done. He stared at it, at the crooked nose and the stubborn chin and the sly look around the eyes, stared at it until he felt tears dripping down his cheeks.

He told himself that, had he heard about Durone's death two months ago, four months ago, four years ago, it would not have affected him at all. Then he gritted his teeth and snarled at the idiocy of spending more than a month on a project that yielded only pain.

He walked out onto the balcony and watched the waves, wondering who else had died, and what had become of everyone else in Fallsville. He realized he'd thought of Fallsville, Massachusetts, as his own Brigadoon—a town swept into existence only once in a lifetime.

Chickie Parmacella, he'd probably become the local Mafia king . . . Hard-on. Had Hard-on found a girl with proper I.Q. to bear his offspring? Had his ditch-digging partnership with his father ever made any money? Vince Parmacella had to be married and the father of a million happy kids, the coach of his oldest son's football team. And Sallie . . . The tears started again. He sat there for a long time, staring out at the ocean and mourning the death of Salvatore Durone.

Gradually, his blank stare turned into an alert look, and then a frown. The personal call, the fact that the lady had wanted to talk to him, the fact that she'd insisted on divulging the name of the dead man. Who went to such trouble with a class-action lawsuit? And Kurtz had said "Sallie Durone." Not "Mr." not "Salvatore," not even "Sal."

Sallie Durone! He began dancing around the room. Who else would use a nickname like that? And she was a "pisser." He laughed out loud. Oh, if *ever* there was a girl who could grow up to be a pisser!

He called Kurtz back. "What was the name of the lady lawyer? The *pisser*, Stan, what was her name?" He couldn't stop jumping all over the place. "No! Wait! Let me guess!" He squeezed his eyes shut. "Was it Marcella Parmacella?"

"Well, yes, as a matter of fact, it was—"

Whoosh. He was flying, really flying. "Did she leave a phone number? An address?" Rod grabbed a pen off the desk.

"Yeah, she did. Do you want her last name?" Kurtz asked. "You only got two out of three. She gave me three names."

All the air went out. "Yes." With much less enthusiasm, he picked up the pen. "Uh, what's the last name?"

"It's a lulu. Here, I'd better spell it for you: C-o-u-r-b-i-e-n-n-e."

Rod fell into the nearest chair. "C-o-u-r-b-i-e-n-n-e," he repeated slowly.

"Yeah. She just spelled it for me. Looks like it's French or something."

"Core-bean," Rod said softly. "That's how you pronounce it."

He hung up the phone and sat studying his scribblings. A *different* Courbienne. It had to be. One of Hard-on's distant cousins. It made no sense whatsoever, the idea that Marci and Hard-on—

Rod stood up and began walking around the room. Hard-on, good old buddy Hard-on, showing up to say good-bye, so touching, so uncharacteristic of him. Hard-on, the planner, squeezing those tennis balls over lunch. What had the ultimate planner been up to that night? The guy who'd never in his life read anything but books on concrete slabs, suddenly issuing reassurances on a friend's fears about homosexuality?

Married to her? No sir. Couldn't be. Not in your life. Not unless Hard-on's personality had been altered surgically. Never.

He looked over at his word processor. There were only a few chapters left to be printed. He went into the kitchen and checked the clock. Plenty of time. The post office did not close for two hours.

32

The Miami Airport public address system blared out another arrival notice in Spanish, and Rod Bingham shifted around impatiently in the check-in line, surrounded by mothers trying to calm crying babies and irritable travelers bristling over the slowness of the procedure.

Bingham stared coldly ahead. He did not feel like being friendly.

It was his second annoying queue in two days. An appropriate introduction, he decided, for reentering New York City life. He counted the people ahead of him. The express delivery line at the post office had been longer.

He played with the buckle on one of his bags. Had she read it? Had he read it with her—the mysterious Mr. Courbienne? Rod Bingham had spent a day and a half contemplating. Rod had addressed the package to her and her alone, but each time he thought about it, he pictured her reading it with Hard-on next to her on a sofa, and a cozy fire blazing in the fireplace, their elbows touching as they turned the pages.

He most certainly would have carved out a very different opus, had he written it for them in the first place.

That, he reminded himself, would have defeated the whole

purpose. It was an exercise—a very personal exercise—and one that had worked.

The mistake was his for mailing it out. Who externalizes an internal memo? Who posts the transcript of his own psychotherapy session to another party? It was the power of the re-creation that had done it. She had become so real to him that he'd let himself blur the lines between internal and external, past and present, passion and reason. The wrong thing to do. It was like being so moved by Tolstoy you wrote a love letter to Anna Karenina.

He kicked one of his bags forward. Most likely she hadn't read it. Most likely she'd just put it aside, too busy to bother. He would find out soon enough. In just a few hours, he would be at the telephone number he had included with his return address.

He wondered if she would call, and then he chastised himself for wondering. Searching for distraction, he reached down to the top of his suitcase and picked up the newspaper he had just bought at an airport vending machine. Time to reenter the real world, he instructed himself, flipping the bundle of pages over so he could read the front-page headlines.

"AAAAAAA!" The loud, shocked cry erupted involuntarily from his mouth. There, smiling back at him from the middle of the front page, was Alexander Dubcek.

Dubcek's hair was thinner, white around the edges. The facial lines were more plentiful, deeper, but there was no mistaking it. This was the man Rod Bingham had last seen holding carnations and waving from a balcony beside Alexei Kosygin.

In the newspaper picture, Dubcek was surrounded by flaming candles. Rod read the caption. "Alexander Dubcek, the man who brought Prague Spring to Czechoslovakia in 1968, returns from two decades of forced obscurity to address 250 thousand pro-democracy demonstrators in Prague's Wenceslas Square."

"Next?" The ticket attendant on the far left was looking at him expectantly. He pulled two of his bags in her direction, pushing the third with his foot. He handed her his ticket, but his eyes darted back to the front page . . . Bulgaria . . . East Germany . . . Poland . . . Hungary . . . datelines from unusual places, describing a wave of democracy that seemed to be sweeping the entire Eastern Bloc.

This was what Kurtz had been talking about!

"Flight Two eighty-two to New York," the ticket lady said as she played with the computer keys.

"Yes." He laughed out loud as he devoured the copy. Reliving Prague Spring had caused him to sleep through something even bigger—the revolution of 1989!

He looked up, squinting, at the departure board behind her. "You have a flight to Boston in forty minutes?" he asked.

"Yes, we do." She offered up her fixed smile and went back to the computer. "Aisle or window?"

He shifted from foot to foot, looking at Dubcek, and then looking at the departure board. "Is the flight to Boston booked?"

"No," she reported as she fingered the keyboard. "There are still seats." She frowned at him. "But you're going to New York, not Boston."

"I'd like to change to Boston." The words surprised him even more than they surprised her.

The woods and pastures he remembered from 1968 had been transformed into a thriving business community, the sleepy roads into thoroughfares. Rod drove by housing developments and modern corporate buildings surrounded by asphalt parking lots the size of football fields, arriving finally at Folgier Estates, a large development of modern, suburban homes set on rambling, grassy lawns.

He checked himself in the rear-view mirror. Worst of both possible worlds: a lined, dissipated adult face with eyes that conveyed the haunting insecurity of the nineteen-year-old boy who had arrived in Fallsville in May 1968.

He drove through the curving, quiet roads until he found what he was looking for. He checked the address. The Courbiennes had done well for themselves. Thirty-three-forty-five Barcroft was a huge split-level home, nicely landscaped with trees and shrubbery that set it off from the neighbors. Two boys were shooting hoops in the driveway, all their attention directed at the basketball net hung high over the garage.

Rod viewed them with trepidation, much the way a mailman views the resident dog. But then, reminding himself that, in his present state, he was viewing everything with trepidation, he parked the rented car in front of the house and got out.

The bigger of the two boys stopped shooting as soon as Rod

turned off the motor. The basketball in one hand, the other on his hip, the boy watched the new arrival with a proprietary air. This one had to be the resident child.

"Hi," Rod said genially. "I'm looking for Marci Courbienne. Is this the right address?"

"Right address, bad timing!" The boy laughed with an air of total confidence. "She's not here." He extended his hand. "Can I help you? I'm her son, Tom Courbienne."

That settled it. She'd married Hard-on. The boy was more muscular and somewhat shorter, but his resemblance to Hard-on was jarring. "Yes," Rod said, shaking the extended hand and not thinking very clearly. "You certainly are."

The boy gave him a look of confusion.

"I knew your father when he was around your age," Rod explained. "You look just like him."

The perplexed look gave way to a mischievous grin. "Not exactly! My mom says the eyes are hers. She says his genes were obviously stronger, except for the eyes."

They were dark brown and animated. "She's right," Rod said. "The eyes are hers." He enjoyed looking at them. "If your mother's out, is your, uh, father home?" Rod asked. Maybe that was better, confronting Hard-on first.

The boy looked down at the asphalt driveway and shifted a little from foot to foot. "I guess you haven't been around for a while." He looked apologetic, as though he was afraid of hurting the stranger's feelings. "He's dead. He died twelve years ago."

"I'm sorry. I didn't know." Rod Bingham felt a spurt of excitement unbecoming of an old family friend. "You're right, it's been a long time. How did he die?"

"A car crash." The boy shrugged. "I was only four years old."

They stood there, the relic from the past and the teen jock, shifting feet on the asphalt.

"Listen, my mom'll probably be back soon. Why don't you go in and wait in the house? It's warm in there."

Rod's New York City sensibilities took over, that and his newly discovered status as an adult. "You shouldn't just let me into your house like that," he growled. "How do you know I'm not a hardened criminal?"

Running his tongue along the inside of his cheek and suppressing a grin, Tom Courbienne Junior took a long, roaming look at Rod's body, from the summer loafers to the thin khakis to the torso shivering underneath the lightweight beige windbreaker.

"You're right." The boy's eyes sparkled. "You might tear the house apart!" Then he broke out laughing. "But you'll freeze if you stay out here! Hey, Frank!" he yelled to his companion. "Let's go inside for a while."

The other boy—smaller and darker than Courbienne—followed them into the house. Rod felt the other kid staring at him and intentionally did not turn around.

The interior of the house calmed him. It was a wonderful place. Not in structure or design, that Rod found rather conventional. But it was furnished in warm colors and comfortable-looking chairs and filled with pictures, trophies, and other family memorabilia. It exuded a sense of coziness.

Rod stopped at a table in the corner of the living room and searched the picture frames for a glimpse of Marci. He stopped when he came across one with a very familiar-looking face—a dark-haired young man in an army uniform. He smiled as he picked it up. "Now *this* is someone I know . . . your Uncle Vince!"

Tom Courbienne said nothing, just nodded awkwardly.

"Your mother's brother? Vince?"

"Yes." The boy gave out a hurt look, not hurting for himself so much as for the poor innocent stranger. His dark brown eyes were pregnant with yet another piece of information he sensed would be upsetting.

Rod felt interior walls crumbling. Not Vince Parmacella, not the vibrant kid he had just joyfully brought back into his life. "No . . ."

The boy nodded. "In Vietnam, October Nineteen sixty-eight."

Rod swallowed. The picture became a blur. He put it down quickly. "I'm so sorry."

"Me too. I never knew him, but from what everyone says, I think I would have liked him."

"Yes," Rod said, surprised at how traumatic this was all turning out to be. "You would have liked him."

"I know who you are . . ." It was the voice of the dark-haired boy who had silently trailed them in and lingered behind in the corner. "You're Smarts!"

"Yes . . ." Rod turned around to look. The face was a little thinner, younger, softer, but it was the same face he had been staring at in watercolor for the last two months.

"And you're . . ." The two visions were fading in and out—the boy, the watercolor—the boy, the watercolor. "You're definitely related to Sallie Durone."

The boy pulled himself up to his full height and threw back his shoulders. "I'm his son," he said proudly. "Frank Durone."

Rod felt his throat constrict. "I just heard about Sal's death," he said softly. "I'm so sorry."

The boy lowered his head.

"Did he——" Rod took a deep breath. "I haven't been around for years and years. The last time I saw Sal he was thinking of enlisting in the army."

"Thanks to you!" Frank Durone grinned. "He told me all about it!"

"Then he *did* enlist——"

"Purple heart in Vietnam," Frank announced proudly. "Four bronze stars!"

Rod's head felt disturbingly light. He turned from one to the other, trembling a little. "You guys have to understand, this is . . . very . . . jarring. I spent a summer working with your fathers twenty-one years ago, and now, now I feel a little as though I'm Father Time, come back, and I'm staring at the two of them, only *they*'ve each gotten even younger!"

The boys laughed.

"Want a soda or something?" Tom Courbienne asked.

"A cold drink might help." Rod followed them into the kitchen. It smelled good, and it had notes and messages tacked up all over the refrigerator. A people kitchen.

The boys wanted stories, and Rodney Bingham gave them stories. Sitting at the kitchen table, sipping a ginger ale, he told them about Hard-on's belting the longest home run of the 1968 summer softball season, but getting so carried away that he forgot to touch third base and got called out.

He told them about Sallie Durone ruling the roost at the factory, instructing the rest of the workforce all to "go out they-ah and build a beddah product!" Oh, he had stories, stories fresh from the written page, and stories that had never made it to the written page but had just been remembered, late at night, sitting out on the Florida balcony.

Never had he had such a receptive audience. They were hungry for the stories, and their hunger touched him. He felt he was doing something special—for them and for their fathers—and then after a while, the tension evaporated and he just felt absolutely wonderful.

The three of them laughed and mimicked as they compared notes, like three boys fascinated by the same topic. For a while Rod actually felt he was back again, "chewing the shit" with the guys, but the more his two companions talked, the more he realized these physical replicas of their fathers were really quite different.

Frank Durone was what Sallie Durone had wanted to be: thoughtful, soft-spoken, and articulate. Tom Courbienne Junior reminded Rod at first of Marci's brother Vince, but then he realized it was just because Vince was a male version of Marci. Tom had his father's body but his mother's personality—quick, devilish, outspoken, sparkling.

"How about my mom?" Tom asked eagerly after a while. "What was she like?"

Rod leaned back and reeled off a whole bunch of stories about plucky, stubborn Marcella Parmacella, controlling the world as best she could from behind the counter of Mongon's in 1968. The anecdotes were a big hit. All three of them were howling by the time he finished.

"She hasn't changed that much, if you ask me." Frank gave Tom a significant nudge. "Like this morning?"

"Yeah! She still gets real carried away when she's determined to do something." Tom turned to Rod. "You wouldn't have *believed* what she was like this morning! Frank came over to shoot hoops, and just as we're getting started, she comes out with this little project she wants our help on. The next thing we know, we're in the car, driving miles and miles away to this place . . ."

"Back to Fallsville!" Frank shouted. "Back to where I'd spent half the morning hitchhiking *away* from!"

"Over to where they're building a huge new apartment complex—"

"And they're *really* building it," Frank interjected. "Like all around us, the bulldozers are going bananas!"

"What for?" Rod frowned. "Why did she want to go there?"

"Beats me!" Tom shrugged. "I guess for some legal case she was working on. All I know is, she got something in the mail yesterday—a whole stack of typed papers? And it set her off, really set her off."

"You don't know what the papers were?" Rod asked.

" 'Express Mail.' " Tom shrugged. "That's what the mailman said. I signed for it, see. The moment she saw it, she went crazy."

"Lindsay said she didn't even eat dinner," Frank Durone offered. "Too busy reading."

"That's right. All she did last night was read. 'Not now.' That's what she said every time we even asked her a question!" Tom winced. "You know, like 'Mom, the house is burning down!' 'Not now.' "

The boys laughed heartily.

Rod joined them. She'd read his manuscript.

"I don't think the trip this morning was for a legal project," Frank said slowly. "I think it was for your aunt. Remember how she spent all that time talking to Louella when you wanted to use the phone? That was just before we left."

"Anyway," Tom continued, "we get there and she tells me and Frank to crawl under this rock and talk to each other, see? I mean, we feel like assholes, right? All these big construction guys and their equipment all over the place, and we gotta climb inside this little cave and talk to each other, just because for some stupid reason, she wants to know if she can hear what we say—"

"But all she hears is the bulldozers!" Frank shrieked, flopping down on the kitchen table. "So, she actually gets them to stop digging."

"As Frank and I, feeling like total morons, climb in real cozylike under the rocks and whisper to each other."

"Like *lovers!*" Frank trilled in falsetto, fluttering his eyelashes at Tom.

"Yeah, like lovers." Tom turned to Rod in righteous indignation. "Can you *believe* it? That's what she told us to do—whisper like lovers while the whole construction crew sat around watching!"

The boys' banter faded out as Rod's laughter chilled to a frozen smile. (Whisper like lovers . . . under a rock . . . in a *cave?* . . . Eavesdropping on lovers in a cave? Right after reading his manuscript and talking to Louella?) His mouth went dry. "This, uh, this place she took you to," he asked the boys. "Was it over a creek? On a kind of embankment?"

"Yeah, it was." Tom said. "Real nice, if you ignore the bulldozers. That's why they're building the complex there, I guess. You know, for the view. Anyway," he said, summarizing, "all I'm telling you is she's still real stubborn when she gets her mind fixed on something!"

Rod forced a chuckle. "Tell me, what was the verdict?" he asked hoarsely. "*Could* she hear what you were saying?"

"Beats me!" Tom yelled. "We were so glad to get outta there . . . who cared?"

"Hey, uh . . . listen, I feel bad about interrupting your game this long," Rod said affably. "Especially now that I've found out about your morning. It's okay with me if you go out and shoot some more hoops. I'll just wait in here."

Tom feigned suspicion. "How do I know for sure you're not a hardened criminal?"

They broke out laughing, nudging and jabbing each other, three old friends sharing a joke.

The boys went outside, and Rod Bingham stared down at the tabletop, overwhelmed by a sense of self-loathing. Was it possible? Had Hard-on really been out there listening to what went on in their most private of all private worlds? Who would have thought it?

He might have, had he thought for one second, instead of—He closed his eyes.

The angry, wronged hero who had sauntered into town to duel with evil forces face-to-face suddenly felt very much like the villain, and yearned to be back in Stanley Kurtz's bed, sound asleep. He began reworking the manuscript in his head, transforming it into the story of an insecure, messed-up kid, so riddled with doubts and so thoroughly self-centered that he'd coldly—icily—walked away from the kindest, most giving person he'd ever known. Not just walked away, walked all over her, trampled her, left her hanging.

He contemplated the rental car parked out front, seeing it now as a get-away car. For a moment he toyed with the idea. ("Listen, boys, it's getting late. Tom, just tell your mom I said hello.")

No. He'd run away once. Had he learned nothing from the past? This time he would stay.

308

33

He could sit alone brooding in an empty kitchen for only so long. After a while the mental stream of mea culpas became tedious. Rod's eyes began searching for clues. He scanned the scribbled entries on the calendar on the refrigerator and the announcements pinned to the kitchen bulletin board. He examined the contents of the cabinets and the refrigerator, and then moved on to the living room.

The perusal of the bookcases took a long time. Then he roamed the room looking at the framed photographs—watching two children emerge from plump bubbles to toddler status, through pony rides and school plays, and team victories and graduations, into the awkward self-consciousness of adolescence, and beyond. Marci was visible only in the corners of photos. It looked as though she had not changed much, but it was difficult to tell.

The proud grandparents were displayed over next to the sofa, both the Parmacellas and another older man and woman he assumed were Hard-on's parents. His eyes roamed from a picture of Mama and Papa Parmacella together, on the front porch of their bungalow, to another one of an older-looking Mrs. Parmacella standing alone.

He looked nervously around the room. Where were the other Parmacella kids? He studied the face of the plump, middle-aged woman with frizzy hair and glasses who seemed to keep reappearing in framed photos, and finally decided it was Louella.

He spotted another familiar face, over in a corner. Tough-guy Chickie Parmacella, glowering in uniform. He looked around for a more recent photo. His lack of success made him anxious. Feverishly, he scanned the fireplace mantel, the other tables, the windowsills.

Nothing. Not one single picture of Chickie Parmacella beyond the age he'd been when Rod knew him. He swallowed hard as his eyes roamed from Chickie to Hard-on to Vince. Young men, frozen in time. What nightmares had she had to face?

He carried the picture of Vince over to a big chair and sat down. He looked at it for a long time, mourning the dreams that had never come true, the promise that had not been realized. However, after a while, the smiling, dimpled face staring back at him began generating warm energy, happy memories.

Rod leaned back in the chair, closed his eyes, and, for the first time in many days, he relaxed, comforted by the pictures, the smells, the sounds of the bouncing basketball outside and the grunts and jeers of his two new companions. He was home, back among the only real family he'd ever had.

A woman's voice and the clatter of heels racing up the front walk transformed him instantly from a welcomed guest into an uninvited intruder. The sound of the front door opening and closing paralyzed him. He sat frozen in the chair, yearning, suddenly, for escape.

He heard the heels click across the entry and stop when they got to the entrance to the living room. He looked up. He saw dark hair, red lipstick, tight jeans, and an oversized aqua sweater. The contours and colors aroused dizzying sensations. "Where have you been?" he scolded. "I was worried about you."

She did a double take, and then walked closer, as though she had not heard correctly. "What?"

He had forgotten how lustrous her hair was, and how thick. He yearned to touch it. "We expected you hours ago."

She moved a few steps closer, her head tilted. "We?"

"The boys and I. What took you so long?"

"Do I *know* you?" she asked coldly.

"Yeah." He smiled. "I'm the guy who shows up every time Communism wanes in Czechoslovakia!"

310

She put her hands on her hips. "Why are you behaving like this?"

"Because I'm scared to death."

Her body relaxed. *"Now* I remember you," she said softly. She collapsed into the chair next to his and looked at him.

It was the same face he had imagined, sketched, and even wept over during the last five weeks, the very same face, only this one was older, laugh-lined, more interesting.

Exhausted too. He noted a redness around the eyes, a blotchiness below, a tear-streaked residue. He searched for words of comfort, a phrase powerful enough to soothe away her tension, but the desire became so fervent it rendered him speechless.

And so they sat, their eyes locked, their hands fidgeting until Marci, at last, broke the silence. "I just spent an hour in a parked car talking to you."

"To me?"

"Yes. It seemed only fair. I'd spent most of last night listening to you as I read your manuscript."

"What did you talk to me about?"

"Everything that has happened in my life over the last twenty-one years." She looked so vulnerable. "All sorts of complicated, strange feelings spilled out, things I've never before been able to put into words."

"Pity I missed the show!" It sounded sarcastic, not at all the way he had intended.

She backed off. "A useful exercise," she announced tersely to the carpet. "Useful for me. A personal catharsis. I don't know why I mentioned you at all."

"Well, I've just spent the last twenty minutes sitting here talking to Vince," he said eagerly, holding up the picture in his lap as if it were his ticket for readmittance to the ball game. "We have something in common."

"Do we?" She rubbed her temples. "Is this really happening?"

"I gather you're not so sure."

"Look," she snapped. "I've discovered—quite suddenly—that everything I thought happened twenty-one years ago did not happen, and a whole lot of things I never knew about did happen. I'm a little confused, a little upset. I think I have—"

311

"Every right to be." He played with the picture frame. "What made you cry?"

She groaned and put her hands to he face. "I must look a wreck."

"No, you look beautiful." It came out louder and lighter than he'd planned. He cleared his throat, but found no words to slip through the newly opened passage. In desperation, he resorted to a practical line of questioning. "Could you hear Frank Durone when he whispered to your son in the cave this morning?"

"Yes."

He shook his head in awe. "How the *hell* did you figure that out?"

"From Louella. She told me she brought Tom down to the embankment one night that summer, when the two of us were already inside the cave. Louella told me that the acoustics were such that everything said inside was belted out loud and clear." Her jaw clenched. "The detective work was relatively simple. A teenager could have figured it out on August twenty-first, Nineteen sixty-eight, if she'd known the facts."

Touché.

She turned on him. "I never told anyone," she said deliberately, her gaze penetrating. "I never discussed any facet of you with another person."

"I believe you."

"He believes me," she snickered to the ceiling. "You believe me? Just like that?"

"Just like that. All it took was twenty-one years, plus five weeks thinking about that summer, and your revelation about the cave." He glared at her. "I'm a real pushover."

"Why did you write it all down?" She sounded like a mildly interested talk-show host. "You needed a boy-coming-of-age vignette for some magazine?"

A fuse blew inside his head. "It was an assignment."

"A what?"

"My agent sent me off to his condominium in Miami on a dare. 'Find something in your life you *care* about' was what he told me. The manuscript I sent you was the result."

She smiled politely. "Why did you come here today? To fulfill another assignment?"

"No, as a matter of fact, it was an impetuous act of passion. I was still operating under the misconception that you had betrayed my confidence, but I didn't care. I'd fallen in love with you all over again."

"With *her*," she corrected.

Right between the eyes. *"Her.* Of course. Anyway," he continued with less enthusiasm, "I came to belt Hard-on, forgive you for your teenage indiscretion, and carry you off on my white horse. Obviously I got more caught up in my own prose than you did."

"Obviously."

"I didn't know anything more than I knew in Nineteen sixty-eight, except the message my agent gave me that Marcella Parmacella *Courbienne* had called. When I heard that last name, I—" He stopped and cocked his head. "Why exactly *did* you call me?"

She ran her fingers through her hair nervously, just the way she used to at the age of seventeen. "I've been working on the Durone lawsuit. It made me think about that summer for the first time."

"So Sallie Durone brought us together?" He laughed and, when he looked up, she was laughing with him, her eyes dancing. Finally, they had found a common joke: The last thing Sal Durone would have wanted to do was bring the two of them together.

"Sal Durone had many dreams," she sighed after a while, "but that was not one of them!" She leaned forward eagerly. "You won't believe this, but I've come to like Sal an awful lot," she confided. "I guess it's because I got to know him for the first time, going over his papers. And then your manuscript."

"I'm glad." It felt so good, this comfortable turf. "Hey, whatever became of Sallie's dreams?" he asked jovially. "Did any of them come true?"

She froze. Her lips smiled but her eyes did not join in. "Where's your family? Your wife?"

"I'm divorced."

"Ahh. What are you planning on doing now that evil old Hard-on isn't around to belt?" She stood up and peeked out the window. "Is the white horse outside waiting?"

He put his head in his hands, yearning for the chance to do a quick rewrite of the entire scene, starting from the moment she walked in the door. "You have every right to hate me," he said.

"Nonsense." She tossed it away with a wave of her hand. "I stopped hating you yesterday."

"What made you stop?"

"Your manuscript." She was walking around the room. "Oh, it raised a whole lot of unpleasant memories, I admit—"

"*Unpleasant* memories?"

"But at least it gave me a history to be proud of." She sat back down in the chair. "It brought *her* back into my life, Marcella Parmacella. She *wasn't* inferior. She *wasn't* a reject. She was one resourceful, plucky little girl. A past to be proud of." She turned to him. "You can't imagine how wonderful it felt, to rediscover her. For that I am eternally grateful."

"*Grateful?*" He winced in distaste. "All the more reason to hate me—for leaving the way I did and raising those doubts in the first place."

"No, no, no," she clucked. "You're missing the point. You helped create her. You set a standard. She'd never had any lofty standards before you arrived in Fallsville. And for three glorious months in the summer of Nineteen sixty-eight, she rose mightily under your tutelage."

"It was not a one-way thing." He picked at the arm of the chair. "She—*you*, for God's sake. This third-person stuff is driving me crazy. *You* totally changed my—"

"There were important after-effects too. All these years, I thought I'd gone to college and law school to spite you, to show you I was every bit as good as you were." She was uttering musical notes, not words. "It wasn't until I read the manuscript that I remembered it was all your idea in the first place!"

She pounded her fist on the arm of the chair. "She *was* too good for her husband, that Marcella Parmacella. She wasn't an opportunist who married him just for the financial backing. She was a victim, one of Tom's many victims." She took a deep breath and exhaled it. "You can't imagine how liberating a discovery that was after spending so many years feeling guilty and grateful. It was very therapeutic, your manuscript."

"I think I'd rather have you hate me. Hatred is at least emotional. You're giving me a book report . . . a distanced intellectual evaluation. I wrote about feelings—"

"Ancient feelings."

314

"Then what was going on in my head never made it to the written page." His jaw clenched. "That's a fairly common problem for writers."

"I've hurt you."

"Don't be silly."

They sat in silence, staring down at the floor. He looked up suddenly. "I take it back. You've hurt me. A million times in this peculiar conversation we've been having, you've hurt me. And I think I've hurt you just as many times. It seems to me that's all we've been doing ever since we started talking—hurting each other." He stood up and started walking around the living room. "I poured out my heart in that manuscript. I lived that whole summer, relived it for five solitary weeks, crying, suffering, going back over the whole thing in painstaking detail, coming up with, I thought, a very poignant love story."

"And for that I'm supposed to give you another Pulitzer Prize?"

"No, I came hoping that you felt it too. You were, after all, the goddamn heroine! And what do you tell me? That it—"

"I felt it! I cried," she said slowly. "Got so caught up in it that I dug into my jewelry box and put *this* on at four o'clock in the morning." She tugged the gold chain around her neck and the flower medallion he'd given her the night before he'd left Fallsville hopped up over the collar of her sweater. Right before the Soviet Union invaded Czechoslovakia and all the dreams were over. Her lips quivered.

"Then why did you act as though—"

"It was more than just a love story." She looked at him with weary eyes. "You have no idea the personal ramifications your truth had. I spent most of the afternoon participating in a session with my father-in-law that no one should ever have to endure."

"Look, I came here, among other things, to apologize. Writing it down made me realize what a totally self-centered shit I was. I certainly think I came here receptive to—"

"Did you march in declaring 'I was a shit'? No, you sat there playing games . . . a tanned, preppy, lighthearted stranger!"

He paced the floor. "Frank Durone said you lent him your copy of *Jeremiah Pruitt*. Did you read it?"

"Yes."

315

"Did you like it?"

She swallowed. "I loved it."

"*That*'s me, if you're looking for a reference," he announced. "That's what I've become. The books were the only things in my life I really cared about."

She walked over to the picture window. "Franklin Dober . . ." she whispered, almost to herself.

"You read the novel too?"

She stared out the window in silence for a long time. "I don't think any character, ever, has moved me as much as Franklin Dober," she said softly, addressing her remarks to the low-hanging branch of the tree in her front yard. "Such a good, simple man trying so hard to understand the complexities of his offspring, never succeeding, always missing the subtlety that was essential, but tirelessly making the valiant effort nonetheless. So loving but so limited. Reminded me of Papa." She shook her head slowly. "I laughed out loud—no, *howled*, that's what I did—during Franklin Dober's political fights with his son . . ." She swallowed. "And I wept as I'd never wept before over the final chapter. Read it and then reread it, sobbing each time, couldn't stop." She turned back to him.

The knot in his throat made him unable to respond.

She looked away self-consciously. "What, uh, what else have you been doing in all these years?"

He winced. "The honest answer?"

"Yes."

He took a deep breath. "Wasted a lot of time stoned on marijuana, drunk on alcohol, womanizing . . ."

She shuddered.

"I've, uh, I've stopped—completely."

"What made you stop?"

"You. Reliving that summer. It was a better high."

She frowned. "What do you want?"

"Everything," he chortled. "You and all your possessions. The house, I love the comfortable warm feeling about your house. I'm absolutely crazy about your son. I want—"

"This is what? The logical follow-up to wanting to be adopted by my parents when you were nineteen?" Her eyes flashed.

"Precisely! Wherever you go, you seem to create this cozy

316

cocoon around you. And I'm always coming in from the cold. There's another consistency, then and now."

"Well, here's an *in*consistency—me. While you've been living the high life, I've become a boring plodder, a dried-up prune, if you want to know, all work, no play. *She*'s not here, that adorable bubbly girl you came to find!"

"What we were was irrelevant when we met in 'sixty-eight. It was what we *became*, what we created for each other that mattered. The grand sum had nothing to do with particular parts!" There was no energy left. He collapsed in exhaustion on the sofa and rubbed his eyes. "I swear, I haven't argued like this for twenty-one years."

"Neither have I."

"You? The feisty one? The terror of the Parmacella family?"

"A terrible thing happened to Baby about two decades ago. Everyone else went bananas and she had to get responsible." She shook her head. "You've sure changed too. You're positively cocky."

"No. I drove up here today very much the way I arrived in 'sixty-eight, thoroughly terrified. If I sound glib, it's the fault of your son and the Durone boy. They made me relax. In one half hour, they transformed me from the way I was at the beginning of the summer to the way I was at the end."

He thought he detected a softening in her eyes. "What do you say we go back and start this whole thing over at the beginning? What was it you told me when I wasn't there?" he asked her. "When you were sitting all by yourself in your parked car?"

She shifted around uncomfortably.

"What's the matter with you? There's a lot at stake here!" He walked over to the table and held up the picture of Chickie Parmacella. "Did Chickie die in Vietnam too?"

"Yes. Well," she said. "As you know, he was not exactly one of my favorite people."

He slammed the picture down. *"Marci . . ."*

She jumped. He did a little too, just at the sound of it. He realized it was the first time he had said her name out loud since she had entered the room.

He walked over to her and lifted her face up so she had to look at him. "Marci." He said it again. She looked receptive, alert, a little afraid too, but more like the Marci he had known than the cool, polished woman who had been arguing with him. "I walked out on you, just like that, thereby accentuating the totally unjustifiable insecurities you had about yourself. It had to make you feel that you were not good enough for that 'other' world out there you always alluded to. Then you lost *two* brothers in Vietnam, one of whom was the light of your life. That must have devastated you . . . *and* the rest of your family. Louella doesn't look like Louella in the pictures you have here on the tables, and your mother is standing there in the most recent shot without your father." He caressed her cheek. "So much loss, so much hurt."

Tears welled up in her eyes.

"You married bland old Tom because you needed the money for college. That couldn't have made for happily ever after. Then he died, leaving you to raise two children all by yourself. And you did. If your daughter is anything like Tommy, you have done an admirable job. But it had to take a toll. It's been a terribly, terribly hard life."

The tears were streaming down her face.

"Isn't *that*, just maybe, what you told me in the car, before you discovered I was a glib idiot you couldn't communicate with?"

She nodded.

"And there is something else too, something that has upset you, really upset you. Maybe that's what you spent the afternoon fighting with your father-in-law about. I can't figure out what it is, but I think it concerns Sallie Durone."

She pressed her face against his chest, crying.

He stroked her hair. "I came in an economy rental car, not a white horse. I had no grandiose plans, just self-centered desires. I think I've come full circle. I need you every bit as much as Kelso's summer college boy needed you in Nineteen sixty-eight." He closed his eyes. "Don't you have needs too—just as you did then?"

"Too many!" It came out in a muffled sob. "That's what scares me!"

"What have we got to lose?" He nudged her. "Help me. You were always the one who was gifted at debate, and, being a lawyer, you've doubtlessly gotten even better at it."

He kissed her forehead.

She looked up at him. "That capsule biography you just intuited about me . . . No one, absolutely *no one* in twenty-one long

318

years, has spent so much energy trying to figure me out, let alone come up with all the right answers!"

"We're even, then." His green eyes glistened. "No one, no reviewers, no editors, no readers that I know of, no one in the world but you and me has ever reacted like that to Franklin Dober."

"Maybe, then, we've finally found a starting point?"

"Maybe." He watched his fingers as they stroked her cheek. "I've never seen a more beautiful dried-up prune."

She closed her eyes and rubbed her face against his hand. "No one has ever moved me as much as you, but no one has ever hurt me as much either. Maybe that's why I put up such a fight. The truth is, I've been calling that New York telephone number you put on the manuscript all day."

"What would you have done if I'd been there?"

"Begged you to come here, or at least begged 'him.' *Him, you, us, them* . . . It's all a little confusing. I've been totally irrational since Wednesday. That's when I went up to the attic and read all your old letters."

He frowned. "What letters?"

"The ones you wrote at night and gave me every morning at Mongon's."

"The ones you promised, at the time, you were tearing up so no one else could find them!"

Her eyes became defiant. "Hey, I got punished plenty for that one minor transgression! Look at all the things I *didn't* do I got blamed for!"

"Forgiven." He laughed, holding out his hands, palms up. "Forgiven!"

"That's what made me call you in the first place, the letters. Then your manuscript, well, that was the finishing touch. I was obsessed. Yours for the asking." She giggled. "Until you came in and actually *asked*. That scared me to death."

"How had you worked out the big reunion scene? You know, during your obsessed period."

She looked away.

"Come on," he teased. "You must have imagined something."

She shook her head. "Wouldn't have worked. Too visceral. Simplistic. Adolescent, really."

"Tell me anyway."

She reached up suddenly and threw her arms around his neck.

He stared down at the face of a brazen woman begging not to be dismissed as an impetuous child. Her eyes bespoke dreams tempered by self-consciousness, yearnings undermined by fears of rejection. It moved him to the brink of tears.

He moaned, wrapping his arms around her, surprised, excited, comforted, wanting to comfort in return. It felt familiar but different. Better. Wonderful. He closed his eyes, lost in the sensation. Journey's end. The bounty. "You're right," he murmured hoarsely, pressing her against him, into him. "Much too simple for two such complicated, mature people."

She rubbed the side of her face against his. "Too intimate for strangers."

He held her tighter, and soon they were locked together, their hands exploring, touching, squeezing. "Visceral."

"Adolescent."

"Just don't let go," he whispered. "Please don't let go."

She looked up at him, apologetic, her eyes filled with tears. "I guess I just need—"

"*We* need," he corrected, kissing her hungrily, and she was kissing him back, just as ardent. He kissed her again, and then again, light kisses on her eyes and her nose and forehead.

They stood there, clinging, kissing, swaying.

"You had a reunion scene worked out too," she whispered.

He laughed, burying his face in her hair. "Mine hasn't started yet."

She looked up at him nervously. "What exactly am I committing to?"

"Well, let's see. There was a bottle of champagne waiting in my room at the hotel. I brought it with me . . . fully intending to down it morosely alone in the car after the confrontation." He ran his finger along her lower lip. "We could start with a toast."

"And then?"

He grinned. "That meat marinating in the refrigerator looks delicious."

"*Dinner?*" she shrieked, backing away. "That's all? You want dinner?"

He laughed and pulled her back. "The neighborhood caroling

event next Tuesday—the one tacked up on the bulletin board? That looked like fun. So did Tommy's game on Wednesday."

"You're into high-school basketball games?"

"Don't know. Never been to one."

She giggled.

He cradled her face in his hands. "Look, neither of us has any idea what the other's life has been like for the last twenty-one years. How about if I'm allowed to hang around town until we get caught up?"

She raised an eyebrow. "Some commitment."

He laughed, hugging her. "Unless you've changed considerably, *your* recitation alone should take a long time."

"I'll talk slowly."

"I know a little about you already—from Tommy."

"Like what?"

"You named your daughter after my sister."

"Only fair. You named me."

"You ended up going to Seaton College after all."

"The college of your choice."

"There are no other men in your life."

"Tommy said that?"

"No." He shrugged. "Wishful thinking."

She shot him a dazzling smile. "Wish fulfilled."

"You cook as well as your mother."

"Hey, there are limits to wish fulfillment!"

"Well, does your mother still cook?"

Her eyes rolled up to the ceiling. "Nothing would please her more than preparing carry-out for you."

She snuggled back against him and they stood very still, holding each other. "Do you know me well enough yet to tell me the rest?" he whispered after a while. "About Sallie Durone and the excess baggage I dumped on you?"

She let go of him and sighed, looking at her watch. She stood for a moment, thinking. "Are you willing to have our champagne toast in an unusual location?"

"Sure."

She walked into the dining room and took two long-stemmed glasses out of the cabinet. "You'll need something warm to wear."

She grabbed her coat and headed for the closet. "Here," she said, handing him a down jacket. "It's Tommy's. You can borrow it."

"Where are we going?"

"For a therapy session."

"Mine or yours?"

She sighed and looked at him sadly. "Ours."

34

"Here?" Rod pulled his rental car off onto the shoulder of the highway as trailer trucks whizzed by in the lane on his left. The car quivered with each passing vehicle and so did he. He turned to Marci, certain he had misunderstood. *"Here?"*

"Here. Turn off the ignition."

He obeyed, against his better judgment. When she opened the door on the passenger side and got out, he asked, "What are you doing?"

"Come on," she laughed. "Don't forget the champagne."

He picked up the bottle and crawled across the front seat. Marci was surveying the steep hill beside the highway. "Over there!" she shouted, pointing to a place where the incline was gradual.

He winced. "We're *climbing* it?"

"Yes." She put the champagne glasses in her shoulder bag and led the way.

"Why?"

"You'll see."

At the top of the hill, he stood next to her and took in the view: highways and freeway ramps and cars and trucks and buildings. He grimaced. "Suburban sprawl at its worst."

"Around here it's called 'progress.' You're standing on top of Bigger Hill."

The name gradually sank in. "Bigger Hill?" he asked incredulously.

"Yup. Sallie's Bigger Hill."

His eyes roamed over the hacked-off tree stumps and flattened rocks. "Bigger Hill has not aged well," he sighed. "It's lost weight and gone bald!"

"That's because they had to blast half of it away in order to widen Route One-ninety."

He gaped at the six-lane highway below. "*That's* old One-ninety?"

"Yes. And, over there to the right, on the other side of the clover leaf about two miles down the road, is Four-fifty, the big Interstate Connector." She smiled up at him. "Right where Sallie guessed it would be." She nudged him and pointed to the other side of the highway. "Look what happened to Fio Marconi's farm."

He squinted into the distance until his eyes made out a semicircular lineup of stores stretched out the length of about three city blocks. It fronted on an asphalt parking lot. In the middle of the parking lot, water shot up into the air out of an enormous circular structure that looked like a reverse waterfall. Rod collapsed onto the nearest rock. "Sallie's crazy dream!" He turned to Marci, aghast. "It came *true?*"

She sat down beside him.

"Ugliest thing I ever saw in my life!" he shouted, gleefully kicking his feet up in the air.

"Progress," she corrected again. "Interstate Four-fifty and the expansion of One-ninety made Orange County an outgrowth of Boston, an expansion area for high-tech industries, laboratories, and all kinds of service organizations to support them—law firms, think tanks, advertising agencies, real estate. That shopping center over there fostered the rebirth of Collier, Massachusetts, its transformation from abandoned factories and impoverished farms into a town with the highest per-capita income in the county."

"Just as Sallie figured," Rod said in awe. "Is that what we're toasting?"

"Sort of."

"I can't believe it really worked!" He picked up the bottle and

324

popped the cork. "I have to tell you, I *never* thought it would." He sat there shaking his head. "I remember in the locker room when I first saw his pathetic pencil drawing on graph paper, I was certain it was just—"

"I think I found that drawing this afternoon." Her voice was expressionless.

"Sal's drawing? Where?"

"In an old file cabinet at my father-in-law's offices."

His face sobered and he put the bottle down. "Marci?"

She was staring into space. "The drawing had someone else's name on it."

He took her hand. "Whose name?"

"Thomas H. Courbienne." She nodded toward the shopping center. "You're looking at the source of the Courbienne family's fortune, the beginning of their real-estate empire."

"Tom stole Sallie's idea? *Tom* was the one who ripped the drawing off Sal's locker?"

"I think so." She was trembling. "Walter Flaherty, the head architect at Courbienne Enterprises, was the one who designed the shopping center. He says it was Tom who came up with the idea . . . the idea and a crude drawing. Walter saved it for sentimental purposes. He found it for me this afternoon."

Rod put his arm around her. "But what about Sallie's friendship with the guy who was going to sell him the farm land—Fio Marconi?"

"Sal told you Fio was related to me, remember? He was, by marriage. His wife Reenie—Irene Marconi—is my mother's favorite cousin. Unfortunately, Sal made the mistake of trying to negotiate with the weaker half. Reenie Marconi has always been in charge of the Marconi family. She's also Louella's godmother. After you left town, Tom got Louella to introduce him to Reenie."

"So he could do what? Offer her more than Sallie was going to?"

"No, he offered her something she'd always dreamed about, something only he and his father had to offer: a modern, well-built house at the other end of their property. That was the trade-off—a house built by the Courbiennes in return for the land."

Rod stared sadly down at the highway.

"Tom was smart enough not to create an uproar. Fio just told

Sal he wasn't ready to sell. Sal took off for the army, and when he came home from Vietnam, he found a shopping center—*his* shopping center—built by the Courbiennes."

"What did he do?"

"What could he do?" She shrugged. "He had no proof. There was no reliable witness, and absolutely no one around here would have believed Salvatore Durone was capable of coming up with an idea like that."

"Was your father-in-law an accomplice?"

"I don't think so. He and I had a horrible argument about it today. He swears he was innocent, a proud father delighted by what he thought was his son's brilliant foresight."

"Do you believe him . . . or do you *want* to believe him?"

She looked up at him with frightened eyes. "Both."

He pulled her closer. "Look, the whole thing is really my fault. If I hadn't run away—"

"You gave Sal Durone the most important friendship he ever had. That's what he told the people he was closest to. He never would have gone to Vietnam had it not been for you, and he came back a hotshot hero with a supply of war stories he managed to keep embellishing until his dying day."

"Did he return from Vietnam enough of a hero to make good on his pledge to marry the prettiest girl in Fallsville and build himself a dream house?"

"Yup. Married Francine Pomola, who wouldn't have given him the time of day before he went to Vietnam. Built a dream house on that godawful bramble-bushy property he used to take you to."

"Did the marriage work?"

"Nope. Total disaster." She smiled up at him mysteriously. "Salvatore Durone *did* find true love, however. One that lasted until his dying day."

"Really? What was she like?"

"Later," she groaned, shaking her head. "Don't want to overload the circuits. Besides, I'm determined to string this telling out as long as I can."

"I'll drink to that!" Rod picked up the bottle, but then stopped and stared across at the shopping mall. "The sight of that fountain is eating away at me. It was so ridiculously important to him. Sallie

Durone's ultimate wet dream," he grunted, shaking his head. "Must have driven him crazy, having someone else take the credit."

"I found out today from the woman . . . uh . . . from Sal Durone's final true love, that in the end, he managed to find peace and even pride and pleasure in the fact that *he*'d been the one who thought it up."

"You've had a very busy day!"

"His last dream—an adequate inheritance for his family—is being handled legally, by me, and mark my words, *that* one is going to come true." She took the glasses from her bag.

He poured the champagne.

"To Salvatore Durone," Marci proclaimed. "The visionary, the *genius* who thought up the Collier Shopping Center!"

They clicked glasses and drank.

Rod frowned at her. "That sounded rather ceremonial."

She nodded. "It's from a speech delivered at the Chamber of Commerce celebration for B.J. last summer." She smiled at the sky. "At least *this* time it's directed at the right person."

Rod pulled her close and waited until her eyes met his. He raised his glass. "To the right person," he whispered.